WE WERE
KILLERS
ONCE

Also by Becky Masterman

A Twist of the Knife
Fear the Darkness
Rage Against the Dying

WE WERE KILLERS ONCE

BECKY MASTERMAN

Minotaur Books

New York

WE WERE KILLERS ONCE. Copyright © 2019 by Becky Masterman. All rights reserved. Printed in the United States of America. For information, address St. Martin's Press, 175 Fifth Avenue, New York, N.Y. 10010.

www.minotaurbooks.com

Library of Congress Cataloging-in-Publication Data

Names: Masterman, Becky, author.
Title: We were killers once : a thriller / Becky Masterman.
Description: First Edition. | New York : Minotaur Books, 2019.
Identifiers: LCCN 2019002289| ISBN 9781250074522 (hardcover) |
    ISBN 9781466886230 (ebook)
Subjects: | GSAFD: Suspense fiction. | Mystery fiction.
Classification: LCC PS3613.A81965 W4 2019 | DDC 813/.6—dc23
LC record available at https://lccn.loc.gov/2019002289

Our books may be purchased in bulk for promotional, educational, or business use. Please contact your local bookseller or the Macmillan Corporate and Premium Sales Department at 1-800-221-7945, extension 5442, or by email at MacmillanSpecialMarkets@macmillan.com.

First Edition: June 2019

10 9 8 7 6 5 4 3 2 1

For Helen Heller, with gratitude for the idea,
and ten years of friendship and guidance

WE WERE
KILLERS
ONCE

CLEMENCY BOARD, DECEMBER 1960

I feel that I should be given consideration for clemency because there are circumstances that at the time the crime was committed that I never had any part in doing. I never participated in the killing of any of the people. That is I never did the actual killing. Also I never agreed to it. The first killing happened when I wasn't in the room. The killing was not premeditated or planned in any way. A witness for the state lied about me, but that I cannot prove. But my main reason is that I never killed anyone.

    Signed,

    Richard Eugene Hickock, Prisoner Number 14746

Being brought up one way and trying to see another way is very difficult.

Perry Smith

Immaculately factual.

Truman Capote

One

Little Brigid Theresa Quinn, with a Band-Aid on my knobby knee from jumping out of a banyan tree on a dare, and a ponytail of red hair that should have been washed four days ago—I'm only six years old when I first hear about the murder of the Walker family on December 19, 1959. Though the decades pass, and I have witnessed even greater horrors than were described that night, I still can't see a Christmas tree without feeling the crime scene, the tree with its ornaments, the glittery packages, the bodies in the living room. Then the memory quickly fades and I'm here and now again.

Whenever I go back there I still find that same little girl.

I don't hear about the Walker mass murder from the television. I get the scoop right in our own kitchen. You know, all the gory details that the news didn't assault you with in those days before they started showing the body bags coming back from Vietnam. Dad's friends from the Fort Lauderdale police department gather together on the Saturday nights when they don't have to work the following day.

I sit on Dad's lap at the Formica-topped kitchen table while he talks and drinks and smokes with his buddies. He smells of beer and cigarettes. The odors don't come from the original source as much as they're channeled through his sweat. December in Florida can be hot and muggy.

Dad's buddies are Ken, Rory, and Mitch. They all look alike as far as I can tell, with flattop haircuts, big hands and bellies. I'm allowed to call them by their first names despite being just a little girl.

Over Dad's shoulder I can see Mom far off in an armchair in the living room. There are only five days remaining before Christmas, and the multicolored lights on the tree cast a glow on her. Mom is needlepointing a seat cover with a big cluster of purple grapes in the middle. The background is blue, what she would call Virgin Mary blue. Mom is systematically covering everything in the house that can be covered with needlepoint. I don't want to grow up to be a needlepointer. It doesn't seem to make Mom happy. She frowns most of the time. No, I want to grow up to be like Dad, drinking and laughing and doing dangerous and heroic things. I don't know until years later that all Dad did was give out parking tickets and maybe get a cat out of a tree once in a while. He'd never even fired his gun except at the practice range.

Ken, Rory, and Mitch are all married, but our house is the only house they can come to and drink because the other wives won't allow "that kind of talk" around their children. That's not how things are run in his house, Dad always says. He says he "rules the roost."

The talk is brutal, all right. Axe murders. Gang rapes. Decomposing corpses eaten by alligators in the Everglades. I've grown used to this kind of talk that other children aren't privy to. These stories I've heard are no worse than the fairy tales I read, like where Cinderella's sister cuts off her own toe to fit into the glass slipper and the blood dripping on the road gives her away.

I think tonight will be just more of that. I can feel the excitement build along with the beer bottles and cigarette butts in the middle of the kitchen table. My heart speeds up with the clinking of glass and the restrained intensity of the talk, even the parts I don't understand. *Go on, go on*, I think. *More.*

The reason they're so excited is that this mass murder has happened right in Florida, our own state. It was in a little town called Osprey, on the west coast of Florida near Sarasota. When they talk about it being

4

so, so close, it gives me a nice little shiver. Like watching *Caltiki the Immortal Monster* before it goes too far and the liver thing dissolves the guy's forearm down to the bone and that keeps me up all night.

"What about that Spencer who confessed?" Dad says, not because he didn't already know about Spencer, but just to encourage the conversation. It's one of the reasons the others like him, because he's willing to play right field. Ken, another beat cop like Dad, doesn't even leave the bench but sits silently sucking down beer after beer. Maybe the main reason he comes is for the beer.

Mitch says, "He was already discredited by the sheriff." He taps his cigarette in his ashtray with a hard tap that shows what he thinks of Spencer. Then he says, "A path-o-logical liar, made up everything. Buncha shit. Sorry, baby." He says that to me because I giggle at the word "shit."

I have gotten their attention with a giggle, so I giggle again to get more. I pull on the sleeve of Dad's white undershirt. I ask, "Who're the Walkers?"

Dad says, "A family of four that was murdered near Sarasota. That's on the other side of our own state." He has never held anything back, or treated me like a little girl. But then he does. "It's like it's . . . right . . . next . . . door." Then he tickles me. It feels more like a thumb punch in my rib than anything nice, but I giggle again even though it makes me jump.

Rory gets up and helps himself to a cold beer from the fridge. Dad passes him the bottle opener and he pops off the top into a separate little pile on the table. Rory says, "We all know who we're looking at for this one. Whoever killed the Clutters."

"Are they liking anyone yet for the Clutter murders?" Dad asks.

"Two guys," Rory answers with a scoff. "You don't know this already?"

If Dad wasn't on his fifth beer he might have taken offense at that. Now, not so much. He only shrugs.

Rory goes on. "Couple of parolees, Dick Hickock and Perry Smith. Some prison snitch came forward and told the FBI he had worked for Clutter. Snitch said that he told Hickock there was a safe with ten thousand dollars at the house. The FBI is looking for them all over the country. They'll find them, all right, but it's a crying shame they couldn't move faster. The Walkers could have been saved."

The rest of the men shake their heads and tsk. Damn that good-for-nothing FBI.

"It's a killing spree," Rory adds after downing half the bottle in one go before sitting down. He takes another bottle out of the fridge so he doesn't have to get up again so soon. "With the Walkers you got the husband and wife shot. You got the two kids shot, a three-year-old and the littlest one drowned in the bathtub. What kind of a bastard has to shoot a one-year-old and then not leave her alone, but drown her in the bathtub? Jesus H. Christ."

Mitch says, "But that's a difference, the drowning. Also the mother was raped. No one got raped before."

Rory says, "That's only because something stopped the killer. Remember the teenage daughter. What's her name?" The men talk for a while about why there was no rape at the Clutter house. They think maybe it was because the Clutter family were all home at the same time, so it was harder to wrangle everyone. No time for rape.

At the age of six, I don't know what "rape" is, though I've heard the word before. I'm certain from the tone of the men's voices that rape can't be good.

"Who're the Clutters?" I ask, confused. I'm also still wondering about rape, so the part about the baby in the bathtub doesn't immediately register. But now the men ignore me.

Mitch says, "Okay, maybe the kids were in the house and they got it first. But they were much younger so not as much trouble to manage, with that big teenage son. And with the Walkers, the husband came home after the three were killed."

Rory says, "No, that's not how it was. The wife was alone in the house, and the killer—"

"Killers," Mitch says.

Rory shrugs and goes on, "—killers got her, then got the father and the two kids when they came home."

Ken and Dad listen to Mitch and Rory talk as if they're experts. No one ever mentions that they're just robbery detectives and not homicide detectives. That would be rude.

6

Ken asks, "How do they know who got there when? There wasn't that much time between the deaths."

And Dad asks, "How can they even tell whether the baby was shot first or drowned first?"

Mitch says, "Oh, those medical examiners, they can tell."

All the men nod like they understand what Mitch means, but after hearing the second time about a baby shot and drowned all I can think of is *right . . . next . . . door . . . right . . . next . . . door . . .*

The talk goes on but I stop hearing it. I can't stop thinking about those children. What did the children see the men do to their mother? What did the mother see the men do to her children? *Stop it*, I think, no, I shout inside my head. *Stop talking*.

My little sister Ariel is four, and my brother Todd is two. They're about the same age as the Walker children. They've already gone to bed but I'm big enough to stay up later. Part of my brain is listening to what the men are saying about the older child, after being shot, crawling to die next to his father. Part of my brain is listening to Dad's voice repeating *. . . door . . . right . . . next . . . door . . . right . . .*

My face gets sort of numb and I guess my ears do, too, because the conversation is muffled and I stop being able to hear exactly what they're saying almost as bad as when I'm under water in the neighbor's pool and someone shouts "Marco Polo." That's okay because I don't want to hear them anymore. I hear a *whooshing* sound and my pulse is beating so hard in the side of my neck that I can feel it. I wish I hadn't heard what I heard. I only wish, I *pray*, Mom will come and tell the men to stop talking about killed children, or at least tell me it's time for bed and take me away from the table, because I can't seem to move on my own.

Prayer doesn't do any good.

Sitting at the table, in my mind I keep hearing shotgun blasts. I keep feeling the cold water in the bathtub sloshing against my face as it goes under. I see the water turn pink. My thumb moves over the coarse hair on Dad's forearm to stop imagining, but I can't get the children out of my mind and how much they make me think of Ariel and Todd. What if someone comes into our house and does that to them? To me?

After silently begging her for so long, I'm finally taken by Mom and put to bed. But of course I stay awake staring at where the ceiling would be if the light were on, with my sheet tucked up around my ears on both sides of my head, as if that can protect me from men who kill children. Men's voices continue to filter into my room. Then the voices finally die, doors open and shut with good-nights, lights go out, and the whole house is dark and still. When I figure my parents won't be coming out of their room I push aside my bedsheets. They're sweaty with my fear. I get out of bed.

Ariel asks, "Where you going?" We share a room and even at four she's a light sleeper.

I say, "Bathroom." I'm hopeful. "You want to talk?"

She says no and rolls over.

I creep down the hall, which is lighter than our bedroom thanks to the night-light plugged into an outlet. I spend that whole night in the hallway outside Mom and Dad's bedroom. You didn't wake up my parents if you were scared at night. They'd just get angry because Dad needed his rest. So I spend that night with my knees drawn up, as small as I can get. My back bones are pressed against their closed door. The muffled sound of my father's snoring is a little comforting.

Maybe I doze off some, but I'm awake to see the sky lightening out the window over Todd's crib in his room. I go in there. Short for my age, I can't reach over the top of the bars, but I can put my hand through them to touch Todd's stomach and feel it go up and down as he breathes. The combination of the dawn and Todd alive and dry tells me everything is okay for now. My vigil is over. I get back into bed by the time Mom opens her bedroom door to come wake us up for mass. She scolds me for my dirty hair, but that's overshadowed by Todd taking an unscheduled dump in his diaper and we're running late.

More than fifty years from now, that killing will touch me again, and with more than childish terror. Cold cases, they call them, as if they're frozen harmlessly in the past without any power to wreak new havoc. Open at your own risk.

8

TWO

I felt Carlo's hand find mine in the dark, and held it just tightly enough to remind myself that Brigid Theresa Quinn was past grown up now. This was the present, not 1959. And home was Arizona, not Florida. And we were safe in bed just telling the stories of our lives. So I felt more indignation than horror when I said, "Mom didn't come get me, she just kept working on that damn needlepoint, the big needle pulling that damn Virgin Mary blue thread up and down through the holes of the canvas. Why did she do that? Why didn't she save me?"

"You told me once that she had given up on your father influencing you," Carlo said. "Could it have been that early in your life?"

"I thought she gave up when I was about ten. I don't know, it all gets vague."

"You understand that was abusive, don't you? Psychological abuse."

"These days it's child abuse. In the fifties, it was just home."

"Oh, those wonderful fifties."

"Remember how we always went to eight o'clock mass because you couldn't have anything to eat before you received communion? Remember those days?"

"Pre–Vatican Two. So that case. The Walkers."

"I suppose I've been fascinated by the Walker family murder ever since that night. Of course, way before I grew up it had stopped terrifying me. Since then I've known other cases, some worse. But that case and its connection to the Clutters, that's the closest I've come to a cold case obsession."

Silence, but I could tell Carlo was thinking about what I had and hadn't said, keeping his breathing light so as not to shift my memory. I imagined I could feel his pulse pumping in his hand.

Then he said, "I remember the Clutters. I was an altar boy at a church not too far from Lansing prison, where Hickock and Smith sat on death row and were executed."

Now my pulse jumped. "You're kidding me. Why didn't you ever tell me this before?"

"It wouldn't have occurred to me that you'd be interested, we were both so young. I had the minimal interest for anything outside my world, like any other preteen boy. More interested in books and baseball . . ."

Carlo's voice drifted off and I asked if he was thinking or falling asleep. Sometimes with him it was hard to distinguish the difference.

"Just remembering," he said. "Later I read *In Cold Blood*, of course. But I don't remember that Capote talked about the Walkers."

"He did. Just briefly because he was convinced that Hickock and Smith didn't kill the family even though they were practically in the same town when it happened. One month after they killed the Clutter family in Kansas, another family of four is killed in Florida. It's always felt like too much of a coincidence, their being so close. But Perry Smith denied it, and Capote believed him."

"The Walker case was never solved?"

"Never. Not in nearly sixty years. It's become sort of a hobby for cold case investigators in Florida. Every once in a while a detective with time on his hands goes back to it. Sometimes I google *Walker family murders* myself."

"When did you check into it last?"

I thought, finally committed to "Long time ago."

"And?"

"Nothing new."

Silence again marked only by the swish of the ceiling fan. Carlo always listened for a long time after I finished one of my stories. He finally said, "You say you're no longer affected by that evening, but I would guess you are. I can hear it in your telling. I hear that child in you."

I was plastered against Carlo's side, our heartbeats long slowed, but his right arm around me drew me even closer. Then we talked. There's no imagining what kinds of postcoital conversations people can have, and there's nothing for honesty like talking while naked.

"My friend Weiss would agree with you, about those times affecting me." Weiss was a psychological profiler for the FBI and my long-time associate. "He says I became an FBI agent because I was chasing my personal demons."

"Did you ever catch them?"

I laughed and rubbed the side of my face against his bare shoulder. "No. They're slippery sons of bitches."

Carlo took his left hand away from mine that he'd been holding, and ran a line with one finger down my forehead. It felt as if I was being anointed. I wondered if he could feel the frowny line between my eyes. He said, "The Greeks believed the daemon wasn't a monster from hell. It was an inspiring force inside of us. Something that drives us."

Like I said, no telling where these conversations will go, especially when you sleep with a philosopher. I yawned. "This I did not know. Do you remember if we let the dogs out?"

"We did," he said. "Our anniversary is coming up next month. What do you want?"

"Such a romantic," I said. "I don't—"

Light snoring. Smile. I had probably worn him out. Our intimacy was usually reciprocal, but I had been the aggressor that night, giving to him what and when I chose and taking what pleasure I wanted. He never said, but I thought this might be a different way for him. I liked to imagine his first wife as something of a prig, passive in bed.

I stayed awake a bit longer, thinking about how long I had left with this man whom I had married only a few years before. Ten, twenty. Thirty years? He had been married to Jane for twenty-five years. Could I beat Jane's record? Was there such a thing as competitive marriage? If there was anything less than perfect it was the fear of losing Carlo after finding him at a time that some would call late in life. This makes sense. When you're young, nothing gets the appreciation it deserves. Love, liberty, life itself is taken for granted. Youth has no sense of its mortality. Later in life, if you're not still consumed with struggling to pay a mortgage and worried about the price of cat food, if you can actually retire, what you have more time for is brooding. Then things you didn't have time to worry about before can prey on your mind more, not less. Sometimes that old-age-serenity thing is crap.

This brooding about the past and future does not just apply to your traditional insecure female. It applies also to a tough old broad who has righted countless wrongs and can still kill a man with her bare hands. It applies also to older men who never paid for the things they did, and become obsessed that someday they'll be called to account.

All that aside, this story is mostly about my regret that I failed to preserve intact the one person I loved most in all the world, you sweet innocent Perfesser. Because even as we spoke that night about the past, it was presently coming for you. And I would discover that the one person I couldn't save you from was myself.

Three

He was short and stringy, with a full head of hair, but mostly gray. The overall effect was of a jockey past his prime. He used these features to his advantage, letting people think he was old and weak, until they got a better look at him. Some were fooled for a longer while than others. Those others shivered or inadvertently turned their back to him, as if affected by something evil at his core.

Prison hadn't made him officially bad. He was already declared bad by the time he was twelve. That was when he killed his little brother with his dad's shotgun. It was 1956. He told the judge, he told all of them it was an accident, but no one believed him. He got sent to a boys' reformatory school outside of Pascagoula, Mississippi. His own parents didn't even believe he was innocent of the homicide, and even if they did they wouldn't forgive him for killing their baby. They figured they saw the writing on the wall and Jeremiah would always be bad. So his parents wouldn't let him back in the house when he was released two years later. No, prison could not have made him worse than he was thought to be.

But it had honed his technique.

"Jeremiah Randolph Beaufort, number 4570937450."

"Yes, sir."

"Your sentence has been commuted. You are free to go without parole. Do you have any dress-outs?"

"Yes." Beaufort thought to add "sir," in his habit of being a model prisoner all these years, but then he thought it was no longer necessary. He didn't have to be a model prisoner any longer.

"We will provide you with a bus ticket to the destination of your choice. Do you have a choice?"

"Pascagoula," he said.

The warden laughed. "Well, that's practically around the corner. You could almost walk. You don't want to go any further than that?"

Beaufort pretended to think on it. "How about Bangkok?"

Now that he was getting out the warden appeared to be more relaxed than usual, laughed again rather than calling him on being a smart mouth. "It's just that, don't you have family or something? In another state?"

"Warden, I've been in here for thirty-three years, four months, and five days. What do you think?"

Not liking the feeling of being on the defensive, the warden shrugged. "I think you're fortunate to be released. Your sentence has been commuted, Mr. Beaufort, but you're hardly innocent of crime." The warden tapped an open file on his desk. "This last stint was your third. You've been in and out of prison for drug possession and trafficking"—he glanced down at the page before him, frowning as if the math was hard—"for almost fifty years."

This is Your Life," Beaufort said, his mood turning dark as he lost patience with sucking up to someone young enough to be his grandson.

Maybe it was how Beaufort said that, or maybe it was that the warden was too young to know the television program. He lifted his chin and looked at the freed man with different eyes, half shaded by his lids. If he had been about to ask whether Beaufort needed a ride to the bus station, now he didn't bother.

"See you soon," the warden said, as he said to all the departing cons.

Beaufort went from the office to a holding area where he could pick up his stuff and change into the clothes his transport had brought him. Thinking about his last interview. What did those bastards expect, that you'd lick their hand gratefully! You put a guy behind bars and take care of him like a zoo animal, three hots and a cot for years on end, fresh sheets you didn't have to wash yourself unless you're assigned to the laundry. They did everything but hold a guy's dick while he pissed. Then they let you out and say you have to be a human being now, lead a responsible life. Beaufort didn't know what he'd do if that was the life he had to look forward to, being grateful for a job bussing tables and sleeping in a cardboard box at the age of sixty-nine.

Beaufort walked out of Central Mississippi Correctional Facility. His transport had been provided via an old associate of his, a guy named Yanchak. The first time he was caught he didn't snitch on Yanchak. It didn't matter that Yanchak would have had him killed if he had, Yanchak owed him big-time.

The transport had brought him some civilian clothes to wear. He had put on real jeans for the first time in more than thirty years, nice if a little too big and too rough, and a shirt that didn't smell of that harsh detergent that bit the inside of your nose. Also a little money, enough to get himself food during the four-hour bus trip to Pascagoula and whatever came after. He didn't ask the transporter's name, but asked him for a little more money, figuring the guy hadn't given him all of it the first time.

"I have to buy a belt, too. You didn't bring me a belt."

The guy forked over the other ten-dollar bill he had held back. Beaufort took it, folded it, and put it with the rest in the breast pocket of his shirt. "Thank Yanchak for me," he said.

It was quiet in the car for a while as they drove. His hearing dulled from the constant noise of the prison population at all times of the day and night, Beaufort could hear nothing but the air from the open window pass his ears.

"So how does it feel?" The guy broke the silence after fidgeting around in his seat, shifting his hands back and forth over the steering wheel. He had a soft southern accent like Beaufort's that showed he was from this area. Beaufort wanted to show that he was the one with power, and not just an ex-con at the mercy of a driver. So he took a good long time before he said, "How does what feel?"

"Being out. After all this time."

Beaufort sniffed the air and found it strangely free of the stench of urine and antiseptic cleaning solution. "I'll have to get used to being able to bend over and pick up the soap."

The guy opened his mouth wide and laughed like it was a joke. "I hear you're someone to be reckoned with," the guy said.

"Some might say that," Beaufort replied.

The guy said, "I can see you're tough, you got this mean vibe coming off you, but Yanchak tells me you were in on that Three Strikes and Life deal."

"Yanchak should mind his own business." Beaufort didn't want to totally put the guy in his place because he needed the ride to the bus station and he didn't want to piss off Yanchak, whom he would need later. But he'd just as soon the guy shut up and let him view the scenery to see what had changed in thirty years.

The guy did not shut up. "So that was in the eighties, right? I wasn't born yet. If they caught you three times you got a mandatory life sentence." He twitched as if feeling the sentence. "Man, that's rough. I was thinking you might be pretty tough, but man, who actually gets caught three times?" He talked like other men might, making fun of someone and calling it conversation.

Not just a junky, but a stupid junky. Beaufort didn't respond. The thing he hated most was someone implying he wasn't smart. He didn't let anyone get away with this kind of talk inside, but it would only be a half hour or so and he'd never see the guy again. Beaufort stepped back out of his own head, noted his restraint, and admired it.

His silence, though, appeared to make the guy bolder. "So what is it with that, how did you happen to get caught three times? I mean, once, maybe twice at the outside, but you have to be pretty dumb or just careless to get caught three times."

"Maybe that's just what they caught me on. Maybe drug dealing wasn't the worst thing I did," Beaufort said, gritting his teeth. He turned his head to look out the passenger window of the car and hummed an old tune. When the tune came to a rest he'd make a little popping sound with his lips as he always did. This continued until they reached the bus station. Beaufort opened the car door.

"See you," the guy said.

"Tell Yanchak I'll be in touch when I'm ready." In prison he had learned that you don't let people get away with anything, or you won't survive. Beaufort took his left hand and put it on the back of the guy's head in what seemed like a peaceable gesture. Then he slammed the head forward, hard, onto the steering wheel. Beaufort looked inside himself and noted that he didn't take pleasure in the act and that he held himself back from actually breaking the guy's nose. He only did it from long instinct, to be tough so you didn't have to look over your shoulder all the time. And it let out a little of the built-up anger. After this he would be more careful to adapt to life outside.

Starting now. He said, "Thanks for the ride," gave his palm a swipe on his jeans to get off the hair oil, and left the car.

Four

Pascagoula had changed some but not much. The same long buildings that made up the strip malls from the eighties were there, they just had different names on them. White Castle was now a Taco Bell. Krispy Klean laundromat was now a Nice Nails.

The bus station was in the same place, only with decades more of grime built up. And two blocks away was the same library. Beaufort noted that.

But first, go to the Ace Hardware (which hadn't changed in fifty years) and get a short hank of twine to keep up his jeans. He stepped around the corner outside, looped the rope around his waist, tied it, and pulled his shirt over so no one could see he didn't have a belt.

Second, use the money he saved on a belt for a large burrito and a strawberry shake to fill his belly for a long walk.

Third, take that long walk. He smiled to himself, thinking how that phrase was one used for men going to their execution. In his case, he was going to make sure it was never used in that context.

On the way out of town, he passed the kind of motel off old Interstate 90 where truckers stayed. He asked if they had rooms and they said sure, plenty.

Would they hold one for a few hours?

Sure. Did he have a credit card?

No.

Then no.

He took a deep breath and remained polite, would have to take his chances there would be a room available later, hopefully before the sun went down and the truckers who were tired of sleeping in their cabs started checking in. He stopped at a Quik Mart next to the motel and got a bottle of water for the trip. Imagine that, three brands of water in bottles. Cold, too.

He walked about six miles without getting tired of walking, even though his prison shoes were not the best. From time to time he'd pick up that tune he knew, the one where he popped his lips at the rest. The sensation of going and going without stopping, without running into a wall or a barbed-wire fence, was exhilarating, almost religious. He didn't mind the humidity or the bugs, they came with the freedom. He felt like he could have walked all night. He was in good shape.

But he didn't keep walking. He stopped at some property past the side of town that was too poor to attract any developers. No one had ever bought this land, a bunch of dirt marked here and there with oak trees sagging with Spanish moss. The only sign of human life that remained on the property was the blackened chimney of a fireplace that had once risen from his childhood home before the place burned down.

His heart started to race as it had not from the walking. He strode over the concrete foundation of the house in a few steps, marveling how small the place was, much smaller than he thought when he was seven years old or so. What he was looking for wasn't in the chimney. It would have been easy to put it there, but too chancy that someone would nose around and find it. He put his back to the back of the chimney, feeling the stonework that had eroded in decades of exposure to the wind and the rain. He put his arms straight in front of him, sighting the line they led to. Then he walked the line.

A good ways off from the chimney he found the first rock, looking like any old rock that had wound up there however rocks wind up. He looked up and saw the next one. And the next. When he got to that third rock, bigger than the other two, but so far off you couldn't easily see it from the house, he moved it to the side and started to dig. Last time he was here he had a car and a shovel, and that made this whole process easier, but you couldn't have everything easy. His nails and the cuticles around them were encrusted with black soil by the time he dug down a good foot and a half to a metal box, somewhat rusted, but not so it wouldn't unlock with the little key hidden underneath the lining of his wallet.

He opened the box and took out the plastic bag. It had a satisfying heft to it.

He didn't hang around to count the contents of the bag. Before he got back to the highway he stopped to put a few twenties from the bag into his wallet and hid the bag with the rest of the money down the front of his jeans. Tomorrow he would get something better.

Beaufort walked the six miles back as the sun was going down, went into the Quik Mart men's room and washed up some so he wouldn't stand out. Nothing to make anyone notice him, dirty hands or anything. The place offered packaged ham and cheese sandwiches and six-packs of beer. He carried these things next door to the motel. They still had rooms. There was a different clerk who hardly glanced at him, instead keeping his focus on a device that looked like a small laptop computer without a keyboard. A movie played on it, a superhero he didn't recognize, but you could tell from the cape and tights. Beaufort had some catching up to do. The superhero was fighting men who were meant to look like bad guys. Bad guys never changed. This reassured him.

He paid cash for one night.

The next morning Beaufort walked over to the truck stop for a real breakfast, nothing that came wrapped in paper or cellophane, and no powdered eggs. He ordered three over easy, sausage patties, and hash browns at the counter. He still felt the euphoria of the day before. God, it was good to be out. He took big gulps of air between bites like even the oxygen was better.

A skinny waitress, with a ring in her nose that made him think of a starving cow, poured his coffee. He asked where was the nearest Kmart.

"Mobile," she said, kind of sullen and snotty, naming a city that he knew was a good distance away.

Now Beaufort, though he was small, had a way of seeming to get bigger until he filled up the space around him. "Is there any place closer than forty miles?" he asked. He kept his voice soft, but the coffeepot shook a little in the waitress's hand as if she'd known mean men in her life and he was one of that kind. Some coffee sloshed onto the counter.

"Now look what you did," Beaufort said, without taking his eyes off her. Watching someone else's fear made him feel better about his own, the fear he could only admit to himself alone in the middle of the night when it kept him awake.

She apologized as she wiped at the spot with a towel and whispered, "There's a Super Walmart closer in town."

His hand shot forward—he was proud of how fast his reflexes still were—and grasped hers, pressed down on the towel underneath. The waitress was too shocked to cry out, and by the time she could have done so he had let go. Then she had no reason to cry out, because he had not hurt her or touched her in an inappropriate spot.

He said, "So I ask you about a Kmart and you don't have the courtesy to tell me about a Walmart. What's the difference?"

She appeared greatly chastened now. "No difference, sir. They have everything."

"Clothes, food, soap."

"Yes, sir."

"That's better. Okay, where is this Super Walmart and can I walk to it?"

"I don't think so. Must be a good two miles north of here. On Denny Avenue. Do you know where that is?"

"I know it." He scraped up the last of the yolk on his plate with a slice of white toast, left enough for the bill and a ten percent tip, and headed out. He left a good tip and he hadn't hurt the girl. He wasn't the same man he had been in his youth; he told himself that this proved it.

Three hours later he was cruising the town on a new bicycle, a large backpack strapped to his back, layered with money at the bottom, some clean clothes and basic toiletries over that, and a small knife, the kind you used to gut fish. It would do in the short term until he connected with Yanchak.

Around lunchtime he found a place called Raising Cane's Chicken Fingers that offered a local paper for free in a box out front. The "fingers" he discovered to be strips of chicken. The paper told him there was a room to rent cheap not too far away. The price of the bike had taken his breath away, and told him just how far his money could stretch these days. He would have to make contact sooner than he thought.

This troubled him, as he had intended to stay clean while he took care of business.

There was some hesitation from the man who answered the door of the place with the room to let. Beaufort was not invited in immediately. Might have something to do with the neighborhood. Staying alive in prison meant reading other people, and Beaufort figured he had this guy summed up pretty quick. Some affliction that caused him to hold his hand in front of his body and a slight limp. Stroke maybe. Getting disability checks. While Beaufort sized up the man he could tell that the man was sizing up Beaufort, and coming to the same initial conclusion as everyone else, mostly. Just like the guy who drove him to the bus station. Just like the waitress. Smallish, old. What harm could he be? If the man felt the hair go up on the back of his neck he didn't trust the instinct.

"I take cash, one week at a time," the man finally said. "Fifty."

"That's okay with me," Beaufort said, and gave him two twenties and a ten from his wallet. "I might only be here a week, is that okay?"

The man looked disappointed but took the money and showed him to the room. Beaufort thought he might have looked less suspicious if he had asked to see the room first, but apparently that didn't matter. Luckily the transfer of money removed any residual hesitation. The room was clean enough and had a private bathroom attached. He had kitchen privileges, too, as long as he contributed to the beer supply. Neither man had asked the other his name.

When the bedroom door was shut, Beaufort finally sagged onto the bed and doubled over from the ache in his gut. It was easy to hide that ache from others, but not from himself. He almost thought he would start to cry, but long years of disuse made it impossible. He got up, put his new clothes in a drawer in the room but kept the money in his backpack. Then he left the house, got on his bike, and headed off to the Pascagoula City Library to do two things: find out how to research things on the internet, and get himself an email address.

He had fears about dealing with the world that had changed so much during his time in prison. Not fears of people, but of changing times and whether he would look stupid in them. Whether people could tell he was an ex-con and how long he'd been put away. Along with the nightmares of killing, he had had dreams of people laughing at him. And he was also afraid, not of anyone in the drug trade, any driver or waitress or man with a room to rent, but of people both alive and dead for a long time.

But most of all, he was afraid of this thing called forensic science.

Five

Because we hadn't experienced so much life together, Carlo and I tried to catch up by telling each other stories, like the one I told him about being six years old and learning about the Clutter/Walker family murders. There was still much neither of us knew, but it was about making the time to know it, not necessarily about keeping it secret.

Except for my feelings when I had killed a few people during my career. I had told him some of the facts surrounding those times, but I had never confessed how deeply satisfying it felt, knowing the terror and pain they had caused others, to watch those bad boys die. I had to carry those demons alone.

The father in the story I had told Carlo about in bed that night was Fergus Quinn. We all managed to survive childhood and followed in his law enforcement footsteps. My sister Ariel joined the CIA. Todd, the baby in the family, went with Dad's outfit, but eventually did become a homicide detective.

I was career FBI until I got into some trouble and was discreetly transferred to Tucson, Arizona, where I hated the boss and opted for early retirement. Shortly thereafter I met Carlo DiForenza, a Catholic priest turned philosophy professor. Hoping to find some serenity, I took his class on Buddhism at the local university. The serenity still eludes me, but I did find love when I married my, as I called him, Perfesser. To him I was always "O'Hari," a blend of my Irish roots and the sultry spy Mata Hari, not the first woman to use her sex as a weapon. Such were Carlo's fantasies about me and the kind of life I had once led.

Carlo knew how to retire with style. While I busied myself with private investigations that sometimes paid more in trouble than in money, Carlo spent his time dabbling in all those pursuits he had put aside first for the priesthood, then for philosophy, then for taking care of a first wife who had been ill a long time. Jane was her name. While I had redecorated the house in my own taste, her ghost sometimes still appeared, in the form of the pugs she had given Carlo before her death, or the smells that struck me whenever I opened the kitchen cabinet where spices like coriander sat waiting to be used. When I thought of her, I imagined her being a really good woman, one worthy of Carlo. And at those times the pugs, the spices, they judged me.

At times like that I had to shake off the suspicion that I didn't measure up to her. There was no evidence for this, as I had resisted asking Carlo to tell stories about their life together.

Not to say we didn't have a full life of our own, apart from Jane. During the relatively short time I had known him, Carlo had started writing a book called *Asterisks and Idols*, which he tried to explain to me on several occasions with little success. With a couple of colleagues and the priest at the Episcopal church we sometimes attended, he was planning a graduate seminar on the interface of science and myth.

Nor was life only about religion. Tackling geology, we had hiked dozens of trails in the Catalina Mountains near our home, and there collected rocks; he could name each one.

But interest in five-billion-year-old rocks was five minutes ago, and Carlo had recently lifted his eyes to the heavens. No, not religion—astronomy. I liked taking peeks through his twelve-inch Celestron, an impressive reflecting telescope with a GPS system. Carlo would tower behind me with his hands on my hips and his chest pressing the back of my head, just to make sure I was in the right position for the viewfinder, he said. I can't forget seeing the Orion Nebula while sandwiched between Carlo and infinity. That and the scent of Gillette aftershave.

Oh God, how I loved him!

Ahem: This is why I was so excited about the anniversary present I planned to give Carlo: a full overnight viewing at nearby Kitt Peak Observatory. Kitt was one of the ten largest observatories in the whole world, and it was only a two-hour drive from our house. In Arizona a two-hour drive is nothing. I planned to drop him off and pick him up the next day, so the gift would include chauffeur service.

I had just finished making the reservation online when the phone rang.

Gemma-Kate, my niece, Todd's daughter, showed up as the ID. I wasn't in the mood to talk to her just then, but when the rings went to the answering machine I heard her say, "Aunt Brigid, pick up the phone. I have an issue."

This was the first time she had ever asked for my help. Shit.

I picked up the phone. I said, "Are you pregnant?"

"Did you really think I would come to you if I were pregnant?"

Oh snap, I think is what the kids say. "I suppose not," I said, thinking of other possibilities. "You need me professionally? Did you assault some frat boy?"

"I take umbrage to that," she said with a mild tone that didn't match said umbrage.

"Don't be coy. How bad did you hurt him?"

Now, one might think these assumptions a little insensitive, and that Gemma-Kate would rise up in shock, angry self-defense, what have you. That's because you don't know Gemma-Kate.

Nine months ago she had come from Florida after her mother died from a long illness, and moved in with us to establish Arizona residency prior to starting at the state university. Bad things ensued. The funny thing was, I discovered Gemma-Kate wasn't gratuitously evil, not like a serial killer or anything; she just didn't have the empathy or moral imperatives the rest of us have. She has always maintained that poisoning one of our pugs was only an accident.

She said.

This was Gemma-Kate's psyche, while sporting a petite physique that had spring breakers in Fort Lauderdale risking statutory rape when she was fourteen, short curly blond hair, and a roundedness about all her features that made her appear as threatening as Betty Boop.

Maybe I know her because, as may be apparent from my remark about the little thrill I've experienced watching bad guys suffer, I tip a smidgen to the left of the empathy spectrum myself.

"Listen," she said, "I've been forced to take a humanities class, so I signed up for something called Oral History. I have to interview someone old by next week."

"I'm not that old," I said.

"Oh, come on," she said.

"No. You already know everything about me that can be known. I'm not telling you the rest."

"But I don't have that much time and I don't know any other old people in Tucson."

"You are not endearing yourself to me."

"I'll cook dinner," she said.

This gave me pause. During the time she had lived with us I discovered Gemma-Kate had become a gourmet cook while taking care of her sick mother.

Seeing that she had me now, she said, "So, yes. I have a biochemistry class to get to."

"What about Carlo?" I asked. "Interview Carlo."

"Why?"

"Ex-Catholic priest, could be a good story in there for you." Frankly, I didn't think there would be anything to interest her, but it was a good way to skirt talking to her myself and still get dinner.

"Was he a priest when he met his first wife?" she asked.

After hesitating a moment, "I'm not sure" slipped out of my mouth. *Why did I not know this?* I thought.

Whether or not she heard that hesitancy in my voice, whether it intrigued her, I couldn't tell. What I could tell is that she felt she had sucked all the value out of this conversation and grown bored. She agreed to interview him.

Then we hung up and I forgot about Gemma-Kate and picked up the latest issue of *Cooking Light,* telling myself I wasn't competing with a dead wife. Of course not. I was too mature and worldly-wise for that.

Six

If you had told Beaufort that a tough guy like him would hesitate at the front of a library, afraid to walk through the door, he would have laughed at you. Yet here he was, conscious of his brain sending the signals to pick up one resisting foot after another, up the front steps of the Pascagoula City Library.

There was information to be had in there, free and anonymous. He had heard from other inmates about the development of what they called the digital age. He didn't have much to do with it himself. Being a lifer meant being in a bad place. Not a bad place the way people spoke of in this modern psychology, but literally a bad place locked up with scum suckers. You didn't get nice perks like computer time. This computer business made him feel like a time traveler from the past. The kid walking down the steps, nearly bumping into him before swerving with an apology, was looking at what they called his "device." Little computers you held in your hand that did everything, add up numbers, look at movies, even act as a telephone or a camera.

Email. Beaufort turned and watched the kid walk down the sidewalk. If that punk could get the hang of this, so could he.

Then somehow he was inside, going to the front desk and asking for help from a woman who held her hair up with a stick. He played humble, old, and ignorant with the librarian whom he could tell liked him even though she must have been a good twenty years younger. It looked like he still had a way with the ladies. Certain kinds of ladies, anyway—the lonely ones who hadn't had a man in a while. With the way he'd kept his body fit in prison he probably looked a little younger than his age when he wanted to.

At his request for computer instruction she showed him to one of the computers that sat in a row along the wall. She pulled up a chair and spent quite a bit of time with him on a slow morning, telling him about search engines and which sources were reliable.

He understood little and grew impatient. "Show me how to set up an email account," he said, and then added, "Please."

The woman cocked her head and for one moment fixed him with one eye like a bird, but if she found anything odd about him she gave no further indication. She accessed her own email and showed him the way the address was constructed. "See, I use my name, PatriciaButts @yahoo.com."

"Got it," Beaufort said.

"Good!" Patricia Butts said. Beaufort wondered if she was a teacher. She acted like a teacher with a student. When he questioned her about getting information from the internet, she showed him how to, as she put it, "google."

When she left him to take care of a frowny woman with a stack of books at the checkout counter, Beaufort set up a Yahoo account for himself, then went back to the internet, where the little blinking line rested on the Google space. He felt like one of those archaeologists opening a long-closed tomb, the suspense of finding something weighing against the suspense of finding nothing. He typed a name. A throb of pain hit behind his left eye, putting him on notice just how tense he was about this. He reached up and rubbed hard at a spot on his forehead as he hit the RETURN button with his other index finger and watched the computer. Within less than the time it had taken to touch his forehead the screen announced 500,000,000 "results" starting with some photos of medical appliances and something called Fashionable Canes. Whatever sound he made had Patricia the Librarian look in his direction. At least he didn't sweep the computer off the table, but for the first time he thought this might be harder than he had previously figured. Taking one of those deep breaths that he had learned in prison support groups, he slid his chair back and decided to go for some lunch.

After all, he kept repeating to himself, this was all just to make sure everything was copacetic, that the thing called forensic science wasn't lying in wait to bite him in the ass. Despite the dreams that threatened him, no one alive knew what really happened.

He chose an Applebee's because it was close to the library. These menus made him nervous. There were so many options for everything these days, it would take some time to stop being either giddy or frustrated by all the choices of eating establishments and the vast menus so big you couldn't see over the top of them. The menu fluttered in his hand when he tried to hold it up, so he put it on the table in front of him, opened to the sandwich pages, and stuck his hands between his knees to steady them.

"Hi. My name is Candy. I'll be your server today," a voice said.

"Give me the Reuben with fries," he said. It was one of the things where he recognized all the ingredients. "And a beer."

"What kind of beer do you want?" Candy asked with an efficient click of her ballpoint pen.

Tired of choosing, tired with the effort of struggling to fit in, he gave her a glare that would have once cowed a gang member one-third his age and growled, "Just bring me a fucking beer."

She cocked her hip in one direction and gave her head a little jerk in the other. "Well, bless yer heart," she said, making him imagine her plunging that ballpoint pen into the side of his neck.

His look must have changed into one of sheer befuddlement, because she said, more kindly, "I'll bring you a Bud."

His meal arrived. While chomping through it, and dipping his fries in extra ketchup, another luxury on the outside (there were so many!), he thought about the conversation in the prison some years before that had started him to worry again.

It was some small-time loser who was doing fifteen on an armed robbery conviction. He talked about how they were doing so much with

30

analyzing folks' DNA. That it was putting a lot of guys in, sure, but getting some off, too. He was going to appeal his case because there was a bit of evidence that might have someone else's DNA on it.

"You think this could get you out?" Beaufort had asked.

"Doesn't hurt to try," the guy answered.

"Did you do the crime?" Beaufort asked.

The guy shrugged. As far as Beaufort knew, the loser was still doing his time, but late at night when he tried to sleep he kept thinking the words *it was putting a lot of guys in, sure.*

Then he heard that they had started reinvestigating cold cases with the new DNA techniques. Rapes and homicides that had occurred years ago. Nicole Brown Simpson. JonBenét Ramsey. Especially high-profile cases like that, that had never been solved.

Like the cases no one ever pinned on him.

It got so he was running through every second of those long-ago events every time his mind tried to rest. Where he might have shed a cell. Whether his semen could still ID him. Even apart from that there was now some massive fingerprint database, all computerized, that he heard could find a match within seconds. He couldn't decide if he should worry more about the DNA or about the fingerprints. It got to be an obsession. He wanted to know if anyone still thought about the case. But he didn't want to know. But he wanted to know.

There's some who would say, Hey, give it up, guy. You're nearly seventy years old, coming to the end anyway. What difference does it make if you go back to prison now? What difference does it make if you spend your final days on death row? You don't have that many final days left.

Funny thing was, you think about the future more when you're old than when you're young.

That was why he couldn't put it out of his mind, whether or not someone, someday, would link him to the things he had done. It invaded his thoughts every ten minutes or so, the way they say young men think about sex, or old men think about death. Nobody ever talks about how a killer might suffer, thinking about being caught. Not every killer was cold-blooded, or not totally, or at least not for a whole lifetime. He brushed the back of his hand against his eyes. Do one thing and you're marked for life.

Appetite suddenly lost, he stared down at his fries getting soggy in the ketchup pool on his plate. Stop thinking, he told himself. Be a man, he told himself. He paid his bill and heaved himself out of the booth to go back to the library.

Beaufort spotted a Walgreens down the street from Applebee's, stopped in there and, after looking again at an enormous number of options on the shelf, with odd names like Zantac, chose a large bottle of Tums and put it in his backpack. Outside the library, he stopped for a smoke, figuring if it wasn't allowed in a restaurant it sure wouldn't be allowed in a library.

Spilling a few fruit-flavored tablets into his mouth, with a deep breath and a curse at the Reuben sandwich mixed with the anxiety that had given him gas, he went back to the bank of computers and tried typing *Walker* again, this time with *Murder*. There on the screen he saw the possibility of *Walker family murders*. His heart pounded and his hands went moist. He wondered if the computer could somehow detect what he was thinking. That he was thinking of the nightmares. But not knowing was worse than the nightmares. He accepted the suggestion.

There were a million results, but the ones he saw at the top of the screen were all on target. He chose the second and read. He read things he didn't know about the Walker family, Cliff and Christine in their midtwenties, and two children, a boy and a girl both under five years of age. This information wasn't readily accessible in 1959, only in the police reports and whatever the police chose to give to the newspapers. For the first time he read about the neighbor finding the bodies, and about the ton of evidence that had been collected:

Some red cellophane from a cigarette wrapper, supposedly from a brand that Cliff Walker did not smoke.

A bloody boot print that did not match anyone in the family.

Witnesses reporting the presence of a '57 Chevy in the Walkers' yard.

Witnesses reporting seeing Hickock with a scratch on his face.

Baby dolls wrapped in Christmas paper that Hickock had sold to a preacher in Louisiana.

A pocketknife with a fruit tree design that had belonged to Cliff Walker and the one like it in Hickock's possession when he was captured.

A fingerprint on the bathtub faucet that didn't match any known individual.

Semen in Christine Walker.

And finally, that they were trying to match Hickock's and Smith's DNA to that semen.

Beaufort looked at the date this was posted. April 2012. It chilled him to think of all the people who might read this, who knew so much because of this computer. Cold cases. The automated fingerprint system. DNA profiling. Could they really test those old bones of the two killers? All this was new in the last twenty years, thirty at most. In 1959 the closest they could get to matching a man to his semen was the blood group. The passing of time might have eased Beaufort's mind, but this, this new world changed everything.

Steeling himself against the burn in his gut, he went back to the place where you could ask a question, and with two fingers slowly picked out the letters on the keyboard: "what happened to Smith and Hickock DNA test?"

An article from a newspaper called *The Bradenton Times* appeared.

Ian Meadows of the Sarasota County Sheriff's Department spent years investigating all the available evidence, both physical, written, and witness, concerning the case that had been cold for nearly fifty years. Then he successfully filed an affidavit to exhume the bodies of Perry Smith and Richard Hickock, the article said. If DNA tests showed that one of them had raped Christine Walker, then it would be one more inaccuracy contained in Truman Capote's "nonfiction novel." Chewing more antacid tablets, Beaufort read, "'Capote began telling everybody he was writing something that was 100 percent accurate,'" said Ralph F. Voss, who in 2011 wrote *Truman Capote and the Legacy of 'In Cold Blood.'* Should the Florida connection be confirmed, Voss said, 'there's going to be a whole lot of reason to write articles about how Smith and Hickock conned Capote.'"

Holy Christ. He remembered he was in a library, and looked up over the top of the computer screen to see the librarian staring at him. She looked away quickly, and he wondered if he had said the curse aloud.

As terrified as he was of taking any chances, Beaufort knew that if he was to have any peace at all the rest of his life, he couldn't stick his head in the sand. This internet business was fine as far as it went, but he needed to track down Detective Meadows, find out what he knew that wasn't recorded here. This forensic science business.

Seven

"I'm supposed to ask if I can turn on this recorder," Gemma-Kate said.

"Sure, that's fine," Carlo said.

GEMMA-KATE, *reading from prepared notes:* I'm interviewing Carlo
DiForenza of Tucson, Arizona. Let's get some of the basics out
of the way. How old are you and where were you born?

CARLO: I'm sixty-seven years old. I was born in Torino, Italy, in
1949, four years after World War II ended.

I had cleaned up the kitchen after dinner while they were talking,
and then put on a sweater and went outside to listen to all this, pulling
up a patio chair near the chaise lounges where they sat keeping warm
by the fire pit. I knew pretty much all of what Carlo was telling Gemma-
Kate, heard it more than once and never tired of it. I thought this was
what it meant to love.

That was a good evening, all of us accustomed to the worst that life
could throw, yet none of us conscious of that melodramatic thing they
call impending doom.

When Carlo gave his date and place of birth he spoke like someone
who knew he was being recorded, carefully and slightly formal.

Carlo's father was a fisherman, with a small boat that he took into the Mediterranean from the coastal town. This was before the whole Cote d'Azur from Montpellier down the Italian coast to Sorrento was linked by wealth, border patrol, and the euro. So Carlo's boyhood was that of the too-intelligent lower-class child, sneaking into the local library as if it was something sinful to read. His mother, Sophia, took him to mass daily at the large church that had been built to house the Holy Shroud. Carlo would stare at it during the mass, squinting his eyes in hopes that the blurring would make the figures more likely to move. He wanted to be the kind of person who saw visions.

GEMMA-KATE: Did you believe the shroud was the burial cloth of Jesus?

CARLO: Of course. We all did.

GEMMA-KATE: It's not. Science has proven it's not.

CARLO: Does it matter? I think the miraculous lies not so much in the physical world as in what meaning we see in it. And how we're changed by the meaning.

Gemma-Kate gave him the respect of not scoffing, while I watched Carlo look at her with an open smile. The smile was one he had turned on me from time to time. It said, *you either feel this or you don't, and I won't try to convince you.*

GEMMA-KATE: Did the shroud ever move?

CARLO: It moved me.

Carlo's father, Antonio, had a brother in the States who pressed the family for years to emigrate to the Midwest. The DiForenza family, Antonio, Carlo, an older brother, Franco, and Sophia, did so in 1959 when Carlo was only ten. But he spoke Italian at home his whole life, and that accounted for a rich undertone of the romantic accent that still surfaced, especially when he was talking to me. Especially in bed. This was not mentioned in the recorded interview.

The shroud's influence, added to his mother's, sent Carlo off to seminary before he graduated from St. Anthony's High School in Kansas City. This was a great relief to Sophia, who had lost Franco to the gangs several years before. Carlo never said, and I never suggested, that maybe he was making up for the loss of his brother, hoping to ease his mother's grief by being the best boy possible. Being a Roman Catholic priest. At that time he didn't realize being a priest would produce its own shame, what it did to his mother when he left the priesthood and married. I knew that part, too.

But back then, the priesthood itself gave Sophia some amount of *agita*. While in seminary, Carlo volunteered to do part of his chaplaincy in the Kansas State Penitentiary—Lansing—the same prison where Franco had died. Sophia was terrorized by the thought of him entering that prison.

GEMMA-KATE: What about you?

CARLO: I let the warden know who I was, and he checked the records and personally escorted me to the spot where it had happened and had me talk to the chaplain who had been there, and who said Franco was already gone when he arrived on the cell block. It felt like a pilgrimage, only backwards, in the sense that I was following the footsteps not of a declared saint, but of a declared sinner. Still, you learn.

Carlo formed a strong friendship with the head chaplain.

GEMMA-KATE: Another priest.

CARLO: No, actually Mark Listewnik was Presbyterian. I learned a lot from him over many rounds of drinks. And he knew all about my order.

GEMMA-KATE: By order you mean—

CARLO: The religious order to which I belonged. I was, I am, a Franciscan.

GEMMA-KATE: You mean you can't stop being a priest.

CARLO: No. Once you're ordained, it's forever.

GEMMA-KATE: But you married. Twice.

CARLO: Yes, I did.

At her questioning, Carlo told Gemma-Kate some stories of his time, as he called it, behind bars. He lived in the rectory of a large church in the city, and drove a dilapidated car back and forth to work every day. There he was cleared by security along with the rest of the prison staff, and had the use of a small desk in Pastor Listewnik's office. He had visiting hours and heard confessions of the Catholic prisoners. He gave last rites on many occasions, most in the clinic where men would go to die of rotted livers and kidneys and lungs after years of chemical abuse. Once he gave last rites while kneeling in a pool of blood when an inmate had been knifed while taking a shower.

CARLO: Convicts die just like everyone else, frightened and sad
   that they hadn't learned how to pray before now.
GEMMA-KATE: How long did you work there?
CARLO: Just three months.

I noticed Carlo's answers were not so expansive as they had been at first. He wasn't exactly curt, but hardly as forthcoming as when he talked about his youth and his family, open even about his brother, Franco, dying in prison. I think GK noticed it, too.

GEMMA-KATE: What about this Listewnik? How long did he stay at
   the prison? Did you keep in touch with him?

He started to cross his arms and then consciously separated them again, refusing to give in to that gesture of hiding oneself. Carlo answered only the last question. "No."

GEMMA-KATE: No . . .
CARLO: No, I didn't keep in touch with him.
GEMMA-KATE: What about your first wife? Where were you and
   how long were you out of the priesthood before you met her?

Carlo paused. I could see him going through possible answers as if he was talking about existentialism rather than the simple facts of his life. That was when I thought again how this was one question I had never asked.

"Gemma-Kate Quinn," I said. "It's a school project, not a *Dr. Phil* show."

CARLO: It's okay, love. After my prison chaplaincy I was assigned to a church as an assistant priest. I worked there for two years, and then had my own church where I worked for three more years. I was thirty years old then. So young, and yet feeling as if I'd experienced all that was possible in a lifetime. Feeling so wise. I think all young people feel that way. And yet, I had what they call a crisis of faith, which must have been brewing, but that I never acknowledged.

That's all he would say. His vocation ended, he was hired as an assistant professor at the local college. He talked about marrying Jane, moving to Tucson, teaching at the university, her death. As always, Carlo spoke of her respectfully, but not at length. I was content with that because I didn't want to know. It was enough that sometimes her presence still haunted the house, in some vacation souvenir that remained on a corner shelf, or that smell in the kitchen cupboard of the spices I never used. I was a newcomer, both to Carlo's life and to the normal world itself. But these were my own thoughts as I listened to Gemma-Kate interview Carlo.

Had he actually answered Gemma-Kate's question about how long he was out of the priesthood before he met Jane? Had he even said her name? I thought not.

GEMMA-KATE: So your wife died, you kept teaching at the university, and that's where you met Aunt Brigid, right?
CARLO: That's right, five years after Jane's passing. I was in the philosophy department. We met when Brigid took my course on the ethics of Buddhism. She was not a very good student, I recall. I kicked her out of the class.

"Oh, go on," I said. "You just wanted to date me."

I interrupted with "It's a sense of right and wrong, dear."
Carlo hid a smile and Gemma-Kate ignored me altogether.

GEMMA-KATE: How much did you know about Aunt Brigid before
you married her? Did you know about what she did with the
FBI or did she give you that crap about investigating copyright
infringements?

I jerked to attention with another sharp word ready, but Carlo raised
two fingers in almost a peace sign. "That's your aunt's story to tell. You
and I are talking about my life right now."

GEMMA-KATE: It seems like you stop me before we get to anything
really good, but okay. Let's see. Did you know anyone famous
who was in prison while you were there?
CARLO: Just like a Quinn, always most interested in crime. No,
there wasn't really, not during my time. But there had been.

Gemma-Kate turned off the recorder, apparently having sufficiently
exhausted the story of Carlo's life. She asked, "Who?"
Carlo looked at me and we both smiled, knowing what was coming.
"Have you heard the names Richard Hickock and Perry Smith?"
Gemma-Kate got sort of a rock-star-fan look on her face and Carlo
noticed.
"Ah, now I'm less boring." Carlo suggested we move inside, so we
left the embers of the fire pit and sat in the living room. He went into
his library in the front room, made some racket, and returned with a
plastic bin. He sat on the floor with Gemma-Kate, rustled around in the
bin until he found a large brown envelope, and from there drew out several articles about Hickock and Smith.
"You told me you didn't have anything on them," I said.
"I just remembered," Carlo said. "It's not much." He raised his eyebrows with, I thought, some air of faked mystery, which made me wonder if he was telling the truth and why he would lie.

"Those are the killers from the book *In Cold Blood*," he said, pointing to their pictures in the article. "Your aunt and I were talking about it just the other night. I assume you've heard of that as well."

"I just know the killers' names because I saw those movies they made about Truman Capote a few years ago. I never read the book," Gemma-Kate said.

"I have a copy." I went into the library where Carlo had gotten the bin from. I haven't said much about this room in my earlier stories. It was to Carlo what garages or other man caves are to other men. Shelves lined the walls floor to ceiling, and more shelves were placed in two rows down the center of the room, with access on both sides of the shelves. Some of the works I recognized, like Plato's *Republic*, and Bertrand Russell's *History of Philosophy*, but only because of hearing Carlo quote from them. No question about it, Carlo and I were different. I was only recently beginning to admit how much.

My own paltry collection rested on a single shelf, so I was able to find the book easily. It still had the original jacket on it, cream-colored background with the title in black and Capote's name in maroon.

"You take care of this, it's a first edition," I said, bringing it back to the living room.

Gemma-Kate opened it to the title page. "'To my little girl on her birthday.' Grandpa gave this to you?"

"Your grandfather didn't have real strong boundaries," I said.

Eight

Beaufort had loaded his bike on the bus to Sarasota. A rental car would have been nice, but he needed Yanchak for that. He had told the man in Pascagoula he might be back and thanks for the use of the room.

It was easy to find the cop he wanted. Even if Beaufort hadn't seen his name on the internet article about the Walker cold case investigation, Ian Meadows's photo was on the Sarasota County Sheriff's Department website. Small towns like Sarasota, where they didn't think they had to worry about gangs, real criminals, they'd be all over themselves being friendly with the populace, that whole community-policing thing. Photographs of each guy in the division. There he was, round baby face with a mustache that didn't help, older guy who might have been a real homicide detective in his heyday, now working cold case homicides.

Beaufort parked his bike around the corner from the sheriff's office, and found a coffee shop close by where he could watch the entrance to the building. From there he saw when Meadows exited the building, and followed him on and off for a week to pick up his patterns. He wouldn't have been able to actually follow the guy home, as he couldn't keep up with a car. But he did find the guy's watering hole, which was within walking distance from the station.

Meadows was never on call in the evenings, which allowed him plenty of free time to drink. And talk like he was still somebody. But mostly drink. Always at the same bar, one of those places that cops frequent where there's always another cop to take them home in case of one too many. The Pelican Pub had dusty nautical decorations, a sign that said HEAD instead of RESTROOMS, heavy boat ropes with a sticky film on them lining the edge of the bar and making it uncomfortable to lean your elbows.

This guy, always on the same days, every other day. That probably meant he had a wife who would complain if he was gone too much. The same place at the bar, too, on this side of the corner. So Beaufort got there about a half hour before Meadows did, and parked himself, not on Meadows's usual stool, but on the other side of the corner.

Meadows arrived, and glanced at where Beaufort was sitting. He gave Beaufort a hurt look, as if the other man had taken something from him that was his by right. But he continued to amble down the bar and squished his body, not on his usual seat, but two away from the other man so it wouldn't look like he was gay. Beaufort had expected that. They were still close enough to talk. Two seats between them, no one would take one unless the bar was totally crowded; that was bar etiquette you could count on, and it had never changed.

Beaufort didn't look up at Meadows's approach, and nursed his beer until the other was through one finger of bourbon. He didn't want to speak until he figured the man was sufficiently relaxed.

Then in that nonthreatening southern accent Beaufort said, "Excuse me, sir."

When the man looked up with a face that didn't mind his particular thoughts being interrupted, Beaufort held up a few fingers. "Do you mind? If you'd rather—"

"No. No, that's okay," said Meadows. "What's up?"

"I'm traveling around Florida by myself and sometimes I get tired of the silence, know what I mean?"

The man nodded an opening, and rather than instantly start asking questions, which would have felt suspicious, Beaufort talked and talked like he really didn't want to hear what the other fellow had to say. He talked about Sarasota, and the weather in early December, how it makes everyone cranky because the summer should be over but wasn't. How the whole west coast of Florida had grown from the time he had lived there as a child. How he had been away from the area for a long time, working in Mississippi.

After a while Meadows's look, formerly melting with the bourbon, got a little icy, like he suspected Beaufort was going to put the touch on him, but he didn't shift his eyes away. So Beaufort kept going, how he was an old man now. How he was making a pilgrimage to all his old haunts now that his wife had died a year ago, God rest her soul. How he grew up in a small town not too far from Sarasota. Osprey, did the man ever hear of Osprey? He was headed there next.

"Where in Osprey?" Meadows asked.

Beaufort was ready for this one, having found Google Maps. He named an address about a quarter mile from where the Walker family had lived.

Like any other cop, as long as he wasn't going against confidentiality rules, Meadows couldn't help spilling about the case he was working on. He said, "How old are you, if you don't mind my asking."

"I'm sixty-three, and proud of it," Beaufort said, shaving a few years off just in case at some point Meadows was to do some math to find out how old Beaufort was at the time of the crime. "But why do you ask?"

"Ever hear about the Walker family murders?" Meadows asked.

"Hell, yeah," Beaufort said. "I was just knee-high to a grasshopper when it all happened, the Clutters and then the Walkers, and I was living in the same town. Remember the Clutters?"

"I guess I do," Meadows said.

"The Clutters was scary enough, and then *blam*, the Walkers happened like a one-two punch just a month or so later. I remember my parents locking the doors for the first time and not letting me go out by myself after dark. Everyone was scared that it would happen again. Times like that, the whole country changed, didn't it?" Beaufort mentioned how he had read *In Cold Blood* when it first came out, and that everyone in Osprey talked about how their town was made famous in that book, just because the men who committed the Clutter family murders were suspected of killing the Walkers, too. "You'd think I could remember the names of those guys. What was their names again?"

"Richard Hickock and Perry Smith," Meadows said. But you could tell he wasn't as interested in the Clutters. He was beginning to get bored and changed the subject back. "The Walkers? I'm on a cold case squad in this county, and I just reopened the case."

"No. Really? You're a detective?" Beaufort said, with that combination of slyness and squirming excitement a person exhibits when they meet a celebrity. He drew his hand across his mouth like meeting Meadows had made him salivate. "Can I buy you a drink? Sir," he said to the bartender, "another of whatever . . ." Beaufort looked expectant, and the man supplied his name.

"Ian Meadows."

"Whatever Detective Meadows is drinking," Beaufort said. "And another Bud for me."

Detective Meadows waved a dismissive hand, but you could tell he was suitably charmed by the reaction, enough to ignore the fact that Beaufort had not supplied his name in turn. It might have also been that he had been bored to an anesthetic state by all Beaufort's chatter, and was relieved to be able to do a little talking himself, and about a topic that no one else cared to hear anymore.

Beaufort asked, "So why are you so interested in the Walker case? You're a damn sight younger than me. Doesn't seem like you're old enough to even be born when it happened."

"That's what they say back at the station. I get ribbed all the time, how I'm looking for a dead man. They tell me the murderer must be in his eighties or nineties now if he's even alive. I dunno. Why are people still interested in Jack the Ripper? Why do they still talk about the Black Dahlia here in the States? The Walker killing happened near here, so we all grew up knowing about the family where they never found the killer. Just like you. Plus there's this possibility of DNA profiling that has opened up all kinds of cold cases."

Beaufort felt his breathing quicken at the mention of DNA and even with the beer had to concentrate on keeping his chest from rising and falling with his alarm. He decided to change the subject until he could get better control of himself. "They kind of have a point, you keep investigating even after the killer is dead."

"What makes you think so?" Meadows asked.

"I don't know, I just figure all this time. Like your friends say."

Meadows nodded and took a drink. "But there's the DNA."

Beaufort shook his head slowly in amazement, better able to talk about it now. "That DNA business. That's really something, isn't it? What did you have to test? And hey, am I keeping you from something?"

"Hell, no! It's my favorite topic and everyone else tells me to shut up about it already. The semen they found in Christine Walker, the mother, was still viable. That's how I got permission to exhume Smith's and Hickock's bodies. It was all high-profile enough to get me some attention, get my sample into the queue at the lab."

"What did you find out?"

Meadows's face fell. "Too bad their DNA was corrupt, but we kind of, *kind of*, got an analysis that showed it wasn't them. Hickock definitely excluded, Smith mostly. I still have my doubts, though."

"I bet you're right, I bet it was them," Beaufort said.

"Sometimes it works, sometimes it doesn't. Maybe we didn't get a match because the semen from 1959 was too corrupted after all. But there's evidence somewhere. There's that thing, too, about matching a family member who has given DNA to research their ancestry."

Beaufort didn't bother to ask for details about that. He was just glad that he didn't have any extended family alive anymore. He grinned to acknowledge his admiration of the detective's perseverance. "Do you think there's anyone else in the world as interested in this case as you are?"

"Well, there was the brother who has been suspected all these years. They were able to exclude him by showing it wasn't his semen. He's really happy to finally be vindicated after sixty years. Other than that, you get a person now and then who's interested in unsolved murders. But not too many, not at this stage anymore."

Beaufort kept quiet for a few seconds, feeling like he was fishing, playing out the line a little so the fish wouldn't get spooked. He took a slow swig of his beer before saying, "So, okay, you didn't get a DNA match with Hickcock or Smith. Are there any other suspects someone can run the results against someday?"

"Someday maybe. The profile lasts forever and will stay on file. If anyone cares." Meadows grimaced and shook his head like he had doubts about anyone caring.

"What about fingerprints?" Beaufort asked. "Seems like with this DNA business nobody cares about fingerprints anymore."

"Where did you hear about the fingerprint?"

"I didn't. I'm just assuming. So you say there *were* prints?"

Meadows looked to his right and left and then leaned toward Beaufort as if he was about to impart something top secret. Beaufort could tell the alcohol had increased the intimacy. Beaufort leaned forward, too.

"Get this," Meadows said. "It wasn't a fingerprint."

"No?"

"It was a palm print."

Well, now Beaufort felt like a man who'd been sitting for a long time underneath a hundred-pound pillow, heavy and suffocating. And now it was gone. One of the things that had preyed on his mind all those decades. Gone. *They never took your palm print, just your fingertips.* They only had his fingerprints on file. Even his voice felt lighter when he said, "Too bad. No way you can match it to anyone, right?"

"Sure we can," Meadows said. "But not necessarily in the way you're thinking. Even at the time it helped exclude about sixty people who didn't match to it. Now fingerprints, that would be a little easier, but . . ."

Beaufort didn't much care about the "buts" of it, and he stopped listening to Meadows while thinking about how the colors in the room were a little brighter and even his Bud tasted a little more beery than it had before. He picked up the bottle with three fingers around the neck and thought of the unlikelihood of anything catching his palm print. His palm print! Shit!

Meadows couldn't tell he hadn't been paying attention. ". . . still adding prints to the IAFIS database, but there are millions of them. Just think, two million people in prison right this minute, and that doesn't count the convicted felons who have come and gone over the past fifty years. Then if you add in the prints taken upon the arrest of a suspect, it's like a needle in a haystack, see what I mean?"

"Yeah, I see," Beaufort said. "Funny how this thing that happened so long ago, people are still interested."

Meadows took a package of unfiltered Camels out of his back pocket, and offered, "Cigarette?"

"No thanks, I'm trying to quit," Beaufort said when he was finally able to speak, yearning with all his soul to wrap his lips around a cancer stick. He wished he hadn't left his antacid tablets back in his room.

Meadows shook a cigarette out of the package and lit it with the flick of his Bic.

"I didn't think that was legal anymore," Beaufort said, lip twitching as he watched. Meadows being a smoker himself wouldn't be able to smell it on Beaufort, but just to be on the safe side he kept his nicotine-stained fingers snug around his beer bottle.

Meadows inhaled luxuriously and blew the smoke in Beaufort's direction. "Nobody but cops frequent this place, mostly. If anyone complains I just put it out," he said.

Beaufort nodded like he knew that. "What's your next move?"

"Retirement," Meadows said, and then smiled. "I don't have a next move. I've been put out to pasture and these cold cases are all I have. Some on the force don't even see it as a job, they see it as a hobby. No, I think I may be the last of the guys who truly care about things like honor and justice." He took another drag off the cigarette. "You remember Kools? They found a bit of a Kools wrapper at the Walker crime scene. I had to research it but I found out they still make them."

"No shit?" Beaufort nodded. "Menthol, right? Do they even make menthol cigarettes anymore? I never liked them."

Meadows nodded back. "Menthol, unfiltered. My research showed that Newport is the most popular menthol brand nowadays." He tapped the ash of his Camel onto the dish the bartender had put in front of him. "This is the cigarette a man smokes. Personally I always thought menthol-flavored cigarettes were for pussies. So for the Walker case, if I ever do find the killer or killers, and it's not Smith and Hickock, I think they'll be pussies."

"If they're even still alive."

"If they're alive."

Beaufort thought this was going pretty well. He forced himself to relax what had become a tight grip on that beer bottle, and let his lower jaw hang down a bit so the muscle wouldn't pop with nervousness. He told himself he was in a superior position, Meadows knew nothing about him, and didn't appear to be a threat. He rubbed his palm on his jeans. When he looked up again, Meadows was looking at him with a glitter in his eyes.

"There's one other thing I just discovered," he said.

The way Meadows said that, it sounded like *I've saved the best for last*.

"What's that?" Beaufort asked, wondering what could possibly top what Meadows had already given him.

"I recently heard something about a confession. It's from Dick Hickock. And, get this, it contradicts anything that he and Smith said."

A confession.

"Hey, buddy, you doing okay?" The expression on Meadows's face, when he finally noticed it, had Beaufort wondering how long he might have been sitting there without answering that question. The answer bubbled up out of his throat. "Sure. Fine. Okay." He didn't dare risk raising the beer bottle to his lips.

"Seriously, you driving?" Meadows asked.

"No. I walked," Beaufort said. He didn't want to know but wanted to know. "What does it say?" he managed to ask.

"The confession? I don't know yet. But what if he finally confessed to killing the Walkers? Man oh man, that would be something."

"If it even exists," Beaufort said.

Meadows nodded, his face looking downcast but his fingers drumming on the bar, drowning out Beaufort's doubts.

Beaufort asked, "Have you had any thoughts about where to look for this thing?"

"Lots of thoughts. But here's one. One of my thoughts was, who do you make a confession to?" Meadows said.

"My defense attorney?"

Meadows shook his head and fixed his gaze on Beaufort in a score-one look. "Your priest."

"Hah," Beaufort said. "My priest."

"I tracked down the name of the chaplain at Lansing during the time just before Hickock's and Smith's execution."

"So you think this chaplain has a confession?"

"He said no. No, you're interested in Hickock and Smith, you should take a look at the Kansas Historical Society Archives. It's all online."

Beaufort shook his head and put a look on his face that he hoped wouldn't show too much interest, letting his eyelids drop a little, but Meadows ignored it.

"They have all the documents associated with Hickock's and Smith's stay at Lansing prison. I had gone over and over those things without noticing this one until recently. In his final days Hickock asked for a priest to hear his confession."

Meadows went on, "He sent a letter to Warden Sherman Crouse. Now, get this, he was specific about wanting a Catholic priest, not the Protestant chaplain connected to the prison at the time. The letter says it's because Catholic priests hold confessions in a higher regard than Protestants."

Beaufort wanted to ask the name of the priest, but he did not.

"In addition, Hickock asked that the confession not be recorded as prisoner conversations often were. He didn't want anyone else to hear what he told the priest. And Warden Sherman Crouse sent a letter back agreeing to this."

With a tilt of his head that disdained the detective's research, Beaufort risked saying only "So we'll never know what Hickock confessed to, or whether it changes the original confession."

Now Meadows delivered his final thrust because he couldn't stand not to. "I know the name of the priest."

Come on, give me a lead. "But he's dead, right?"

"Nope, and he's not even far from here. Priests are like the rest of retirees, they all move to Florida. He's living at a Dominican abbey."

Give me a name, for God's sake. Beaufort struggled to get control over his lips, which were jumping around on their own accord. He clamped his hand over his mouth and forced out a single word between his fingers. "So."

Meadows nodded. "I contacted him. He told me he might have something he's allowed to share with me, did I want to come up and visit him. He's apparently very ill, so I may be just in time. I thought I'd drive up there next week. It's a nice area and a good excuse to get out of town.

Away from the wife. You okay? You got pale before and now you're a little flushed. How's your blood pressure?"

"I don't remember it being so hot here. I guess my blood needs to thin." With all his attention on keeping his hand from shaking, he put the payment for both his and Meadows's drinks on the bar with a small tip, and left.

Meadows looked disappointed.

Going up against a seasoned investigator, that might not have been the smartest thing, but how else could he find the information he'd just received? His face felt cold with fear despite the Florida heat as he made a beeline three blocks away where he could run into a Quick Stop and get a pack of Newports.

After a couple of those he told himself he was safe. Meadows hadn't even asked his name. There was no record of him anywhere, except for those fingerprints taken decades ago, the last time he was arrested. They were probably still sitting in some file with the other millions of prints, waiting to be scanned into the FBI database. Even if that happened, the Walker print wasn't a finger, it was a palm.

Only with the possibility of that confession, and this Meadows on the verge of finding it, whether it was in writing or whether that no-name priest would testify to it . . .

He brought the cigarette up to his mouth and looked at his palm. Which of the lines etched in it had been left on the faucet? Which lines could indict him? He rubbed his palm on the side of his jeans.

He wasn't safe. He had gone into the bar thinking he was following up on the Walker case, and come out knowing that there might be a document that linked him not only to the Walkers, but to the Clutters, too. He couldn't be sure he was safe unless he got to Hickock's priest before Meadows did.

Beaufort knew how to do things at this point. He found the closest library and the computer bank therein. He googled *Kansas Historical Society Archives*. Over seven hundred separate documents covering everything from Hickock's plea for clemency to an envelope addressed to the warden from Hickock's mother. Long, neatly handwritten letters from Hickock asking for a radio. For drawing materials. Reading those letters put Beaufort back into the past and he didn't want to be there anymore. He was reaching the end of a short fuse and was about to pop when he finally found the letters written seven days before Hickcock's execution:

April 7, 1965

Dear Warden Crouse:

As you know, I am to be executed on April 14, 1965. Before that event I wish to make my confession. As the chaplain in the prison is a protestant minister, and because the protestant religion does not hold confession in the same regard as the Catholics, I request that a Catholic priest be called in to hear my final confession. In addition, I request that no recordings are made and that no one else be allowed to hear what I tell the priest. Our long relationship is nearly at an end and I hope you will grant me this last request.

Respectfully,
Richard Eugene Hickock
Prisoner number 14746

And the very next document after that was the response from the warden.

April 8, 1965

Dear Mr. Hickock:

I am going to grant your request. We have located a priest at a local church who will be here at two o'clock pm tomorrow. He has agreed to hear your final confession and grant absolution. A guard will be posted outside the door, but other than that your time with the father will be private and unlimited.

Warden Sherman Crouse

Is it asking too much that somewhere here there should be a goddamn mention of the goddamn priest's goddamn name?

The library had a second floor. He ran up the stairs and down the aisles of shelved books until he got to an area that was empty. He drove his fist into a collection of large hard-bound copies of *National Geo-*

graphic. They resisted and gave with just the right balance so as not to damage his fist. The magazines bounced back and hit whatever was on the shelf on the other side, those books spilling onto the floor. He breathed in and out the way they had taught him in prison, and that calmed him. In case anyone might be coming around to check on the noise he moved casually back to the stairs, down, and to the computers.

He needed to approach this from a different angle. Getting control of himself again, he searched *Dominican abbeys in Florida.* There was only one, about an hour's drive north of Tampa. And in that abbey he hoped there would be only one very sick, very old priest.

Nine

The night was so cold I brought a heavy wool blanket out to the back-yard where Carlo was on one of the chaise lounges studying winter constellations. I lay down on top of him so we were both staring at the sky together, and pulled up the blanket. I was feeling a recent neediness that made my body want to touch his more often. He didn't object.

There was a little while of silence, just the two of us except for the pugs, their small shadows moving about the yard like beige moons, before I said, "Tell me a story." I was being cagey, with something specific in mind that I couldn't let go of after Gemma-Kate's interview. That question about Jane he hadn't answered.

"Well." He thought. "Okay, I've never told you this one. I was teaching this course on the history of witchcraft and this one kid—" The sentence was interrupted by his laughter, laughing so hard I could feel his gut jumping beneath my back.

I interrupted him. I heard myself interrupting him with a coyly innocent voice while the self-possessed, secure Quinn inside of me yelled *leave it alone, you idiot.* "Not that. Tell me something about your first marriage. About Jane."

His gut stopped jumping. "Why?"

"You've never talked much about Jane."

"You never asked me."

That was evasive. Was his breathing harder beneath my back than it had been a moment before? Could it be that my sweet honest hubs had a secret as big as any of my own? Lying on top of him could be the next best thing to a polygraph. I tried to keep my own breathing in check as I said, "Come on, tell me something good."

"What would you like to know?" he said, sounding a little cagey himself.

Is this how we always had been, or was it new?

"She sounds like such a *good* person."

I must have managed to keep the sarcasm out of my voice, because he said, "Oh, she was that."

"So tell me . . . tell me how you met," I said, and then focused on keeping my breathing light and regular.

"Are you sure?" he asked.

"Why not? Are you okay with talking about her?"

"Of course."

I think we both lied, but he began anyway.

In those days, Carlo said, the earliest of the feminist movement, and way before denominations other than the Roman Catholics routinely ordained women as ministers, there was no such thing as a female chaplain. When Carlo DiForenza, during his pastoral training, went to work at Lansing, the office was in the women's prison.

There he met Jane, who was a volunteer doing literacy training.

"She and I worked together over the course of the three months I was at the prison. We shared an office, compared notes on different inmates, which ones had potential for change and which were the unredeemable bad apples. She was grateful for my advice."

I'll just bet she was.

"During your pastoral training. That happens before you become a priest, right? Not after?" I recalled those times I'd been responsible for an interrogation, keeping my tone mild and my questions nonconfrontational. Giving the suspect the opportunity to say the things I knew he wanted to say. This felt like that. The sane Quinn inside me hated me for my deception.

"That's right," he said, without offering more. "She was a passionate woman, totally dedicated to her work and to the church. I even remember in our talks, at some point she shared with me that she had always wanted to be a priest. Of course that's impossible in the Catholic Church."

Good Lord, not that, too. So is this what it was like when saints mated? No wonder off and on I'd felt haunted by her presence in the house. I looked at Al and Peg, who had wandered back to the porch and were patiently waiting to be let inside. The pugs that Jane had given him just before she died.

Jane was suddenly not feeling like a ghost anymore. She was taking on more and more flesh by the second.

I didn't say any of this. Instead, "There. I knew we could do it," and felt all smug and grown up. It would only be later, after I'd a chance to think about stories about Jane and stories about me, that I'd start the comparisons. Like the fact that she had a rock-solid faith and I'm a mushy atheist. Like the fact that I put people in prison and she taught them to read. These things started eating at me. Was she good in bed? I wondered. What if she wasn't a prig after all? But even I wasn't dumb enough to ask that.

Ten

Beaufort went to the Quik Mart and asked the clerk at the checkout, "Do you sell throwaways here?" He measured his voice carefully to sound like he knew what he was talking about. The kid pointed to a rack, and Beaufort chose a phone and was relieved to see it came with instructions.

He called Yanchak.

"You hurt my man," Yanchak asked. "Why should I talk to you?"

"You sent an imbecile to get me. Business must be bad."

"Not so bad."

He met Yanchak in another bar, in another part of town. You'd expect it would be a sleazy joint given Yanchak's dealings, but it was an upscale place on the water. You'd expect them to meet in a dark corner, but they sat outside on the patio. You always expected these guys to look like malnourished scumbags, but not so Yanchak. He showed up in a navy blazer, white shirt. Loafers, no socks. Good haircut, more silver than Beaufort remembered. In short, what actual Florida drug dealers looked like.

"You look old, but otherwise not so bad," Yanchak had said. "With a little doddering, a little shaky hand, a lot of cops wouldn't bother to look in your trunk."

"So do we have a deal?" Beaufort asked.

Yanchak had balked at the fact that the target was in law enforcement.

"You realize this isn't even a firm thing," Beaufort had said. "I drive the cash no matter what. Then if the fix becomes necessary, I call you. Otherwise, we're square."

Yanchak ultimately agreed to have it done, and said he could make it accidental, but it came with a higher price. Yanchak knew he could trust Beaufort to transport some funds to El Paso for him. Someone you could trust was worth a hit. Beaufort balked in turn at the destination.

"I don't want to drive to El Paso. That's, what, a thousand miles?"

"More like fifteen hundred. Hey, I'm sure you can find someone else to do the fix."

"Okay, okay." With just a little thought Beaufort decided the deal wasn't bad at all. It was as if the hit was a bonus. He'd have the cash Yanchak offered him for the drive, a fake license and vehicle registration. And he got to keep the car. There must be a lot of cash in that car, he thought. Good deal for all concerned, except Meadows. And even Meadows might survive this if Beaufort could get to the priest first. If at some point another piece of evidence started to implicate Beaufort, all it would take was a phone call. Then all the cold case files on Walker would be put away because who else cared? No one, according to Meadows.

He just had to make sure that he got to the priest before Meadows did.

He'd got the beige Hyundai in Tampa and a license made out in the name of Jerry Nolan as he requested. Yanchak even threw a gun into the deal. Sweet, as the younger ones in the joint would say.

It had taken him a while to figure out all the modern gadgetry, the automatic windows and such. The sound and sudden movement when he accidentally found the right button made him jump. This whole new world business made him jumpy. Then he'd got on I-75 and headed north about an hour to where St. Dominic's Abbey was tucked just outside the small town of Tarpon Springs.

He'd found the monastery and announced himself in the reception area, said that he was interested in becoming a monk. He hadn't been sure how to say it, but they seemed to buy it. Someone named Abbot Franklin greeted him, said that Brother Eric was the usual guest master, but would Beaufort enjoy a brief tour? Of course he didn't actually say "Beaufort," as Beaufort had given him the name of Jerry Nolan.

Abbot Franklin had pointed out different areas as they strolled through the abbey: the refectory, the pilgrims' quarters, the monks' quarters, the infirmary.

Infirmary. That sounded right.

Beaufort asked how big the infirmary was, how many monks it could hold.

They had paused outside the closed door, and Abbot Franklin lowered his voice. "It only has a couple of beds. If one of us is really sick we're taken to a hospital. Except Father Santangelo, he's in hospice here."

"What's wrong with Father Santangelo?" Beaufort had asked.

"Pancreatic cancer," Abbot Franklin had whispered. "Lot of pain. When he first came here after retirement he was the sort of saint who could raise a glass while whipping you at the pool table. He's not expected to live much longer. He'll leave a hole in our community that no one could expect to fill."

"Is he a young man?" Beaufort had asked.

"Oh, no. And that's the blessing of it. He turned ninety-six on his last birthday."

"Poor old guy. Does he have family?"

"Apparently he was the youngest. No one is left."

Beaufort put on his best sympathy face. "What about friends? What about people visiting him?"

Abbot Franklin glanced at Beaufort, but if he thought anything was odd about the questions he was too polite to not respond. Oh, how helpful, these monks. So lacking in suspicion. So eager for members that you could go there and say you wanted to be a monk and they believed you. Bending over backward to show the world how good Catholic clergy could be, that they weren't all money-grubbing pedophiles.

"Someone has called from time to time," Abbot Franklin said, answering his question, and when Beaufort didn't say anything, added, "A Father Carlos . . . something, I don't quite remember a last name. But I don't think he's called in a long while."

"Well, I'm gonna pray for him," Beaufort said as he made the sign of the cross before the door of the infirmary. "I'm gonna pray that God won't make him suffer much longer."

Abbot Franklin smiled his appreciation. "Would you like to see the grounds? We have a lovely grotto dedicated to Mary."

That was Monday and this was Thursday night. He had told himself it was wiser to wait at least a few days before returning, less chance of someone connecting his visit. It had been sixty years, for God's sake, and Meadows didn't seem to be in a hurry to interview the priest.

Now Beaufort waited in that same grotto until he saw the last of the lights go out in the abbey, signaling that the monks were dreaming their little monk dreams. He put on the monk's robe he had bought at a costume shop. He put the hood up over his head. He hadn't seen anyone with a hood up, it was too hot, but he couldn't take a chance of being recognized.

He moved around the outside of the building and broke into the door leading to the pilgrims' quarters. The door was a flimsy little thing, and no match for anyone who had lived outside the law. Despite the robe that made sure no pilgrim would question him, he discovered himself to be lucky so far. All the doors to the rooms were open, and not a pilgrim in sight. Probably because of this, the door between the pilgrims' quarters and the monks' quarters was unlocked. By the dim hall light he followed the linoleum squares to the door that they had kindly marked for him—INFIRMARY.

He opened the door, this one also unlocked, stepped inside, and lowered his hood. There was a bright night-light attached to the wall that illuminated the room enough for Beaufort to detect a hospital room with two beds and a moderate amount of equipment. An enormous clock was on the wall, next to an empty cross of equal size.

"Hello," said a voice from the hospital bed, a stronger voice than belonged in this darkened sickroom.

Beaufort jerked with the shock of hearing it, but recovered and played his part the way he imagined it would be played. He saw the figure now, with the back of the bed raised up so the figure could see him as well.

"Hello, Brother," he said, remembering what Brother Eric had been called. "I didn't think you'd be awake."

"I don't want to miss anything," the man said. His left hand fluttered over his sheet, as if it searched for something, and then found it and was still.

Beaufort came closer to the bed, and saw that the thing the priest was handling was a device with a button, probably for dispensing morphine. "Are you Father Santangelo?" he asked.

"The very same," said the man.

"Do you know who I am?" Beaufort asked.

"If you're who I think you are," Santangelo said, "I've been waiting for you a long time."

"How do you know?"

"If someone checks on me at night he's usually in his shorts. No brother would enter this room in the dark of night dressed in his robe. And especially with the hood up. It's too hot. Also, you rented the wrong color robe. It should be brown instead of black. It makes you look like the Grim Reaper. Also, you called me 'Brother.' I'm a priest, not a monk. The others know to call me 'Father,' if not just 'Victor.'" Santangelo's voice ground down to a whisper on the last words.

"Well, you got me there," Beaufort said, noting the first name.

Santangelo's hand fluttered over the morphine button again and then must have realized it was too soon for another dose and reluctantly rested on the priest's chest. "That's right. You might be evil, but I'll bet no one ever accused you of being a genius."

Nothing bothered Beaufort more than being thought evil. Unless it was being thought stupid. His urge to punch the priest's face was at odds with his need for information. "What did he accuse me of?"

"He?" Santangelo asked, and then apparently decided not to be coy. "As you know, I'm not at liberty to tell you that."

Beaufort wanted again to clock him then, but that wasn't his sole purpose. "I'm not going to hurt you."

Strength came back to the voice even though he spoke through clenched teeth. "Do I look like a chump to you?"

"No. And you don't sound like a priest either," Beaufort said, thinking of the gullible Abbot Franklin.

"How many have you known?"

When Beaufort stayed silent at that, Santangelo said, "I'm in great pain. Not feeling particularly pastoral. So get on with your business."

"I just want to ask you a few things, and then I'll go," Beaufort said, not taking the time to confirm or deny knowing priests.

"Go ahead. As long as it doesn't violate the seal of confession or threaten harm to anyone, I'll give you the answers." The priest's tongue darted out of his mouth and whisked from side to side. "I'm not used to talking this much. Could I have a drink of water?"

Santangelo indicated a bedside table with a glass of water on it, half full. Beaufort took the glass, held it to the priest's lips, and hoped the guy wasn't a better con than he was. If the man was scared, he wasn't showing it. Santangelo put his paper-dry hand over Beaufort's that held the glass. Before he could take it away, Santangelo pulled the hand to his face.

"Your hands are cold and sweaty," Santangelo said. "The sweat smells like fear." He sniffed again, as if sampling a new wine. "And a little like damnation."

Beaufort drew his hand away and put the glass back on the table without letting himself be taunted. Then he said, "Okay. Talk."

When Santangelo did not talk, Beaufort picked up the morphine dispenser and moved it to the table next to the bed.

"There was a confession," Santangelo said. "The penitent said you were still alive and dangerous. That you threatened to hurt someone. I always suspected that included me."

"The penitent. Dick Hickock," Beaufort said. "Say his name. We both know it."

"Richard Eugene Hickock. Was everything true, what he said about you?" Santangelo asked.

Beaufort felt like the priest was baiting him, and tried not to feel that. "What difference could it make?"

"You're the one who's still searching for the answer."

"And you're the one who can give it to me. Tell me what he confessed to."

"Sorry, no can do. I don't make up the canonical rules. I just follow them."

"You smug bastard. Was it in writing?"

"Interesting question. If I had a document, and the document made clear who the penitent was, what would I do with that document? Now that I'm dying, who would I give it to? These are great mysteries, yes." Saying all that exhausted Santangelo, and his head seemed to sink further into the pillow afterward. His hand fluttered over where the morphine dispenser had been.

Beaufort took his index finger and found the pulse in the side of Santangelo's throat. For a dying man it was pretty strong. Maybe the fear he said he didn't feel made this so.

"Have you talked with Detective Ian Meadows? Maybe just over the phone? Did you tell him you have the confession?" Beaufort asked.

"That's three questions and you are, as they say in baseball, striking out." Santangelo's eyes gleamed in the dark. He may have been a priest, but he would have made a damn good poker player. He went on, "Do you know, I can tell someone that someone meeting your description was here without breaking the seal of confession? A very small man, with a full head of silver hair, and a face like a weasel's."

Somewhere a bell sounded.

"What was that?" Beaufort asked.

"That's the call for midnight prayers for the die-hards. One of them will check on me."

"We're running out of time. Do you understand what I can do?"

"You think it matters to me whether I get another twenty-four hours? I'm near death and can think of less banal ways to spend my last moments." And the smallest of smiles, or a grimace of pain.

Beaufort knew he had to send a stronger message, that he meant business. He pulled up the hem of his brown robe until he could get his hands underneath it. He lifted his covered hands and pressed them to Santangelo's face. Through the cloth he pinched the man's nostrils shut with one hand and clamped the other over his mouth.

He had caught the priest by surprise. After trying and failing to take one breath the man lay still. When he thought the priest had gotten the message but was still conscious, Beaufort pulled his hands away. The priest opened his mouth and sucked loudly at the blessed air.

"I don't want to kill you, old man. No matter what you think, I'd take no pleasure in it. Last chance," Beaufort said. "Where's the confession?"

Beaufort could barely see the slight move of the head that indicated negation, but negation of what he couldn't know. He cut off the priest's air the same as before and whispered as loudly as he dared when he had pulled his hands away and Santangelo had gotten his breath once more. "Where is it?"

"It's all there, everything. Everything you did, and it's far away and safe."

"Where? Did you leave it at Lansing?"

There was almost a flicker of sympathy in those eyes that looked on Santangelo's killer. "You're in such a hell. It almost makes me want to absolve you."

"Did you give it to Father Carlo?"

Taking that chance was worth it to see the old man's face. Even that bit of name finally cut through the priest's composure. His eyes and mouth opened wide.

But then he tried to shout for help.

Maybe what they say about the religious living longer because they lead such healthy lives had some truth to it. Even with stage four cancer it took a longer time than Beaufort had expected for the priest to die.

Beaufort picked up the priest's right arm that dangled off the side of the bed after his struggles. He pressed the palm of the hand to his forehead as if even after death the priest had some power to cool the burning in his brain. It did no good. So, first arranging the arms next to the body, he straightened out a few wrinkles in the bedsheets. It was too dark to tell if the face was reddened where the cloth had been pressed against the man's face. Not too suspicious, Beaufort thought.

He heard a sound out in the hallway. Beaufort slipped behind the bed, which was out from the wall and raised a bit at the head for the ease of the patient. He hoped the monk coming in was too sleepy to notice any shadows he might cast on the floor.

The monk came over to the side of the bed and seemed to lean over Santangelo, though from his position, and holding his breath, Beaufort couldn't be sure. The three men, two living and one dead, were separated by less than three feet. After a few moments—perhaps he was trying to rouse the man, or at least determine if he was sleeping comfortably—or feeling for his pulse—the monk ran out of the room.

There was no time to see how long it would take for him to rouse the other monks and bring a whole troop of them into the room. Beaufort stood up and sped out, closing the door not as quietly as he would have liked, and ran left down the hallway toward the pilgrims' quarters. There was noise in the hall behind him, so he didn't bother to relock the outside door.

Running back to his car, past the statue of Mary, he thought about how good he had felt arriving here this night, and how unexpectedly bad he felt now even though he had a decent lead on where the confession was. Santangelo's last words, about Beaufort being in hell, kept repeating . . . he couldn't stop those words. How did the priest know?

But then if Santangelo were still alive Beaufort would tell him that it wasn't hell he was in. Hell was permanent. This was purgatory because he was finding a way out.

Eleven

My questions about Jane weren't the only things fired up the night that Gemma-Kate interviewed Carlo. I remembered mentioning to Carlo that night in bed how I'd checked from time to time about whether there'd been any progress on the Walker family murder case. So here I was sitting at my computer on a slow day, googling. I also made a mental note to get back the book I'd loaned to Gemma-Kate.

That copy of *In Cold Blood*? My father gave me that first edition for my twelfth birthday. I read it then and several times since. For anyone who isn't familiar with Truman Capote's masterwork, here's the story according to Capote: Two guys, Richard Eugene Hickock and Perry Smith, meet in prison where they're doing time for petty crimes. Hickock tells Smith that another prisoner, Floyd Wells, has told him of a well-to-do Kansas farmer named Herb Clutter, for whom Wells has worked. Wells says that Clutter keeps ten thousand dollars in a safe in his house office. Hickock gets Smith to help him rob Clutter. *In Cold Blood* relates their adventures, on road trips from Mexico to Florida, passing bad checks for cash, including the night when they go to the Clutter place in Holcomb, Kansas, and with a knife and shotgun slaughter Mr. and Mrs. Clutter, and their two teenage children.

They find less than one hundred dollars.

Ultimately, the two men are captured by the FBI in Las Vegas on December 30, 1959.

Smith confesses to killing two of the Clutters, but later changes his confession to say he killed the whole family. When questioned, he says it's because he feels sorry for Hickock's mother, "who is a sweet woman." No one, not Capote or Special Agent Alvin Dewey, questions the motivation for this reversal. The men at the Kansas Bureau of Investigation are so happy to finally find the killers they don't care about the fine points of their confession.

While Hickock and Smith are incarcerated, it's discovered that they were in the area of Osprey, Florida, at the exact time that the Walker family was killed. That was late December, just about a month after the Clutter killing. Prime suspects, they're polygraphed, which is thought to confirm their innocence. Despite some witnesses reporting them in the area, and considerable physical circumstantial evidence, such as scratch marks on Hickock's face that could have been made with a high heel, the state doesn't press its case. This is nuts. Maybe the state doesn't want to delay hanging them, and the Clutter case is enough to accomplish that goal.

Subsequently, they're convicted only of the Clutter murders, and executed in 1965. *In Cold Blood* is published shortly after.

Now here's the thing that has always intrigued me.

It's not news that there are discrepancies in Capote's telling. This is well established. For example, there is no proof that "Willie Jay," said to be a religious mentor of Perry, and an early cellmate of Dick's, existed. Invented by Capote, or invented by Perry Smith? I often wondered if it was because most of Capote's interviews were with Perry Smith, and all he got was Smith's account of the events. What we get from that account is that Smith is a poor victim of childhood misfortune and abuse. Sensitive. Liked to paint and play his guitar. A TV series they made once had him crying and wetting his pants.

Hickock, on the other hand, comes across as a sociopath, stupid and cruel. Smith painted him as the ringleader who kept insisting "they would leave no witnesses." A pedophile who wanted to rape Nancy Clutter until Smith bravely stopped him—by killing her himself.

But if you go to the Kansas Historical Society Archives you see a different Dick Hickock. This one has been reading law during his five years on death row prior to his execution. He's writing letters that show a degree of articulation and intelligence unlike the man portrayed by Capote. Sure, that he's a murderer, and a cold-blooded one, that cannot be denied, but the man has more depth than what we read about him in Capote's account.

Was Smith telling the whole truth? And if not, why not? Was it to weave a sympathetic portrait of himself with just enough villainy to titillate an author like Capote?

And was it sheer coincidence that the two men were in the neighborhood when the Walker family was murdered?

Questions like that have obsessed more than a few over the years.

My internet research brought me to a cold case investigator named Ian Meadows, who operated out of Sarasota County. He had actually gotten permission to exhume the bodies of Richard Hickock and Perry Smith, to check their DNA against that in the semen found in the underpants of Christine Walker, the mother who had been raped and shot. The DNA was pretty corrupted in both the bodies and the pants after so many years, but the analysts thought it was good enough for testing. No match was found.

For the umpteenth time I thought, *Who killed you?*

A welcome distraction. I made a mental note to one of these days call the detective, or even go over to Sarasota to visit him the next time I was in Florida. Find out if he had a next move. These guys loved to talk about cases. Seriously, give them an opening and you can't shut them up.

Twelve

Beaufort's drive took him west on I-10, a straight shot out the panhandle of Florida through Alabama, Mississippi (passing back through Pascagoula), Louisiana, and finally Texas. Only not so finally. Texas was the worst, more distance from side to side than all the other states put together, and El Paso was at the farthest point west. He drove five miles over the speed limit the whole way to make the best time possible without making a highway patrolman suspicious.

He wasn't expected in El Paso until three nights later, so he took his time, doing about five hundred miles a day, stopping at motels now that he had the extra money. It was easy to find computers at each stop, twice at small libraries, and once in the lobby of the Holiday Inn Express. From one of those locations he sent an email under the account he had created. The librarian in the Pascagoula library was right about being able to use his email account from any computer. From one of the places he stopped he sent an email to the current chaplain at Lansing. He said he was doing some genealogy research (from TV commercials everybody seemed to be doing it) and was looking into a relative who had been a chaplain there. Did they have a record of every minister who had served there, and could he get it? Hopefully with the years they were there?

He hoped a chaplain would be a little more cooperative than a government bureaucrat. It didn't appear that way, though. The next time he was able to get to a computer, the next night, there was no response waiting.

Instead, he went back to the Kansas Historical Society Archives and continued to pour through Hickock's and Smith's files at Lansing Penitentiary. Hickock had a never-ending stream of correspondence, five- and six-page single-spaced, handwritten letters addressed to the warden and his attorney Joseph Jenkins, going on and on about how it wasn't fair that death row prisoners should have to be incarcerated next to the petty criminals who were generally more rowdy at all times of the day and night so he couldn't sleep. Another letter explaining why he should be allowed to have art supplies in order to spend some time drawing. Another letter begging for a radio to help the death row prisoners preserve their sanity. Even a brief one requesting watermelon. Except for the art supplies, most of his requests were rejected. Beaufort had to read every word in every document because he wasn't totally sure what he was looking for, and a clue might be contained in a phrase anywhere in any letter or legal brief.

There was the letter from Capote asking Warden Crouse for permission to interview the men—initially denied—newspaper articles about Smith going on a hunger strike in order to "cheat the gallows," a telegram from Smith to Capote sent the day before his execution, asking if Capote would come visit him. A letter from Hickock's mother that mentioned him finding God. *Fat chance on that, Mom.*

Letters from Hickock to his attorney. None of the letters talked about a separate document, any confession that would supersede the official one he'd made. Just to see how far this internet could get him, Beaufort googled the name Joseph Jenkins. Nothing likely, just a real estate agent somewhere in Idaho. *Joseph Jenkins Attorney*, he typed. Nothing. Man long dead, probably, even the law firm defunct.

There was an article published in the December 1961 issue of *Male* magazine, in which Hickock himself told his life story. Beaufort scanned the article as fast as he could read, holding his breath to the end to see if Hickock had ratted him out there in any way. True to his promise, though, Hickock said nothing about Beaufort, didn't even mention "the boy and his grandfather" that Smith had told Capote about, leaving the identity of the pair anonymous as they would appear in the book.

He did not enjoy doing any of this. He did not like to remember his time with them. During his association with Hickock and Smith, and in the aftermath of the Clutter and Walker killings, Beaufort could never have anticipated how famous Smith and Hickock would become because of Truman Capote's book. Damn bad luck. If Beaufort had known that would happen he never would have hooked up with the two of them.

When he stopped in the early evening, in Houston, Beaufort found the library still open and finally got the message he had been waiting for. Someone named Phillip Payne, the Reverend Phillip Payne, wrote that the list of chaplains serving at Lansing prison was quite extensive, and would he be able to narrow down his search by date?

Beaufort wrote back that he could narrow the search to 1960 to 1970.

Payne must have been at his computer, because the answer came back immediately.

> **DEAR MR. NOLAN:** In 1960 during the time in question the chaplain at Lansing had been Werner Krause, and was replaced in 1965 by Mr. John L. Hurld who continued well into the seventies. Does this serve your purpose?
>
> **DEAR REVEREND PAYNE:** Were either of these chaplains Catholic?
>
> **DEAR MR. NOLAN:** No, Mr. Krause was Lutheran, and Mr. Hurld was Presbyterian.
>
> **DEAR REVEREND PAYNE:** Was there any Catholic priest working at the prison during that time?
>
> **MR. NOLAN:** One was on call when needed, a Father Victor Santangelo. Other than that I can offer that there was a seminarian doing his chaplaincy at Lansing. A note in the file said that he was recommended by Father Santangelo. That was for three months beginning in 1972. I know that's outside your date range.

Payne gave Beaufort that seminarian's name. Carlo (not Carlos as Abbot Franklin had said) DiForenza.

Santangelo. Son of a bitch, Santangelo. Santangelo calling him stupid still rankled, would sometimes be the first thing he thought about when he woke in the middle of the night, and it gnawed at him. *I gotcher stupid right here*, he thought.

It felt good to finally be doing something. When Hickock and Smith were still alive he had lived in fear that they would rat him out. Then he stopped worrying when they died. Then he started worrying again with this whole forensic science business. Meadows had eased his fears for just a moment before telling him about the suspected confession. Then Santangelo had confirmed the confession, and now Beaufort knew where it might be. Having become an expert with internet searches, he found he was headed in the right direction, toward Tucson, Arizona, where this Carlo DiForenza lived. He was a genius, and lucky to boot. Genius and luck put him only a ten-hour drive from his next target.

Common sense told him he didn't need to worry, he only had to follow the clues and he would find the confession.

He told himself this. So why in the middle of the night would he wake with the fear coiling up from his guts like it was a living thing inside of him, under its own control? As if the fear wanted out, like a monstrous parasite, coming to stand outside himself, beside himself? He didn't think he could take it much longer.

As he drove the rest of the way on I-10 Beaufort had too much time to think about how he was on the same road that he had traveled with Hickock and Smith so many years ago. His grandfather dying somewhere along this road, he couldn't remember where. If he'd never met up with Hickcock and Smith, who would he be? What if he hadn't done what he'd done . . . he could hardly remember why he did it . . . to prove to them and himself that he was bad?

And the nightmares. He probably wouldn't have the nightmares if it weren't for Hickock and Smith.

The next night Beaufort was in El Paso, where he handed off the money to his contact.

Thirteen

Here's something I held on to, something we had in common: Carlo and I both liked to read. Granted, we read very different books. Carlo read a lot of philosophy, theology, and science, and sometimes books that combined all three. And more recently, books with titles like *Peterson's Guide to Stars and Planets*.

Me, I gravitated toward Ken Bruen, who sets his tough crime dramas in Galway. They're raw, but not in the sense that some use the word, as in smutty. Raw like the wounds of Jesus. Reading about the tortured alcoholic detective Jack Taylor pumping bullets into the face of some bollix made me, by contrast, feel girlish.

I stopped at the line "She noticed me staring at her neck. Nuns, like cops, see everything." Did that go for priests, too? And how much like a nun was Jane? Was she submissive and plain?

"If she couldn't be a priest, did Jane ever consider entering the convent?" I said aloud. Having once said her name, it had become easier to say it again.

I thought I noticed Carlo shift his butt in his recliner.

"She did, I think. But decided she loved the world too much."

The whole world? Or just your spot in it?

I glanced at the cover of the book he had just opened.

"Trollope," I said.

"Strumpet," he replied, smiling but without looking up.

"Very funny. The book," I said, squinting so I could read the title. *The Way We Live Now*. Is that a novel?"

"It is," he said, and kept reading.

"I've never seen you reading a novel before."

That didn't seem to require a response.

If Carlo had been more forthcoming I wouldn't have nosed into the book that evening when I begged fatigue and he went to walk the pugs by himself. Inscribed on the blank page when I opened the cover was "To my dearest Lady Carbury, with undying devotion from your obnt srvnt, Mr. Broune." And the date, more than two decades ago. The handwriting was Carlo's.

They had playful pet names for each other, like ours. Only theirs were esoteric literary allusions. And a date that showed how the young unlined Jane would always live in his memories, while I had brought more of a sixtyish body into our relationship.

Had he chosen this novel to read because I'd awakened his memories of Jane with my questions?

I closed the book and went into Carlo's library, just to see if there were any more of Anthony Trollope's novels. They were easy to find because there were so many of them. Like almost two dozen lined up on a shelf at eye level. I pulled just one out and found a message from Lady Carbury to Mr. Broune.

That wasn't all. Next to the Trollope novels was a book called *Wiping the Slate Clean: Reducing Recidivism Through Prison Literacy Programs*. By Jane DiForenza.

She was not only a better person than I was.

She was more intellectual, on Carlo's level. They didn't just read together, they wrote together.

She didn't just bake things and have poor taste in decorating.

She was probably strong.

And Carlo never told me any of this, why? Because he didn't want me to compare myself to Jane and feel that I was lacking?

Things you think have been put to rest, resolved, snuck back into your mind when you least expected, catching you off guard. You have to do battle with these obsessions again and again, even if you're one tough broad who doesn't take shit from anyone.

Self-worth: my right to occupy a spot in the universe no taller than five foot three inches.

How tall was Jane? Such a trivial thing, but those are the things that break us. The camel's straw. The nail in the tire. The wicked mustard seed that grows inside our mind, and encroaches on our delicate mental balance. Is this what happens to everyone three years past the initial infatuation, or just to me?

The security screen door is heavy and banged shut when Carlo returned with the pugs. I moved quickly away from the books (I did not run) and out of the room because how often and with what reason did I ever go in there? Luckily the computer in my office was still on, and I sat there with my hands poised over the keyboard, heart beating hard enough to notice.

"I'm in here, honey! Just doing something I forgot!" With both exclamation points at full throttle.

He replied, something in a softer tone that I couldn't hear, one of those things that's not necessary to hear. I thought of how easy it becomes to lie.

Fourteen

When he first arrived in the Tucson area, Beaufort had checked into a motel in Catalina, this one just about a mile away from his target. His goal was to find someone he could live with for free rather than pay for a room. She needed to be old enough so she wouldn't laugh in his face, but young enough and good-looking enough that she could still believe she was worth it. No hookers. Tits would be nice but not essential. Sometimes women with big tits thought too much of themselves and got picky because they thought if you had those you could snag a guy with them any time you wanted.

He had gotten some new clothes, khaki trousers and a navy blue jacket at a local thrift shop called the Golden Goose, good-looking but not flashy enough to draw the wrong kind of attention.

It didn't take long. He found her about seven miles away at one A.M. on a Thursday, an hour before the bar closed, when the good girls had gone home and the bad ones hadn't given up hope.

Except for having some Mexican name like most bars in the area, this bar at the corner of Oracle and Houghton didn't pretend to be upscale by having a theme, like the maritime theme at Pelican Pub. The theme here was Bar, pure and simple. A couple of men were left, looking so low they'd have to reach up just to tie their shoes. Losers. There were four women, two sitting across from each other in a booth, one jabbering loudly to the other that she shouldn't go home to that creep, any guy who'd hit a woman blah blah blah she deserved better than that.

Another woman who looked like prime property sat alone in another booth. Her clothes were tight but not slutty, clearly giving it away rather than selling it. A little grim faced, staring into her whisky on the rocks like it was a crystal ball and the fortune was bad. He arced his way leisurely toward her booth, and ran his fingertips over the edge of the table, to send a message. She didn't look up when she said, "Get lost."

Women had changed since the seventies, Beaufort thought. Better know that now than waste his time with a bitch. He turned his attention to the only other woman. She was sitting at the bar, and that was a good thing. Being alone at a bar at one A.M. signified a lot of things.

This time he played it more cool, sitting two stools down the way Meadows had at Pelican Pub in Sarasota. The woman didn't look up, same as the one in the booth, but her chest rose and fell a little more rapidly to show that she knew he was there. It felt like she was a patient fisherman and he was the fish, the bait being an odd top with the shoulders cut out and jeans tight down to her ankles, what kids would wear. She was no kid. She'd had enough alcohol so her hand was steady when she reached for her purse, hanging by its strap over the back of the barstool, and took out a packet of cigarettes.

Beaufort took his lighter out of his jacket pocket and laughed shyly at his awkwardness leaning all that way over to light her cigarette. She smiled at him laughing at himself, and it seemed to relax her. Her face looked younger, and more appealing, as she cupped her small fingers around his.

In the light of the flame he could see she wasn't bad-looking, just too sad to encourage strangers much. Her hair was a dry red wine with a little gray growing out around her temples. Her lipstick matched her hair, or had earlier in the evening. Now most of what had been on her lips was on the rim of her glass. This wasn't the kind of woman who made him nervous. He could handle this kind easy. She offered him a cigarette after she took a puff of hers.

"No, thanks," Beaufort said. "I'm trying to quit."

That started the conversation. "Me, too," she said, and winked.

"Though I'd suppose that if I was really trying to quit," she said, and paused as if there would be a punch line, "I wouldn't carry a lighter." Her chin dipped and her eyebrows rose as she said it.

Beaufort took that as a cue to chuckle. "My dad taught me that a man should always carry a lighter to light a lady's cigarette."

He knew he had her on that one, but just to seal the deal he added, "Also it's a habit. My wife smoked."

Her eyes flickered, going over his probable story in her head, calculating whether she should stay or go. She stayed. "Is your wife . . . gone?" she asked, choosing the word cautiously.

"Six months ago. This is my first time sitting alone at a bar since she died," he said. "It took me all evening to put on a jacket and walk in here. Am I too late?"

"I don't think so," she said.

Beaufort had learned quickly that while he was gone the world had gotten nicer, and he knew not to start out with a moron joke. Instead he asked her about herself.

Her name was Gloria Bentham and she said she had a place in walking distance off Houghton where she didn't have to drive in case she'd had a little too much to drink. Tonight she had had a little too much to drink, so she was a little less distrustful than she might have been. You could see her, as they talked, him about his wife and kids he didn't get along with, and his career with race horses, disappointingly a little too tall to be a jockey, but training paid well, her flippant about two divorces just to show she hadn't been left on the shelf her whole life, and her job as a doctor's receptionist, trying to figure out if he was the real thing, and worth it. You could almost see the oh-what-the-hell change come over her face when she said it was time to go. Who would lie about being a horse trainer?

She was cautious enough to ask where he lived, making her sound like a real estate agent qualifying a potential buyer. But just because she was careful didn't make her a women's libber.

"Hotels right now." Cheap motel, actually, but hotels sounded more like he had money. "I sold my place in Weston. Know where that is?"

She shook her head no.

"Southeast Florida, but not on the coast. More land there. I had a couple horses of my own, but sold them with the house. Now I'm traveling around, looking for the next part of my life."

She said she liked the way he said that. "Today is the first day of the rest of your life," she said, nodding a little too vigorously.

He didn't comment because he was busy paying for their drinks. When she got off her stool he saw he had guessed right, she was just petite enough that she wasn't taller than him. He walked her home, humming softly and now and then popping his lips.

"What's that tune?" Gloria asked. "I know it."

"My mom used to sing it to me when I was a little guy. It's called 'Humoresque.'"

"You're different," she said.

Beaufort darted a glance at her. *What am I doing wrong now?* "How so?" he asked.

Seemed she could tell that bothered him and quickly replied, "Wearing a jacket anywhere in Tucson, but especially to that dive bar. Liking classical music." She paused and then said with a flip of her hair that was probably meant to make her look girlish, "I like it."

"Well, I like you," Beaufort said. As he said it, he realized he meant it, too.

If she had had feathers she would have preened them then. But take it slow, he thought, man who just lost his wife was the kind who encouraged trust. He wouldn't jump this gal's bones right off the bat. He did walk her home and go inside of her small prefab house when she opened the door to him. It wasn't ritzy, she had a lot of plaques on the walls about loving yourself. Newish furniture in the Southwest style. A chrome-and-glass shelving unit filled with ceramic statues she called Yahdros. He said they were great, and she pointed out her pride and joy on the matching glass coffee table, a whole scene on a porcelain base with shepherds and sheep.

Yes, this would do. He got close to her, and when she looked up expectantly, he played shy again and gave her a chaste peck on the cheek. She jumped at the chance of seeing him again. Who was the fish and who the fisherman?

He let it take a couple of weeks to move in with her, not liking to spend all that money on a motel room, but knowing how you have to play it with a woman who had a nice place and a respectable job. Smart, too, with more than one book lying around. Beaufort picked them up when she wasn't looking and read the descriptions. Sometimes he would feel almost dizzy at the amount he didn't know about the world that other people did, as if he had been on another planet for thirty years. Looked like a kid's book. Should he know an author by the name of J. K. Rowling? Was he famous? Beaufort had to be careful about what he should know, and it made him tense and sometimes a little testy with Gloria. But except for worrying about where he might need to catch up to her, he thought she was perfect. An old-fashioned broad, not too smart for her own good. But overall he bided his time, didn't rush things even in bed.

With Gloria's approval, Beaufort had subsequently adopted a dog from the local shelter. There were lots of pit bull mixes that no one wanted, but he chose a three-legged dog with scruffy fur and big eyebrows. The assistant at the shelter told him it was a mix between a poodle and a schnauzer—a shnoodle named Achilles. They were so glad someone wanted that dog they treated Beaufort like a saint. No one suspects a man walking a small dog, especially if the dog's name is Achilles, especially if the dog has only three legs. Beaufort had never had a dog before, but when he brought it home Gloria looked at him like he was a saint, too. He didn't realize what points the thing would score. When all this was over he wouldn't just dump the dog somewhere, he'd take it back to the pound. Or if they really got along, then he'd take Achilles with him when he left.

He had gone to the little library annex in a strip mall next to the motel where he had stayed. There on the computer he brought up Google Earth and located the satellite image of the house. Sweet. Neighbors on both sides, nothing in the back but a hill that sloped down to the Cañada del Oro wash with scrub cactus threaded by smaller washes that were bone dry this time of year. A path had been worn along the top of the arroyos that made for easy walking and had no cactus to lodge itself in either man or beast. Good place to walk a dog.

He felt nervous, now that he was getting closer, and the nerves caused that acid in his gut that made him chew handfuls of Tums without much effect. But he told himself over and over and over that, even if this guy knew what had actually happened, it didn't mean he would recognize Beaufort. Nobody would. And if the guy had in his possession what Beaufort thought he had—it made sense, didn't it, that he had it?—the guy wouldn't know what he had. If he did, he would have sold it, and Santangelo would have found out. Everyone would know.

Know what? What did Hickock say? The thoughts tumbled over themselves, gravel in a concrete mixer. His mind wandering, his feet didn't pay attention. Beaufort slid down the steep slope of a small arroyo off the path, and crashed to his knees while the dog, still attached to the leash, had managed to stay up on the edge and was now looking at him with some curiosity, possibly thinking the human would be better off with a third leg. Beaufort stood, found that he hadn't damaged anything, and lifted the dog across the arroyo to the other side before scrambling up there himself.

The fall actually helped to dislodge his momentary panic. When he had walked past the fence in the backyard, maintaining a decent distance so as not to appear to be snooping, he saw everything working his way. DiForenza was on the back porch fiddling with what looked like an oversized telescope. Beaufort had walked up to the fence and called out.

Fifteen

The temperature was in the midsixties, chilly for early December in Arizona but balmy for the rest of the country, which was having recurrent blizzard conditions. The windows were open to let the place air out, so I heard the voices in the backyard. When I went to the door I saw Carlo standing at the back fence, talking to someone on the other side. The man was short in stature, though his head came nearly to the top of the metal railing on the fence. He was elderly by most standards. Another head barely cleared the concrete block base at the fence. Dog with floppy ears and big white eyebrows.

Bored with the skip trace I'd been working on, and lured by the fine day, I went out back to join them.

"This is Brigid," Carlo started.

"Jerry," the man said with a creamy southern accent.

He doffed his baseball cap. "And this here is Achilles," the man continued in his good-old-boy voice.

"Ha, that's a good one," Carlo said.

The man looked at him as if he expected more without knowing why. Carlo read the look.

"You know, Achilles . . . Homer . . ."

The man stared some more.

"The *Iliad* . . . Achilles was killed with an arrow to his heel . . ."
Nothing. ". . . and there's your dog without a hind leg . . ." Carlo trailed
off, giving up any further attempt at classical allusions.

Jerry laughed, trying to look like he got it.

"Is he a rescue?" I asked, to let the poor man off the hook.

Didn't work. He gave me a blank look before saying, "No, I got him
at the pound."

Abandoning the topic of dogs altogether, Jerry gestured at the telescope. "That's a big mother. Sorry, ma'am," he said, doffing again.

"Carlo is the astronomer," I said, resisting the urge to assure him I
thought the scope was a big motherfucker, too. I'm trying to refine my
sensibilities. "It's all I can do to tell the difference between the Pleiades
and a hole in the ground."

Jerry chuckled appreciatively again as if he knew what I was talking
about. Fairly smooth recovery for a guy who says "this here" and has
never heard of an adopted animal being called a rescue. "That thing
looks heavy," he said. "It's mighty impressive."

"It's not that heavy, really. If you detach the scope from the stand
it's only about sixty pounds," Carlo said. He pointed to a square of flag-
stones close to the fence. "This pad I made?"

"You made that pad?" Jerry asked, and then whistled, "Hoo."

Carlo nodded. "I need to get the telescope out here. It's awkward to
carry because of the diameter. You have to sort of hold it out from your
body. It makes it heavier than it actually is."

"Let me help," Jerry said. "It might not be as heavy as it looks, and
I'm stronger than I look."

Carlo welcomed the help, and I wondered for a moment why he hadn't
asked me. Then I looked doubtfully, not at the man but at his dog. "Tell
you what," I said, "I'll get the pugs back in the house while you walk
around to the front gate. Achilles here can come into the yard that way
and make nice slowly."

Al and Peg had meanwhile been up on their hind legs, front paws on
the concrete ledge, already making nice with a very placid Achilles.
While Achilles wandered off with his human companion around to the
front gate, which Carlo had opened for them, I herded our guys in
through the back door and shut it. They were not so content, but amused

themselves by snotting up the glass while they watched Achilles take over their territory, methodically going from sage to planter to wall to birdbath, marking each. With his right rear leg missing he didn't have a problem balancing on his starboard side.

Jerry had put Achilles's leash down on the patio table, and took a handkerchief out of his back pocket. He wrapped it around the handle of the telescope, saying his hands were a little sweaty, and he got a better grip that way. He and Carlo lowered it to the ground. Then they carried first the tripod and then the scope out to the pad, where they counted three and swung it up to the tripod, jiggling it a bit until it popped into place. The man wiped his hands and put the handkerchief back in his pocket as Carlo thanked him and asked if he'd like a coffee.

The couple invited him to have coffee. Well, Carlo DiForenza did. The wife looked a little put out, like she had better things to do or didn't think much of the bum in her yard. That's right, he thought, she was one of those people he'd heard about, Saddlebrookians or some such up this way, who had some money and wanted to distance themselves from those who did not.

The wife, Brigid, her name was. There was something of the women's libber about her style, the way she dressed and spoke. Were they even married? Yes, there were wedding rings on both their hands. She must be one of those libbers. Pretty old for that, he thought. At least she made the coffee, and brought two mugs out to them, and then went back into the house, leaving the men to sit on the back porch and watch Achilles sniff every piece of gravel individually. After a few minutes she opened the door again and let their dogs out.

"What kind of dogs are those?" Beaufort asked to be polite.

"Pugs," the woman said.

At first the pugs seemed bent on driving the intruder from their yard. While keeping their distance they set up such a ferocious barking no one could be heard over them. The wife quickly went inside, and came back out with a piece of cheese she handed to Beaufort.

Alerting to the smell of the cheese, the pugs rounded back to the porch.

"Here, break that in half and give it to them," she said. "They'll calm down."

They did, and went off to sniff Achilles, and that was pretty much that.

"I have to get used to gravel everywhere instead of grass," Beaufort said, picking up the conversation where they left off. Beaufort would have liked to go inside the house, case the joint, but Carlo suggested they sit on the back porch, chairs facing a particularly craggy section of the Catalina Mountains.

"Ah, we're connoisseurs of gravel out here," Carlo said. "There must be a dozen different kinds, in different sizes and colors. That spot where Achilles is peeing now, that's called pea gravel. Not because of what the dogs use it for, the size." He took a sip of coffee. "Amazing how your dog gets around on three legs as if that were the natural way of things," he said. "Al, stop that."

"It's okay. It's just a dominance thing. This is Al's territory. Nice place you have here," Beaufort said, as he sipped from a mug with a red, white, and blue A on the side. He was careful to just touch the mug on the handle, and even then he rubbed his fingers back and forth discreetly to smear any prints left there. "Been here long?"

"Decades," Carlo said. "Even so, we were the last house in the development to get this view."

"It seems that everyone I run into asks the question 'Where did you come from?' like nobody is actually from Tucson."

"That's the case," Carlo said. "I was born in Kansas, but came out here when I was still young. My wife is from Florida."

Kansas. Right. But Beaufort didn't follow up on that. Instead, though he had never actually lived there, he went with "Florida! What a co-inky-dink. I'm from Florida, too."

The woman came out to ask if they wanted more coffee.

"Jerry is from Florida, too," Carlo said.

"Where in Florida?" the woman asked.

He hesitated, not wanting this to go further, then tried, "East coast."

"Me, too," she said. "Did Irma get you?"

Taken off guard, "Who?"

"Hurricane Irma."

"Oh, Hurricane Irma. No."

"Would you like more coffee?"

Beaufort took another sip. "It's delicious, but I'm fine, thanks."

The woman retreated back into the house, and Carlo continued with the job talk. "I'm retired from the university."

Beaufort thought he couldn't stand much more small talk. But then he couldn't just bring up Santangelo right off the bat. So he asked a few more questions about Carlo's job. Acted impressed. Said he had been a jockey before he retired. He might have given Gloria a different story but what could it matter? He needed something classier for these people.

Despite the cool weather Beaufort had started to sweat. He rubbed his palm on his jeans.

"Are you doing all right there?" Carlo asked him.

Beaufort looked up, startled, fearing Carlo could see his tension. But then Carlo said, "Are you sure you don't want a refill?"

"Maybe coffee's not such a good thing," he said. "I think I'm still used to the northern temperatures."

"I thought you said you were from Florida," Carlo said. "By way of the Deep South, perhaps? I think I can detect a bit of an accent."

"It's true, I did some time in Mississippi," Beaufort said.

Carlo tipped his head as if acknowledging a joke. "I've heard other people speak of it that way, too."

Sixteen

The new neighbor didn't stay that long. I picked up the mug he left on the patio table and carried it into the kitchen, where I put it in the sink for washing later. Carlo came in and poured himself another cup from the pot I had made.

"It's probably bitter," I said. "I could drink it. Give it here."

"It's okay, I'm getting to appreciate rancid coffee," he said.

"So that guy," I started, turning and leaning against the counter while Carlo got some creamer out of the fridge to make his coffee more drinkable. "Who is he?"

"I'm not sure what you mean, O'Hari," Carlo said. He could take apart any sentence and examine it five different ways.

"I mean, who actually says 'co-inky-dink' instead of 'coincidence' anymore? Didn't that have its heyday for about five minutes in the eighties?"

"You were eavesdropping?"

"I heard him when I came out to offer coffee. It was kind of weird when he didn't know what a rescue dog was. That's why I mentioned Irma. It wiped out the Keys last year."

"I remember."

"Even if they don't remember specific names of hurricanes, anyone who ever lived in Florida would know what we mean when we ask, 'Did Irma *get you*?' What does he do for a living?"

"He said he's retired."

"Retired from what?"

"He said he was a jockey."

I felt my eyebrows edge up toward my brow. "He has sort of a large ass relative to the rest of his body. Did you notice that?"

"I can't say that I noticed his ass as much as you did, dear." Carlo sipped the coffee, added a little more cream, and sipped it again. Then he put the creamer back in the fridge before fixing me with that calm but firm expression that says he's about to cut me off. "Honey, have you ever heard other couples in conversation? It usually doesn't sound like a police procedural. Why are you going on like this?"

"There was something off about him. All the usual things people know about. Not knowing what I meant by a rescue. He sounded like he's been in a coma for ten years."

"Well, maybe he has. Honey, aren't you being a trifle . . ." Carlo paused and I saw his lips press together as if he was going to say "paranoid," and then they remolded themselves around ". . . suspicious? Just because you got burned once it doesn't mean everyone in Arizona is a villain."

That made me a little angry, mentioning how I'd let myself get suckered. I wanted to tell a real funny lighthearted story about how many times I'd been caught for underestimating villains.

Like the time I saw the man in the wash while I was collecting rocks there, and knew immediately that he had a thing about raping older women, and I thought I could get the truth out of him by letting him drag me into his van. No, that wasn't funny.

Or like the time I thought someone had to be okay because of a good sense of humor. Until I found out they'd killed a child.

Or like the time I watched a man bleed out and only regretted he died so slowly . . .

Nope, nothing funny going on here. What came to mind was a slideshow from my FBI years, getting shot in the leg, and Laura having her ear stapled because I couldn't see what was in front of my face, and men who liked to fuck mummies, and Jessica, oh the worst of all because

Jessica died and it was my fault. Those were the stories I could tell but never had, and now I never would because they weren't like the stories Jane would tell, lighthearted and funny and, and *good*.

Amazing how quickly we can think all of that. Instead of saying it, I said, "I got burned because I forgot that everyone is a potential villain until I prove they're not. This guy. He's a type. I worked with forensic profilers enough to recognize a personality type."

"Am I a type?"

"Oh stop. I'm talking about an intensity. The way he stared without blinking while he was trying to project the good old boy image, like he was trying to read our reactions. There's something mean and hard about him, underneath all the cap doffing and ma'aming, that's all I'm saying."

Carlo fixed me with that gaze that made me wonder if I'd been speaking aloud what I supposed were only thoughts. Not for the first time I thought if I wasn't careful he could make me confess to anything. He said, "It has been a while since we've had guests. Maybe it's time. I invited him over for stargazing. As a thank-you for helping me. I'm sure he won't murder us in our beds."

"I'm sure you're right," I growled softly, then got myself a refill and went back to work on the skip trace. At least it was something different to think about.

Seventeen

There were so few places of business up in Catalina it was easy to appear to just happen on someone coincidentally. Beaufort threw a few things into his shopping cart at Bashas', the only grocery store in at least ten miles, the same one where he picked up flowers for Gloria. He stopped at the Starbucks counter to get a coffee. They didn't used to have coffee shops inside grocery stores either.

Carlo was sitting at a small table near the Starbucks booth with two other men, all intent on their conversation. Beaufort had a rubber hedgehog that he had picked up for Achilles in the pet aisle. As he paid for his coffee he squeaked the toy to get Carlo's attention. It worked, and Carlo called a hello to him.

Beaufort maneuvered his cart to the table. He was not invited to sit with the men, but he sat down anyway in the fourth chair. "Who do I have the pleasure of meeting?" he asked, hoping it sounded classy enough.

Carlo introduced him to Father Elias Manwaring, from St. Matthew's Episcopal Church, and to Harold Maas, an astronomer who taught at the college and was also part of the Mars Rover project. Carlo explained that they were getting together regularly to talk about a seminar they were planning on the interface between science and religion. When

Carlo was finished explaining, the three men looked at Beaufort expectantly, maybe thinking he would be off now so they could get back to their discussion, but he didn't go. So the portly man identified as a priest stepped in politely.

"So, how are you two acquainted?" he asked.

When Beaufort explained that he had met Carlo over the backyard fence, so to speak, and helped him move his telescope, Maas's lip curled as in "You call that a telescope?" and Manwaring asked with a smile, "You're familiar with the daunting Ms. Quinn, then?"

"I'm sorry?" Beaufort said, not recognizing the name.

"Mrs. DiForenza, I should have said. Carlo's wife."

"Her name is . . ."

"Quinn. Brigid Quinn," Manwaring said. "I'd been told she kept her name." He glanced at Carlo. "Not that there's anything wrong with that."

Maas said, "Man, Elias, for a liberal clergyman you're way out of step."

Beaufort asked, "But why do you say 'daunting'? I think she's a lovely lady."

Manwaring winked at Carlo. Carlo said, "Elias is being ironic. My wife is an ex–FBI agent. You see, there was some trouble at the church, and that's how—"

"Trouble my ass," Manwaring said, while Beaufort thought it unlikely for a priest to speak that way. Was he really a priest and reflected more of the changing times, or were the others shitting Beaufort and he didn't get the joke?

"She saved my life," Manwaring added.

Carlo laughed and sipped his coffee. "Elias is exaggerating as he often does," he said. "There was an incident that involved the church. Brigid took care of things."

Behind their conversation Beaufort cursed to himself while he felt his grin stretching wider and wider like an idiot's and hoped no one was smart enough to notice he was close to hyperventilating. He rubbed his palms on the edge of the table, took a deep breath, held it for a couple of seconds, and then released it and said, "So, how did Brigid get to be a superhero?"

Whereupon Carlo told him all about her fabulous career foiling villains for the FBI, awards from the president, a strong woman who still made him proud.

"Still?" Beaufort said, and it sounded to him like a croak.

No one noticed that either.

"She retired," Carlo says. "But she's still a private investigator."

Beaufort still made no move to leave, until finally, in the silence that grew a little more awkward with each second, Carlo said, "You know, that offer of an evening of stargazing still stands. If you give me your telephone number I'll call you."

Beaufort got out his wallet, took out the receipt from the restaurant where he and Gloria had been last, and handed it to Carlo. "Would you mind if I called you instead? I'm having trouble getting messages off my cell phone."

"I know how that is. I don't even own a cell phone." Carlo took the scrap of paper, and with a pen that was lying on the table between the men next to a pad where they'd been making notes, he wrote down his landline number. "Call soon, while the moon is new," Carlo said.

Without asking what the hell that even meant, Beaufort tucked the phone number back in his wallet and disengaged himself with thanks for the company. Harold Maas, who had sat quietly looking bored for most of the time, now said a cheerful good-bye. Beaufort remembered that he should buy at least what was in his basket, and went through the checkout line.

Patting himself on the back for getting the man's phone number without giving up his own so that Gloria couldn't get wind of what he was doing, he got back to the house, fired up Gloria's computer, and googled *FBI*. But useful as this internet was, there was no way to tell when Brigid Quinn had been an agent, or which office she had worked for, whether Tucson or someplace else. So he wrote down the number of the nearest FBI office, which seemed like a likely place to go, and called them.

"Hello," he said, using that airy-old voice that had worked before, "I'm looking for an agent. Brigid Quinn."

"I'm sorry," the woman at the other end of the line said, "there's no agent here by that name."

"Golly," he says, "I'm trying to connect with her about my missing granddaughter. I'm told she's an excellent private investigator now and is still in the area."

The woman excused herself for a moment, and then a man's voice came on. "Hello, Mr. . . . ?"

Beaufort was using Gloria's landline, and he knew that the office he was calling would probably have caller ID. "I'm Frank Bentham? Staying at my sister's place in Tucson." Beaufort repeated the business about wanting Quinn's aid in locating his granddaughter. He embellished a bit about her having run away.

"Well, Mr. Bentham, I can't tell you her whereabouts now, but I can say that she did work with the Arizona Bureau. Perhaps if you checked directory assistance you could find her."

"Thank you so much!" Beaufort let a little quaver seep into his voice. "You've helped an old man to hope." Beaufort hung up the phone. So the men weren't kidding, his target was married to an actual FBI agent who apparently still had some balls.

Switching to his approved cell, he called Yanchak.

"Brigid Quinn? Never heard of her," Yanchak said.

"Can you check around? You've got connections all over the place."

He could almost feel Yanchak glowing with the compliment from two thousand miles away. Beaufort knew he knew how to play people.

"What do you want to know about her? What business do you have?"

Beaufort wouldn't say. Not even Yanchak knew anything about him from before the time Beaufort started working for him. As the seconds ticked by without Beaufort saying anything, Yanchak said, "Is this anything I should be concerned about? Do I not want to get involved?"

"Nah, it's just a curiosity question."

"Right," Yanchak said. He promised to check around and call back.

Beaufort found himself telling himself he wasn't stupid. No, he was smart, smarter than that woman. He was going to know everything about her, while she knew nothing about him. Didn't that make him smarter? Santangelo, that bastard, saying Beaufort was stupid that night at the monastery. The priest didn't know a thing about Beaufort.

Beaufort timed his call to Carlo late in the afternoon when he thought Carlo might be there and before Gloria got home from work. He accepted

93

an invitation for dinner the following night, while the moon was still dark. He knew how to be careful now that he knew who the Quinn woman was. He would take his bike to the house in case she started to get suspicious and wanted to run his license plate. He was smart, staying on top of every eventuality. And possibly overly cautious, but why take a chance?

Eighteen

You didn't have to go to a florist for flowers the way you used to. So it was easy to bring Gloria a bouquet regularly. Not a balloon. He saw some with HAPPY RETIREMENT! which meant it wasn't a kid thing anymore, but he couldn't cotton to the idea of giving a balloon to an adult. Liquor was a different thing. You could get liquor in grocery stores in Arizona, so with the flowers he picked up a bottle of Grey Goose to restock her liquor cabinet, show he wasn't a freeloader.

Every time Beaufort handed Gloria a bunch of chrysanthemums she'd start to cry. He had to wait until she was finished before they could get on with the evening, but he sort of liked it. She said she cried because she'd had two abusive husbands and Beaufort was so good to her.

He told her he was celebrating with the flowers and the vodka because he had gotten a part-time job working with horses at a local riding stable down the road at the edge of Catalina State Park.

It wasn't true.

Gloria pretended the vodka was for her and kissed him on his nose.

He had to admit he actually liked this woman. She could be a real cut-up and make him laugh even if he didn't always get the joke. Like tonight, her wearing a shirt with flamingos done in sequins, with dangling flamingo earrings to match. Rocking her head to make the flamingos dance, she strutted out of the bedroom. When she saw his doubtful expression, she started to giggle.

"Too understated?" she asked.

Beaufort didn't quite understand the question or how to answer it, but took her into his arms and kissed the tip of her nose back and that seemed to do the trick. He was happy in a way he'd never been before.

Gloria hip-bumped him and went back to cooking dinner. Beaufort took the bottle of Pinot Grigio out of the fridge and read the label as he poured her a second glass and got one for himself. Ecco Domani, the label said. He was growing to actually like wine, and had noticed that even this had changed, that they didn't offer Chablis in restaurants anymore.

Gloria had her back to him, sautéeing some cut-up peppers and onions on the stove, when she said, "I told Steph about you today."

Within a heartbeat he was at her side. Leaning with his back against the counter next to the stove, swishing his wine in the glass the way he had seen people do on television. "Who is Steph?" he asked, trying to keep his tone easy.

It must have worked, because she didn't look alarmed. "One of the med techs at the office. She was happy for me." Gloria stopped sautéeing and smiled at Beaufort. "She said a group of them were going out for drinks and a movie this Friday and did I want to bring you. I'd never been invited like that before. I think maybe it's because I'm happier. That I've changed somehow, made people like me more." Now she looked back at the pan. "I think it's because of you."

Beaufort went over the details of himself that he had given to Gloria, true and false. No harm done, really, but, "I have to tell you, I'm kind of a private person, not much for the group thing," he said. "I'm not ready to go out with other people just now. And I'd appreciate you not talking too much about me either."

Gloria didn't look up this time, shyly or in any other way. She just kept stirring and stirring.

"Understood?" he asked.

"Sure, Jerry. I understand."

So she wouldn't take it too hard, he took the wooden spoon from her hand and put it down on the counter. She gripped the spoon as if she was afraid he was going to hit her with it, but then she let go. He drew her to him and folded his arms around her with his hands on her ass. "Maybe for a while I want you all to myself."

That did it. She kissed him and looked happy again.

"And if you keep talking about me, they'll keep asking, and that might make things uncomfortable between us."

"Careful, it will burn," she said, frowning, and turned back to the stove. "I got a couple of steaks, with A1 sauce the way you said you liked it. Do you want to fire up the grill?"

He had learned before now that that meant turning on the gas, and went out back to do it, thinking about things as he took the platter Gloria handed him and proceeded to cook the meat.

Thinking that all his life he had missed out on a woman bringing him steaks to grill and he wanted more of it.

Thinking that he hoped everything went well and he would have a lot more time with Gloria who wasn't such a bad old gal.

Thinking people were of two kinds. One kind made him nervous. The other kind he could see was weaker than he was, and he could have his own way with things. He prided himself on being smart enough to tell which person was which. Gloria was the weak kind. He had lucked out finding her.

No, it wasn't luck. It was brains. A mind as sharp as a surgeon's scalpel. His time with junkies, his time in jail, he had learned how to find out who the weak ones were, the ones who could be separated from the rest of the herd.

He was smoking on the back porch after dinner when Gloria came out with the remains of her wine.

"I didn't think you smoked," she said.

Interesting how a woman could go from good old gal to annoyance in a moment. Beaufort didn't like people trying to control him in any way. He'd had enough years of that in prison. "I just started," he said, not bothering to apologize or explain.

Whether or not she could accept that, Gloria was distracted by something bigger. "Jerry, your hand."

He looked at his hand when he raised the cigarette. The palm was raw. At first he didn't know how it could have gotten that way, and then he realized he must have been rubbing it on the adobe wall of the house while he was thinking. Gloria kissed it, took him inside, put some antibiotic ointment on it, and placed a large square Band-Aid over the raw place.

"You've seemed tense," she said, rubbing his back at the top.

"I'm not."

"You've got stress knots."

"Ouch. Stop it."

"If you wanted, I could give you the number of someone I've used."

"Are you saying I need a shrink?"

"No. He's more of a life coach."

That's another new one, Beaufort thought. But he had become accustomed to not speaking out loud when he didn't understand. If he let people keep talking it usually became clear what they meant.

Gloria finished her bandaging, led him from the bathroom, and patted a place next to her on the bed. He sat down, waiting. She was so cute when she tried to take charge.

"He taught me some meditation techniques you might use," she said. "You put your fingers like this and tap each one with your thumb while you say, 'Sah. Nah. Tah. Mah.'" She illustrated, and looked at him expectantly. Beaufort could not bring himself to do something so idiotic, and he sat there watching her, wondering what planet he was on.

Gloria didn't appear to notice. "There's breathing that goes with it, too," she went on. "Breathe in on a count of three, then breathe out on a longer count of seven. Try it. Sah. Nah. Tah . . ."

Beaufort placed the backs of his hands on his thighs with the fingers up and slightly curled. He stopped short of saying the nonsense, but tried the breathing and the finger tapping. After a couple of rounds he couldn't force himself to go on no matter how well-intentioned Gloria was. So this was the world, he thought, with its pathetic pretense that it was more civilized and in control of itself than the world he'd been part of for thirty years. He started laughing, and took her into his arms. "You don't need a life coach anymore, babe," he said. "I'll take care of you, and you're never going to be hurt again."

He had one of his dreams that night, woke up to Gloria holding him, stroking his damp hair and cuddling him like a mother. The sight of her face was what told him it was only a nightmare, all the screams and bloodied flesh. He wished he could tell Gloria the joy he felt upon waking, because in the dream he had tremendous remorse about the killing. A monster wouldn't feel bad like that about the killing, would he? Maybe not even have nightmares at all. Certainly not feel joy upon waking and realizing he hadn't done it this time.

Beaufort stroked Gloria's face the way she was stroking his while he thought *if you really knew me you would not love me.*

At that thought, as quickly as if his emotions were on a toggle switch, the joy plunged back into the despair of the dream. He could find Hickock's confession, and the nightmares could stop. To do so, he could kill every person in his way, and loathe the necessary killing with all his heart. But the only thing he could never do, he could never stop being Jeremiah Beaufort with Jeremiah Beaufort's past. He was stuck with all of himself.

Nineteen

I thought this was a good opportunity to see if our new friend was just lonely, or stalking lonely, or on the con in general, or targeting me in specific. So, dinner as well as stargazing.

"You just had me over for dinner because you knew I'd cook," Gemma-Kate said.

"Untrue. I also had you over for dinner because I want you to give me your take on this guy who showed up in our backyard and sort of glommed on to us."

"How long have you suffered from paranoia?"

"It's not paranoia, it's instinct."

Standing over a pot on the stove, Gemma-Kate smirked as she tasted a pad thai noodle, considered, and added a splash more fish sauce. "Oh yes, I'm well aware of your instincts." Gemma-Kate was referring to a time in the recent past when I'd been royally suckered, and then mistakenly blamed her for it.

"I learned my lesson, never let down my guard," I said. "So shut up and cook."

Gemma-Kate put down her spoon and looked in the cabinet next to the stove. "You forgot to get peanuts."

"There's a new jar in the pantry." Not being a total lump in the kitchen, I went there myself, got out the jar, and handed it to her.

She said, "So what's with this guy?"

"I'd rather you were left to form your own opinion," I said.

"What about Uncle Carlo? What does he think?"

"He thinks everyone is destined for sainthood. Even you."

"What's his name?" Gemma-Kate asked.

"Jerry."

"Jerry what?"

"He didn't say."

The doorbell rang with the *Eine kleine Nachtmusik* tune that was left over from Jane. Tonight the tune made her blink into my mind, her ghost walking through this living room, dusting a table (I had always pictured her using a feather duster while wearing an apron), focusing on a new recipe with an adorable smudge of flour on her cheek, giving Carlo a light kiss in a way that was hers alone. Then I remembered she read literary classics and wrote books, too. And then she blinked back out again. There are a thousand things that spur these memory flashes, not just Jane. I say this to show it's not jealousy, or not always.

But back to the doorbell. Jerry had arrived.

Gemma-Kate wiped her hands on a kitchen towel and beat me to the front door, opening it as wide as the smile between her plump cheeks. Before letting the man in, she stuck out her hand and said, "Welcome! I'm Gemma-Kate. Gemma-Kate . . . Quinn."

The pugs, too, had rushed the door as soon as it opened, and were doing their best to save us all from the intruder. The man shouted over them as he put out his hand, "Hello, Gemma-Kate. I'm Jerry."

Nice try, I thought. But then Gemma-Kate, with her usual lack of aplomb, shouted back, "What's your last name?"

Jerry paused, looking far from plussed, and then said, "Nolan."

Meanwhile I was trying to hook my fingers around the pugs' collars and failing. They twisted around and I let go when I felt my circulation being shut off.

The man who called himself Jerry Nolan took a small plastic bag out of his golf jacket pocket and extracted two pieces of cheese for the pugs.

Al and Peg fell to silent gobbling and then remembered the reason they liked him.

"Ah, you remembered," I said. I looked out at the driveway for his car. "You rode a bike."

He nodded. "I live close, and it's a nice evening," he said.

"It will be dark when you leave," I said.

"The bike has lights," he said.

I took his jacket, ushered him into the living room, and offered a glass of wine or a cocktail. He said he didn't drink. I wished he did, because the way he grinned at nothing was making me nervous. I got myself another Chardonnay.

After some stilted exchanges about the desert life and his job at the local riding stables, we sat down to dinner, Carlo and I at either end, with Gemma-Kate facing him across the table. He ate like a gentleman and managed table conversation, which I tried to steer from general to personal as the meal went on.

How unseasonable the temperatures were all over the country. Predictions of an early cold snap after an Indian summer.

How we were in the dry part of the year and couldn't expect any rains until late December.

When the rattlesnakes went into hibernation, September or October?

When we had all moved to Tucson, and what brought us here.

Then I asked Jerry where he had come from, and he said Mississippi. Maybe he saw me react, and changed his story. Originally, he said, before Florida. Wouldn't say where in Mississippi, but instead segued into being baptized as a Catholic. Drifted away from the church, he said.

"Brigid and I go to an Episcopal church," Carlo said. "You should come sometime. There are lots of Catholics there."

"How can you tell?" Jerry asked.

"They always want you to know," Carlo said. "Where were you baptized?"

I happened to glance at Jerry, and he had the look of someone who had just been dealt a straight flush. I watched him.

"At St. Anthony's," Jerry said.

"I used to be an altar boy at a St. Anthony's," Carlo said. "In Kansas City."

"That's the one," Jerry said. "Small world."

Between Mississippi, Kansas, Florida, and now Arizona, Jerry had gotten around in that small world, I thought.

"I should say so," Carlo said. "You and I are around the same age, I bet. We might have both been baptized by Father Victor Santangelo. Vic was very important in my life."

I saw Jerry lick his lips and swallow. Rather than take the next question and ask how Santangelo was important in Carlo's life, he turned the conversation to when Carlo had become interested in astronomy.

Carlo said it was a recent hobby.

"He's very passionate about it, though," I added. "My anniversary gift to him is an overnight up on Kitt Peak. Have you heard about their programs?"

"Not yet," Jerry said.

I explained, several huge telescopes, six thousand feet elevation, an expert on hand. Sleeping quarters and sandwiches. Carlo filled in some of the details I didn't know while tilting the wine bottle in my direction. I moved my index finger up in our subtle sign that said I was done.

"When do you plan to go to this place?" Jerry asked Carlo.

Carlo told him. With some questioning, with too many questions? Carlo told him the date and how long it would take to drive there. Gemma-Kate caught my eye from across the table.

Jerry changed the conversation to what Carlo did for a living.

Carlo reminded Jerry that he had been first a Jesuit priest, and then a philosophy professor at the university.

Jerry said that sounded hard, philosophy, and Carlo didn't mention that Jerry had already said this the first time they talked, but joked that yes, it was a tough racket.

That was another opening.

"So what do you do, Jerry?" I asked, pretending I didn't already know, and toying with a noodle on my plate to indicate I didn't much care.

"I'm retired," he said. We waited. And then he finally gave up some information. "But I had an interesting career. I was a jockey."

"Flat or harness? Steeple?" I asked.

He paused, and picked at his own pad thai before answering. Apparently he didn't like it as well when someone else was asking the questions.

"Flat," he said finally. "I was never stupid enough to do the steeplechasing. Too easy to break yourself. Do you ride?"

I cocked my head in a noncommittal way and pretended to be too interested in him to talk about myself. "Where did you race?"

"All over the South. Nothing high stakes like the Derby. Nothing famous. Ever hear of Mother's Little Helper?"

"No, sorry."

"He was one of the horses I rode for a while. Placed a couple of times but never won a race. I guess you could blame me."

"Ever race at Pompano Park?"

Another pause, then, "Sure."

"When?"

I kept my eyes on his face, but the dining room table has a glass top and through it I could see him picking at a bandage on his right palm.

"In the seventies," he said.

Then and throughout the evening he seemed both a trifle edgy and overly polite, like a man who's socializing in a different class and is insecure about it. But there was more. The feeling lingered that he was playing me as much as I was playing him. That one of us was the cat and one the mouse and I wasn't sure who was which. That didn't allow for either of us to get anywhere, like evenly matched chess players.

After dinner Carlo said he was going to fire up the telescope, sight it, and enter some coordinates for interesting spots he had picked to view. He rubbed his hands together as he said that, and looked expectantly at Jerry.

Jerry wanted to help with the dishes. I tried to shoo him away, but he insisted. Specifically, it appeared he wanted to put his own dishes in the dishwasher. I watched him as he rubbed his thumb and index finger vigorously over his knife and fork before placing them in the utensil compartment.

He spent some time with Carlo and the telescope, used the bathroom before saying he needed to be on his way home, and left.

Twenty

Beaufort was taking a chance, and he knew it, but didn't have a choice if he wanted to get in their good graces and make it easier to find out what he needed to know. The woman's niece was there, too, and stared at him half the time as if she was dissecting him in her mind. Gemma-Kate was her name. She had fixed the dinner, something oriental but not like what he'd ever gotten in a Chinese restaurant, made with shrimp and crushed peanuts. And noodles instead of rice, what was it with that? Next dinner was going to be a big steak and mashed potatoes, he decided.

"Interesting aroma," he said. "What is that smell?"

"You're probably smelling the fish sauce," the niece said. "It's kind of like soy sauce but heightens all the other flavors better."

If the dinner was long and dull, the time with the telescope was pure torture. Carlo kept training the telescope on one area after another, stepping aside to let Jerry exclaim over pale smudges of light while Carlo kept advising him on how best to see them, looking out of the corner of his eye, for example. Telling him about star clusters, nebulae, the moons of Jupiter. Could he see the four spots of light that were the largest moons? Could he see the bands across the planet itself?

Could he keep from slamming Carlo's face on the eyepiece? He had held it together through the dinner, and mostly through the telescoping, but the effort of not simply shooting the three of them and searching the house at his leisure was almost too much to bear. What rotten luck, that the priest had gone and married an FBI agent. Retired or not, she wouldn't think the way other people do.

This is what he was thinking about while pretending to see the things that Carlo was pointing out. Beaufort thought he did pretty good with the conversation, sidestepping most of the questions. But he'd gotten a little cocky by the time the jockey business came up. What was with all those questions? And him offering unnecessary information. Was Pompano Park even around in the seventies? Stupid! Jerry said he had to use the bathroom, and the young girl showed it to him. There he held his hand up and saw it shaking in the mirror. The bandage on his palm was peeling around the edges. He sank to his knees in front of the john as if he would throw up, and actually did heave a bit. He let his forehead rest on the toilet seat a moment. A little better, but standing in the backyard wasn't getting him anywhere near what he was looking for, and it was time to go.

As he did with the utensils at dinner, Jerry was careful not to leave a print in the bathroom in case the wife began to suspect him. He didn't suppose he had given her any reason, but you never knew what those people were thinking. Could she get his DNA somehow? Would it have been left on the fork that he put in his mouth, or even on his plate? As he thought about this his stomach wrenched again, but he took a deep breath and it passed. He used his wrist to flush the toilet, and likewise to raise and lower the water faucet handle. A piece of tissue worked for the door handle. Goddamn forensic science.

Telling himself that he was overreacting to the horse track business, and that just getting inside the house was progress, he felt a little calmer now. When he opened the bathroom door, to the left he saw two more rooms in darkness except for a shaft of light from a ceiling fixture in the hall. In the room on the right he could barely make out what looked like an office desk with a file cabinet next to it. It could be there.

In the room on the left he saw bookshelves that ran not just along the wall the way bookshelves usually do, but down the center of the room as well. It looked like a little library. He stood at the entrance to the room despite himself, as if it had hypnotized him, was luring him into its darkness. It could be there instead. He started to hum his old tune absentmindedly.

The overhead light went on, and Beaufort, jumpier than he thought, jumped.

"I'm sorry, Jerry. I didn't mean to startle you," Carlo's voice behind him said. "Do you like to read?"

"Some," Beaufort said.

"What are you reading?"

Beaufort thought of the book he saw at Gloria's place. "I'm reading one by J. K. Rowling and it's good," he said. "I think I'll get some more of his books."

"Ye-s-s," Carlo said with a look that Beaufort couldn't read. He walked over to a tiny desk against the wall under a window and picked up a manila envelope darkened to orange with age. "Speaking of Father Santangelo. Just the other day I was talking about that time and dug this old thing out. Maybe you'll be interested." Carlo opened the flap that had once been sealed with tape that had lost its stickiness long ago, and pulled out a sketch of Richard Hickock. "Do you recognize this?"

He knew it from the moment Carlo had mentioned Victor Santangelo. At last. At fuckin' last! "No," he said. "Who is it?"

"It's a sketch done by one of the killers of the Clutter family, you know, *In Cold Blood*."

"I remember something of that. How did you get it?"

"It was part of some things Victor gave me when I left the active ministry. He wanted me to know that he still had faith in me even when I didn't have faith in myself." Carlo slid the sketch back inside the envelope and put it on the desk. "Do me a favor and don't tell Brigid you saw it. She doesn't know I have it, and with our anniversary coming up I thought it would make a great gift."

"You're going to give her a sketch of a murderer as an anniversary gift?"

Carlo smiled. "Macabre, I know. You'd have to understand Brigid."

Beaufort ached with wanting to ask Carlo what else Santangelo had given him, what else might be right in that envelope, but *don't be too eager*, he told himself. *It's all about keeping control so don't rush it.* It's not like what he was looking for would be out in plain sight for him to pick up.

"Well, thanks for the evening," Beaufort said. "I'm thinking I'd better be getting home. It's past Achilles's time to go out."

Twenty-one

Sometimes you can't rid yourself of an obsession, but you can replace it with another. Which is almost as good.

Uber had brought Gemma-Kate up to the house, but I wanted to take her back to her dorm so I could talk to her about the evening, and about the man. I figured, being a psychopath (not that she's been formally diagnosed, but we all know it) she'd be able to tell if he was somewhere on that spectrum.

"Come on, we're going," I said, putting on a thick sweater and giving Gemma-Kate hers as soon as I saw Jerry get on his bike and turn left at the first street. That meant he would be leaving the Black Horse development on the western side.

"But I wanted to ask Uncle Carlo a few more questions," she said.

"No time right now," I said. I hustled her into the car and took the long way around, out the north entrance, and turned left on Golder Ranch. I picked up his bike reflectors crossing Twin Lakes, heading north. I followed far enough behind so I could see him turn right on Hawser, and head to an area where the pavement ended. Not too many houses down there. I pulled the car off the road.

"You wait here," I said. "I'll be right back."

"Aunt Brigid, you worry me sometimes," Gemma-Kate said.

Here in the desert there's precious little shrubbery to hide behind and the tree trunks are hardly wide enough, but on Hawser I managed to slip from sage to mesquite to bottlebrush without, I think, him knowing I was there. I made it to the corner in time to see his rear reflector light stop.

I sprinted after him to make sure I saw which house he stopped at, then hid again to watch him unlatch a gate.

I went back to the car, moving at a more leisurely pace now, and Gemma-Kate looked at me with some disdain as I buckled in, drove off, and asked her what she thought about Jerry Nolan.

She didn't have too much to offer right off the bat. "He's definitely odd. And the steatopygia is odd."

"What are you talking about?"

"He has unusually large buttocks for a man," she said. "And what was that tune he was humming when he walked off after dinner? It sounded familiar."

"To me, too," I said. I hummed a bit of it. "But I don't know if I've ever heard the title. I bet Carlo has."

"He knows everything." She almost sounded a little peeved by that observation.

"So tell me what you think."

"I think he's creepy. I don't mean in the sense that he shouldn't be around children, not that kind of creepy, but more like he's trying really hard to be what he imagines is human. It makes him nervous."

"Where would you judge his IQ at?"

"Top half of the bell curve but just barely. He strikes me as thinking himself much more clever than he actually is."

I agreed. "And the name Nolan. It's old. No-Last-Name."

"Now, Aunt Brigid," Gemma-Kate said. "I'm sure that some people actually have that name and are not trying to con you."

"Why do you think his rear end is significant?"

"Well, everything about him screams jockey, the short stature, the thin frame, the wiriness. Except for those buttocks. I would think it could affect his horseback riding. And why were you badgering him with all those questions about his being a jockey?"

"Because he was never a jockey," I said.

Twenty-two

Beaufort remembered there was a bigger purpose for cutting out of that house. Apart from finding what Carlo had from Santangelo, he needed to find out when Pompano Park had been built. So that was the reason he was already a little on edge when he walked through Gloria's front door to find her in her bathrobe, with Achilles in her lap, sulking. At first she appeared to want to give him the silent treatment, but he couldn't be lucky enough to have that kind of woman.

"Where were you so late?" she asked.

The whining grated on his nerves, but he forced himself to keep his composure. "It's nine o'clock. That's not late." He couldn't help adding, "It was two in the morning when I picked you up."

"You're not answering my question." Her voice quaked a little with the courage it took to say that, and he knew it was because she was a little angry, and a little scared, both of him going and him staying.

"Oh, baby," he said. "You think I was out with another woman?" He went up to the chair, leaned over and tried to kiss her. She turned her head away and he ended up with a lick from Achilles instead. "I swear you're enough woman for me."

"You didn't take your car."

"Didn't you see, I took my bike. They needed me at the stables," he said.

"What for?"

"There was a night ride. Then I had to take care of the horses. Then I had a drink with the owner and shot the shit for a while. Any other questions?"

"Night ride? Sounds something like a submarine race. And I've seen the owner. She's young and pretty."

"When were you there?"

Abused women can always tell the smallest change in a man's voice, some inflection that predicts violence. Beaufort wondered for a second why it never stopped them. If only they'd stay quiet they wouldn't get so beat up.

"Oh, I was never there," she said cautiously. "I just saw her, across the parking lot at Bashas', not even close enough to talk."

Beaufort tried to keep that dangerous inflection out of his voice. There might come a time when it would be useful but this was not one of them. What was of benefit was that the tables had turned and he was now questioning her. As gently as he could, "Then how did you know it was the owner of the stables?"

"She had one of those magnetic signs on the side of her truck. I swear, Jerry"—this was a good sign, when they started to protest in their own defense—"she didn't even look in my direction."

Was Gloria spying on him? If so, it was only a matter of time before she started snooping around, asking questions, and finding out he didn't work at the stables at all. He needed to put this to rest or find himself looking for another place to stay before he had gotten what he came to Tucson for. He was too close to screw it up now.

Beaufort took Achilles off Gloria's lap, and he knew he still had her from the way she let the dog go, as if she knew what was coming. He leaned forward and reached into where her bathrobe closed. Her hips moved in response.

"There you go," he said. "I'll show you I haven't shot my wad yet." That came out before he could think about whether it was the best way to say it.

She didn't seem to think it was crass. "You could have left a note," she protested, but weakly now, as if begging him to lie.

Beaufort stood up, left Gloria in the chair with her knees spread slightly, went to the desk, and turned on her computer. It was that conversation with the wife that set him on edge. Was that racetrack built after the seventies? Is that where she caught him? He had taken an awful chance with saying a time when he had raced there. He googled *Pompano Park history*. It was built in 1964. Close one, but safe. He was getting good at this computer business.

Gloria's voice got to him before she did. It made him jump. You were always on alert inside for someone coming up behind you. She didn't seem to notice, though, when she said, "I understand, Jerry. Sometimes a man has to look at a few porn pictures to get in the mood." Then he could feel her standing behind him, looking at the computer screen. "A racetrack?" she said.

Beaufort's hands hovered over the keyboard, frozen in space. It wasn't the racetrack question that alerted him. That could be innocent with Gloria thinking he had worked with horses. It was the remark before it. His mood had definitely soured. He stood up, his back to the screen, the desk chair pushed aside rather than coming between them. "What did you say?" he asked.

Gloria got that scared puppy look she got sometimes when she knew she had said the wrong thing, the thing that might make a man hurt her or, what would be worse, leave her. But he knew she couldn't imagine anything worse than that. Gloria, for all her charm, had a very limited imagination.

Beaufort said again, "What did you say?"

Gloria stumbled and bumbled her way around the words. "It's just . . . I saw . . . you know . . . every man does . . ."

He rolled the desk chair back between them, facing her. "Sit down," he said.

She sat. He turned the chair around so it faced the computer, and stood behind her. "Show me how you know."

She pointed to a group of boxes underneath the Google search line. *Macy's*, one of the squares said. And there was *Pompano Park* where he was just looking. And *Weather Channel*. And *Movie Tickets*. And *YouTube*. And *Facebook*. And *Sexy Girls*. He had never noticed this before.

"See? It's okay. It's not like you were looking at children, or violence." She turned to look up at him with a tone that was meant to encourage. "You're just a red-blooded American male," she said, and turned the chair slightly to nuzzle his crotch, which was at about cheek level. "They all do it."

"So you looked at what I was looking at?"

"I just—"

"What do you do, click the cursor on that box and it takes you there?"

"Well yes, I—"

Jerry put his hands on her upper arms, which was more a gesture of get-out-of-my-chair than let's-have-sex. There was no mistaking one for the other as he added, "Go to bed, honey."

"But. Are you upset that I looked at your sites?"

His hands tightened, allowing no opposition. "Just go to bed. I'll be there in a while."

"But tell me you're not angry at me," she all but whimpered.

"If you insist, I've got this thing about people snooping around, watching what I do. I guess your life coach would call it a hot button. Do you understand what I'm saying?"

"Sure," she said. "I'm sorry."

He was tempted to say *you certainly are*, but refrained. She stood, more like heaved herself out of the desk chair, and dragged herself into the bedroom without looking at him. He was happy for a moment, thinking how much more manageable Gloria was than the priest's wife.

When the bedroom light went out he went into the kitchen. From the cabinet under the counter next to the stove he took a bottle of bourbon from Gloria's liquor stash and poured himself just a couple of fingers. He'd have to have sex with Gloria one of these days, he thought, but for the time being her wanting it would keep her in line better than satisfying her.

As for her being able to snoop on what he was doing on her computer, he realized he would have to be more careful, go down to the library to use their computers for his continued monitoring of Meadows's progress on the Walker case. Close one.

For now he wrote "bourbon" on the grocery list she attached to the refrigerator door, then crossed it out thinking he should get it himself as a gesture of forgiveness. Jeez, flowers, dinners, make them come first, but hurt their feelings once and they never forget it. Is this what he'd dreamed of, all those years in prison? How long would it be before this kind of life just seemed like another sentence?

Beaufort gave a world-weary sigh and sat in the office chair at the desk. Achilles had come out from wherever he was hiding and laid himself down with his head on the man's foot. Achilles always seemed to know when to make himself scarce and when it was safe to come out. Dogs were smarter than women that way, he thought.

Beaufort clicked on the square that showed the Pompano Park site. It didn't take him long to find out where Quinn's questions had been leading. She asked if he did flat racing or steeplechase. He knew the difference between those, and had answered flat.

Only as he looked at the photographs of the track, at the horses pulling surreys rather than the jockeys riding them, and then as he read more, he discovered the point of that conversation. Pompano Park wasn't a racetrack that offered flat racing. It had always been and was still exclusively for what they called harness racing. He said he only did flat racing. And that he had raced at Pompano Park. His thumb and index finger jerked involuntarily and hit the glass of bourbon, knocking it onto the carpet. Shaking, he picked up the glass and went into the kitchen for more while he thought about what Carlo's wife had done.

She had not only caught him in a lie, the bitch had set him up for it. She must be on to him.

Maybe it was time to stop being so cautious. He could just kill the two of them in their beds and burn their house down to destroy the evidence. That would take care of all the problems, get rid of the confession which was probably in there somewhere, and anyone who could connect him to it.

But then he thought *probably*. There was no guarantee that DiForenza had the confession in the house. Unless he put his hands on it, unless he read what Hickock had said about him, he would never feel any safer than he did now.

It was probably a better idea to get the wife out of the way before he did anything else. This was necessary. He stepped outside the house to light a cigarette, see how good he was about not smoking in the house? And called Yanchak.

Twenty-three

When I got home from dropping off Gemma-Kate I found Carlo unloading the dishwasher. I went into my office to use Google Earth to locate the address where Jerry No-Last-Name was living and who owned it. Then I poured myself the last of the wine, sat on one of the counter stools, and enjoyed watching Carlo scrub some food off the stovetop. It's important for philosophers to engage in something physical now and then.

"You were very kind to give Jerry dinner," he said, breaking our companionable silence. "I don't necessarily agree with you about his being mean. He seems to be more of a loner, and a little lonely. Very much on edge."

"When you invited him, did you tell him to bring a date?"

"Just as you asked me to."

"He didn't."

"I suppose he doesn't have someone to ask. New in town and all that."

"He lives with someone," I said. "A woman."

"How do you know this?"

"I got his address and looked it up. The house is owned by Gloria Bentham. Did he mention her?"

Carlo frowned and shook his head.

"Interesting that he came to dinner by himself. Why would he accept an invitation to dinner without at least mentioning her? Or mention her at least one time during the evening?"

"Maybe she's a relative. Or maybe he's renting a room."

I asked him if he had formed any opinion about Jerry No-Last-Name.

"He seems like an average man, no better no worse. Jumpy, though. Intense. Perhaps a little socially inept. And he thinks J. K. Rowling is a man. I wouldn't think you'd have to be particularly culturally literate . . ."

I took the utensil container out of the washer, set it on the counter, and started putting the knives and forks away. If there were any prints on Jerry's, they might have survived the washing, but not the rubbing I saw him give them.

Kitchen tidied, Carlo turned all the living room and kitchen lights out, put on his red astronomy goggles, and headed back into the darkness of the backyard. I followed him by the glow of his special flashlight that also shone red, picking my way carefully around the chaise lounges on the patio.

"That tune he was humming," I said. "Did you hear it?"

"I did," Carlo said, his mind on keying star coordinates into his GPS, which made the scope turn slowly with a *burrrring* sound.

"It sounds familiar, but I don't know the name of it."

"Neither do I."

"I thought you might. He didn't hang around long to look at the stars."

"He was very enthusiastic at first, praising my abilities at astronomy, telling me how smart I am to be able to find the deep space objects. But his interest waned quickly. Many people are like that. It can be disappointing. You see these grand photographs in magazines showing brilliant colors, and then find that through a telescope everything is shades of light."

Carlo focused his attention on the eyepiece for a moment. "Want to see Jupiter?"

"Sure," I said, and stepped up to the telescope as Carlo moved away.

"Can you see the moons? Only four of them, little pinpricks of light surrounding the planet." Without waiting for my little hum of assent he went on. "He also seems to have a tobacco addiction. As soon as we got outside he tried to light up, and I had to tell him that the light would affect our ability to see. He seemed incredulous at first, waved the glowing cigarette in front of my face and laughed as though I were making a joke."

You can only appreciate the moons of Jupiter for so long. I gave up my place at the telescope. "Did he put it out?"

"Finally, yes. It took another ten minutes to get my eyes to readjust. I was mildly annoyed."

"What did you talk about besides stars and planets?" I asked as I watched him reposition the scope to examine the Orion Nebula.

Not turning away from his gazing he said, "He asked how much I paid for the telescope. Other than blatantly currying favor—"

"Is that like sucking up?"

Carlo gave me that look he gives when he knows I'm just taking him down a peg. "He was very curious about my time as a priest. Whether I worked at St. Anthony's after I was ordained. More questions about Victor Santangelo, how close I was to him. He kept bringing the conversation back to that time and place, I noticed, but without making it clear why. And he asked questions about you."

"Like what?"

"What it's like being married to an FBI agent."

"How did he know that?"

"Elias mentioned it to him when we met at Starbucks. He also said that you and I seem so different from each other. Asked how we met. He asked if you were a rider, of horses, and I said I thought you had been at one time but had had an accident and your back couldn't take the jolting anymore. And he mentioned again that 'my lady was lovely.'"

"Again?"

"Yes, I do recall he also said that when I saw him at the grocery store yesterday. Bit of a sycophant, as I said. I told him he probably didn't want to say that to your face. He asked, 'What, she doesn't like being told she's beautiful? I thought every woman liked that.' I said, 'No, she doesn't like being called my lady.' And he said, 'Women these days,' and shrugged." Carlo frowned into the dark sky as if his thoughts were somewhere up there, and said, "And that was about it. I think he has a little crush on you. Either that or empty flattery." Then he turned his head toward me and looked hard and long, fixing me in place with his gaze the way he still did sometimes. It still made me feel like I was being caressed by a spirit. I'll never know how long it would last because I was always the first one to look away. But I felt loved, even if I wasn't the first, even if I wasn't the only

Leaving Carlo with his telescope, I got my forensic kit out of the kitchen drawer, took out the powder and brush, and gave the faucet and flush lever in the guest bathroom a light dusting. Nothing. Now that might just have meant that the guy didn't wash his hands after going. If that was the case, though, there would have been something, an old print from Carlo or me. But nothing. Someone had very recently wiped down the sink. The lever on the toilet, too. The toilet had been flushed, so there should at least have been the sign of human contact on the lever. The man was being careful not to leave any trace of himself in the house. Sometimes an absence of evidence could be suspicious. Gotta be a con.

I went back to my computer and googled Jerry Nolan, a shot in the dark. Girard "Jerry" Nolan, born 1946, rock drummer. The age was right, but the photo didn't look like my Nolan. Plus, he was dead. Tried Facebook and found well over a hundred Jerry Nolans. Gemma-Kate was right, some people actually did have the name Nolan without being grifters. Half of them on Facebook provided profile pix if you didn't count the dogs, motorcycles, superheroes, or that one with the two girls in bikinis. Even so, that left over fifty Jerry Nolans without pix where I couldn't do a visual match, and who knew how many Jeremys or Jeremiahs?

Plus I wasn't getting paid for this.

Best to just be careful and see what the guy's game was.

Twenty-four

The next day around noon I considered taking Al and Peg for a walk over to the house I'd found. But I dismissed the idea, as they wouldn't be thrilled about it, the lazy bums. There's more than one reason pugs look like old potatoes. Instead, I put on my sneakers, and took comfort in the fact that it was now cool enough during the day to go for a run. By cool enough I mean in the low seventies. By run I mean run, none of this slow lope that people my age are thought to tolerate. And I took the long way, down Golder Ranch and across Cañada del Oro Parkway to Hawser, so if I did see anyone I'd look a little spent.

There were no cars parked out front of the house where Jerry Nolan was living, and the gate in the chain link fence wasn't locked.

A perfect place for an unsuspecting fingerprint is the latch on a door handle where you press your thumb. I didn't even have to break inside. I took a roll of packing tape out of my pocket, cut off a thumb-sized piece, and pressed it against the latch where Jerry had entered the night before. That's when I heard tires on the gravel drive behind me.

I turned around to see a worn-out woman getting out of her car with weary legs. Her jeggings and a peasant blouse untied at the neck made me think of a fifty-year-old flirtatious kitten. As she approached I saw those vertical lines between her eyes that no amount of moisturizer can eliminate. Two more lines setting off her frown. She was a woman whose unhappiness was etched into her skin deeper than a tattoo that said HURT ME. I remembered what I had thought about Jerry being the kind of man who beats his wife.

She came toward me with a question, but I went first.

"I'm Brigid Quinn," I said. And for now no more. I hated to do this to her, knowing where it would lead, but I had to know what was up. This, too, I regret.

The woman's eyes shifted to a sign next to the door that said NO SOLICITING. She asked, "What are you doing on my property?"

"I'm actually looking for someone." I paused because I couldn't be sure what name he had given this woman. I went with first only. "Do you know Jerry?"

I watched more than weariness play across her face. All the things I'd seen before in my career were there. Suspicion, jealousy, anger, sadness, and fear. Everything could be explained by my presence except the fear. We both knew I meant her no harm, but someone else apparently did.

"Why do you want to know about Jerry?" she asked. At another time, I thought, she might be a polite sort of person, but the threat of another woman had at some point become great enough to make her forget her manners.

My usual inclination at a time like this would be to make something up, to invite them to church the way Carlo would, but I just couldn't be that dishonest. It would be victimizing her even more, and it wasn't worth it just to satisfy my curiosity. Instead, I found myself wanting to help her.

Silence makes people want to fill it, and I discovered I'd been thinking too long when she said, "Does he know you?"

The unspoken messages were coming thick and fast now. *Does he want you instead of me?*

"Look," I said. "I live in the neighborhood. Jerry helped my husband," subtle emphasis on *husband*, "move his telescope. He just happened to be passing by and they met. Has he mentioned Carlo?" Again, a little emphasis on the *Carlo*.

Now, with all the other emotions coming and going across her face, I noticed a new one: shame.

"No" was all she said, and I could tell she was ashamed of not knowing such a simple innocent detail about her husband's, boyfriend's, whatever's, doings. Then she looked suspicious again, sending the lines between her eyes deeper. She wasn't even buying the truth. At least, she would be feeling at some unconscious level, it was better than being ashamed.

She wasn't moving toward the door, which I realized I had been blocking. I stepped out of the way now, but she stayed where she was with a hateful, narrow-eyed stare. Whatever I was, whatever I had come for, I was the enemy. For some time now, everyone had been the enemy. I had no reason to stay, but I couldn't just leave this woman to herself and—what else? Was it Jerry Nolan who had made her this way? Or had he just found her and made the most of it? Were they married? I didn't need to ask. I could find out everything on my own now.

One more try. "I wanted to invite both of you over for dinner. Sometime," I said, implying that Jerry had told us all about this woman. I hoped in the course of things she didn't realize I hadn't called her by name just in case it wasn't Gloria Bentham.

"Thank you," she said, summoning the woman she might have once been, polite, gracious. "But I don't think—"

"Just something casual. Carlo will grill something." Okay, so we didn't have a grill but I was sure I could get one and one of us could learn how to use it.

"No," she said, her voice a little harsher now. "We're just not really . . . sociable." Then she either saw the look on my face or realized herself that I was there because Jerry had been, indeed, very sociable. Sociable how, exactly? The jealousy and shame had equal play now. She turned her head to the right and left, looking down the street. Clearly, she didn't know he had already been at the house for dinner just last night. But she was thinking about it, where he had been, where he said he had been. She wasn't stupid.

"I was out taking a run," I said, pretending to wipe perspiration off my brow. I assumed she was looking for my car and not seeing it. Also she might be wondering how the hell I knew this was Jerry's house. Then I heard the dog bark. "I can tell your dog's bark. That's how we met, Jerry and Carlo, I mean. He was out walking your dog." That was a slip—why would I assume it wasn't his dog? Of course it was obvious, but why would Gloria think it would be obvious to me that they weren't coupled enough to share a dog? Oh Lord, I couldn't say two words without making it all much worse than before I began.

With the license plate I noted as I walked away, I was able to check records and find that it along with the house belonged to Gloria Bentham, decent credit rating, employed as a doctor's receptionist, unmarried. So Jerry Nolan was a moocher. Not only a moocher, but an abusive one to boot. Possibly not physically, but emotionally. Gloria was one of those women who was willing to put up with anything but loneliness.

When did your average insecurity turn into pathology?

And how could I figure all this out? Here's how: I occasionally volunteered at Desert Doves, training women to defend themselves. As with villains, I'd seen enough of this kind of woman in my career to be able to profile her within the time of our conversation. The only thing I couldn't know is whether she would tell him about meeting me, what her attitude would be. Timid? Angry? And what would the meeting tell him about me? That I was looking for information about him? I hoped Gloria would tell him about my visit, because his reaction might flush him out and confirm my suspicions.

Twenty-five

I've always been a little competitive, so it was with a particular sense of triumph that I had given Carlo the anniversary gift of an evening on Kitt Peak. It's hard to know what to get a philosopher as a birthday gift. Everything Carlo really treasured (except me, I assured myself) was inside his own mind. This would also get his mind off of Jane. I bet she never gave him a night on Kitt Peak. Of course he wasn't interested in astronomy back then, so.

I also liked the idea of depositing Carlo on a mountaintop to keep him safely out of the way in case Mr. Nolan found I'd connected with Gloria and decided to get aggressive. So far, however, we hadn't heard from him, and it had been a week since he came to dinner.

The skies are clear in Arizona and in many areas darker than most populated places on earth. Consequently, there are four major observatories within driving distance from our house, one that I can see on Mount Lemmon from our backyard. On a cloudless day, driving south from Tucson, you can spot a white speck that is one of the domes of the observatory on Kitt Peak. It's about a two-hour drive from us, and is the most dramatic location open to the public. On that afternoon in early December we descended into the valley that is Tucson proper, and then ascended again slowly to the base of the mountain. After that the climb began rapidly to a height of a little over six thousand feet.

I've dangled from too many rooftops to suffer much from serious vertigo, but the narrow road that curved around the rocky outcropping on the left side and plunged thousands of feet to the valley below on the right still made a nerve in my neck tingle and made me happy I wasn't in the passenger seat next to the drop. Even in my new Miata, nice and low to the road and with splendid maneuverability, I was more than happy to stay within the speed limit, which at some of the hair-pinnier turns slowed to ten miles per hour.

Okay, maybe I would put the car to more of a test on the way down, but I wasn't going to say this to Carlo. Despite my being poisoned, attacked by a therapy dog, and splashed with the guts of a serial killer—and that just since we were married—I still felt he worried unnecessarily about my safety. More than once, and especially these days, I thanked my lucky stars that Carlo had never actually seen me in action and what happens to the other guy at those times.

Back to the mountain. Everyone thinks of the desert as just hot and hotter. The fact is, thanks to a stronger than usual El Niño the Arizona temperatures were already in the forties at night. With the higher elevation, Kitt Peak promised to be colder than that after sunset, and it was already freezing on the summit on the afternoon we arrived. I was secretly glad that I was dropping Carlo off and taking Gemma-Kate out for a late dinner and a show. I had given her the choice of a new Bruce Willis movie or a live performance of *The Nutcracker*, which neither of us had ever seen. I was also glad she chose the movie.

As you come around the last curve you begin to see immense glowing white buildings that feel like an alien way station. There should be that music from *2001: A Space Odyssey*. Really impressive, so I didn't just dump Carlo off and run. I stayed long enough to show an interest in the huge complex, which he shared with the enthusiasm of an eight-year-old at Disney World. His glee was contagious, and I willingly walked up the hill to the elaborate four-story structure through which you could view the sun without being blinded. Then over to the opposite side of the compound, passing a low building with a sign outside that said, QUIET, ASTRONOMERS SLEEPING, and from there onto a narrow service road that curved along the cliff from which the big momma rose.

You take an elevator up to the top of this observatory where the telescope thrusts itself at the heavens in a way that seems arrogant. As if it could really see what can never be seen. The scope itself is about thirty feet tall and ten feet wide, so big that when you're standing on one of the observation decks next to it, you can see the eyepiece. The observatory is not heated. The heat waves would create too much shimmer.

"It's f-freezing up here," I said, trying to draw my down jacket closer but never getting it close enough. We were standing on an inside catwalk that went all the way around the tower with windows overlooking miles of harsh desert punctuated with mountain ranges, and far off to the east, where the city lights couldn't cause pollution in the dark sky, a glimpse of Tucson. "Are you sure you have enough warm clothes?" I asked.

Carlo lifted his sweatshirt to show another beneath it. "You should know. I think you emptied the coat closet into that duffle bag we brought," he said, and then paused, something more interesting coming to his mind. "Your nose is so cute when it's pink. You look like a bunny." I put on my tough broad face, but he bent down from his considerable height to my inconsiderable one, and kissed said nose. The man does not let me get away with myself.

We had a bit of a better cuddle later when he walked me out to the car.

"It's getting on to dusk," he said. "You should start down."

I gave him a final hug and said, "You stay warm, and I'll be back to get you after breakfast. Breakfast is part of the package, right?"

He smiled and nodded.

I thought about how married couples are, how they look after each other in small ways. But I didn't get all mushy. "Have a wonderful time, and happy anniversary," I said.

"Same to you, and don't let that Jerry come prowling around," Carlo said with a wink. While I had neglected to mention lifting the print, I had remembered to tell Carlo that I was certain Jerry was living with a girlfriend and that men always mentioned their mate to show they weren't on the prowl. After some consideration, Carlo had said that was likely a hasty generalization.

There were a few other cars in the parking lot, but they were either staying there the whole night, or else would be driving down the mountain after a ten P.M. viewing. Once on the road the descent started almost immediately, at about a six percent grade. Even being able to see well enough, I decided I'd take it slow, figuring I'd put the Miata through her paces on another day, and this time live to pick up Carlo in the morning.

Because of that six percent grade I tapped my brakes a couple of times to make sure they were working, and when the road got steeper I downshifted into third and then second gear to make the engine do some of the work. There was no moon; we had planned it that way to optimize the viewing. It was the last smidgen of day, the sun having set but leaving a reluctant red-orange stripe just above the horizon line. With my headlamps off, a Kitt Peak rule to avoid light pollution, I could still make out the boulders going slowly by on my right inches from my passenger door, and was glad the drop-off into the valley was on the other side of the road. Even with my lights on I might not have seen the patch of black ice. It hadn't been there on the ride up, or else was only forming on the opposite side of the road.

I felt my wheels lose traction but didn't panic. Rather than trying to apply the brakes—a dangerous move that could have made me skid off the edge of the cliff—I concentrated all my attention on keeping the car on one side of the road or the other, preferably close to the wall of rock. But the car was thrust forward and I barely made it around a sharp curve going twice as fast as the probable speed limit on a sign I couldn't see. I felt my wheels skid over the narrow dirt shoulder on the left side of the road. Then I felt the wheels grip the macadam again.

Feeling confident that I was past the danger, but still unsettled, I ignored the rule about keeping the lights off after dark and turned on my headlamps, at the same time applying the brakes to stop and let my gut simmer down after a close call.

The brakes didn't engage.

Twenty-six

Seven days had gone by between the time Beaufort decided that the Quinn woman needed to be eliminated, and now. Enough time for Yanchak to locate a guy in Arizona who was willing to do the job, and enough time for Beaufort to case a couple of homes he thought were likely candidates for him to hit. It was simple, just discover the pattern of the inhabitants, when they were in and when they were out. Watch what couples left for work in the morning and hit there. The first house, in the development east of the one where the DiForenzas lived, he'd done three days ago. The second one, by the Lago del Oro Parkway, he'd done yesterday. It was secluded, up one of those steep driveways where you practically needed four-wheel drive just to visit. Surrounded with nothing but hills and arroyos, wild saguaros, prickly pear cactus, and chollas, no one would see his car if he stayed up there all day. And no one to see while he took his time with the lock on the door leading from the back porch. No security. Lovely view. It took him less than an hour.

Today he got to the third house as dusk was descending. Right on time.

Just to be on the safe side, in case their paths should cross, Beaufort had taken Gloria's car that morning with the promise of getting the oil changed, and he had kept his promise. The car was one of those lime green Volkswagens that must have been popular in another decade. Now you didn't see so many of them. It was a sign of Gloria's clinging to the edges of middle class that she hadn't traded hers in. Beaufort thought it was a little noticeable, but it was better than someone tracking his own license plate.

He drove two streets beyond his destination, turned left, and parked the Beetle on the side of the road in one of the undeveloped lots. A cop drove by on Golder Ranch, possibly looking for signs of whoever had burglarized the first two homes, but didn't even turn his head. Beaufort smiled, thinking, *Who would suspect a lime green Beetle?* He grabbed his backpack, pretty empty right now, from the passenger's seat and drew it over one shoulder. Then he marked the time on his watch to see how long it would take him to walk quickly but not run, which would draw attention to himself from any passing vehicle. In just one minute he had walked across the street and into the area of cacti and ravines where he had first walked with Achilles. This time, though, instead of keeping to the high ground, he entered a deep arroyo that ran fairly parallel to the yard lines of the neighboring houses and hid him from sight.

In another three minutes he had climbed up out of the arroyo and walked the ten or so paces to the low wall that separated the DiForenza house from the wildness of the desert. He stepped up onto the concrete block at the top of the wall and boosted himself over the fence attached to it, glad as always that he had kept in shape. The telescope on the pad nearer to the fence, with its protective cover, provided a good shield so he could glance around to make sure no one saw him. A hound barked in the yard next door, but otherwise the neighborhood was quiet. Everyone minding their own business, not staring out of windows.

He checked his watch again. It had taken just six minutes from the car to here. He had to keep that in mind if he needed to make a sudden getaway, if someone spotted him. Once he was inside the house he should have plenty of time, as nobody was going to be coming home. He stepped carefully over the gravel, noting that he didn't make any prints among the larger stones. He avoided an area of smaller gravel where that would be the case.

When he got to the back door he drew from the backpack a couple of tools he'd learned to use while in prison. The bolt lock gave him some trouble. He was rustier than he thought, and considered that he should have practiced on one of Gloria's doors. Luckily, the second lock, a spring, hadn't been engaged.

The dogs inside knew him well enough to remember he was the Treat Man. From his pocket he withdrew a gallon-sized plastic bag and dumped some cubed cheese on the living room carpet after giving both the dogs a brief belly rub. While he did one belly the other one waited his turn. These were a couple of well-behaved dogs. And boy, could they eat. "Achilles sends his greetings," Beaufort told them as he pulled on a pair of latex gloves. He was pleased that a few lights had been left on, probably for the dogs. That meant that Brigid had intended to come home after dark. She had no idea.

First: The bedroom was the most likely place to go to make it look like the other jobs. There was the jewelry box on the dresser in there. He was careful to grab a random handful of the junk and leave one or two things that looked real. He wanted to make it look like he was not a gem expert, but only some punk. He shoved the items into the plastic bag that had held the dog's treats. He pulled out a couple of drawers and left the contents, mostly women's accessories here, men's underwear there, scattered on the floor. The bedside tables yielded something better. Third down on the right contained a box with a gun. That would be taken, of course, no matter who the burglar was. He checked the chamber and found it unloaded but didn't waste time finding the ammo. He could always get some. He put the weapon in the bag with the jewelry.

To make it more realistic he coursed through the other rooms in the house, making a little mess here and there, too. Take a butcher knife from the kitchen? That seemed authentic. No, waste of time. Overthinking it, Gloria would have said, with that new talk he was learning.

The dogs ignored him, engaged as they were in licking the cheese residue off the carpet.

With the can of red spray paint from his backpack, he made a mark on the wall leading to the master suite. It was distinctive without being too complex. A circle with two lightning strikes through the center.

Now for the real part. He went first into the most apparent room of the house, the priest's office. Only when he got there he discovered it wasn't his office at all. Awards hung on the wall and photographs, good God, was that one of her shaking hands with Ronald Reagan? Much, much younger, but unmistakable. This was her office, a business office where she did her private investigating work. Maybe they shared that file cabinet.

She didn't bother with a lock, luckily, and he went through all the hanging folders in each of the four gray drawers. Difficult to move quickly. Many of the folders had crime scene photos in them and they distracted him from the task at hand. He looked at his watch. Just to keep up the look of the invasion he pulled out half a dozen folders from the last drawer and threw them across the floor. Random mess, like a punk would make.

The doorbell rang.

Somehow all the plans had failed. Brigid, at least, had returned. This is what he thought.

The blinds were open, and the window of the office looked out to the front walk. What happened next happened within seconds. Beaufort looked at the driveway, but there was no car parked there. He swung his eyes right to the front door. He saw a man at the door, angled with his back to him. He didn't have enough time to recognize whether the man was Carlo or not, because on their own his legs buckled. He let himself drop to the floor and crawled on his stomach closer to the wall, rolling over and pressing his back against it, in case the man looked in the window.

The dogs started barking, then ran into the office to see if Beaufort was going to do anything about this. He stared at them staring at him. "Scram," he muttered under his breath. Finding him useless, they ran back into the living room and recommenced their protest.

Without a response to the bell, the man tried knocking on the security screen door, which reverberated throughout the house and made the dogs bark even more loudly. "Carlo?" he called. Waited. "Brigid?"

Idiot, he told himself. If it had been one of them they wouldn't have rung the doorbell. Beaufort found himself holding his breath as if the man would be able to hear him. The blinds next to the door were open, too, weren't they? Was the man nosy enough to look inside? If he did, would he see the red mark he had painted on the wall? What would he do then?

Idiot, he thought again. He'd made the mark in a side hall where the man would never be able to see it no matter what window he looked in.

The man finally left, but there was no telling what he had seen or what he would do next. Beaufort had better make the most of the next few minutes and then hightail it out of this dump.

The library was daunting, but it was the only room left. Beaufort, nervous after the unexpected visitor, practically ran down the four or five aisles of books, as much as one could run in such a tight space, scanning the titles for one that would provide a clue that the thing was tucked inside between the pages. But he didn't know what title that would be, nor if the thing was actually small enough to be contained within a book. In frustration he kicked the books on one of the bottom shelves so hard they tumbled out the other side. That was okay, it just looked like more vandalism.

He turned this way and that, seeing nothing as the shelves in the middle of the room extended up to within a foot of the ceiling. The only thing left in the room was a closet with two sliding doors.

He looked at his watch. What the hell was he doing looking at his watch? What difference did the time make? With a shrug he pushed the door on the right to the left.

Shelves in there as well, from the ceiling of the closet down to the floor.

More books. More. Fucking. Books.

He seized the sliding door and ripped it off its track, with a curse throwing it down one of the aisles where it bounced off a shelf and landed on the floor. First frightened by the unexpected visitor, and now enraged by his failure to find what he was looking for in his carefully plotted search of the house: These were feelings Beaufort was not accustomed to. He imagined Hickock and Smith somewhere in hell, Hickock laughing at him.

Beaufort slumped on the floor and looked at his watch and wondered where the woman was right now.

Twenty-seven

I was on an eight percent grade now, going around a turn, and aware from the trip up that the road continued like this for over a mile before entering a long straightaway that led from the mountain. I pumped the brakes to get as much out of the hydraulic system as possible. Nothing.

Speeding up now with the mass of the car on a downward slope, I didn't dare to look at my speedometer but figured I was doing almost forty miles per hour and the emergency brake would only zig or zag the car ferociously. Zigging I go over the cliff. Zagging I hit the boulders on my right—and then bounce off and go over the cliff.

If I tried turning off the ignition I'd lose my power steering and at this speed would never be able to make the hairpin turns.

I had already put the car in its lowest gear when I downshifted on the fly, and couldn't brake the engine itself any more than it was already. Except for some real fancy driving, the only other thing I could do was to roll all the windows down and create some wind resistance. Fat lot of help that would do, but I pressed the button anyway.

And kept on. One curve after another, taking them at speeds far exceeding the limit but thank God for the sporty chassis that kept my center of gravity as low to the ground as possible. You're halfway there, Quinn. Just focus. And hope this thing can still hug the road doing forty miles an hour on a hairpin turn. Just as I thought that, the tires squealed as if the car itself was expressing its doubt.

Jesus, it was cold with the windows down and the air rushing in.

I rounded the next turn and was beginning to congratulate my reflexes, which hadn't slowed as much as I might have feared, even if I had left my heart about a half mile back.

Then I picked up the reflection of some taillights not far enough ahead of me.

Closing in rapidly, I honked and kept on honking. If you're just aware that I'm here, I thought, and can see that I'm barreling down on you like a maniac, maybe you'll understand what's happening, turn your own lights on, speed up just a little . . .

Nope, it's an astronomy geek who has no idea I'm in trouble. Thinks I'm a crazy who in addition to the reckless driving has no regard for the rules about keeping your headlights off and not polluting the mountain with light. I was not only going to have to keep my car on the side of the mountain, I was going to have to pass this idiot by switching to the outside lane. Please let it be on a swing to the left.

Nope, swing to the right.

Please let there be guardrails on this stretch.

Nope, no guardrails. I felt my car skid on the dirt followed by a sensation that the back wheels were swinging over nothing. My stomach followed. At this rate if I survived I wouldn't have any organs left. I gunned the motor and the front tires caught hard and kept catching. The back wheels followed suit.

Some vestige of my mind made me unclick my seat belt on one short straightaway, and then crack my door on the next. If I was going to go over the edge, this way I'd have a chance of jumping to a less certain death rather than going down with the vehicle. It's what you do when you're descending on an eight percent grade with multiple switchbacks and no brakes.

At least I got past that jerk without either of us plunging into a bomb-like explosion. I yelled an obscenity at the top of my lungs as I sped by him. His windows were closed and for all I knew he had his iPhone plugged into his head, so I feel fairly sure he wouldn't have heard what I called him.

Funny how as I look back I talk about speeding, but I couldn't have been going more than forty, forty-two miles an hour. It's all relative, and nearly impossible to take a 380-degree switchback turn while going that fast. After I got back in the proper lane I had the sense that the grade was easing now, maybe just five percent, and that would mean that the drop was only a few hundred feet. But three hundred feet would kill me just as dead as a thousand feet, and I wasn't slowing down on my own.

One curve, two curves, three. I was operating on sheer instinct now. Like an animal with a driver's license.

And then just as suddenly as I had begun the terrifying descent, I was free of the mountain, escaping from its curves as from the tentacles of a giant octopus that had finally let me go. My brights showed that nice long straightaway, and now that I was safe I let my hands shake a bit on the steering wheel and my lungs take in all the air they wanted. At least I still had my lungs. About midway down the road I coasted to a stop.

And stayed, shivering as frantically as an overcaffeinated Chihuahua.

Having continued on its way as a sane person who stayed within the speed limit would, after five minutes the car that had been behind me pulled up beside me. Time had gone by, but anger had not subsided. The passenger window rolled down, the other driver fumbled at something and cursed. Then a flashlight, not that strong but enough to blind me after the dark, and a man's voice yelled in something like a British accent, "Don't you realize this is neither the time nor place for joyriding? You could have killed both of us!" Maybe he was responding to my red sports car as much as his own adrenaline, but I really wasn't in the mood just now for road rage, whatever the excuse.

My window was still down and I managed to say without shouting, "My brakes failed, you fucking nimrod. And turn off that fucking flashlight, motherfucker."

That calmed him down in an instant, especially when he took a close look at my face, which may have been glowing white in the light he shone on me. He turned it off. He must have dropped it, because he cursed and bent over and fumbled around. When his head came back into view I still couldn't make out his face, but I could see him lean forward and tilt his head to see that I was alone. His doing that made the nerve in my neck spark, but he didn't get out of his car to offer *help*, he just asked if I had Triple A. That made me give my brakes an instinctive tap, to find that they were working just fine now. The brakes were working.

"Yep," I said, mystified. "I'll call them. You go on, I'll be fine."

His voice sounded doubtful when he asked if I was quite sure.

"Yes, I'm sure," I said. I smiled cheerily to assure him. Then I thought about how we'd been in such a dry spell. "Did you hit that ice?"

I saw the brim of his baseball cap nod in the shadows. He said, "I managed to recover. Only the one spot. That was freakish." I picked up an aged note in his voice now that he wasn't yelling, reminiscent of bedsprings and a slow air leak.

Remembering that I had cracked my door open in anticipation of jumping for my life, I opened it wide in order to close it properly. When the man in the other car saw me do that, he gunned his engine and sped off, taking the left turn on the main road with his tires squealing. What was it with that? Did he think I was experiencing delayed road rage and was going to attack him with my tire iron? It was only much, much later that I thought his British accent sounded like an American actor portraying any other nationality.

Twenty-eight

I picked up Gemma-Kate in front of her dormitory and told her I wasn't in the mood for a movie because I was a little shaken after losing my brakes on the road from Kitt Peak. Would she please come back to the house with me, spend the night, and drive Carlo's car to Kitt Peak in the morning? I would follow until the mountain road started, and leave the Miata parked at the bottom while we fetched Carlo. That way we could drop her off at school again and continue on to the dealership. She agreed to do that while appearing unconcerned by my near-death.

On the drive up to Catalina I asked questions because she wasn't talking.

"Have you been back to visit your dad?"

"No."

"What about Christmas? Are you going home?"

"I don't think so."

"You should decide pretty soon before you can't get a ticket. Do you need money?"

"No. Dad said he would pay."

I sighed, thinking about spending Christmas Day in bed with Carlo alone, getting out only for a new book and occasional sustenance. "You could come spend the holiday with us."

No response to that. Instead, "So do you have anything more on that Jerry Nolan character?"

"I got a print and sent it to Weiss, but nothing yet."

We stopped once at Mr. An's for some takeout sushi. Along the way I kept tapping the brakes, taking a long time to coast to a stop at lights so I wouldn't hit the driver in front of me if the brakes failed again. It was like a different car from the one on the mountain road, as it had been up to that point, no trouble at all.

We walked into the house through the garage door and let the two pugs snort and bounce around us with unrestrained joy. Maybe even more joy than usual, which I attributed to Gemma-Kate's presence.

Out of habit I yelled, "Couch time!" and we all headed to the living room and sat down for rubbings. Gemma-Kate didn't sit down with us, but leaned over and patted the head of one of them the way she had the first time she met them, pat, pat, pat, no real feeling for animals. Or anyone else, for that matter. I never could figure out why the dogs liked her, seeing as how she'd nearly poisoned one. Perhaps pugs are forgiving creatures.

"Is this one Al or Peg?" she asked.

I confess to sneaking a peek at the dog's privates. They looked alike to me, too, and we were still getting used to differentiating between them rather than calling them simply the Pugs. "Peg," I said, seeing no male appendage. At that point both dogs had taken whatever love they needed from me, and jumped off the couch. Gemma-Kate, too, had moved on, undisguisedly checking out the place for anything that piqued her curiosity.

"Well, this is not like you," she said, going to the back door. "Are you actually my aunt Brigid or have you been taken over by aliens?"

No more distracted by either dogs or my thoughts about Gemma-Kate, I looked up.

"You left the back door unlocked," she explained.

She was right, I don't do things like that. I might forget which pug was which and whether I had my Miralax, but I don't forget to lock the doors before I leave. Gemma-Kate inadvertently reached out to open it, but I stopped her with a whisper, almost just a movement of my lips. "Don't touch it."

Gemma-Kate was a cop's daughter and understood when I removed my cell phone and my weapon from my tote bag. I tossed her the phone, which she caught neatly. I watched her press her thumb on the three numbers and then put the phone to her ear without speaking. All she did was breathe through her mouth loudly enough so that only I and who-ever was on the other end at emergency services could hear her. *Good girl*, I nodded.

Her eyes were tracking as she did so, and now she pointed to the short hall that led to the master suite. On the yellow wall someone had spray-painted a good-sized circle in red, and inside it two lightning bolts.

I listened with all my ears until all I could hear was my mild tinni-tus. Even the pugs were still, watching me. I moved first to the master bedroom area, clearing that and the bathroom. The room itself was a relative mess, drawers pulled out and clothes strewn about. The lid of my small jewelry box was open. I would deal with that later. For now I was just making sure we weren't about to be killed by some burglar, cornered and desperate.

The drawer to my nightstand was pulled out more than I remem-bered leaving it, and knowing what was inside I took the time to pull it open. The box with my other weapon in it was still in the drawer, but when I lifted the lid I found it empty. So someone had it in their pos-session. Were they still in the house?

I really didn't need this tonight. You might think someone like me could risk death on a mountain road and then come home and fight off a guy hiding in the shower. Well, maybe I could, but I'd rather not.

Gemma-Kate had been left unguarded in the living room. I moved more quickly now and found her where I'd left her. I motioned for her to go into the bedroom, and as she passed by me I whispered, "Lock this door, then go in the bathroom and lock that door, and tell the nine-one-one dispatcher there's a break-in. Not sure whether perp is still on premises." The pugs, who had been watching everything with mild in-terest but no apparent alarm, followed her when she silently tapped the side of her leg in a *come* gesture. Times like this, they were as useful as a fly swatter in a locust plague.

Weapon at the ready I moved to the front of the house, to the laun-dry room on the right, quietly throwing the bolt on the door to the garage so if he was hiding in the garage he couldn't get in now. Then the TV room, then my office, noting that the fourth file drawer down had been pulled out. Some of the files had been taken out and thrown on the floor, but without any apparent reason. It looked random, like something vandals would do.

Then I went into the other room, which was the best place for someone to hide, with Carlo's four shelves of books running through the middle of the room. The person had been in here as well. One of the sliding closet doors had been ripped off its track and thrown against the shelves, upsetting some books but not with enough force to turn over the shelves themselves. The closet in that room was crammed to the gills with more books and storage bins filled with Carlo's dissertation notes, articles he had written for various academic journals, and several drafts of *Asterisks and Idols*. It would not have room to hide a small goat, so I didn't draw aside the other sliding door to look inside for a person.

Finally the guest bath. Oh, that shower curtain. How much more contented our lives would have been without *Psycho*. I stepped forward in my bare feet without a sound, without turning on the light, and ripped the curtain aside as I fell to my knees in the opposite direction from which an attacker would instinctively aim a blow.

But no, the tub was clear.

It was only on my way back from the front of the house that I spied a plastic grocery bag on the floor by the window in the library. Carlo's? I moved toward it cautiously and could easily see through the thin plastic that it contained my own things, including my other weapon. One that wasn't registered. No matter what the cops found, they should not find this. I gingerly opened the top of the bag with the back of my hand and drew out the gun.

I started breathing again, and went to the bedroom door and knocked. Then I called out. Then I remembered GK couldn't hear me because she was locked in the bathroom, which was a bit of a remove from the door of the bedroom. I pounded harder, and yelled, and was interrupted by the doorbell playing *Eine kleine Nachtmusik*. Funny how Jane could come to mind even at a time like this.

I tucked my extra weapon under my sweater in the back of my jeans, went to the front door, and threw it open to see Deputy Max Coyote in a defensive stance partly behind the wall where the front walk led to the driveway. Another deputy I hadn't met before stood by the white thorn acacia in the yard.

"It's clear," I said. "Someone was here, through the back door, but they're gone now. Except I haven't checked the perimeter."

Without bothering to greet me, Max walked into the house with his very young partner, who he introduced as Deputy Eric Stamen. He placed a call for another unit to patrol the area around the neighborhood and walk the arroyo in back of the house to see if there was any sign of them coming over the fence, any footwear impressions in the arroyo beyond it, or in the gravel in the yard.

Gemma-Kate merged from the bedroom still gripping the phone as if that was her job and by God she was doing it. "I saw the blue-and-reds reflected on the bathroom window and figured it was okay to come out," she said.

Max didn't sit on his usual place on the couch with the pugs banking him on each side, where he would have gone another time. He ignored Al and Peg as they snuffled around his cuffs, trying to figure out where and when they'd smelled this guy before. For his part, Max stared at me with narrowed eyes. We had been friends once, a bit more than a year ago, but we weren't anymore. He would probably tell a different story, but the short version is that I'd saved his life once and he never forgave me for it.

"What do we do next?" I asked, deferring to his position.

This time he was all business. He pulled out a computer tablet and said, "Take me around."

I showed him the mark on the wall first, and he blinked without comment, revealing his lack of surprise. That was the first clue that our home wasn't the first.

"You've seen this before," I said.

He continued into the bedroom.

I said, "Okay, in here he pulled out some drawers and messed up the clothes." I looked in the wooden box with the glass top on my dresser. "All that's missing from here is some junk jewelry, like a random handful. See, here's an emerald cocktail ring."

"They didn't take that?"

"No, it's still there." I gave the room another cursory glance, saw that Carlo's bedside dresser drawer was cracked open.

"Anything missing from there?" Max asked.

"I don't know. I can't say as I ever opened this drawer." I peeked in there now, feeling as if I was invading a space, and feeling silly about feeling that way. My eye went to a pair of wedding rings, a man's and a woman's, tied together with a bit of yarn. Jane.

Max said something.

"Hm?"

"Medicine cabinet?" he repeated.

"I didn't see it opened." I went into the bathroom area and checked. What drugs we used were still there, some sleeping pills and Valium that I only take when I can't rest and need to be on my game the following day. Carlo's blood pressure meds. All there.

We came out of the master bedroom area and went into my office at the front of the house. I pointed out the filing cabinet drawer. Looked through that quickly, and pulled out the other three. "I wouldn't know from this if he took out a single paper or something, but it didn't look like he found the files important." I thought about it. "Why would a burglar leave an emerald ring but take the time to look through a filing cabinet?"

Without an answer handy, Max went into the next room, the library. Whether or not you're doing an investigation, I find there are two kinds of people in the world: those who look at the books that others have on their shelves, and those who don't. Max and I were both of the latter kind. He walked up and down the rows that the metal shelving formed down the center of the room, ignoring those titles as well as those on the bookshelves that covered the walls from floor to ceiling on three sides of the room. He stepped around the closet door that was in the middle of the room and pulled aside the door that was still standing upright, to expose some large plastic bins, three of them stacked on top of each other. Max looked at me expectantly.

"As far as I know, these are manuscripts of books that Carlo has written, materials for the classes he taught, things like that. I'll find out more when he's back home if you want."

"Where is he?"

"Overnight at Kitt Peak."

"Nice." Then Max shrugged, clearly as puzzled as I had become. Why would someone paint a gang sign on the wall and then look through file cabinets and libraries? This guy wasn't looking for valuables or even prescription drugs. Whoever had been here was looking for information.

They were looking for something in particular, and they were either not professional or in a hurry. Maybe we surprised them. Or maybe they didn't care if we knew.

Max made notes on his tablet about the materials thrown out of the file cabinet and the books shoved off the shelves, frowning at the more random acts of vandalism. This was new, I thought, not like the other incident, or incidents.

Also new was the fact that the stolen property in a plastic bag had been apparently forgotten on the floor of Carlo's library. We both stared at it. When I looked over at Max he was blinking the way I had been. "I imagine all the stuff from my jewelry box is in there, but I haven't touched it yet," I said.

"Could it be the burglar was frightened off? Do you think he heard you coming?"

Now it was my turn to shrug. "You're the cop," I said.

Then he asked if we could sit down. We went back to the dining room, where Gemma-Kate was, without effort, enchanting Eric with her dimples.

"She's only seventeen, and I can see you're married," I suggested, pointing to his ring. "Can I get you guys something to drink? Coffee? Water?"

Max said no, but Eric took a glass of water. He appeared new on the force, a bit deferential to Max. He looked at the glass of water like that was maybe not the right thing to do, and he didn't drink any. Maybe Max had told him something about me. Not everything by a long stretch, but something that was not flattering.

Max knew he was dealing with someone who knew how this worked, so he asked, "Point of entry?" knowing I would know.

"Back door. No damage, must have picked the lock. Bolt."

Max could see the back door from where he was seated at the table. "Not the spring lock, too?"

"No. I figure the bolt will stop most people. But not this one."

"I thought you knew better."

"I think I've gone soft, Max."

Max snarfed lightly and asked, "How long were you away from the house?" Fingers raised and ready to fill out the template before him.

I gave him all the details with the time of each segment. "About seven and a half hours. It took a couple extra hours on the way back to pick up Gemma-Kate at the college and stop for sushi. So you figure they were here sometime after six when it was dark? Not much of a window."

"Not necessarily," Max said.

He knew something I did not. "What were the other break-ins like?" I asked.

Max almost nodded, apparently reluctant to share even this. "Two others, one on the other side of Golder Ranch and one down the hill in one of the homes on Lago del Oro Parkway. One of them was late afternoon before the owners got home from work. So the burglar or burglars knew something about them. Did some homework."

"Who are the other victims?" I asked, casually, knowing what conclusion he would draw. Which he did.

"Let us do the investigating," he said. "I don't want you making people more upset than they already are."

"So the sign on the wall, this happened at the other houses. But these aren't just kids. Kids would have broken a window," I said.

"And that sign is staged," he said, still not admitting that's what had happened before. "In the few minutes that you went around the house, did you notice anything else?"

"Like what?" I asked.

Max shook his head like he didn't have a clue like what, so I said, "Hardly anything. I was looking too hard for someone who might try to kill me. That was after losing my brakes coming down from Kitt Peak. I've been a little tense," I added, rubbing a nerve that jumped under my right eye.

He stood, clearly as uninterested in my near-death experience as Gemma-Kate had been, and gestured to Eric that they were done here.

"You're not going to dust?" I asked.

"We did at the first two houses and got nothing. He's wearing gloves. This looks like the same MO. Just hard to tell if it's a pro or an amateur. Seems to be signs of both. Either. You don't want me to mess the place up, do you?"

"Rather you didn't," I agreed.

When Max got up and gestured at Deputy Stamen that they were leaving, I said, "Max, Carlo misses you."

He didn't say *I miss him, too*. Guys didn't say that. He glanced at Eric and Gemma-Kate as if he did want to say something, but not in front of them. The two deputies left, not bothering to reassure us that we were safe. Max would never think there was a doubt about whether I could take care of myself.

"The burglar apparently didn't want these," Gemma-Kate said, pointing at two things that looked like yellow-and-black-striped pillow covers, draped over the back of one of the living room couches.

I balled up the costumes and threw them on the shelf in the coat closet. "The pugs were bumblebees for Halloween."

Gemma-Kate looked at me, her little round features flashing into an expression of disgust that gave her the passing look of a gargoyle. "You got costumes for the dogs. Aunt Brigid, do you think you're trying too hard with this suburban housewife schtick?"

"*You* should learn how to blend in as well as I do," I said, finally putting my pistol down on the kitchen counter. I took a bottle of opened white wine that still had a few glasses left in it out of the fridge.

"Got saki?" Gemma-Kate asked. "All this stress, I could go for some hot saki."

She didn't look all that stressed to me. Now, me, I was a little stressed. I said, "Do you mind? I've been robbed. Besides, you're underage, so you'll drink Pinot Gris and like it." I poured Gemma-Kate a glass of wine and put our sushi takeout on plates.

After a couple of bites of eel roll I was able to change the subject. "How did that project of yours go?" I asked. "The interview of Carlo?"

I thought of those rings in his nightstand. Refocused to hear Gemma-Kate say,

"I didn't do it."

"What do you mean you didn't do it? You didn't do the assignment at all?"

"No, I just talked with the instructor and said I had a more interesting idea but I'd need a week. It's still about interviews, just not about mine, so it's a different angle. The book you gave me."

"How much have you read?"

Gemma-Kate looked like she would have rolled her eyes at me but it wasn't worth the effort. "All of it," she said. She picked up a piece of her rainbow roll, dipped it in the soy/wasabi mixture, and got it to her mouth without dripping or dropping. She took her time chewing it, and her only reaction to the wasabi was that her eyes watered. That's how she would look if she ever cried, I thought.

"I started doing some checking, and reading other sources. One book called *Truman Capote and the Legacy of 'In Cold Blood.'* And the Kansas Historical Society Archives of prison documents. Really interesting stuff."

"How so?"

She shook her head. "Not ready to talk about it yet. I'm still formulating conclusions."

We ate a little while in silence, letting the sushi relieve the stress. Gemma-Kate got the last piece of crazy monkey roll because I was thinking about what I would do to find the asshole who broke into my house. Right after I beefed up the security. I was kicking myself about that. Later I would kick myself harder for not suspecting Jerry Nolan, but at that stage it would have just been paranoid. Plus right then I didn't have any evidence of prior criminal activity. Plus if he was burglarizing more than one house why would he choose someone he knew already? He might not be the smartest guy, but I wouldn't have thought he was that stupid.

Gemma-Kate cleaned up the kitchen while I straightened up the small messes the burglar had left. I folded the clothes back into the drawers and closed them, shut the lid on my jewelry box and the drawer with the wedding rings in it, and went into the library. I wasn't sure whether to just leave it to Carlo to put everything back the way it was, or whether it would bother him less if he didn't see what someone had done. There I was, protecting him again like some delicate flower, a man who had known prison life and once admitted to thinking of bludgeoning someone to death with a champagne bottle.

I sat down before the bins in the library closet. I had never opened this closet, never noticed the bins. I could look in them now. Just a little. I took the lid off the top bin and found paper yellowed with age, and carbon copies of old papers, with dates going back to the seventies when he got his PhD in philosophy and the late sixties when he was in seminary. There was a badge from a conference, identifying him as SPEAKER. I thought I would ask his permission to look through more of these papers, because it made me feel closer to him as a young man. I had never seen photographs of him from that time. What had he looked like with his hair all one shade of dark brown, without the lines in the face I loved, eyes not yet sobered by life, some half-finished creature? I felt a sudden mush of missing, stronger than what I'd felt with all the personal and professional distractions of my time in Florida not too long ago. It seemed like forever since I'd dropped him off at the observatory, and it was only four hours. Is this what it was like to love someone? To be held in a kind of thrall that can hurt without warning, despite every intention not to care so?

Ah, here was a photo after all. It showed a couple, youngish from my point of view, dressed in waders, in the middle of a running stream. She was petite and willowy, with her hair tied back in a ponytail, the way I often wore my hair. Vulnerable, needing him, she clung to the man as if frightened that the river would carry her away. Her mouth was wide open in that kind of a laugh. He had one arm supporting her, while his other arm held out a fly-fishing rod. He was grinning at whoever was on the bank taking the picture. I got to thinking about the first time I'd worried about losing Carlo, and figured seeing this photograph right after I saw the wedding rings was what made me think that way.

I thought back to the time when I was new to the wife game, did not know the real Carlo well, and was crazy worried that he would find out what kind of woman he'd married. With my petite stature and little-girl looks (at least at that time), the FBI thought it found in me a gold mine for undercover work. Giving me the status of Very Special Agent, one that even many FBI agents don't know about, they pimped me out across the country to use as bait for serial rapists, killers, human traffickers, child pornographers, and the low-life scum that got involved with these people.

In order to keep my cover, it meant doing things I don't like people to know about at the potluck lunches at the Episcopal church Carlo and I occasionally attend. I don't like to talk about the things I did with anyone, the groups I infiltrated, or what I did to nail them. How I skirted justice, how many I killed, most in the line of duty.

That I hadn't killed anybody in about a year didn't feel like a huge point in my favor.

Needless to say, my life hadn't involved much fly-fishing. As I've said, my idea of nature was something you needed to get through in order to get to the next building. I wasn't the sporting kind and up to now didn't think Carlo was either.

Now I knew what the woman who had been a ghost for the past couple of years looked like. I hadn't realized how much I physically resembled her, and it made me feel like the one who was the ghost. Or was that my imagination? I tucked the photo back, against the side of the bin next to the stack of papers.

"Aunt Brigid."

I looked up at Gemma-Kate standing behind me, and wondered how many times she had said my name before I heard it. I shook myself out of the silly thoughts. What I needed to be thinking about was finding the burglar and making the home more secure.

"Are you still worried about the break-in?" she asked.

"Yes, that's it. I think I'll turn in. The sheets are on your bed."

Twenty-nine

Waiting for the call, Beaufort sat at the same bar where he had met Gloria weeks before. He didn't know much about brakes, but he knew Yanchak, and Yanchak knew everybody. At least that's what he said. Beaufort thought it was a simple matter of cutting the brake line. So when the guy called him to report what had happened, and Beaufort stepped out in the parking lot to talk, he felt confident that he'd be told Quinn's car went off the mountain as planned. But that wasn't the story he got.

It started with the guy talking like he was from a different planet, all about remote SMS and bullshit. If he hadn't been able to send the SMS remotely, he explained, there was a risk that they'd find evidence after the crash of the brakes being cut. Or even worse, the woman would have known immediately upon leaving the parking lot that they were disabled.

Beaufort didn't give a shit about what "SMS" stood for. Did the guy see the car go off the edge of the cliff? Was the woman dead?

No, the man had to explain every detail of the setup, and the drive down the mountain, and his conversation with the woman at the bottom.

"What do you mean, at the bottom? Are you saying she's not dead?"

That's what he was saying, the man said, but it was all very professional, so Beaufort didn't have to worry about the woman suspecting anything.

"I didn't want her unsuspecting, I wanted her fucking dead!" Beaufort screamed. Then he screamed that he wanted his money back.

The guy told him to come and get it, easy to say when Beaufort didn't even know his name and it was unlikely that Yanchak back in Florida would ever give it to him. Good old Yanchak, he managed to let Beaufort take the fall for the drugs all those years ago and he was still screwing him. Why had he ever trusted the Polack? The way he saw it, Yanchak owed him one. He owed him a big one.

Beaufort had finally hung up the phone without another word, as there were no words in his head. Oddly, his thoughts turned to Gloria Bentham. She had been so easy. He thought he could play Brigid Quinn the way he could play Gloria or any other woman. Now he knew there was more to Quinn than met the eye. Who was this woman who could get off a mountain without brakes?

The whole day had been a bust. He didn't find anything at the house, in his haste and frustration he left the bag of loot there, and now this.

Still steaming from the conversation, Beaufort got into his car, drove the short distance home, and pulled into Gloria's driveway. He bolted from the car, walked into the living room, and threw his car keys on the glass coffee table, where they hit one of the porcelain figures that Gloria loved so much. The porcelain toppled. The glass won.

"Jerry?" Her voice came from the bedroom, all questioning and timid. That made him angrier.

"Jerry!" The voice was in the room now. He whipped around to see her standing in some baby-doll getup, the black lace struggling to support her sagging tits and her saddlebags spilling out from beneath the panties. His life was unraveling and all this idiot cared about was sex.

"You broke my mother's Lladró," she said, too shocked to hide her sadness or her body.

"Sorry," he muttered, but even he knew it didn't sound that way.

Maybe his tone was what set her in a different direction, not reading him well, not realizing the kind of day he'd had and taking it as a warning. "You don't sound sorry. You sound like you've sounded for the past week."

"What have I sounded like?"

"Like you don't care about me anymore. Like you don't notice that I'm hurt. Look at me! I'm hurting, Jerry! My life coach today said I should share my feelings with you."

"So share."

"I did! I am! Ever since your little friend stopped by."

"What friend? When?"

"I told you. A week ago."

Beaufort got himself under some control. He was able to ask the question without grabbing Gloria and smacking the answer out of her. "What friend?" he asked.

"She said her name is Brigid Quinn. She said she knew you. She didn't appear to know about me." Gloria's sadness and hurt were taking over now, and if she noticed the change come over Beaufort when she said the woman's name, she ignored it. "You don't want to go out with my friends, but you have your own and you don't invite me. Her."

Beaufort lifted the coffee table, and the pieces of broken statue dusted the floor around it. He threw the table across the room, where it hit the flat-screen television set and made a funny slash in the surface rather than cracking it the way it would if it had been glass. The television tottered on its base and then fell forward off its stand.

Beaufort darted here and there in the room, cursing and looking for what all to break. He noticed Gloria and his brain clicked to breaking her.

She saw him coming. Rather than fight, or run, she slid to her ass in the corner of the nook leading to the bedroom. She drew her knees up close to her and folded her arms around them. She ducked her head to make herself smaller, as small as she could get. It appeared she knew how this drill went, from other times and other men, and she knew that she stood the best chance of survival if she cowered.

Beaufort watched her tighten into a little seed of a person. His brain clicked from that to the rage that swelled from his groin through his chest, rage that had been tamped down through all the prison years. It

clicked to all the things in the room that he could yet destroy. It clicked
to how it was better to destroy with an audience in attendance, the way
it was the first time. Then, as quickly as the rage had exploded, it subsided. The only sound was his breathing and her breathing in a post-
orgasmic way.

What now? He didn't regret the damage. It felt good and eased his
heart. But he watched Gloria balled up in the corner in her stupid lin-
gerie, and felt a feeling that was . . . bad. He told himself he wasn't a
monster, and he could prove it. He went to her, sagged down beside her,
and put his arm around her. She flinched, but he kept his arm there until
he could feel her relaxing in his grasp.

"I'm sorry, baby," he said. "I'll replace everything. I've had a helluva
day, and now this."

"What happened?" she asked, her sympathy taking over the way he
predicted it always would. He could tell from the way she raised her
hand and placed it on his knee that, at least this time, everything would
be okay. She was grateful for the apology.

Rather than make up something about the helluva day, he asked her
to tell him about Brigid Quinn's visit.

"She was at the door when I came home for lunch one day last week,"
Gloria said. "She didn't have a car, but said she had been running. She
asked about whether I knew you." Gloria ended with a placating "I've
been afraid to say anything. Because . . . " She gestured timidly at the
mess around them.

Brigid Quinn was a crazy bitch, he told Gloria. She was a patron at the
stables, he said. She was stalking him. She was crazy. He never went over
to her house for dinner. That was a lie. Gloria shouldn't talk to her again,
and if the woman came around Gloria should tell him immediately.

As he talked, he thought about Quinn tracking him down and
making this connection with Gloria. What else did Quinn know
and what would she tell this woman? Right now Gloria was basking in
the newfound intimacy of what Beaufort had convinced her was a
common enemy. She would believe the lie because she wouldn't want
to imagine where the truth might lead. But what would happen if he
had judged Gloria wrong? That business about challenging him and

how he spent his time, having his own friends and ignoring hers. Was she respecting him enough? If not, one of them would have to go, and that would be complicated. Complicated if he had to find another place to live.

Complicated if Gloria didn't show up for work.

Thirty

The Miata was still under warranty so I took it in the next day, with Carlo following behind in his old Volvo. The Volvo had lost its AC some years before, and I was grateful this was the winter so he wouldn't bake all the way down to the dealership near the Tucson Mall and both of us bake all the way back if I had to leave the car there. The brakes didn't fail again, but tired as he was after being up late on Kitt Peak, he still insisted on coming.

They weren't busy, so while the mechanics checked out the car we waited in one of those smelly waiting rooms that apologizes with bad coffee and grimy televisions you can't turn off because they're mounted high up on the wall as if they fear you'll run off with them, or worse, change the channel.

When they called my name Carlo and I both went to the repair window, where I anticipated hearing what was wrong, but the guy who managed the customer service desk said the brakes checked out okay. The name on his shirt said HAL.

"But they failed, Hal," I said.

"They're fine," he assured me, his face with the expression of a cabinet nominee at a confirmation hearing.

"I was driving down from Kitt Peak and they went out. Do you understand? No brakes. Nada. I could have been killed."

Hal gave Carlo a *How do we put up with this?* look. "Lady, it's like being a doctor. If you come in and tell me you passed out and I do a brain scan and don't see anything, what can I do?"

"The brakes failed," I said.

Carlo added, "False equivalence." Which made both Hal and me look at him like he wasn't helping.

"Maybe you just did something wrong," Hal said thoughtfully, rubbing at his face with the back of his knuckles the way men do when they have facial hair, which Hal did not. "Or maybe you had a plastic water bottle wedged under the brake pedal. That happens sometimes. And then you panic."

"I don't panic," I said. "And I know how to drive very well. And there was no water bottle in the car."

"That will be eighty-nine dollars for the diagnostic," he said, having run out of logic.

"Fuck you," I said, at the same loss.

"Come on, lady," he said. "I'm not a mechanic, I just do the paperwork. Don't give me a hard time."

"Then let me talk to the mechanic."

He gave Carlo another put-upon look, but Carlo just smiled. So Hal left and brought back a guy wiping his hands on a greasy towel like they always do. He must have been warned, because he didn't meet my eyes, at least not in a consistent kind of way.

"Hi, Phil," I started, reading his name on his shirt and not wanting to startle him.

"Hi," he said.

"You checked my brakes?"

"Yes," he said, cautiously, as if it was a trick question and answering wrong might set me off somehow.

"And there was nothing wrong with them?"

Phil glanced at Hal. "Nothing," he said.

"They failed on an eight percent incline coming down Kitt Peak. Then I got to the bottom of the mountain and they worked fine. They haven't stopped working since yesterday, driving around town."

Phil shook his head sadly, as in, *what a strange and complex world it is*. Clearly, I wasn't going to get anything out of him with his boss giving him the stink eye. Said boss tried to get me to pay for the diagnostic again, and I tossed the paper back at him, saying they hadn't diagnosed shit and besides, the car was under warranty.

I said, "Now, Phil, given that I'm a really experienced high-speed driver, and the floor mat wasn't wedged against the brake or anything like that . . . are you ready for this next question?"

Phil nodded.

"Under what circumstances could brakes give out on a car that's less than a year old?"

Phil gave it all his thought. He looked to the right and the left. Then he looked straight at me like he'd just remembered the answer to the test question. Then he shook his head no.

"Come on," I said. "Tell me whatever you're thinking no matter how crazy it feels."

Phil said, "The only thing I can think of is that someone could send an SMS message using the OBD II dongle."

I vaguely knew that he was talking computer jargon, but I never had much to do with the guys in the internet crime division unless it had to do with distributing pornography. So Phil's words made about as much sense as listening to someone say *nick-nack-paddy-wack-give-a-dog-a-bone*. Hal could see it on my face and smirked, thinking the old lady would now go quietly.

I stood my ground and said, "OBD stands for—"

"On-Board Diagnostics."

"And SMS—"

"Short Message Service."

"As in sending some sort of wireless message. Like text messaging."

Phil said, "That's correct."

I didn't need to ask what a dongle was because I had enough information to figure out that with all the computer software they install in cars these days, it's possible for someone to hack wirelessly into your braking system and put it temporarily out of order.

I said this.

Phil acknowledged that was what he was getting at.

"Ma'am," Hal started. "Are you going to say that someone hacked into your car intentionally and disabled your brakes?"

"No, I'm not," I said. "But you might. You're going to call the manufacturer and find out if there have been any recalls for this reason. And then you're going to call me to bring the car back in and check to see whether the on-board diagnostic computer registers such hacking."

I left Hal glaring at Phil, waiting for me to be out of earshot so he could start yelling about lawsuits. Poor Phil.

Now, if my job hadn't made me sort of a suspicious person to begin with—not talking paranoia—I would have ignored this angle, simply hoping that it wouldn't happen again. As it was, I thought about the other car that had been on the road down the mountain with me, the only person within a mile, a driver who could have been the one to put my brakes out of commission temporarily. Who drove off in a hurry when he thought I was getting out of my car. Who was that man?

With the evidence in hand, that someone had staged a burglary at my house looking for some information . . . the strong possibility that someone had tried to kill me on the mountain . . . I could only reach the conclusion that someone was after me.

After *me*. Goddammit, isn't that the conclusion anyone would come to?

Thirty-one

They didn't have everything that I needed at Home Depot, so I ordered the rest online and had it shipped two-day. I also made an appointment with a company that could replace the windows in the back of the house with unbreakable ones.

Because I had my contacts but no control over priority, it also took that long to get a callback from David Weiss. Weiss was a forensic psychologist who would retire from the profiling division of the FBI in another year or so. We had those nicknames for each other that can only develop when you've known another person for decades. He called me Stinger.

"Hey, Sigmund," I said.

Turns out it was a clean print, and it wasn't Gloria Bentham's.

"I was able to have the print you sent me run against IAFIS," he said without preamble, how's life and all that. That's how Weiss is, not high on the emotional intelligence spectrum.

"Anything interesting?"

"It matches to the booking print of a Jeremiah Beaufort. Precisely three bookings, as a matter of fact. He was one of those poor shmucks who were part of the Three Strikes and Life deal that Clinton signed during the war on drugs."

"So what's he doing out of prison?"

"That new thing they were doing for nonviolent criminals with over-long sentences. He was commuted and released."

"Are you able to track him to Tucson?"

"His current whereabouts are undetermined. All I can say is that he was released a little more than three months ago from Mississippi State Correctional Facility. I did a superficial check on him and find him operating under the radar, no record of him buying a plane ticket or anything big. No car. Not even a credit card. Which makes one wonder what he's doing that he doesn't want to be found. Now tell me. What kind of trouble have you gotten yourself into this time, my old buddy? And what will you do for intel after I retire?"

"Where was he charged those three times?"

"Let's see. We got one in Mississippi . . . the first two were in Florida. So he was operating in the Southeast. I realize you worked for the Florida Bureau office for a while, but you were never involved in drug trafficking investigations. And he doesn't seem worth your time. He's a very petty criminal, nothing violent. Seriously, Stinger, what do you have to do with this man?"

"I don't know. I only know he's now in Tucson, living somewhere within walking distance of our house. He made casual contact with Carlo first, and has been working himself into our favor like a regular con artist. I questioned my instincts at first, but with what you've said about him I don't think his showing up is a coincidence, or that he's just your garden variety con. Stuff has happened, a burglary, what may have been attempted murder."

"Murder. Who?"

"I think he's after me. I just have to find out why. Where in Florida was he picked up?"

"Hm, offshore between Tampa and Sarasota. That was the second time in Florida. The first time was just on a small possessions charge, but at that time you could get five years. The second he was suspected of already dropping off his load of cocaine he'd gotten from a boat coming in through the Gulf. But he didn't get a longer sentence that time because all they found was some residue in his boat. Three years that time." Weiss moved on to something he did not already know. "So tell me, how is everything by you? Has your psychopathic niece tried to poison the dogs again?"

Weiss had been of moderate assistance when I thought Gemma-Kate was trying to kill me a while ago. At the time he was convinced of it, and it was partly his fault I nearly died, but you don't hold things like that against old friends. "Gemma-Kate is doing fine, keeping up with her classwork, and I told you I'm certain that poisoning thing was just an accident. She's actually been helpful with this Beaufort, trying to profile him."

"As in 'it takes a killer to catch a killer'?" he asked.

"Stop. She says she's never killed anyone. At least not for fun, and only if they truly had it coming. At least not in a long time," I joked back.

"All in the family," Weiss said, and it stopped being a joke. "Did you know that forty percent of our behavior is genetically determined?"

I considered bantering, but the Beaufort thing was more interesting.

"One more thing," I said. "Where was Beaufort born?"

"Pascagoula, Mississippi."

"That's funny, he told Carlo he was baptized in Kansas City."

"That could happen. People move around."

"Maybe not. In those days a good Catholic had a baby baptized within the first week so they wouldn't end up in limbo if they died. I doubt they would have rushed him from Mississippi to Kansas for a baptism."

We exchanged a few more pleasantries about budget cuts and politically motivated layoffs, who was still there. We didn't say any names because you never knew when calls were being recorded. It went something like:

"Mr. Manhattan?"

"Gone."

"Good, he was a dick. What about Rising Star?"

"Still rising and with considerable power. She's with Homeland Security now, connections to the TSA. Not a big enough fish to get on anyone's sonar for termination. It doesn't hurt that she was always good at keeping her opinions to herself."

"Plus that's one department they won't be defunding any time soon. Tell her I said hi."

"Are you serious? She wouldn't want me to know that you know her."

Then we lied about how swell it would be to see each other again, and hung up.

With his prison record it was easy to find his mug shot; make that plural because of his several arrests. In shot after shot I could see him aging from his middle twenties to late thirties, and confirm my guy was Jeremiah Beaufort. After that it got harder. Try as I might, I couldn't find any trail after he left prison three months before. No credit cards, no bank accounts. As Weiss said, this was a man who was flying under the radar, cash only, which made me wonder how much of it he had and how he got it.

His birth certificate corroborated Weiss's finding that he was from Pascagoula, Mississippi, but records were scanty when I tried to access his background there. I kept coming up with one of those messages: *Removed from public view in accordance with restrictions of Mississippi Privacy Act.* There was something there they didn't want me to see, probably a document that mentioned a juvenile.

What did you do, Jeremiah Beaufort? Or what was done to you?

Only the last drug charge was brought in Mississippi. The first two were in Florida, before the drug wars started in earnest and the entire Florida coastline was open for business. When things got hot there he must have moved up the coast before he was snagged the third time and put in for what everyone would have assumed was life. As far as any violent crimes were concerned, he was clean.

Jeremiah Beaufort may have been good in the drug racket. Maybe he thought he was smart, because he managed to avoid the greater charges for which he was guilty. The investigative report had him as a suspect for running cocaine from Nicaragua by boat to the Florida Keys. He was in charge of the operation after the lead guy, a Guatemalan, was "lost in a boating accident," and Beaufort could have amassed a tidy fortune that nobody was ever able to locate in any offshore account. But in actuality it was no harder, and maybe it was easier, to ply this trade in the seventies. Millions of tons got through, hundreds of dealers were never caught. The investigators could never prove the major deals, and settled for getting him twice on possession and once on selling a couple of ounces. But in the end it didn't matter, he still got life.

So Jeremiah Beaufort would consider himself a criminal mastermind. But here's the thing that doesn't take a professional profiler to deduce:

A smart guy doesn't get caught three times.

Hunting a smart professional is like playing chess. There are certain prescribed moves you can predict more often than not. But dealing with someone who thinks he's smarter than he is, well, that guy is more like sitting down with someone to play chess, and he starts playing Candy Land, and you can't call him a jerk and walk away, because he'll kill you. He doesn't know that killing someone in law enforcement, retired or not, is a stupid move, and should be avoided.

No, of all the possible chess moves you might expect from a seasoned pro, all you can be certain of is that the stupid criminal will do something else because he doesn't know any better. And that is liable to get you dead, or someone else who you really don't want dead.

But all that said, just because someone is a crook doesn't mean they're after me, necessarily. Could be he was a scumbag low-life, a mooch, and an abuser, but that didn't mean he was after me. Him running into us, that could just be a co-inky-dink.

I mounted the motion detectors in the front and back entryways while Carlo was at another meeting with Elias Manwaring and the science professor whose name I couldn't remember. This was good because Carlo would have offered to help and he is not really as good as I am with either ladders or power tools.

I tested the motion detectors, which came equipped not only with football stadium lights guaranteed to illuminate the front and back yards for twenty-five feet out and to the sides, but also were connected to a closed circuit camera. This might sound high tech, but it's no more than parents are using with nanny cams. Everything was working. I was not content, closing the barn door after the cow . . . but no use crying over . . . I managed to stop my mother's platitudes from ganging up on me before I went any further.

All the outdoor stuff was battery powered, but electrical wiring, I must admit, is not among my gifts. Luckily someone was available to come out the same day and install the indoor security. His ringing the doorbell set off the pugs, who bounced their bodies sideways against the screen door. When I answered the door he shouted over their barking, "I probably shouldn't mention this, but you couldn't have better security than these guys."

"These guys? They're pugs. Who's afraid of pugs?"

"There are too many houses without dogs to take any chance going into one with. They might alert the neighbors. They might be small but they still have teeth. On top of that, you have two of them."

I didn't bother to tell him that we'd already been broken into and they hadn't helped much that day. For the first time I wondered why not. Probably because the house is so well insulated the neighbors wouldn't hear the dogs barking, I thought first. Then I thought, so why didn't it deter the vandals, thieves, punks, whatever they were, the way the alarm guy said they would? Then I thought, who knew us and the pugs well enough not to leave the house alone and go to one without dogs, where there was no chance of being attacked?

I would think more later, but for now I told him to go ahead with the alarm system, which he installed within an hour. He showed me how to program it with a passcode, and explained how the sheriff's department would be alerted if it went off. I knew all this but I let him talk. I'd been dealing with security my whole life. The only difference is that I had let my guard down living here with Carlo, in Jane's house.

That made me remember the doorbell played *Eine kleine Nachtmusik*. Call it petty, small-minded, insecure, what have you, but this was one reminder of Jane I could eliminate. I mentioned it to the security guy.

"I don't think I can reprogram it easily. Would you like me to disengage it altogether?"

Nice man. I said yes. Visitors could knock. Carlo wouldn't mind. Neither of us was very social, and so few people came to the house he probably wouldn't even notice. That made me think, who, besides the occasional salesperson or evangelist, had rung the bell in the past six months? And who had made nice with the pugs?

I started to link together all the little points of the past couple of weeks like a dot-to-dot picture. Showing up at the back fence. Living within walking distance. Being so helpful with moving the telescope. Happening to see Carlo at Bashas'. Getting an invitation to dinner. Not mentioning the woman he lived with, let alone asking if she could join him. Lying about where he was born or lying about where his family went to church. Lying about being a jockey. Ingratiating himself with the pugs.

I got down on the floor, which was the signal for Al and Peg to rush me. I sniffed them as if I could detect cheese on their breath, silly, I know. They both tried to French my nose.

"What do you know, pups?" I asked them. "Come on, talk to me."

They remained inscrutable. As I belly-rubbed them simultaneously, one on each side, I wondered what Jeremiah Beaufort wanted from me. Was it revenge? Or was it something I had in my files that could incriminate him for something far greater than the risk of getting caught for burglary? Was that his goal, to search the house? And in order to do so without anyone around, would he have set up the whole charade of making it look like gang members were breaking into neighborhood homes for the sole purpose of finding something in ours? If so, what was that thing he was looking for?

Thirty-two

Max agreed to meet me at Carlota's, which up in Catalina was about as far as you could get from Tucson proper without leaving the county. But we didn't meet on Taco Tuesday when the place was packed. And not even at lunchtime. Three in the afternoon found the restaurant empty, and even so we sat at a table in the back corner behind a pillar with some vines painted on it. He showed no surprise when I said, "I know who committed the burglaries."

"Who?"

"This man." I put the most recent mug shot on the table. "He's close to seventy now, but this was him about thirty years ago. He goes by the name of Jerry Nolan, but his real name is Jeremiah Beaufort."

Max shook his head. "I can't believe what you're telling me. A seventy-year-old man broke into three houses and painted gang signs?"

"I know, improbable. But he's been stalking us. And maybe worse."

"Stalking. Give me more."

"He showed up first at the back of our property. Made nice with Carlo. Helped him move his telescope."

"He sounds like a real threat to the public weal. Brigid. It's Arizona, and people are friendlier than in the East. Strangers wave. You've been here several years now. Get used to it. Have you got anything I can use?"

Max put up a finger to keep me from answering while a waitress came up behind me and put a dish of salsa and a basket of tortilla chips on the table between us. "That's not the hot, did you want hot?" she asked, referring to the salsa. Then she took a pad out of her apron pocket to take our order. Max was about to shake his head impatiently, but Carlota's was my Mexican restaurant (everyone in Tucson has this kind of loyalty) and I didn't want any hard feelings no matter what was going on. "I'll have the topopo salad with pulled pork, please," I said, handing her the menu I didn't need to look at because I had it memorized.

She seemed satisfied that the order was large enough even though Max was only having an iced tea.

"When I was checking to see who might have gotten out and I hadn't been notified, I found out about this guy. Jeremiah Beaufort, a petty drug dealer who got let out with that recent release of nonviolent criminals."

"So. He was in prison. And he's not even paroled, his sentence was commuted. You're still not making a connection."

"With all his visiting, why didn't it ever come up in conversation?"

"You're being overly sensitive. He's not a sex offender, Brigid. It's not like he has to register. He was under no obligation to tell you he's an ex-con. How did you even find out about him?"

I took a deep breath. "I found out where he was living, in one of those prefab jobs on Hawser. I lifted his print off the door handle and had it run."

"Good God, woman. And you say *he's* being creepy?"

"You don't trust me," I said.

He gave me one of those *no shit* looks. Ignoring it, I told Max about everything, the vibe I got from the woman Jerry lived with, the fact that the pugs hadn't objected to the burglar, and . . . the pièce de résistance . . . how he might have disabled my brakes. As I said all these things, they seemed rather less compelling than when I had thought them earlier that day. I could see by his face that he was thinking the same thing.

Max dipped a chip into the salsa now that he figured he was dealing with a nonissue and was allowing himself to relax a little. His tone was condescending as he asked, "If you think he's after you, what's his motivation?"

I ignored the condescension. "I don't know. I don't know that yet." The topopo salad arrived and I forked some out of the fried tortilla shell that served as a bowl. "So you won't help me?"

Max looked mildly disgusted by my question, treating me like an ignorant civilian, an old woman with possibly some paranoia. He said, "Help how? I get involved when a crime is committed. So far what I'm hearing is suspicion—"

"Instinct—"

"—without any substantiation, simply based on the single fact, no, two provable facts, that the guy didn't tell you he was in prison, and that he gave you a different name. Brigid, we got bigger problems than that. And here's another thing. You said you were going to keep a low profile. The only one I can see breaking the law here is you. Prowling around some man's property is not a low-profile thing to do. Stop it."

"We used to get along so well, didn't we? Playing poker. Talking philosophy."

"That was Carlo."

Having lost any appetite I might have had at three in the afternoon, I took out a twenty and laid it on the table. "I'll tell you something, Max, this is what happened the last time. You didn't trust me before, and it nearly got us all killed. You're a bullheaded bastard, you know that?"

"Anybody ever tell you you're a loose cannon? I worry more about what you'll do than what anyone else will do."

I got up and grabbed my tote bag from the corner of the chair. "Okay, have it your way, but don't say I didn't warn you. I'll take care of this on my own."

Max rose, too, like he totally got the threat. "Don't you do anything, Brigid. I'd just as soon arrest you for trespassing as try to pin something on that poor old man."

"Poor old man. Bite me, Coyote. Times like this I wish I had a dick for the sole purpose of telling you to suck it," I said. "Plus, you really going to arrest me, and where might that go? You want to be held accountable for a cover-up?"

Max knew what I meant, the case that broke our friendship and caused this animosity. The waitress ran up when she saw that I had stood, and it wasn't to make sure I wasn't stiffing her. They knew me better than that. She tried to hand me a takeout container. "You want to take that with you?" she asked, pointing to my hardly touched salad. I summoned a smile and said no thanks.

Well, that didn't go very well. I had an alternative that I didn't want to use, going around Max, I mean. But it looked like I had no choice. Well, sure I did, I always have a choice, but what the hell.

We've got a neighborhood online chat group. You can sell your dining room table, offer to walk dogs, and ask about a good landscaper. You can also post alarming messages about having your house broken into, warning others. I was counting on this when I pulled up the chat group and found the other two victims. One of them was old enough to still have a landline that was available through directory assistance. I called and got Artie on the phone.

I got right down to it, said I was another one of the houses broken into, and asked, "You hear of any progress in the investigation?"

"Not a thing. My wife is so jarred by the break-in she's afraid to leave the house. That business with the graffiti on the wall threw her for a loop. She thinks it's satanic."

"I wouldn't jump to that conclusion. It looked more like a gang sign."

"I don't think that will comfort my wife. What do you know about gang signs?"

"Watching crime shows on TV. What did they get?"

"Mostly jewelry, but it didn't look like they knew what they were looking for. Got mostly junk, and left her mother's engagement ring. They left the laptops. That's why we were told it was probably some kids. I hate kids." He paused, waiting for my agreement.

"Yeah," I said, not wanting to go off on a tangential rant.

Satisfied with that, Artie said, "My wife wants me to call a home security company. I don't know where to start."

I gave him the name of the company I had used. And thinking he would trust me enough at this point, I asked, "Tell me, do you have a dog?"

"No. I hate dogs."

"What about filing cabinets?"

I half expected him to say he hated filing cabinets, but he said, "No. We keep our important papers in two of those containers with a lid and a handle. That's all we need."

"Where do you keep them?"

"Under a desk in one of the guest rooms. Why?"

"Were they disturbed at all?"

"Not that we could see. You know, I hadn't thought until now how weird that is. All our Social Security information, passwords, all kinds of important things are in those files."

"Oh, maybe not so weird. Burglars more often go for tangible items they can fence."

So I didn't get any information about possible suspects from the other victim, but I got a different way of looking at my own. With the other home they went for small valuables. My place they went for files—after making it look like they were stealing other items. Max missed this angle. What were they looking for, and why did they go through the elaborate ruse of making it look like multiple gang break-ins?

Thirty-three

While Gloria was at work, Beaufort took Achilles to the local dog park and threw the tennis ball he'd bought for the dog. He was still angry about having failed to dispatch the Quinn woman, but it eased his frustration to watch Achilles run on his three legs as fast as any dog on four. *When life hands you lemons*, Beaufort thought, thinking of another plaque on the wall in Gloria's house. Dog wasn't too smart, though. When he got to the ball Achilles looked at it and then at Beaufort as if saying *Now what?* As Beaufort walked to the ball, threw it, and walked to the ball again, he assessed his situation. He thought he was smart that way. He thought he could look at all the elements of a problem, link them together, and formulate a good plan. Here is where he stood:

With the appearance of that sketch of Hickock it seemed likely that if DiForenza had that much, he had the other thing that could incriminate him.

He had received that thing from Father Victor Santangelo, who was now dead.

Question: Did DiForenza know he had the document? This was not certain.

But if DiForenza knew he had it, and had read it, there was nothing in it to connect Beaufort to either the Clutter or Walker murders.

He must not have read it. He might not even know what he had.

DiForenza was not a problem.

The problem was his wife, Brigid Quinn, the FBI agent.

Brigid Quinn suspected him, but how could she?

Maybe she did without knowing what she suspected him of.

What he did know is that she was harder to kill than he had at first thought.

What should he do now?

A pragmatist, that's what he was. Not a killer. He sat down on the ground with his back against a mesquite tree, not needing the scant shade that the tree could provide on a summer day. Achilles lay down beside him, panting from his ball chasing, his back pressed against Beaufort's thigh.

"You know I'm not a bad man, don't you, boy?" Beaufort said, stroking the bump where the dog's leg had been. Achilles licked his hand. "If I was a bad man we wouldn't get along so well. And you're the only one I can talk to. I can't talk to anybody else. Not even Yanchak." Maybe it was screwy, but as he spoke to Achilles just then it felt very natural, talking to a dog.

But Beaufort knew he couldn't tell even Achilles what he had done in Garden City.

As he had watched the progress of the case with Dick Hickock and Perry Smith back then, there had been headlines about the two changing their confession. Smith took the rap for killing all the Clutters. This was a sure sign to Beaufort that he was in the clear. Hickock must have agreed, maybe figuring that he'd at least escape the death penalty.

But when the verdict came in, and the penalty for both of them was execution, things weren't so clear-cut anymore. Beaufort watched the weeks go by with the pair not talking, but the gnawing at his mind grew worse despite, maybe because of, their silence. He felt confident of Smith, but what of Hickock?

"I had to send a message to Hickock, that he needed to keep up his side of the bargain no matter what," Beaufort said to Achilles. "I didn't have a choice." Achilles turned his head and gazed at Beaufort, who felt like he was being hugged with the look. Beaufort hadn't felt this way before, not even with Gloria. He stroked the soft fur from Achilles's neck to the spot where the dog's tail sprouted. Achilles rolled over onto his back for a tummy rub, and Beaufort obliged.

Beaufort had done what he had to do, and when it was reported in the Garden City newspaper, he clipped out the article and put it in his shirt pocket. He thumbed a ride a safe distance from the home where Hickock had lived with his parents, and where Mrs. Hickock lived alone now that the father was dead. Beaufort walked the rest of the way, off the road close to the trees and tall shrubs that lined it, so as not to risk ever being discovered.

When he got to the house it was early evening and the lights were on, so he was able to easily see Mrs. Hickock sitting at the kitchen table. When he snuck in the door that led straight to the kitchen, he saw she was just sitting there, staring at her hands clasped on the tabletop. Intent, as if the hands held a secret that they weren't giving up. So intent was she that it was easy for Beaufort to come up behind her.

She jumped when he brought his hands down firmly on her shoulders.

"Don't turn around," he said in his deepest voice, which you'd never think would go with his stature and his boyish face.

When he thought that she would obey, he said, "I want you to visit your son, Dick. I want you to tell him that he better keep his mouth shut."

"I don't under—" the woman began.

"It doesn't matter. He'll understand. And he'll understand when you tell him that if he doesn't keep his mouth shut people he loves will be hurt bad. You." He slowly lifted his hands from her shoulders, but she seemed frozen in place. He drew the newspaper article out of his pocket and tossed it on the table in front of her eyes where she could read it without moving her head. "Show this to him. It's my guarantee," he said, and slipped out the back door while she read it.

It wasn't nearly as sensational as all the news surrounding the Clutter family murders and subsequent capture and trial of Hickock and

Smith. Just a small article, an incident that nobody thought critical to the public well-being. Just a kid's prank, they must have thought.

Ten dogs had been poisoned around Garden City.

"You know I'd never hurt you, don't you, boy?" Beaufort said, getting to his feet. That seemed good enough for Achilles. He rolled the ball into his mouth and stood up, ready to go home.

Thirty-four

Down at the corner of Oracle and Golder Ranch Road there's a shop that caters to the wealthy enclave of Saddlebrooke, about five miles to the north, selling local art and doing a first-rate job of custom framing. That's where we take our occasional business, so when Drew from Framing and More called with a question about "the job," I thought I was only having a senior lapse.

"What job?" I asked. "Did I forget I gave you something to frame?"

"No, your husband did."

I haven't totally lost my brain. I knew immediately this was an anniversary gift, but I had more serious things on my mind at the moment. "Tell you what, he's down at Starizona getting some telescope computer thing fixed. Could I ask you to call again in a couple of hours? I think this is supposed to be a surprise."

"Oh, sorry. It's not actually finished, I just had a question about what I should do with the letter I found between the sketch and the cardboard backing. Carlo didn't say anything about the letter."

Sketch? A letter behind the sketch that Carlo didn't know about? What the hell? My attention swerved. "What sketch?"

"I'm sorry?"

"What's the sketch of?"

"It's a man's face. Done in pencil."

"You know my husband. Is it him?"

Drew paused, like taking a second look. "No way."

"What does the letter say?"

"It starts out, 'To whom it may concern . . .'"

"Yes?"

"'My name is Richard Eugene Hickock. I—'"

"Holy shit," I said.

"What? You know this guy?" Drew asked.

Anniversary surprises be damned. With my brain fuzzy as if I'd just taken some mind-bending drug, I put the break-in on temporary hold, hung up the phone without being sure if I said good-bye, and drove the few minutes down to the framing shop, hoping there were no cops lurking on a side street to make up their ticket quota by end of month.

At the drive into the shopping center I pulled hard right with only the tiniest squeal of the tires, parked, ran into the shop, and had to cool my jets behind a customer who was picking up another job. I waited while Drew packaged the newly framed work in brown paper. I waited while he rang up the charges and took the guy's credit card. I ground my teeth and waited while the two talked for a few minutes about the weather. People in Arizona usually aren't in a hurry except for those instances of road rage, where we rank fifth in the country. I remained quiet, my heart idling. I'm working on patience.

When the other customer was gone after exhausting his discussion of the merits of the unseasonable coolness in relation to global warming, Drew gestured me over to his workbench, where a pencil sketch lay next to a handwritten letter. The cardboard backing where it had been sandwiched was faded on the outside and darker in the middle where the sketch had rested. That alone told me it was pretty old. Pretty authentic.

"Nice sketch," he said, rubbing his ink-stained fingers over his beard as if to muffle the words he felt he had to say. Like I'd done it myself and it was crap. I don't know where Carlo found it, but the fifties hoodlum look was unmistakable, that long thin face ending in a pointy chin, and the narrowed eyes, one slightly higher and more slitty, that I had seen in so many photographs. As Capote himself had described it more capably, "composed of mismatching parts as though it had been halved like an apple, then put together a fraction off center, the eyes at uneven levels and of uneven size." In the lower right-hand corner were the initials P.S.

I failed to stifle a gasp. "Do you recognize who this is?" I asked, ever curious about the extent of the younger generation's cultural illiteracy.

"Looks familiar. Maybe from a television program?" He seemed embarrassed, more and more certain that I had done it myself and wanted recognition for it.

This beat my Kitt Peak present all to hell. I felt like one of those people who discovers a Van Gogh in their attic. I decided not to tell Drew that this was a sketch of Richard Eugene Hickock, almost certainly drawn by his partner in crime Perry Smith. I was leaving it in his hands and thought it better not to reveal its potential value. We're talking hundreds of thousands of dollars at auction. I leaned closer to the single page of lined notebook paper next to it, only confirming that the name was there as Drew had read it to me over the phone.

"Did you read this?" I asked.

"No," he said. I'm sorry if I'm biased against youth, but I wasn't surprised at his lack of interest. Maybe he couldn't even read cursive. I carefully picked up the letter and asked for a folder to get it home safely. The creases where it had been folded in half and then folded in half again so it could be hidden behind the sketch were making the paper tear.

Drew focused on his job. "Your husband asked for this simple wooden frame with a two-inch matting, apricot. How do you like it?"

What I really wanted was to get out of there and get home where I could examine the letter more closely, and do an internet search to make sure it was something original rather than a copy of something already in the archive. "Sure, sure. Fine," I said about the matting choice. "About the folder?"

Drew touched the Scotch tape that had been used to stick the sketch to the cardboard backing. "This is old stuff," he said, scraping at a corner of the yellowed, brittle tape. "I should trim that away from the paper. It will make it just a little smaller but there's no other way. Do you want the backing or should I throw it away?"

"Might as well pop it in the folder there. Good," I said, restraining myself from screaming at him. Thinking more, I almost told Drew that I couldn't leave the sketch there after all, that it was too valuable. But it felt as if more than one person had been accusing me of paranoia lately, and I took it to heart. Pretending to scoff at myself for worrying so, I did ask him if he had a safe he could leave it in overnight. He did.

Thirty-five

I forced myself to drive the short distance home without reading the letter to make sure I could get there before Carlo returned so he wouldn't know I'd seen his present. Then I regretted my delay when I saw Carlo's car in the garage. I could have lied and said I'd been to the grocery store, but had no groceries to show for it. Easier to simply confess.

"Well, look, you've spoiled the surprise," Carlo said, though without any apparent hard feelings.

"Where did you get that sketch?"

"There you go with the interrogation again."

I sat down at the dining room table. If my tote bag had contained diamonds I would not have clutched it more tightly. I patted the space next to me and he complied.

"Not a chance, Perfesser. You're the one who's always telling me we should have total honesty between us, right? Why didn't you bring this out when Gemma-Kate was here and we were talking about *In Cold Blood*?"

"Of course I expected to tell you the story of its acquisition when I gave you the present. But if I showed it to Gemma-Kate that night you would have seen it, and I wouldn't have been able to surprise you, would I?"

Well, that was intriguing and made my focus shift momentarily from the folded-up letter on the table to Carlo. "What story?" I asked. "How are you connected to this?"

For the first time since I'd known him, Carlo actually looked uncomfortable. A little bit of a grimace on his face at some disagreeable memory. "Let's look at the letter first," he said.

That was what I wanted to do, so I took the letter out of my tote bag, placed it on the table in front of us, and very carefully unfolded it so it wouldn't tear at the folds. We read together:

Dear Father Santangelo:

My name is Richard Eugene Hickock. I was convicted of being an accomplice in the murder of a family by the name of Clutter. My attorney, Mr. Joseph P. Jenkins, has petitioned for a stay of execution. If that is not approved, then I am going to be hanged, so this is my only chance to tell part of the story no one would know otherwise. The truth would not be important if I was the only one involved. I do this because people I love have been threatened and I fear for their lives. These people include my mother and brother, two ex-wives who I do not bear any grudge against, and my four children who at the time of this writing are seven, eight, twelve, and thirteen years of age. I may have done terrible things, and I deserve my fate. But I am not totally vicious the way they paint me, and the way I paint myself.

The confession I have written superceeds any other I provided. If my attorney is successful and my sentence is commuted to life, I will be an ongoing threat to the person who threatens to kill my family. Howsoever, I am caught "between a rock and a hard place," because if I tell the whole truth now, the appeal will certainly be denied. So I am allowing the lie to continue in order to save my own life, not just my family.

I am going to give the confession for safekeeping to you, under the seal of confession when you come to see me a few days from now. I place this letter here with instructions to share my confession with the authorities if at some time someone in my family feels threatened. I understand this may be useless and even stupid, but I don't know

what else to do and I am half crazy with fear of that boy! Still, I take
what steps I can. I have been a bad father, not caring for my children.
But I don't have to die a bad father.

I hope you are a good man who can keep a secret, and share my
story if that becomes necessary.

Sincerely,
Richard Eugene Hickock
Kansas State Penitentiary, Lansing
Prisoner Number 14746

Carlo and I both read quietly, maybe two or three times, then just stared at the document.

"What boy?" I finally asked. "And he threatens to kill Hickock's family? I take it you got this from Victor Santangelo?"

Carlo scowled. "It must be bogus," he said.

"Why do you think?"

"Look at the linguistics. 'Howsoever'? Bit of archaic elegance. Except for the several misspellings there's an articulateness here that's far beyond what I've known of Richard Hickock. It doesn't sound like the voice of Hickock as Capote portrays it. Look, he spelled 'supersedes' wrong, but it's a marvel that the word is in his working vocabulary. Keep in mind I've read the book as well, and saw the movies, too, not only because everyone did, but because I was working at the same prison that executed these men. Smith's style has a poetic lilt to it when Capote quotes him, but Hickock has the voice of a . . ."

"Depraved, ignorant savage?"

"Yes. That."

"Well, the interesting thing is that this style actually matches other letters Hickock wrote in prison, which makes the letter feel more authentic. Plus you got it from Santangelo. Santangelo must have got it from Hickock and tucked the letter behind the sketch for safekeeping." I felt goose bumps rising on my forearms. "Oh my God, I know someone who knew someone who was one of the last people to speak with Hickock just before his execution."

"Santangelo is definitely the priest who visited Hickock. He told me about it, but he didn't break the seal of confession. Like I said, when it came up in conversation I didn't tell you because I wanted to hand you the framed sketch at the same time."

I felt myself stutter over my next words, aware of what they might mean. "He must have had the confession, too. He didn't give it to you?"

"No, he didn't. At least not that I can remember. There might have been something else."

"Like what, exactly?"

"I don't know. Some other information he said he couldn't share. But he would send me things from time to time. Books. Articles he'd written that he wanted me to comment on."

"And you've never wondered about what information he might have on the Clutter case? Probably in the top five homicide cases of the twentieth century? Up there with Charles Manson and Jeffrey Dahmer?"

"Oh, Brigid, stop. Not everyone in the country continues to be obsessed with the Clutter case. It happened when you and I were both kids. When Vic gave this to me it was about fifteen years after the events and he might not have remembered he put the letter with it. And neither of us were thinking about the case." The corner of Carlo's mouth went up on one side as he said, "I wasn't thinking about much of anything except Jane."

"It had to mean something to Santangelo. Otherwise why give it to you?"

"Vic didn't own much. Vow of poverty and all that. Maybe this was all he had to give. He said he was giving this sketch to me as a symbol of his trust that I was an honorable man." Carlo hung his head a bit and shook it. "He was wrong about that, about my being honorable." Carlo's face took on an expression that was at odds with his general placid philosophical bent. You could tell there was a hurt that would last forever. He said, "That crisis of faith that I told you about, that made me leave the priesthood, it doesn't gnaw at me in the way of some grievous sin, but it's still a failure. You see, Brigid," and I knew this was serious because he used my name, "it was all about Jane."

My thoughts had been rushing hither and yon while we were talking, but now they lighted on what Carlo had said a minute before, about not being so interested in a fifteen-year-old case because he was only caring about Jane. I suddenly remembered the night I sat listening to my dad's friends talk about the Walker murders, how I wanted to say *stop talking*, but could not. We don't change much.

"This is going to be about sex, isn't it?" I said sweetly, feeling my face turn a lovely shade of green.

Thirty-six

Just as lightly, not suspecting that I really cared, Carlo said, "Isn't it always?"

I felt my chest rise and fall more rapidly with what I might be about to hear. But hadn't Carlo listened to everything about my past that I was willing, that I needed, to share, no matter how gruesome? There were likely pictures in his head that would never leave. I had to be willing to carry the same kind of pictures, though in his case I imagined they would be lovely, lovelier than any he had about me. In at least two cases, pictures of me included blood. I suppose this is what they mean when they talk about a late marriage and the baggage that comes with it.

The picture of wedding rings in a bedside table drifted into my mind again. "This story seems important," I said, using a blander statement than the accusatory *Why haven't you told me this story?* It struck me that I hadn't realized I'd been anticipating it these past two years, like waiting for what comes after "shave and a haircut." There was something big to know, and those rings were confirmation. "So tell me."

He shook his head, and examined my face the way he does, and seeing what I didn't want him to see, said, "I've never told you this story because it wasn't mine to tell. Jane got into some trouble, so it's her story. Telling it to you feels . . . it feels disloyal."

"No." I turned more in his direction, putting one of my feet on the crossbar of his chair but not touching him. I kept my face still so he couldn't see the hurt that his excuse had caused, that he would keep a secret from his living wife in order to stay loyal to his dead one. She was dead, for Pete's sake. Why would she care more than me? There was something fucked up about that. "You could have kept it to yourself before you started. Now you have to tell the story."

He looked alarmed at that, like a suspect who knows he's been found out. Then he started in an unexpected direction, not one with hearts and flowers and a slightly prim love story like I would expect about him and Jane.

Carlo said he knew that when it came to working with inmates there was a delicate balance between being helpful and being a patsy. Carlo understood getting conned. He knew all about it from watching the grief his brother, Franco, had put his parents through. But Jane hadn't had this counsel.

"Shortly after my work at the prison was finished, she called and asked to see me. She was crying. Oh, how she cried."

I don't cry much. "It just rips your heart out when they cry," I said, but Carlo was too wrapped in his memories of dear innocent Jane to notice the irony.

"So what did they do to sucker her?" I asked.

"I can't remember all the details. Some routine setup, a prisoner asking her to mail a letter for him, which—"

"Is verboten even though it seems like such a harmless thing," I finished for him.

"It escalated slowly, with this and that little favor, you know how it goes."

"I do."

"Until he said he'd turn her in if she didn't have sex with him."

"The poor lamb," I murmured rather than *I cannot believe she fell for that.*

Carlo, clueless to my subtext, continued, "Jane asked me what she should do, and I told her I'd go with her to tell everything to the warden, and vouch for her. She did that, and was told she couldn't volunteer at the prison anymore, but they wouldn't press any charges."

"Thank God," I said.

Carlo told me how they went out to lunch after that, and then lunch again, and then dinner. At first Jane asked him to be her spiritual director, and they started talking about theology, but it always got off track somehow and went to what novels they were both reading, what movies they'd seen. Serious novels, serious movies, I assumed. No, not movies. *Films.*

"I bet she loved Italian food," I said, and went on before he could catch the snark in my voice. "So when did you actually become lovers? After you became a priest? Before?"

Carlo sighed. "About a month before my ordination. And after. We were lovers well into the time I had my own church. I couldn't stop, but Jane was a better person than I."

Now who's the sucker?

"At some point she said she couldn't go on that way, being secretive. But I tell you, Brigid. There was nothing sordid about it. Jane was my *grande passion*. At the time, I had to make a choice between God and Jane, and I chose Jane."

Of course he did. After all, Jane was a saint. It may be apparent by now that I am not.

If he could understand how I felt just now, he was too lost in his Carlo thoughts to see it. No matter what he *said*, what I *heard* was that a person only has one *grande passion* in their life, and that I was not Carlo's the way he was mine. I had to get us off this train of thought before the track ran out.

"Do you like fly-fishing?" I asked, assuming a negative on that.

"God, no. I don't even like anyone who does." He looked at me with an expression that clearly was not connecting my question to anything we'd been talking about. Maybe there were so many photos of him and Jane having fun that he had forgotten this one. Or maybe, I thought hopefully, the trip was such a disaster that he'd forced it from his memory.

"I saw a photo of Jane when I was cleaning up the mess after the burglary," I said. "You were fly-fishing. I never took you for a sporting kind of guy."

He still wasn't warned. "Ah, that vacation." He turned his left palm up and pointed to his thumb. "See that scar? I caught a hook there." And smiling at the scar that he would always have, "I would have done anything for her," he said, clearly without thinking through his words before he spoke them.

That did it. The rings, the intellectual pet names, the shared ministries, the book she had written, her baking skill, for fuck's sake, the photograph with the laughing face that he would have done anything for, and then the *coup de grace,* a tragic death. I had the whole picture now. Carlo's *grande passion* had brought together romance, mutual faith, and loss, an almost combustible erotic combination.

I could tell that was the moment I lost my poker face, and he knew it because his face finally mirrored mine. There was nothing he could say, and he had the grace to realize this and move on to our original topic. There was nothing else to do. You can't apologize for a feeling.

Instead he said, "Vic was the one who had mentored me from the time I was an altar boy. He encouraged me to do part of my pastoral training at the prison. And he counseled me through the whole process of discovering whether my destiny lay with the priesthood."

I allowed him the truce for now. "Did he try to get you to stay in the church?"

"Not at all. He told me to follow my gut rather than my intellect. And I did. That sketch became a symbol of how much he honored my decision."

The mention of the sketch swung my attention back to Hickock's letter and its promise of more. "Is this all he gave you?"

"I'm not sure. I have so much garbage that I've never thrown out, and here you've just found the letter I never knew I had. So many years had gone by, with no one from Hickock's family contacting him, Santangelo probably forgot it was even there."

"You're telling me Santangelo didn't get the full import of what he had? Truman Capote made Hickock and Smith famous."

"Now we can say that. You take a parish priest from Kansas in the late fifties and there was a good chance he never heard of Truman Capote."

"Oh, come on."

"You come on. The country didn't use to be as small as it is now. Vic would likely have known about *In Cold Blood* at some point, and that might have been what made him think the sketch had some value, but that could be as far as it went. I didn't even think it was a big deal until now. Not all of us are true-crime aficionados like you are. And new confession or not, I think you'll agree it's a moot point that Hickock and Smith killed the Clutters."

I thought of all the stuff crammed into the closet in Carlo's library. "Are you absolutely sure you don't have the confession?"

"I don't. Or at least I don't think I have it."

Conflict forgotten for the moment, we both stood up at the same time and went to the library closet. He pulled out four large plastic tubs, spread them on the floor, and we sat down to go through them. I was glad I had shoved the photo of Jane way down on the side of the top bin, and hoped it wouldn't emerge. Though driven by wanting to see if Carlo had Hickock's confession, I didn't think I could bear to see Jane just now. *Out of sight, out of mind,* Mom would have said.

We pulled out stack after stack of articles typed on manual typewriters, and Xeroxes of sections of books he had been reading for one project or another, and syllabi of courses he had taught over the years . . .

"Oh, look," he said. "Here's one of my early sermons on the Transfiguration."

"Focus," I said. But then I remembered going through the papers just like this after the burglary And that made me remember Jeremiah Beaufort again.

I didn't altogether stop sorting through the papers, but at the same time I told Carlo everything I had found out about the man who had identified himself to us as Jerry Nolan. Everything. What he was in prison for. How his sentence was commuted. All his slipups. All my suspicions. Then there was one of those little leaps that made the nerve in my neck spark. Some might call it genius. Some might call it my continued failure to make the connection between Beaufort and Carlo.

"Perfesser. Could Jerry have seen the sketch the night he came for dinner?"

Carlo described that moment when they were both in the library and he had shown Jerry the sketch. How Jerry had appeared impressed by it, and said he remembered the case although he was a boy at the time.

Just a boy. I thought:

Beaufort had been the only person other than Carlo to know about the sketch.

Beaufort might know how valuable such a thing could be.

If our home had been the only break-in, and the sketch was stolen, Beaufort would be suspected.

Our house, and the sketch, may have been the true target.

"He's a criminal, and he's made some pretty stupid mistakes," I said after I'd spoken my thoughts aloud.

Carlo's eyes got that vacant expression they get when he thinks of something that, most of the time, has nothing to do with his current circumstances or whereabouts. "Bonhoeffer," he said.

"Bon-who-fer?"

Without getting up from the floor, like a boy he scooted on his butt back into the bookshelves and scanned one toward the bottom.

"How do you find anything in—"

He interrupted my question by pulling out a worn tome from the right side of the second-to-the-bottommost shelf, waved it at me like a victory flag, and flipped it open to the back, where he scanned the index, then to a different page. "Stupidity is a more dangerous enemy of good than malice," he read, and kept going. "One may protest against evil; it can be exposed, and, if need be, prevented by use of force." Here he looked up and nodded at me as if I represented said use of force. Then he looked down at the book again. "Evil always carries within itself the germ of its own subversion in that it leaves behind in human beings at least a sense of unease. Against stupidity we are defenseless." Carlo looked up at me and finished the quote by heart. "For that reason, greater caution is called for when dealing with a stupid person than a malicious one."

"What if the person is both stupid and malicious?" I asked.

"Then I believe you're screwed," Carlo said mildly.

I genuinely grinned, happy to feel as if we were back to how we always were. "Well, that was helpful. But the question is, what am I going to do?"

"Do?" he asked, his eyes still a little glazed with the thought of what he had been reading.

I kicked his foot with my own. "Hey, Perfesser. Snap out of it. Let's get back on the original topic, the possibility of Hickock's confession. What do you know about Victor Santangelo? Is he still alive by any chance?"

"If he is, he's over ninety. We kept in touch over the years. The last I heard he's living at St. Dominic's Abbey, near Tampa. I should call him sometime."

"Yes, you should. You should call him soon. Like right now? Now is a good time."

Carlo nodded. He's not the kind of person who goes instantly from thought to action. At the moment he looked like this was one of the things he would think about for some weeks, and then possibly forget as he thought about something more captivating. Also, in typical guy fashion, he wasn't one to stay in touch with friends. I could be the same way. If I had friends.

I snapped my fingers to get his attention again. "Is that a coincidence, Beaufort operating around the Gulf Coast before he went to prison?"

"Not so big a coincidence. It's not like there are Dominican monasteries all over the country."

"Still, all of this seems to be pointing to a single general location in Florida, that area between Tampa and Sarasota. Remember the Walker family lived outside of Sarasota. I could take a little field trip over there and find out more about this Jeremiah Beaufort and the circumstances of his arrest in Florida, and maybe how that connects to me. Also check out any links to Father Victor Santangelo at the same time."

I helped Carlo put all the papers back in the bins, and then he went out into the backyard to pull weeds from the gravel coating the ground. I knew him well enough to know that pulling weeds was what he did when he wanted to think.

For my part, I retreated into my office, my thoughts shifting back and forth between Jeremiah Beaufort and Jane in the smooth way that thoughts can. It was that thing where someone pops you in the jaw with their fist and for a brief time after the initial shock you're numb until the serious pain kicks in.

I was single for the first sixty years of my life, but I'm not totally unromantic. Like all single people I would sometimes wonder what it would be like to have a mate, to be in love forever with the same person, to be in sync. Then I knew too much about the world. Now I knew too much about Jane. I think overall I would have preferred not to have known how much he loved her. How funny that I had felt this way a couple of years ago, and over an incident much more critical to Carlo's and my relationship. I thought I'd gotten past that insecurity. Brigid Quinn, vulnerable. Did it ever stop? Do you ever just relax in a relationship? Why did things have to bubble up from time to time like ancient tectonic plates crashing against each other, sending little shock waves that weaken the land we think we live in? Was it Carlo's fault? Or was it Jane's? Or a combination of everything. Everyone. Me. Not being Jane.

The self-pity overwhelmed me once more, spreading through my chest like a balloon pressing the air out of my lungs. I felt so low I got down on the floor where my spirits were. But that was no good. The pugs, who had followed me into the room, took it as play rather than an expression of despair, which took most of the drama out. They threw themselves at my head until I laughed at myself.

Oh, grow the hell up, Quinn. You're sixty-five years old, for Pete's sake, and at some point you have to stop thinking like a teenager. Romance, my ass. Look at that poor Gloria Bentham.

When does your average insecurity become pathology?

There but for the grace—no. No, I don't need anyone else, not God, not nobody. I can manage on my own just fine. I made the decision in a flash, deciding I wouldn't love Carlo quite as much as I had to this point, because that much loving hurt too much. Yeah, that's the ticket.

I rubbed my cheek against the Berber carpet to get rid of any remaining Jane thoughts, got up off the floor, and called the Sarasota Sheriff's Office. I didn't have any trouble getting through to Detective Ian Meadows when I told the receptionist I might have some information about the Walker case.

Then I called St. Dominic's Abbey and asked to speak to Victor Santangelo. Dead, cancer, someone called Abbot Franklin said. When I asked

191

how long ago he had died, Franklin gave me a date about a month before. I told Carlo what I had discovered, and thought I could detect an almost physical shift in him as the past returned to grieve him. So many events happening simultaneously, I thought.

Thirty-seven

Gloria started to be something of a problem, moping around.

Beaufort had replaced the television the very next day after he'd broken it. And using some superglue he had been able to repair the figurine that had broken off the base of her favorite sculpture. It wasn't as damaged as he had thought.

Or maybe Gloria's moping had something to do with the Quinn woman's visit to their house. Maybe Gloria hadn't told him everything. Damn that Quinn woman. Whatever the reason, dinner was a little strained the night after their row, and the next one, too. So was the sex that Jerry attempted. Gloria was like a limp dishrag and it was her fault if Beaufort was, too. Without comment, without even saying good night, they gave up and rolled to their opposite sides of the bed.

Beaufort fell asleep quickly as he always did, but woke up to find the moonlight coming through the blinds. His cell in prison had been totally dark, and he hadn't gotten accustomed to the light that came into Gloria's bedroom. Tossing a couple of times, when he didn't hear light snoring, he realized that Gloria wasn't in bed. Gloria, who always slept like a rock.

He lifted his head slowly from the pillow and looked toward the bathroom, which was darker than the bedroom. Then outside the bedroom door he saw the bright pinpoint light of a small flashlight. It held steady like she was standing in one place in the living room.

Beaufort turned rather than pushed back the covers so they wouldn't make so much as a swishing sound, and slowly drew out his feet and put them on the floor. He didn't bother to put anything on but walked naked one step at a time into the living room, hugging the doorjamb and then the walls where the light of the flashlight didn't go.

Gloria must have been holding the flashlight between her teeth, because when he put his hands on her bare shoulders she screamed and the light dropped. Beaufort gripped her strongly enough so she couldn't bend down, and they stood there in the dark with what light there was spilling uselessly across the carpet.

"What are you doing up?" he said, pretending that she was just startled by his sudden presence.

"Just. Up," she said, having no excuse prepared.

He put his arms around her from behind, ran his hands down her arms and felt that she was holding something. His wallet, open, in one hand, a piece of paper in the other.

"What are you looking for?" he asked, taking both from her unresisting hands. Though it was dark with only the thin beam of the flashlight across the carpet, he knew the paper was the receipt with the DiForenzas' phone number written on the back.

When he put it back in the wallet and bent to retrieve the flashlight, Gloria ran. She stubbed her toe against something in the dark. He could tell that by the way she stumbled and yelped. It slowed her down but she was still able to get into the bedroom and lock the door before he could reach her. That was stupid, trapping herself that way. Beaufort remembered other women in their bedrooms. No way out.

In another decade he might have pulled the phone line out of the wall. Unfortunately, there were now cell phones, and Gloria kept hers on her bedside table. Beaufort hoped she wasn't doing anything stupid in there.

"Honey, let me in. I'm sorry I scared you."

"Oh, no problem, I'm okay."

"You locked the door. Open it up so we can talk."

"Okay, sorry. I'm coming."

But of course she didn't come unlock the door. He considered trying to break down the door, but flimsy as those things were he didn't think it would be so easy. He remembered how they usually put those tiny wrenches at the top of the doorjamb in case you have to get in and the door is locked from the inside. He was just tall enough to run his fingers along the top of the door until he felt the thin piece of metal shaped like an L. The wrench had likely been there when they built the place, and it was still there.

He wasted no energy being silent about it, but jammed the wrench into the lock, felt the internal lever give, and opened the door.

She was being stupid in there. Gloria held her phone, which in the dark room illuminated the fear on her face. Her thumb, shaking, hovered above it, ready to summon help.

"You said you didn't go to her house for dinner!" Gloria yelled. Good golly, could she yell when she wanted to.

Beaufort raised his hands palms out as he would to a skittish colt if he actually knew that much about horses. "Gloria. Babe. I didn't."

"I never said she said you did!"

"Did what?"

"Go to her house for dinner!"

Beaufort forced himself to walk smoothly and without apparent haste to the other side of the bed where she stood. He took the phone from her hand, and looked at it. The display read NEW LIFE. She wasn't about to call the cops, but her therapist, life coach, what have you. He put his arms around her as if to comfort her. Her body was slick with her sweat and she slipped his grasp but didn't run again.

Beaufort turned on the bedside lamp and sat on the edge of the bed, smiling now that the crisis was past, no real damage done, and they were having this argument in the nude. He pulled the sheet over his groin. "Honey, sit down a second."

Gloria took the housecoat she always left at the end of the bed and put it on. Then she sat as far away from him as she could without it looking like she was doing so.

"I'm sorry I was upset," he started. "I was upset that you were going through my wallet in the middle of the night. You would be upset, too. Why did you do that?"

Gloria thought about it. "I was . . . thinking about how that woman came over and you said that she was lying about you going over there for dinner. But she never told me you were there for dinner. And I couldn't stop thinking about that. I wanted to see if you had her telephone number or something in your wallet. I, I love you."

He didn't say *I love you* back this time, it was too pathetic, and too late. "Well, that was a real spunky thing to do, going into my wallet. But I have to say, somebody who loves somebody doesn't do that. And doesn't feel like they need to call their shrink in the middle of the night," he said.

"I—" She had started to say she hadn't done that, and then gave up. "I was s-scared."

"Now why would you be scared of me? I told you I would never hurt you. And I never will."

Gloria didn't have an answer for that.

Beaufort said, "Why were you looking in my wallet? Was there anything interesting in there?"

"I didn't see anything."

"You didn't see what was on that piece of paper?"

She looked at him as if trying to gauge whether admitting it would get her into more trouble. Then she shook her head, cautiously. "No. You grabbed me before I could look at it."

She was a lousy liar. She was lying and he knew it. She knew that what was written on the piece of paper was a telephone number, and if she called it she'd know that at least one of the people living there was that Quinn woman. But chances are, even if she had seen it, she wouldn't have been able to memorize it.

"Well, you can believe it wasn't that woman's phone number. I did go over there, but they're really boring people and the husband had been pressuring me to look through his telescope. I got it over with and came home. I didn't tell you because I figured you'd be jealous. And look at you."

Gloria smiled her best, most trusting smile.

Beaufort looked at the time. Three A.M. He knew how to tell whether Gloria was still his woman, or whether he had to make other plans. He went to the dresser drawer that had been allotted to him, pulled out a T-shirt and shorts and put them on. Leaving the drawer open, he went to the closet for his suitcase and put it open on the bed. He packed his clothes slowly and neatly to give her time to think.

That's what she did, stand there watching him and thinking. It was a game of chicken they played in the night. But Beaufort won the game.

Gloria, defeated, spoke first. "What are you doing?"

"Clearly there are trust issues here, and I don't think it's good for me to stick around," he said. Trust issues. He was picking up more and more of the lingo of this new world.

She didn't beg him to stay so he pushed a little more, but kept his voice calm. "First you're nosing around in my computer. Now this?"

That did it. Rather than point out it was technically her hardware even if they were his searches, she all but fell to the floor and hugged his ankles. "Jerry, please don't go." It went rapidly to crying after that.

"Have I ever struck you?" he asked, and his tone was aggrieved. "Have I ever so much as laid a finger on you in anger?"

"No! You've been great!" she protested.

"Then don't embarrass yourself. You'll feel lousy about it tomorrow."

"I'm sorry. I'm so sorry. It's my fault, I had no business looking in your wallet. I'm sorry."

"Honey, nothing has happened. I moved in for a while and now I'm moving out. I didn't take anything from you that you didn't want to give, am I right?"

Gloria nodded, still sobbing and not bothering to wipe away the tears.

Beaufort was glad to not move out. Right now he didn't think she would do anything. What could she do? And on what grounds? So far he hadn't committed any crimes. It wasn't a crime to be an emotional freeloader and he had been careful not to step over any lines, never stole anything from her. Never even bruised her, though he had come to think that wouldn't be a deal breaker for her. She was pretty much his.

She followed him to the door, where he stepped into the shoes he always left in the front hall at her request. He had always hated doing that but he never objected. She tried to go into his arms, to let him feel her nakedness under the nylon material that covered it. Beaufort put down his suitcase, held her to him, and said, almost tenderly, "I wouldn't tell anyone else about this. Not even your life coach. You wouldn't want anyone to know."

She would know what he meant. She wouldn't want anyone else to know her shame. Her desperation. Fags, junkies, lonely women. They were all the same, willing to do anything for a little love.

For now he decided to stay.

Thirty-eight

When the framer was finished with it, and Carlo presented it to me with pride and a kiss, I would have hung the sketch of Dick Hickock in a place of prominence in the living room, but I realized there are lines you shouldn't cross. So I put it on the wall next to my desk and admired it there. I imagined Smith doing it from memory while sitting in his cell on death row. The eyes were almost laughing, and the mouth wasn't grim, a man in easier times. *When were you?* I thought to the picture. *Was this before or after you killed the Walkers? Because you did kill the Walkers, didn't you, Richard Eugene Hickock?*

The sketch would have been a magnificent gift by itself, but that letter had turned the sketch into what felt like a treasure map. The thought that Carlo and I were likely the only ones, besides Victor Santangelo, who had evidence of a new confession stirred up as nothing ever had my old excitement in the Walker case.

I had spoken to Carlo about my plan to visit Meadows, see what I could find out about the mysterious confession, maybe go up to St. Dominic's and talk to Abbot Franklin about whether Victor Santangelo had left any effects. No matter how confidential a confession was I couldn't see him throwing out a historical document. At the same time I could do a little checkup on Jeremiah Beaufort in old records of the sheriff's department.

Carlo was being very gentle with me, like I might be troubled about what he'd told me about his relationship with Jane. He kept giving me these looks, but we didn't speak of her, and how she had become so much more than just a ghostly presence with culinary skills. No, I had my feelings well in hand. I didn't even want to look at their wedding bands to see if there was something engraved inside. I was big-girling all over the place.

You want me to confess? Okay, God's honest truth. Of course, yes, I was going to Sarasota to see what I could dig up on Jeremiah Beaufort. And while I was there I'd talk to Meadows, too, about him and his investigations into Hickock's and Smith's DNA. But I also needed to get away for a bit, to wrangle my feelings for Carlo.

I need to be perfectly clear here, and forgive me if I'm repeating myself but that's post-menopause for you. It wasn't Carlo leaving the priesthood that stuck in my craw. It wasn't even about him boffing Jane; I wouldn't care if he'd done it in one of the church's pews. I'm not a self-righteous prude. This was sheer jealousy over another woman, didn't matter whether she was living or dead. Why oh why couldn't it have ended in divorce rather than death. I would have felt better. Jealousy, simple but hardly pure.

I thought about this. Okay, I didn't just think, I obsessed about it, and wished there was someone I could talk to about girl stuff. A female friend? I had one once but that hadn't worked out so well.

Sigmund? He wasn't so good at relationships himself. Plus I knew him well enough that I knew what he would say if I told him I was feeling like a second-string wife. What he would tell me:

Try not to think about it.

The stinking fact that was smacking me in the face like a rotting mackerel was that if I couldn't talk to Carlo about something, I was pretty much alone.

But then I realized I had been alone for most of my life. I didn't need anybody.

• • •

Instead, I focused on things that couldn't threaten the equilibrium of my marriage. "I want to draw out Beaufort, and I'm trying to decide if it's better to tip my hand and let him know I'm going to be in that area 'asking some questions,' or whether it's wiser to go first, see what I find out, and then surprise him," I said.

"That's your expertise," Carlo said. He seemed to have lost interest.

It was the afternoon before my trip to Sarasota, and I had an early flight the next morning. I made a decent dinner, chili, something I could count on because I'd made it before. But something drove me to do things I hadn't tried since the earlier days of our marriage. I opened one of Jane's cookbooks that were usually out of sight in one of the kitchen cupboards, and rather than choose something at random, I paged through until I found a page with a spot on it. Something she had made for Carlo, I was sure of it. Strawberries in a meringue cloud.

Was I doing this to, in a way, thumb my nose at Jane's ghost by summoning her? Or did part of me want to watch how Carlo responded, what other memories the dessert would reveal?

While a small voice in my head kept telling me to have some self-respect, I set about making the meringue clouds. My goodness, they really did look like little clouds. I put the pan in the oven and closed the door.

Felt satisfied.

Remembered that I had neglected to add sugar. That couldn't be good.

I took the pan out of the oven, scraped all the meringue into a bowl, added the sugar, and remixed it. I was feeling less satisfied as I spooned the white crap onto the cookie sheet again, and put it back in the oven.

When they came out, they didn't look bad at all.

The nights were chilly now even at our elevation, and Carlo made a fire in the pit on the back porch. We sat there wearing sweaters, getting extra warmth from the hot chili. We didn't talk much. We had already talked out all the logic behind me going to Florida, how Hickock's letter had me interested once again in the Walker case and how I could kill at least three birds with one stone, showing the letter to Meadows to see if he had any leads on where the confession might be and what it might have to do with the Walker case, finding more about Jeremiah Beaufort's activity in Florida, and visiting Abbot Franklin. No, around 5:30 P.M. we were just a couple of old farts eating chili out of cracked ceramic bowls. No candles, no white tablecloth, no fancy dress. No romance. Who needs it?

Denial is highly underrated.

When we had finished the chili I took in the bowls, told Carlo to stay put because I had a surprise, and pushed two of the clouds onto their own dessert plates. I was glad the meringue didn't break apart when I pushed them. That should have been my first warning.

"Want coffee?" I yelled through the open back door.

"No thanks," he yelled back.

Romance, ha. Better this way.

I took the plates out to the table and set his down with a flourish. I admit that I watched his face to see if I could tell whether he thought of Jane. Why did I do any of that? Why would I do that to myself?

He didn't look nostalgic for times and loves past, if there is a look for that. After commenting that it looked really good, he picked up the dessert fork and applied it to the meringue.

The meringue didn't budge. I thought back about how I had mixed the stuff twice, once without sugar and then after I had added some. Does that do something bad?

It's rare when dessert calls for an executive decision. Carlo stood, picked up my plate and his, and headed inside the house. When I walked into the kitchen the garbage disposal was running, but it sounded like it was losing the race. I flicked off the switch and carefully extracted the meringue from the disposal. Carlo held open the lid of the garbage bin where he had thrown the other.

"Is that a hint I should give up cooking?"

"No, I'm trying to show you different people are gifted at different things. And that you should stop trying to bake things."

My mouth going, as usual, to a point from which there would be no return, I asked, "Well, then, what am I good for?"

Carlo stood there, processing, possibly wondering how we got from a bad dessert to an existential dilemma.

"See, there's an example," I said. "I impulsively open my mouth and things spill out, but you, you think it all through before answering the question 'how are you.' For me most of life is like, like the garbage disposal switch. On. Off. Alive. Dead. Good. Bad. I like action movies and you like art films."

"I actually enjoyed *Guardians of the Galaxy*."

"You're a man of deep faith and I'm an atheist."

"I acknowledge if there is a God, She's got a lot of explaining to do."

"You're a Democrat and I'm a Republican."

Now he paused. And leaned back against the kitchen counter. He said, "You're a Republican?"

"Aargh!" I said.

"Seriously. Who did you vote for in the midterms?"

I slammed the top of the garbage bin down on the travesty that had been the meringue shells. "How the fuck did we end up together? And why do I feel like you're committing adultery?" I asked, feeling grief in my voice, and mentally kicking myself for talking like every woman in every romantic comedy I'd ever endured.

Carlo looked at me longer than anyone normally does in a conversation, before saying, "Adultery?"

"You said you didn't want to be disloyal to Jane. Is that how I make you feel?"

Again he paused longer than normal people do, at least the ones in my family when there's an argument in process. This was possibly why Carlo and I never argued—it took too long and we'd both get bored. Then he frowned, and stared, and processed some more, and finally said, "I think we may have a misperception," as if he were disagreeing with an academic colleague over some complex point. But then he bent down and swept me into his arms, so unexpectedly I couldn't think about resisting.

"Your back," I warned, relishing the thought of him hurting himself.

"You're not that heavy," he said.

"I'm small, but I'm dense," I said.

With that less than erotic exchange, he carried me all the way into the bedroom and put me down on the bed as if I was breakable.

"Just like a man," I said, nursing my resentment with full-on gender bias while curious about what would come next. "You think sex solves everything."

"No, I don't," he answered. "I promise you, this isn't about sex."

Sentimentality is out of fashion, so instead of letting myself feel, I reached playfully for him. If that's how he wanted to go, who was I to turn down an orgasm?

"Right. So tell me, what am I gifted at?" I asked. "This?"

He drew a sharp breath. "This and that." He sighed.

"Oh. That."

Then he said, in a tone of voice that said we were having any old conversation, almost as if he was talking quietly and solemnly to himself, "Come, Madam, come, all rest my powers defy, / Until I labor, I in labor lie."

While he whispered those lines he was gently unbuttoning my blouse. He had never spoken to me in poetry before. Was it part of his nature that he thought I wouldn't have understood? That I would laugh, or wasn't intellectual enough? How would Jane have responded? I struggled to keep Jane out of the bed.

"That's hot," I said, still guarding myself with detachment.

He didn't answer immediately, his mind on other things. More curious than aroused, I helped with a slight rise of my hips so he was able to pull off my jeans, and then I watched him next to the bed, doing the same, slipping off his jeans, leaving his shirt on but unbuttoning it the way he had unbuttoned mine.

"Want more?"

I shrugged.

"You're going to have to tell me you want more."

"More, please," I said, but still playfully.

He lay down beside me, his fingers roaming as he whispered, "License my roving hands, and let them go, before . . .

behind . . .

between . . .

above . . .

below."

This time I was the one to catch my breath. I lifted my chin and closed my eyes. I lost the contact of his hands. Then I sensed more than felt him over me, but while I anticipated what would come next, he stayed still.

"Brigid," he said. "Open your eyes."

I did, and found his face close to mine, his own eyes staring into me as he started to move. "No, keep them open," he said in response to my natural reaction. "Keep them on mine."

"It's hard." I smiled. "To keep my eyes open."

Instead of kissing me he rubbed my nose gently with his own.

"Open your eyes, my love," he said softly.

And when I did, he repeated, "Keep them on mine."

"Why?"

"Because, my only Brigid, this is what it's about. I want to assure you. I want you to know for once and for all, that when I'm making love to you, I think of no one but you." His eyes, wide open in mine, were deep, and dark brown, and true.

"And at every other time," he said, "I see no one but you."

I trusted him, because what else can you do? "Okay," I said. "Now can it be about sex?"

"Okay."

Then the conversation ended.

His head resting on my belly. My heart feeling safer than it had felt in a while.

"Who were you quoting before?"

"John Donne. A sixteenth-century rogue turned Anglican priest."

I said, "I never knew poetry that old could be that sexy."

"Yes, unfortunately we're still living with the fallout from the Victorian era. But enough of the small talk. I'm so sorry I hurt you. I wish I could go back and not hurt you."

"I admit, you could have lived a long and successful life without telling me all that."

"I know you won't believe this, but you're nothing like her, and that's a good thing."

205

I noted that at this point he wouldn't even risk saying her name. "Why is it good?"

"Without being disloyal to her memory, I think I can say that when you're in a relationship for a long time, you understand why bubbles are made to burst."

"Please. You don't have to try—"

"Too bad you don't like sci-fi much," he continued. "There's an old *Star Trek* episode where Mr. Spock says, 'You will find that having is not altogether so good a thing as wanting. It is not logical, but it is often true.'"

His struggling to make it better, and with a *Star Trek* quote no less, was only making me incredibly sad. That to some extent, in order to love me, he needed not to love Jane. I managed to say, "So much for grand passions."

"Yes. Are you sure you'll be safe?" he asked, rapidly switching gears so as not to restart the argument.

"I'm sure. Just promise me you won't let that man, whatever his name is, inside the house."

Carlo promised.

"Now tell me," I said. "What is my gift?"

"I'm sorry?"

"You said I couldn't bake, but that I had my own gift. What am I gifted at?" Grabbing hold of my old jokey self, I reached out and put a finger on his lips. "And before you speak, you better come up with something better than I've got a great ass."

Carlo stayed quiet, and I thought I might have maneuvered him into a corner, but it was only that philosopher habit of his. He was thinking about the words to express his thought as seriously as if the question had been asked at a conference with four hundred people in the audience. "Dr. DiForenza, does your wife's primary quality lie in her ability to bring you to orgasm?"

He finally rolled over to his left side so our eyes met once more. I tried to match his gaze, but I was still the first one to look away. He said, "Sex is terrific, but you. You take all the pretentiousness and posing of the world, even mine, and smack it down with a single look. You're an original, Brigid Quinn DiForenza. You're such an original that I confess I've sometimes feared that you would grow bored with this tired philosophy professor and leave me for someone who could offer you more . . . danger. And, forgive the cliché, I hope to God I die first, no matter from what disgusting and painful disease, so I never have to know a life without you in it."

Thirty-nine

Beaufort had called the house while the Quinn woman was taking a shower, awfully convenient for his purpose. Carlo had answered the phone, and Carlo was no match for his brains.

Beaufort had said he was calling to invite the two of them out for dinner. It had been meant to show that he acknowledged Gloria as his live-in, what they used to call a "significant other" and what they now called "partner," which he discovered from hearing the term used that it could mean gay or straight. It was also to quiet down Gloria, who appeared to be less and less trusting of what he might have going on with the Quinn woman.

Beaufort had thought he could detect some new hesitancy in Carlo's voice as soon as the other man knew it was him on the line. He congratulated himself, that he could read people without even seeing their face.

"Gloria, my partner, I mean, she's a little shy," he had said. "I thought it would be good for her if the four of us could meet for dinner. You're so easy to talk to. Say, tomorrow night?"

"Um . . . Gosh, Jerry. I'm sorry, but Brigid will be . . . away?"

"Away? Where's she going?"

There had been a pause in which Carlo obviously tried to lie, and failed to some degree. "Tampa? Area?" he added, the uptick at the end of each word making it sound more like a question than an answer.

"When will she be back?" Beaufort had asked, and then so as not to sound prying, said, "So we can get a date on the calendar."

But then there had been some sort of commotion and Carlo had welcomed someone who'd come in that didn't sound like Brigid. Carlo said he would have to call Beaufort back. Beaufort had said good-bye and hung up the phone, putting two and two together to come up with the realization that Quinn was on to him, though how that could be he didn't know. All he had known was that "Tampa" must mean she was going to talk to Detective Ian Meadows, and that had been enough to get him on the phone with Yanchak.

Once this was all over he had to take care of Gloria. Over the last few days she hadn't seemed as perky as she had been at first. He'd had to put her in her place that night when he caught her going through his wallet, right? You'd think she would have gotten over it by now. Maybe flowers were getting a little old. Some Russell Stover's maybe? Or even a trip up to the Grand Canyon. She said she'd been there, but he'd never seen it. They could take Achilles.

As for wondering what to do about getting rid of Brigid Quinn, it looked like she was doing it for him.

If there had been any more possibility of talking, Gemma-Kate spoiled it. She had let herself into the house with a stack of books in her arms yelling (at least yelling insofar as Gemma-Kate is capable of expressing her emotions) something I couldn't quite hear.

I had left the bedroom door open when I went to take a shower, but Carlo, who had put his jeans and shirt back on, was in the living room and knew to close the door. I thought I heard the phone ring, but found the pugs trapped with me and barking madly to get out to Gemma-Kate, though again I couldn't imagine why. They must know something about her that the rest of us do not, I realized. By the time I had dressed and come out, Carlo had poured three glasses of tawny port and was listening to GK like his life depended on it. How strange for me to think of it that way.

Now much more her subdued self, when Gemma-Kate saw me she halted the conversation to ask, "What's with the surveillance equipment? If you were any more fortified you'd have drones bombing you for potential ISIS intelligence."

"Too bad about inheriting the Quinn sarcasm," I said. "How did you get here and why did you come?"

"Uber," Gemma-Kate said. "Uncle Carlo says you're going to Florida tomorrow, so I'll stay here and you can drop me off in the morning on the way to the airport." She sat on the couch barricaded with two pugs, at least seven books, and some thick manila folders. "I need to talk to you about *In Cold Blood*," she said, answering the second part of my question.

"You told me last week you read it. So what's the big epiphany?"

Gemma-Kate shot me a look intended to wither, a special look for aging aunts. "I didn't just read *In Cold Blood*. I read all of Capote's works, autobiographies, critical analyses, and whatever was online in archives. Dad helped me get access to the police reports from Florida, too. Capote got a lot of it wrong and I can't tell whether he did it on purpose or was duped by Perry Smith. I'm totally obsessed."

"You've done more research than I ever did. Did you find out anything new about the Walker family murder?" I asked. "We know they killed the Clutters, but it's the Walkers who're still the mystery. That's the important thing."

Gemma-Kate shook her head no and sipped her port with a deflated air of regret. "Maybe you can make her understand," she said to Carlo. "I'm not sure I have the energy."

Well, that was snarky.

Carlo thought. Gemma-Kate seemed fine with the length of time he was taking. Feeling the post-sex munchies, I took the opportunity to get out a tumbler and spoon myself a generous helping of Cherry Garcia, then took it to my chair where I poured my glass of port over it. By the time I stirred the concoction into a milkshake, Carlo was ready to talk.

"Here's an example of what Gemma-Kate was telling me before you came in," he said. "She says Hickock and Smith told Capote they took forty dollars from the Clutter house. That was in their confession as well. But the prison archives show, in a post-conviction hearing for clemency, Hickock admitted they took over a thousand dollars."

"No shit? That's a huge difference," I said, letting the ice cream melt on my spoon and drip back into the glass. "It would account for how they got the money to travel to Mexico and from LA to Miami and back to Las Vegas before they were caught. In those days a grand would do it." Then I put the glass down, got up from my chair, and went over to the couch because I could see dozens of pink stickies protruding from the pages of my book. I opened it. "You underlined my first edition!"

Ignoring me, Gemma-Kate went to the fridge, got out the container of Cherry Garcia, popped off the lid with her thumb, grabbed a tablespoon that was in the dish drainer, and started eating out of the container, all without losing her train of thought as she came back to the couch.

"And what about Smith changing his confession to take responsibility for all the murders, and Hickock agreed to it, and no one, not a single person, ever pressed him on why. Why did he take responsibility for killing all four people?"

When I heard her mention a confession I gave up on expressing outrage over the desecration of my book and went to fetch the sketch from my office and the letter from my carry-on. I put them on the coffee table in front of her. "You get a sticky note anywhere near these and you die," I said.

Gemma-Kate gazed first at the sketch and then at the letter, and then at me with all her questions in her eyes. I'll be damned if she didn't lose her composure for the first time ever, her voice trembling as she said, "Why didn't you show me this when I was here the first time?"

Carlo explained that he wanted to surprise me with the sketch as an anniversary present, and that we didn't know about the letter until the framer found it.

"Do you know what this means?" she asked.

I was enjoying too much breaking through her usual cool lack of affect to let the moment go. I let her dangle there before saying, "With you coming in the door without knocking I'm thinking it means I need to have the locks changed before your uncle Carlo and I want to make love again."

Gemma-Kate gazed at the letter the way some people would look at a sliver of the true cross. "That does it. I'm writing a book. Do you have the confession?"

"That's one of the reasons I'm going to Florida tomorrow, to talk to the detective who talked to the priest."

Like a child hearing that her parents were going to leave her with the babysitter while they went off to Disney World, Gemma-Kate's plaintive cry startled the pugs from their slumber. "Let me come!"

On top of the cry Carlo said, "That's right, Gemma-Kate's starting in about this business made me forget. While you were in the shower Jerry Nolan . . . whatever his name is . . . called."

"About what?"

"He asked if we wanted to go out to dinner with Gloria and him."

"What did you say?"

"I said I thought you were going to Florida?"

"Oh, Carlo. No."

"I was taken off guard."

I said to Gemma-Kate, "If Beaufort is guilty and it has to do with me, and if he has the connections he could have, he'll send someone after me. I can deal with that. But if he comes here to quiz Carlo—"

"Excuse me—" Carlo started.

"I should stay here until you're back," Gemma-Kate said, looking at me.

"Look, I hardly need—" Carlo started again.

"I could skip a few classes," she continued as if Carlo hadn't spoken.

I considered. "What if he takes you off guard again?" I asked, finally addressing Carlo.

Carlo spluttered. I didn't recall seeing him lose control before, except for that time he got upset with Gemma-Kate and me and threw a book at the wall. "I'm a six-foot-three man," he nearly bellowed.

Gemma-Kate finally acknowledged him. "As opposed to what, a short woman? Aunt Brigid, tell him how Dad trained me."

"You mean about breaking a collarbone? She can break your collarbone," I said to Carlo. "Or push the bridge of your nose into your brain. What's that bone called, GK?"

"Nasal bone."

"Duh."

"Oh for God's sake, she can't even reach it," Carlo shouted and then looked embarrassed at letting himself be in the same room as this exchange.

"That Nolan is short," Gemma-Kate said.

"I will not contribute to this inane reasoning. No, no, no, and no," Carlo said. "Look at me. Do I look like the child in *Home Alone*? Nothing is going to happen in the seventy-two hours you're away."

"I'm here already," Gemma-Kate said, as if that clinched it.

Carlo glared at me. It was a lot different from his gaze of just an hour before.

"Can I talk you into staying in the house?" I asked, thinking of all the security I'd installed.

He still looked sheepish but said, "With the doors locked."

"And you won't let Beaufort in no matter how he tries to con you? You don't know anything about me going to investigate my connection to him, right?"

Carlo didn't grace that with an answer. Against my better instincts, and in light of how adorable he was to me at that moment, I gave in.

Except for one last shot. Knowing how she thought, I said to Gemma-Kate, "Do not, do not get involved with this. Understand?"

Gemma-Kate tried to look innocent and failed. "Nobody hurts Uncle Carlo," she said, batting her round blue eyes.

"Nice act," I said, batting her back. "I hear you've tried anything with this guy and I'll report to the university that you lied about being an Arizona resident." Ah, threats, part of the Quinn family dynamic.

Forty

When I had spoken to Detective Meadows on the phone from Tucson, I had identified myself, and told him about my interest in the Walker case and about looking into drug cases on the west coast of Florida in the eighties. Had he been working there then? He said yes. I asked if he knew the name Jeremiah Beaufort, and he said no. He said he could tell me what he knew, but seemed to be more interested in the Walker case. He asked why I was interested. I said that I had a lead on a new confession purported to have been written by Richard Hickock shortly before his execution, and that I suspected the confession would show, if not the sole responsibility for the killing of the Walker family, then some involvement that he had not revealed.

Meadows didn't sound surprised about a confession, but he did say, "Written?" as if that was a piece of the puzzle he had not had. He wanted to know where the confession was, and I told him I didn't have it yet, and was wondering if he did. We danced around like that a bit, him sounding cagey, which was odd. Most investigators are happy to talk about cases, especially if they're cold and talking won't destroy the case. Maybe he was working on a book. Maybe my vague comments about a written confession intrigued him. Maybe it was just because he didn't know me from Adam. If I wanted to come to Sarasota, he said, he'd show me his files. And we could discuss the drug activity, too.

I flew into Tampa, picked up a rental car, and met Meadows at what appeared to be his favorite office, a stool at the end of the bar in the Pelican Pub. He told me there about how he, too, had read the request by Hickock to see a priest. "Asking for a priest felt suspicious, and I wondered if he might have confessed to killing the Walkers, thinking he could ask the priest to keep the seal of confession because he was slated to die anyway. So after the DNA testing came up with nothing, I tracked down the name of the priest through the prison chaplain from that time. His name was Victor Santangelo," Meadows said.

"I know," I said. He looked surprised, like he thought that was something only he knew. I explained my husband's involvement.

"You know someone who was tight with Santangelo?" Meadows looked at me like I was two degrees of separation from God. "I was certain he could give me something substantial. Unfortunately, he's dead. He was in the final stage of pancreatic cancer, and before I could get up to the monastery, he was gone."

"Carlo doesn't have anything of use," I said. "So with Santangelo's death you're at another dead end."

"I can see it in your eyes, you're suspicious that it wasn't natural. Even if he was very old and dying."

"Old, sick, what have you, the timing sounds a little too coincidental," I said. "Just before you could get up there to talk to him."

"I'm still going up. Maybe they know something up there."

"Like who Santangelo was in contact with other than you and my husband?"

"Bingo."

He looked at me expectantly, so I gave him what he was looking for. "But if there's something in writing . . ."

Meadows wiped his mouth with the back of his hand. "Changes everything." His eyes drifted off like he was calculating something. "Could be a very valuable thing," he said, and the way he said it made me think of eBay or a large advance on royalties, but Carlo would call that uncharitable. "Now what makes you think there's something in writing?"

I hesitated, but thinking of what I wanted from him in the way of history on Beaufort, I took Hickock's letter out of my tote and laid it on the bar, safely away from the condensation on his glass.

Meadows read the letter. Either he was a slow reader or he went over it several times before finally admitting, "I knew it. This is the biggest thing since I got Hickock's and Smith's bodies exhumed."

I nodded. "This could be the biggest thing ever."

Meadows was smart enough to not ask if he could keep the letter. I asked if I could join him when he went to visit the abbot. We talked a bit more about what he knew, and he corroborated the progression of Hickock and Smith down to Miami, then their stopping for a couple of days in Sarasota around the time the Walkers were killed. Then he finished his drink and we agreed to meet at his office the next day to go over the files he had. Yes, yes, he said, the drug cases, too. He offered to drop me off at my hotel, but I told him I had a rental car and would just as soon have another glass of wine to relax after the long flight.

So he left first. I watched him go out the front door and start to turn left to where I knew he had parked his car. I looked down at the check he had signed, and that was when I heard that old noise of a car backfiring, only this was three cars all backfiring in succession. My head jerked back up to see the rear end of a white car going past the front window, and Meadows thrown backward against the plate glass. He slid down the glass leaving a trail of blood. The window didn't break because Meadows had stopped the bullets. Must have been small-caliber semi-automatic and the assassin was a good shot.

I often wonder whether if I had left with him, I'd be among the dead now, too.

Forty-one

The following afternoon, Beaufort was on the phone with Yanchak again, though this time not as confident.

Yanchak was saying, "So you know already?"

"News travels faster these days. It was broadcast within less than an hour. How did you do it?"

"Didn't the news tell you?"

"All they know right now, at least according to the reports they gave CNN, is that shots were heard, no one else in sight at the time. All they showed on camera was blood on the window and the sidewalk."

"Drive-by. We had to set it up in advance to make sure it was clean."

"What do you mean set it up? Didn't I tell you the best place and time to get him was at that bar?"

"Excuse me, but I didn't want to take a chance. I had someone watching his movements. He was in his usual watering hole where we'd been scoping him out. It's off the beaten path. No one saw. Not even the bartender. Or if he did, he knows better than to talk."

"Are you sure he was dead when you left?"

"Oh yeah, got in a lucky head shot."

"Not exactly subtle. You're sure no one saw?" Beaufort asked.

"The only other patron in the place was some woman sitting at the bar. Maybe it was his wife. Maybe it was a stranger he was hitting on."

That old acid pang stabbed Beaufort's gut. "What did she look like?"

"Hard to tell. Small? You realize we're talking drive-by shooting, right? White ponytail. Yeah, ponytail is certain."

Beaufort took a deep breath and let it out with a yell. "You imbecile. That was the woman you were supposed to kill in Tucson. That job you botched. You were supposed to get Meadows before he talked to her. Now who knows what she knows?"

Would either of them have thought to discuss the Santangelo connection? Or not yet? Their conversation was clearly over, at least for now, if Meadows had been leaving the bar. If Quinn knew about the monastery, and went there, would the monks ID him? Probably not, they said there were pilgrims coming and going all the time, and he had never mentioned Santangelo specifically. But what if they said Santangelo had had a visitor besides Meadows? What if they described what Beaufort looked like? If they gave a good description of him she might make the connection with the man who befriended her husband. This was getting messy and had to be cleaned up before it got worse.

Beaufort said, "Listen, you need to finish this job, and finish it before she gets to the monastery."

"This is sounding a lot like you're ordering me around. I don't like that sound."

"If you had taken her out when you were supposed to, we'd never be in this spot."

"And I agreed to kill the cop in return. The deal is done."

"The thing is, I didn't kill a cop, you did."

"You idiot. If I go down, you go down as accessory to murder one, so stop threatening me."

For a few seconds, heavy breathing on both ends of the phone. Then they got their wits about them and went back to their corners.

"I want that woman dead," Beaufort said.

"And I've had it with you," Yanchak said. "I've put my neck out more than I should have already, and from here on, you're on your own."

And that was that. Beaufort disconnected, his mind darting from one idea to another like like a squirrel who couldn't remember where he left his nuts. Everything had been going so well. *Think,* he thought, *think.* The Quinn woman was nearly two thousand miles away and there was nothing he could do about her. But the evidence against him wasn't two thousand miles away, it was just around the corner.

All Beaufort had to do to be certain of that was remember the look on Santangelo's face when he had said the name Carlo. What he could do was finish what he had come here for, get Carlo to give up the confession, which Beaufort was certain he had, and then get out of town.

Forty-two

I had thrown myself off the bar stool onto the floor, yelling at the bartender and anyone else in the place to get low. Then I crawled across the floor to the door, and by the time I got there the sound of the gunshots had been gone for a while.

So I stood up and ran outside, wishing I'd been able to bring my gun. With a glance to recognize that I could no longer see the car that had driven by the bar, I knelt next to Meadows and put two fingers against the side of his throat while dialing nine-one-one on my cell phone with the other.

I screamed, "Officer down." And gave the location. Within a minute an ambulance and three squad cars arrived, but I had known it was too late. I told the officers who I was and how I had come to be at the bar with Meadows, both of which they could easily corroborate. But not all. If this had to do with me and Jeremiah Beaufort, or the Walker case after all these years, who knew who else might be in danger. Better to keep it vague, just an interest in his cold cases because I was ex-FBI, that kind of thing. I gave them my contact information and told them I'd be in town until the next day if anyone wanted to get in touch with me.

I thought about Meadows, dead. The only thing I had to connect his death to was that he was working this cold case, and that he was intending to visit the abbey. Who knew this? And what information might still be found there now even after Santangelo was gone? Could he have known something about Beaufort's drug deals, something that was serious enough to still get him in trouble? Was Beaufort's reach this far and this strong? That seemed unlikely after all this time, but Meadows's body told me otherwise. No, the monastery was the only lead I had. After the police let me go I checked into a Marriott in Sarasota, and called Carlo to reassure him that yes, though I had been talking to Meadows before he was killed, I was quite safe and Carlo shouldn't worry no matter what he saw on the evening news, and that I was going to call St. Dominic's to follow the only lead that Meadows gave me.

Brother Eric, who identified himself as the guest master, picked up and, when I asked, told me that Abbot Franklin was in prayer.

"This is very important. Please tell him that someone from the FBI is on the line, and needs to speak with him. It's urgent." I usually don't wave those letters around, seeing as how I'm no longer with the FBI, but I didn't have the time.

Brother Eric sounded a little aggrieved when he said that evening prayer was of the utmost importance to the abbot, and did I realize it was evening?

"If you won't do it, then please have Jesus tell him that Detective Ian Meadows was shot to death a few hours ago and I'm concerned that someone might harm the abbot himself."

Apparently I called it right and they weren't keen on that whole martyrdom thing.

"Abbot Franklin here," a deeper, older voice said, not trying hard to disguise a little irritation at the interruption to his prayers mixed with concern for the safety of himself and his monks.

I explained what had happened with Meadows and how I suspected it had something to do with him intending to visit the abbey. Again, I didn't at that point connect it to myself. "What can we do?" he asked, his concern crackling over the line.

"Tell me if you know anything about Victor Santangelo that might help me find out who did this," I said.

"I can't see what I could possibly know. All I can tell you is that

Detective Meadows called here to speak with him. Is that why you're calling, because you knew of that connection?"

"I did, and I think Meadows must have been on to something. I think he was on to someone so dangerous that Santangelo's death might not have been any more natural than his own."

"Victor . . . are you saying he was murdered?"

"I don't want to tell you anything that might put you in danger. How much can you trust the other monks in the abbey?"

Franklin couldn't help but laugh. "They've all been here for years. They're getting on. We haven't had a new brother in two decades. No, I can assure you these men can be trusted."

"Had to ask. What about some visitor? Did anyone call or come by asking about Father Santangelo? Wanting to see him?"

There was a too long pause, I gathered not because he couldn't remember that happening, but because he could all too well. When he spoke, it was with a cautious affirmative.

"Man? Woman?" I asked.

"A man."

"Did he give a name?"

"Funny, he might have said, but now I don't recall it. So many visitors come here, and names are the least important thing about them."

"And did he ask about Santangelo?"

"No. Well, I'm trying to remember, and we did talk about Father Santangelo when I showed him the infirmary, but I can't recall which of us brought it up. Mostly I was thinking he was one of those lost souls who hope to hide their demons under a robe. And the reason I remember him more than any other is that something about him made me uncomfortable. You'll think I'm odd . . ."

"Try me."

"I've known so many religious, and I think I can tell a vocation when I see it. With this man, there was no vocation. I felt there was suffering there, but not goodness. That's all I can say."

"And how long was it after his visit that Father Santangelo died?"

"Only a couple of nights. But do you . . ." His silence was only broken by a soft crying.

"I'm not suggesting . . . you said he was near death."

"But now that I think about that man? What might Victor's final moments have been like? He came to us for peace. And I couldn't give that to him. You must understand, nothing ever happens here. We go through our hours of the day as if the whole world is doing a frantic dance, and all that we do is keep time with the music. That we should have a visitor, and you should suspect that visitor, and the next day, these events are singular and all of them connected. Now what must I do? Should I report it? Should I have his body exhumed for an autopsy to see how he really died? Are there others here who might have recognized the killer and be in danger as a result? Tell me what to do!"

"I think what you should do is not jump to conclusions. Let me ask you one more question first. Did Father Santangelo ever speak about another priest named Carlo DiForenza?"

"Oh my goodness. Why do you ask that?"

"He's my husband. Did you know he left the priesthood and married?"

"Victor has spoken to me about this man at some length, about his life. You must be Jane. Victor thought the world of you."

A spark of annoyance, but nothing dies forever. "That was his first wife. She died about seven years ago, and I've been married for two years. Carlo said he called Victor some time ago."

"Yes, I know, that's when Victor told me about him. And that's not all. When we went through Victor's few effects after his death there was a sealed package with a note that it was to be sent to Carlo. It was practically the only thing he had, and I don't know what's in the package. I'm afraid I haven't gotten around to sending it yet. Shall I do that now?"

"No, I don't think we have time. And while I don't think anyone knows which hotel I'm in, I don't want to get out on the road and head in your direction in case someone is following me. Is there any chance we might meet in Tampa?"

"I can be there first thing in the morning." He sounded a little excited as his voice slipped into a Deep Throat impression. "Can you get to Temple Beth-El in Tampa without being spotted? The security is better there."

The next morning I called a taxi to pick me up and drop me off outside of a Macy's, and then called another taxi for the rest of the trip. There were no cars following. Now I was walking up the center aisle of the temple, toward an immense wooden ark that was the focal point. No statues, no pictures, stained glass with geometric designs. A man in a black suit sat facing away from me in the first pew on the right.

"Abbot Franklin?" I asked.

He stood and shook my hand when I introduced myself. Then brushed a hand over the arm of his jacket. "I came in disguise, you see," he said, apparently pleased with himself. "And I'm old friends with Rabbi Norwitz so he let me in. I thought this was all safest."

"Well done," I said. "Really well done."

"Now, before I give you—would you happen to have some identification?"

That was going a bit far, and he had no idea who Brigid Quinn really was, but I showed him my driver's license and he seemed contented. He handed me a nine-by-twelve manila envelope with a clasp and tape over the closing flap. From the look of the tape it didn't appear he or anyone had opened the envelope.

"Now what do we do?" he asked.

"Abbot Franklin, I'm coming to this late and I have no right to advise you. But if I were you, I'd keep this just between us for now. Let me do a little investigating and see what turns up. Don't even talk to the brothers about it, for their own safety. Can you do that?"

"I can." He sounded somehow absolved of sin and receiving his penance.

"Does Rabbi Norwitz care if I stay here a bit longer?" I asked.

"Are you Jewish?"

"You might say I'm everything and nothing."

He nodded as if he understood better than I did. Patted my hand and said, "They're Reformed. I'll let him know on my way out."

I eased up the yellowed and hardened tape that might have been applied over fifty years ago. If this thing was authentic, I would be the only person alive who knew the complete truth of what had happened. As I started to read, I could hear the voice of the writer in my head. The voice sounded true.

Forty-three

Hickock's Confession

First of all, I have to begin by saying that some of this is repeated from my official confession, but that is necessary. It is impossible to tease out the facts that are not yet known from the official story, some of which is true and some of which is a lie. What with the stories that Perry and I told to Agents Nye and Duntz, then the one to Agent Dewey, and then the official confessions we signed, and me telling my story to another journalist, and the one I wrote myself, and what was told to a man named Truman Capote who wrote what he says will be called *In Cold Blood* (he is very famous for other books) plus God only knows what he actually wrote . . . well, you get the picture. Now I am going to "tell it straight."

The letter attached to this account explains the purpose of me telling the whole truth now. I am putting it behind a sketch Perry did of me and giving it to the priest who is coming to hear my confession. This part will explain what really happened with the Clutter family in 1959, and also what I know about the Walker family.

Sometimes I think Perry took the chance because, if it goes into the book, it will be like a letter sent to the boy, sort of a love letter, that Perry is protecting him. I don't know what happened between Perry and the boy, but I want to go on record that I have always behaved as one hundred percent normal, not like a queer or as a pedophile.

But I should start closer to the beginning.

I met Perry in Leavenworth where we were cellmates for only two weeks. But it was then he told me he had actually killed someone in Nevada once, and I thought he would be a good partner in crime for this reason, that he seemed to be open to all kinds of possibilities, and not much of a conscience. I had never killed anyone, and did not think I could do it. I got paroled first, and talked Perry into meeting me shortly after, when he was released. That's how we hooked up, at a restaurant in Kansas City. It was there that I laid out the plan to get a car, drive across the state, rob the Clutters, and be back in Olathe in the same day so as not to make anyone suspicious. Perry agreed to the plan.

I had been working as a mechanic in an auto shop in Olathe near where I was living with my parents on their small farm. It was easy to borrow a car from that place, load up a shotgun I had, pick up Perry who had moved into a motel in town, and head out very early one morning.

Our destination was a small town outside of Garden City, four hundred miles away. This is where the Clutters were, and I was only thinking about the job. But Perry was thinking about Mexico. He talked and talked about what we would do in Mexico, what cities we would go to, as if the Clutters were just a stop for gas or food. I said would you please shut up about Mexico already and keep your mind on what we need to do tonight? He did not lose his temper at me the way he did sometimes, he just stewed.

We were about fifty miles west of Olathe and had a long ways to go. I did not relish the thought of Perry giving me the silent treatment for the rest of the trip. When you are doing a job together you need to be together. Well, within a few miles of Perry's silence we encountered the boy and the man, the boy waving wildly at us to stop. As we got close, I could see the man was old. He stood still next to the boy like a sad statue.

It is true that they were on the side of the road and flagged us down, and that I was against picking them up. But it is more complicated than the story Perry ultimately told. And it was not about bottles.

Because he had been giving me the silent treatment for so long, I was relieved when Perry finally spoke to me, but then it was to say let's pick them up. I said are you kidding me? Do you want witnesses who can say we are in this part of the state today? I kept driving while Perry stared at them as we went past, and then looked back with his head out of the window.

I thought that was that, but then Perry said pull over.

I kept driving, and said you are just doing this because I said negative things about Mexico. I promise I will take you to Mexico when we are done. We just have to focus on the job.

Perry said pull over or I don't go with you.

Oh, how I wish I had stuck to my guns and not given in to Perry. He talked me into bringing those two along, acting like it was a good deed and not re-venge for me waffling about going to Mexico. He said we would drop them off in the next town. I said that's Le Loup and he said that town is too small, let's take them to Emporia. I'll never read the book, and I suppose I'll never know for sure what Perry told Capote, but I'm not as stupid as they both think I am. I'll bet that happened a lot, that Perry came across as good while I came across as bad, even though it was Perry who started the whole mess that brought me to this place in my life, facing the gallows. I would not be sur-prised if somehow Capote helps Perry get life while I am hanged by myself. But I digress.

I backed up along the shoulder of the road and the boy and his grand-father got into the car. The boy said he and his granddad got kicked out of where they were living and were hitching their way from Pascagoula, Missis-sippi, all the way to an aunt's place in Colorado. The kid asked us where we were going and Perry almost told him but then I said Wichita because I saw it on a signpost we had just passed. The kid asked could we take him there instead but I said it was not on the way to Colorado.

Perry asked the boy how they managed to hitchhike so far, where did they sleep and how did they eat, etc. The boy responded that along the way they had been picking up bottles and turning them in for cash to buy food. He said the sides of the roads were covered with them because everyone threw them out the windows of their cars and no one cleaned up. There are some now, he said. You could see the sun glinting off the glass. Could we stop?

Again, I was very angry at this turn of events, and it felt like Perry was taunt-ing me when he said sure. So the three of them got out of the car and col-lected about two dozen bottles before they got back in. The grandfather was somewhat sick, but not sick enough to stay in the car. He helped a little.

Now the way Perry tells it is that all this happened much later, after Mexico and California and maybe even after Florida. I can't remember very well. But I do remember Perry made a whole lot more of the story, with a whole lot more bottles. He said he told Capote we must of picked up 1,000 bottles at 2 cents per. That got us twelve dollars and some change that Perry and I split fifty fifty with the kid and his grandfather. When we cashed the bottles in I was all for leaving the two of them at the quick stop, but they wanted to come with us further, and this is where Perry stopped telling the truth. He says we left them there. But we did not.

I need to make this very clear, that we picked up the boy and his grandfather <u>before</u> the Clutter murders, <u>not after</u>. But even that is nowhere near everything I have to tell.

About a hundred more miles down the road Granddad was coughing pretty hard and when I looked at him in the rearview mirror I could see he was pastier than before. We had been driving for a couple of hours and the kid said he had to "take a piss." I pulled over to the side of the road and we all got out and relieved ourselves except for Granddad. When the kid buttoned his old dungarees he looked across the land and said he saw a glittering that looked like a pile of bottles. Perry said we had enough, and I was ready to drive on too but the kid insisted. He laughed and said picking up those bottles was kind of an addiction, once you started you could not stop. He got Granddad out of the car and said come on you help. There was an old sack that we had used for some of the bottles on the floor in the back seat, but they did not take the sack.

I could not see what good Granddad would do to pick up bottles, he was not even walking too well. The kid supported him with an arm over his shoulder and they weaved like a couple of drunks. Perry and I watched them go far off the road. I remember our conversation during this time. I said I had not noticed before, watching him from behind, there's something different about that kid.

Perry watched but did not say anything.

I asked Perry can you see the bottles he's talking about? Can you see the glitter?

Perry said yes, I think I can, Dick.

The two kept stumbling over the uneven ground until they were a good one hundred yards away. They looked kind of small but we could still see them. I expected them to start bending over, like they were picking up bottles, but they did not.

I looked on the back seat and said to Perry that they did not take the sack with them, but Perry did not answer.

I watched the kid take Granddad's arm off his shoulder, and sit him down on the ground. He turned around and he waved at us, watching him. Then he started to walk back to the car.

I asked what do you think that kid is doing?

Perry said he had no idea.

I started up the car. Something gave me the "heebie jeebies" about that kid before now, and the feeling was getting worse.

Perry put out his hand to stop me from putting the car in gear. He said wait for the kid.

I said why? Why are we waiting for him? I said we should get as far away from him as fast as we can.

Perry said we're a hundred miles from nowhere, we could not just leave him here.

Well, my mouth dropped open at that one. Perry did not seem to get that he was saying we could not do to the kid what the kid was doing to his grandfather. Perry just stared at me with his eyes wide and a little smile. His eyes glittered like the bottles in sunlight. I did not think I could talk any sense into Perry, so I tried getting him to view the business end of the deal. I was spitting mad but I tried to keep calm like Perry was.

I said I did not put in for three of us, Honey. I called him Honey not because I am queer, but because I always knew he was and he liked me to call him that. It made it easier to get him to do things my way. Plus he was always saying he thought I liked little girls which is untrue. Calling him Honey got back at him a little. Anyways, I said ten thousand split three ways isn't much worth the drive to Holcomb.

Perry said that poor kid, what else can he do? He's got nowhere to go, no one but us. Now that his grandfather is gone, that kid is all alone. It's like we're his family.

I said do you hear what you're saying Perry? That poor kid is alone because he's killing his own grand-dad.

Perry said he isn't actually killing him, Dick. You can see that yourself.

I said he left him in that field to die, that's even worse.

Perry said Dick, that man was pretty sick. He'll probably be dead before evening.

I said you can't know that.

Perry said sure, I can, Dick. Some things you just can sense. I got a strong feeling about this.

The way Perry kept saying my name, Dick this and Dick that, all the time keeping his voice easy, it did not take a mind-reader to see he was digging in his heels on this. I felt myself fidgeting in my seat and he just sat there cool as a cucumber. Perry Smith was the real killer, I thought. Cold blooded and all. And I could tell he knew it. If I turned Perry loose with this boy, what would I do then? And what if the two of them decided to leave me in the dust (or dump me somewhere the way he dumped his own grandfather!) and go get the Clutter money themselves. I tried once more.

How do we know we can trust him to keep a secret, I said.

Perry shoved his thumb out to the field where the old man sat. That's the proof right there, Perry said. If he can trust us knowing that, we can trust him with a simple robbery.

If you ever read what that writer writes about us, you'll probably be led to believe that Perry Smith is some poor soul who had a rough childhood with a mother who ran away, and who got badly wounded in the military so he was half crippled and in pain all the time. I heard it all myself on our drives across the country. I can practically hear the two of them, him and Capote, sobbing on each other's shoulder and it makes me want to "puke." I bet Perry will say I was the really bad one, someone who was raised in a happy family and just has one of those evil, criminal minds. That is what he will say. I am saying that is a goddamn lie, please forgive my language.

So the boy climbed into the back seat of the car as if nothing had happened and said okay, let's go, and Perry said, kind of jokey, what, no bottles?

They's all broken, the boy said. He started to hum this tune, slowly. At the end of some lines he would make a popping sound with his lips. Perry said he recognized the tune but did not know the name. The kid said his mother always used to hum it to him when she was alive.

The kid started up the humming and popping again and that was when he caught my eyes in the rearview mirror. I tell you, I was afraid to turn around and afraid not to turn around, the way you are when you know there's a mean dog behind you. Will you set it off if you pretend to ignore it? Will you set it off if you turn around and let it know you know it's there? I didn't turn around, but finally put the car in gear and headed on. It is true there were bottles out in that field. I can still picture them glittering like a pond in the sunlight, and that old man sitting among them, dazed like he still did not understand what was happening, and looking like he was treading water.

You know where this is going. When we got to Emporia where I wanted to get some supplies for the job, I again said this is where we drop off the kid. And the kid said, you know you missed the turn for Tulsa a while back there. I know because we came through it. Where are you really going? He refused to get out of the car and Perry refused to come with me if he did. Perry seemed to be enjoying the whole thing. I even thought maybe that this was Perry's way of avoiding doing the job altogether. But I kept on. I picked up some duct tape that we would need at a shop and we headed on.

Now I did not know what would happen. With about a hundred miles left to go before we would reach the Clutter place, we stopped in Great Bend for dinner. It was a good meal with steak and all, because we had all the money we collected from the bottles. Perry started to talk. He told the boy about how he and I were in prison at the same time, and how I had come to him with a story I had heard from another prisoner.

Tell him, Perry said. You tell it.

You shut the fuck up, Perry, I said.

Perry would not shut up. He told the boy how I was in for grand larceny and Perry was in at the same time for something I cannot now remember. Perry told the kid the same story he had told me, where he had killed a man in Las Vegas with a bicycle chain. He watched the kid as he told the story, as if he was looking to see how the kid would react. Kid leaves his grandfather to die in the elements, what did Perry expect? The kid did not look shocked. The kid hardly looked interested. But he did look at Perry with more interest than he looked at me, and I started to wonder who was heading this operation anyway.

Anyways, whoever is reading this knows about the robbery from the news and our trial, but in brief here is what Perry told the boy without me being able to stop him. A prisoner named Floyd Wells had told me all about this family by the name of Clutter who was well to do and lived on a ranch just outside Holcomb, Kansas. This was not far from where we were in prison the first time, in Lansing. Floyd Wells said that he had worked for Clutter seasonally, along with a lot of other men, and that Clutter paid them in cash. He said Clutter always had money in a safe in his office which was on the first floor of their two story house.

The boy asked who was "they."

I said it was Mr. Clutter, Mrs. Clutter, and a teenage son and daughter, according to Wells. There was an older daughter who did not live at home any more.

The boy said then it's a good thing there are three of us.

Perry said that was so.

The boy asked how Wells knew about the safe.

I said Wells told me he had seen the safe, and the money in it.

The boy asked how much money.

I had sort of given up hope of being able to extricate ourselves from this little weasel boy, and started to answer ten grand, but Perry, who was sitting in the booth next to him, winked at me and said five thousand dollars. In a second I loved Perry again for at least doing this, for lying about the money so the boy's take would be less than two thousand and Perry and I could split the rest between us. It made me very happy, which I think Perry meant to do, so there would not be bad feelings among us going in. It's better to feel this way when you have to work together.

Forty-four

Not wanting to appear too eager, Beaufort went over to the DiForenza house the morning after Brigid left for Florida. Of course she must have discovered something about Beaufort's connection to Smith and Hickock and to the Walker case or she wouldn't have gone there. Likely she didn't know all, but if Meadows had happened to describe the small old man he'd talked to before Yanchak got him . . . if Brigid had connected that man to Beaufort . . . if she had found out something from that abbot at the monastery about him visiting . . . but then she would have called Carlo and warned him, wouldn't she?

Beaufort took his car this time, no worries about the license being checked, parked in the front drive, walked up the front walk, and rang the doorbell. The surveillance camera was new, and the motion detector lights went on, showing that she expected to be gone that night and didn't trust her husband to activate them. The woman wasn't totally stupid, but he wasn't worried about being caught on film. By the time she saw it he would have found what he was looking for, and then he and Carlo would both disappear without a trace, Carlo to be disposed of once he was over the border where that kind of thing happened more easily.

He doffed his cap at the camera.

No one was coming. He rang the doorbell again, and that was when he noticed there was no chimey sound from inside the way there had been on his previous visit. He rapped on the screen door instead. The impact reverberated through him and set off the dogs inside.

Carlo pulled open the main door but left the screen shut, and, presumably, locked. He seemed uncomfortable. No, it was more distraught. "Well, hello, Jerry," Carlo said. "Sorry, I was watching the news. Really upset that Brigid was with that poor man just minutes before he was shot."

"That's terrible," Beaufort said, casting around in his mind for the thing that would open the door. Finally went with "Could I come in?"

"I was actually, just . . ." Carlo might have said any number of things. Going to walk the dogs. On his way to a dental appointment. But Carlo was not a good liar, at least not off the cuff, at least when his mind was so preoccupied with his wife's safety. His "just" trailed off in the style of an evangelical minister who has run out of prayer ideas and is trying to fill the gap.

Beaufort pulled off his cap and said the only thing that would likely make this sucker open the door to him. The one thing Carlo could not resist. "I want to make my confession," he said.

Forty-five

Sitting there in the synagogue, engrossed in this document that felt like some ancient parchment holding long-lost mysteries, I had let the time slip by. When I glanced at my watch I saw I had less than half an hour to get to the airport. I put the pages back into the envelope as quickly as I could without damaging them, and hustled my way into the parking lot, empty except for my rental car.

I made it to the airport, was happy to find no line ahead of me where I ditched the car, and dashed into the terminal. At first glance I thought it was just a busy morning. A very busy morning. The line at check-in was one hundred strong. A kiosk was open, but when I tried to print my boarding pass I got a message that said check with attendant.

Never a good sign.

I got in the line with everyone else, now wondering whether I would miss my plane or whether there was simply no plane to miss. I asked the person in front of me what was going on, some poor mom with two small children in tow.

"Didn't you hear?" she asked while waving like a two-armed octopus to maintain some control of the kids. "There've been freakin' blizzards in the north since early morning. All over the Northeast and Midwest. Flights are canceled. Like five thousand of them."

"Mommy, what's *freakin'*?" the bigger of the two asked.

"It's insane," she answered, "and stop licking your brother's hair."

At any other time I would have dreaded being in the same row as these people, but today that was the least of my problems. I had a connection through Dallas where it wasn't snowing, but that didn't make a difference. Only one of a herd of cattle hemmed in on both sides by a strap and other cattle in front and back of me, by the time I got to the agent the flight had not taken off. Delayed two hours, she said.

Powerless, I stepped away from the counter and let those behind me surge hopelessly forward.

With plenty of time to kill, I went through the TSA PreCheck line and on to the new concourse assigned to the flight that might leave in two hours, though one can always assume that's just a sop they're throwing you to keep you quiet. There was a Cinnabon, beckoning me. I never get one of those monster pastries unless it's a moment like this, when I'm needing carb comfort of a most excellent kind. With a large coffee.

I sat down at the gate that showed Tampa to Dallas in two hours, and called Carlo. No one answered, but I wasn't concerned. I left a message telling him it was a good thing I'd driven myself to the airport so he didn't have to stay on top of flight times. I also told him I had a surprise for him, but didn't go into details. For one thing, this was probably more exciting for me than it was for him, and for another thing, it would have taken too long to explain before the message machine shut off.

Someone once said, if you're being screwed and there's nothing you can do about it, you might as well lie back and enjoy it. Now, I think whoever said that should have his testicles removed and shoved into his ass, because I've know too many women who've been screwed when there was nothing they could do about it, and enjoyment doesn't enter into it. But I can agree with anyone who says when you're trapped at an airport, eat an entire Cinnabon. When I finished it, I stopped into a nearby restroom to wash my fingers so I wouldn't get sticky on what I was coming to think of as Hickock's confession.

Forty-six

Despite Beaufort's requesting a priest, Carlo had still hesitated opening the door.

"Jerry," he said, "I'm not in that line of work anymore. Haven't been for decades. How about I get you in touch with Father Elias Manwaring. You remember meeting him once at the coffee shop inside Bashas'?"

"I don't want to talk to someone I don't know. I just want to talk to you."

Carlo still hesitated. That wasn't like him. Beaufort thought he must know something. So he put aside the ruse. "Carlo, I know why Brigid went to Florida. She's looking for information about me, from another time when I did some bad things. And you know, all she had to do is ask and I would have told her. That's what I want to tell you about."

Carlo finally turned the lock in the security door and opened it. Beaufort stepped inside and took a deep breath.

"Can I get you something to drink?" Carlo asked, apparently noticing Beaufort's stress and thinking it was about his confessing his misdeeds.

"Got any bourbon?"

"My goodness, this must be a dark secret indeed." Carlo moved comfortably to a cupboard next to the stove, opened the door, and pulled out a sliding tray with a half-dozen bottles on it. If he remembered, the priest didn't remind Jerry that he said he didn't drink. "Let's see, gin, Scotch, vodka, Brigid is the vodka drinker . . . here's an old bottle of Jim Beam from when she tried to make bourbon balls last Christmas." He held up the bottle and grimaced as if remembering that the bourbon balls weren't all that good.

"That'll do," Beaufort said. "Join me?"

"I don't mean to be a stick-in-the-mud, but it's a little early for me. I'll have a glass of tonic."

Carlo poured generously, got his tonic over ice, and the two sat down, Carlo in a wing-backed chair next to his desk, and Beaufort at the end of the couch nearest him.

"I'm really sorry I worried you," Beaufort started. "I guess I should have said something before now."

"We had no business knowing about you until you chose to reveal it. It was a coincidence that Brigid was in law enforcement and naturally suspicious. How did you know that she had thought something was . . . amiss?"

"You mean that I was in prison? Well, you might get out of prison and go straight, but that doesn't mean you lose your contacts. A guy in Tallahassee called to tell me he had word some elderly white-haired woman was nosing around, asking questions about me."

Carlo had smiled at hearing the description of Brigid as elderly and white-haired. "Well, your cohort had it partly right," he said.

The next part was easy, because Beaufort was telling the truth. He explained how he had been a disadvantaged youth, a trial for his mother after his father died in the Korean War. (Well, that part was a lie, but Beaufort was warming to his story.) A young hoodlum, he was arrested for possession of marijuana when that could send you to prison for a couple of years. Then getting out, more hardened than before by his time, he hooked up with his former supplier and started selling. Got picked up on the street again by a sting agent. Did more time—

While he was telling his story, the phone rang. Beaufort stopped in midsentence and looked around the house for where the phone might be. Carlo looked, too, in the direction of the kitchen area across the great room. At the phone on the counter over the liquor cabinet.

"Do you need to get that?" Beaufort asked, not wanting to show he was on edge. "If it's important. I can always pick up the story when you're finished."

"Let it go to voice mail," Carlo said. "We get so many telemarketers calling we don't even get up unless they leave a message."

They both stopped while the phone went through six rings and then changed to voice mail. "Hello, Carlo? It's Elias. I know you screen calls, I'll wait for you to pick up."

Carlo smiled at Beaufort. "Could I freshen your drink?" he asked.

Beaufort shook his head, and after a couple of beats the voice went on.

"Okay then, you're not within earshot. Call me. I'll be at the church for another hour. Good—oh, it's around nine right now. Bye."

Carlo nodded at Beaufort to go on with his story.

On the third go-round Beaufort had decided to take a step up in the marketing chain and supply the drugs himself. He bought a small boat and was transporting the goods up through the Gulf of Mexico to safe harbors along the west coast of Florida. This went on for a while, but coincided with the Three Strikes and Life law. "Do you remember that?" Beaufort asked.

"I do. It was part of the war on drugs. You got caught then?"

"Yep. Third time was the charm. I was in for life, no parole. Whether it was fate or God, those years in prison changed me, and getting released not too long ago was like salvation. I truly had my second, hell, sorry, Father, my fourth chance at life. And I wasn't going to screw it up this time."

"So you were never a jockey."

Beaufort shook his head ruefully, imagining his segue into finally finding out where Carlo had that document. If he could somehow trick him into revealing it without having to strong-arm him. What if, somehow, some way, it wasn't necessary to kill Carlo? That would be nice. He didn't want to hurt Carlo even more than he didn't want to hurt Gloria. "No, I made that up. I could see you were good people and I didn't want you to think bad things about me." He took another sip, and watched Carlo, who looked at him with such kind eyes as he had never known before. No one in his whole life had looked at him in just such a way. Was that love? And then he heard himself talking.

Beaufort talked for a long time. He told about when he was twelve years old, taking out his pop's shotgun that was kept in the closet, and playing cops and robbers with his eight-year-old brother. He never liked his brother, that was for sure, because he knew Howard was his mom's favorite. She never looked at him the way she looked at Howard, or made the things he liked to eat as much as she made them for Howard.

He shot his brother dead, but he told the judge he didn't know the gun was loaded. He was pretty sure he didn't know, anyway. But he got sent to reform school just the same. His mother didn't believe it was an accident at all. The reform school was hard. He got pushed around by the other boys because he was smaller, but worse than that was the matron, a woman whose armpits smelled of frying onions and garlic when she leaned over him. For some reason those times made him angry, and he took it out on the other boys, once beating a kid's head so hard with a brick he came back from the hospital with his face all wired together.

They must have told his parents, because when Jeremiah was released from the school two years later, his parents wouldn't let him back in the house. What was he going to do, where was he going to go, and only twelve years old? The house burned down. He didn't know his parents couldn't get out. He went to the next town, lived with his mean old granddad for a while, and then they lit out west . . .

All the things Beaufort had kept to himself, as if the deeds were large things that he needed to keep hidden for so many years. Meeting up with Hickock and Smith, and what happened at the Clutter place, that was just the beginning.

He saw the Walkers in a diner in Sarasota, and heard them talking about buying a car they'd seen: a '57 Chevy.

He watched them split up. The father took the two small children. The mother went home.

He followed her.

He sat outside the house getting his courage up.

When he finally got out of the car and walked up to the house, he could see her through the screen door. She was putting some groceries away. The screen door was unlocked, but he knocked anyway so as not to alarm her.

He said he had heard them talking and wondered if they'd like to buy his car.

She said her husband was just out getting cigarettes and would he like to wait.

She offered him some sweet tea but he said no.

He sat at the kitchen table. There was mail on the table that she opened. One was a Christmas card which she placed so you could see it on top of the refrigerator.

He surprised her when her back was turned to him, took her into the bedroom, raped and shot her. He dragged her body off the bed and into the front room. He didn't know why he did that, nor why he covered the blood on the bed with the spread.

He saw a cedar chest where people usually kept things that were important to them. He thought it would be good to take something from it, so the cops would think it was someone who knew the family. He found a majorette's uniform folded neatly in the chest. He took one of the pieces from it and left the lid of the chest open.

He heard the front door open and ran back into the living room.

He shot the father. It took two bullets.

He shot the older boy because he might be old enough to tell.

The mother was not dead, but had crawled to where her husband lay with his dead son. She was on her knees when he shot her again in the back of the head.

He shot the toddler but it didn't die immediately. The gun was out of bullets now. He took the baby into the bathroom where he laid it facedown and turned on the tap. It didn't lift its head.

He turned off the water and didn't think about whether anyone could pick up his print when he put his hand on the bathtub faucet to get up.

Looking for a wallet, he went through the father's pockets but only found a pocketknife, which he took.

Finally, he picked up two wrapped presents that were underneath the Christmas tree.

And left. Had he felt pleasure in the killing? It was hard to remember how he felt then. There was no pleasure in the recollection now. He felt more like an observer, distinterested. If he felt anything, it was that it hadn't happened. The important thing is that he was a killer then, but he wasn't now. Now he only killed when there was no other option. Now he—

He heard, "Jerry? Jerry, are you all right?"

Beaufort looked at Carlo and wondered how much he had said and when he had stopped talking. From Carlo's face it didn't appear that he had said very much. He heard himself say, "If a person does something bad, but they never do anything that bad again, then is the person still bad all through?"

Carlo tilted his head and looked puzzled at the question, was about to ask one of his own when Beaufort shook himself out of the strange mood he'd been in and changed the subject. He had realized he was about to get into worse things that maybe it wasn't wise to reveal, especially as he was looking for that confession. Maybe someday he'd have more opportunity to talk with Carlo.

Forty–seven

Here is a good question. If Perry Smith was so much smarter than me, why was I the one who knew how to grift, and I had to coach him how to do it? And if he was so tough, why was he such a "scaredy pants" when it came to walking into a shop and scamming an ignorant sales clerk?

We got a lot more money from cashing bad checks than from picking up bottles, let me tell you. Every shop we went into I got an extra twenty-five dollars or so. The checks were fake. When you go from town to town, a couple shops here, a couple shops there, this adds up.

This was before we went to the Clutters, when we needed money. I just wanted to mention this to show that Perry was not as smart or as tough as he looked in photographs in the newspaper.

Back to my story now. The shotgun I took from the house was intended to frighten the Clutters. Also a hunting knife. Now this is an important point. Perry told in his confession that I was the one who said we would not leave any witnesses, meaning that we would kill the family with the gun. He said I brought the gun with the express purpose of killing the family. But if I said we would kill the family so as not to leave any witnesses, then why would Perry think of getting stocking masks to wear? We would not need masks if we were going to kill the Clutters. You see, it does not add up. Do not believe everything you read.

Anyways, we drove up to the Clutter ranch after dark and parked within view of the place, waiting for the lights to go out. The kid was still in the back seat. He was humming that tune that he always hummed, very slowly, so that it sounded like something you would hear at a funeral ceremony. When Perry saw the house he lost his cool demeanor. He started knocking his back against the car seat as if he couldn't wait to go on a carnival ride. I thought it was because he had never lived in a house that was so grand, and he hated anyone who did. I grew up poor, too, but live and let live, I always said. It wasn't the Clutters' fault if their father was better at making a living than Perry's or mine was. This is how I thought, but I suppose no one will ever believe it.

There was a small porch on the side of the big house, with a door that we knew led to the room that Mr. Clutter used as an office. We could go in there and not take a chance of someone seeing us go in the front. It was perfect. Perry knew about locks, so he got us in. I kept a look-out while he went through all the drawers in a big desk. There was no money there. It would have been easy if there was money in the desk. I looked around for the safe that Floyd Wells said he had seen in the room, but I could not see it. I thought it might be in another part of the house, somewhere more private.

But we were surprised by Mr. Clutter who found us. You can imagine he was surprised, too. I was always the talker, so I took charge here. I told him to get up and open his safe, wherever it was.

I was the one holding the shotgun at this time, and you could tell it bothered Clutter, though he did not appear to be all that frightened of us.

Clutter said he did not have any money in the house, or not very much. He also said he did not own a safe. Clutter was actually very polite, and said he thought we could work this out, but I was getting very nervous. I had not been involved in a robbery up to this time. I thought it would all go much easier.

The kid, who had been standing by the door as if he was ready to bolt at a moment's notice, yelled at me, what was Floyd Wells talking about a safe! He said he had seen the safe! There must be a safe!

Perry put up his hands and shushed the kid, and told him it was better if we did not say anyone's name. You see, this was another hint that we would leave without hurting anyone, because if Perry did not intend to leave Clutter alive he would not have said that to the kid about not saying Wells's name.

When Perry got the kid calmed down he asked Clutter who was in the house, and Clutter said his wife and son and daughter but please not to wake them up because they were sleeping. He repeated that we could work this out, and he offered to write a check. Then Perry flared up all of a sudden and said what do you think we are, idiots? Perry usually acted like a cool character but he would get offended if anyone insinuated that he was not smart.

He pushed Clutter towards an open door which we discovered was the stairs to the basement. I went to follow them down there, and that was when I wondered why the kid wasn't with us, but when I looked around I did not see him in the downstairs area. I said this to Perry.

Forget him, he said again, while strong-arming Mr. Clutter down the basement steps. That was when I thought we did not have masks on. Again, names did not matter if someone could tell what we looked like. But things were moving quickly by then, and I did not think about it more.

While I stood holding the shotgun on him, Perry tied Mr. Clutter to a pipe in a room off the main basement area. He made him lay down on the floor which was cement, and very cold. I was the one who found a cardboard box standing against a wall, a big one that could have held a twin sized mattress. I put it on the floor so Mr. Clutter would not be so cold. He still looked pretty uncomfortable, with his arms stretched out over his head and wrists tied around the pipe. Then Perry wrapped duct tape around his ankles. Now Mr. Clutter began to look very fearful and kept saying please don't hurt my family. My wife is sick.

By the time we went upstairs to the bedrooms, we found that the kid was ahead of us. He had already locked Mrs. Clutter, Kenyon, the son, and Nancy, the daughter, in the bathroom. He had the hunting knife and was using that to make them do as he wished. At this point I kept thinking this is not how it was supposed to go, but I did not know what to do. I admit I was getting upset, beginning to lose what little cool I had when we first entered the house.

The kid let the son out of the bathroom and took him downstairs when we told him about the basement. He said he would take care of tying up the son. While he was doing that, we tied up Mrs. Clutter in her room, and Nancy in her room. I was holding the shotgun, it was mine after all, and when they saw that they did whatever we told them to do. While Perry tied Nancy up he was telling her to be quiet and no one would get hurt. I admit at that point I could not see how we would leave with no one getting hurt.

The girl asked where her father was, was he okay.

I heard humming, then the kid came into the room. He had the knife tucked into his belt. I glanced at it, curious, but I did not see any blood. I was about to ask him what did he do with the Clutter boy, but he pointed at the girl on the bed and said look at this, this girl is young, about my age. Maybe younger. Dick, you would like her. Unless you think she is still too old.

That was when I knew that Perry had talked to him about me liking little girls. Which is not true. But it made me mad. I said let's finish up here.

But he could see that I was agitated, moving from foot to foot, and my being agitated seemed to encourage him. Go ahead, he said. We have time. Perry and I could step outside the door if you want privacy.

Perry laughed. It was more like a snort, because a little snot came out of his nose and he wiped it with the back of his sleeve. He looked embarrassed, like that was the worst thing that would happen that night.

I said is there money in the house or not? You should spend your time looking for the money and stop fooling around.

He said oh go on, Dick. Maybe she is only twelve. Or at least you could shut your eyes and pretend. We all know you like little girls. Have you ever had one? This is your chance.

I was confused and just said I don't want to.

He said don't want to or can't? Then he said you talk about having an ex-wife and children, but we don't know that for sure. Perry did you ever see a photograph of his wife?

Perry said no.

I did not know what to do. The girl was staring at me, and I could not stand the terror in her eyes, wondering what would happen to her. He continued to taunt me, and Perry did nothing to stop him. He just watched me with that little smile of his.

The girl looked like she was trying to form words maybe to say please don't hurt me, but her lips were twitching so much they could not form the words and she had no breath.

Stop it, I yelled. I felt like I was there but not there. I yelled stop it again and my voice, which had a buzzing quality to it, seemed to come from someone other than me.

No one will ever know. We are the only ones who will know what you did. Or didn't do. I don't know which is worse. The kid said these things.

The girl's eyes bugged out at me. They could not have been bigger. Her breath was harsh now, in and out.

Can you get it up? He would not stop.

I do not know why, but I raised the shotgun and screamed shut up. I don't know if I was screaming it because of the taunts, or at the girl because of her loud breathing. There were those eyes. I told her to turn her head to the wall. She did. Then I fired the shotgun. I will never know why I did that, but I had to stop her from looking at me that way. I hated her for being so afraid of me. Why was she so afraid? I would not have hurt her otherwise, in any way. I am not a bad man. I had never killed anyone before. Or after. Maybe I had some strange feelings now and then, but I had never even molested anyone, and I do not know where Perry came up with this.

So that is what makes this part of my telling a real confession. Perry was telling the truth shortly after we were arrested, when he said I killed Nancy Clutter. Before we changed our confession so Perry took all the blame. I wish to be forgiven this sin before I go to the gallows.

After that the money was forgotten. Things happened fast. The kid made a whooping noise, took the shotgun from me, went into Mrs. Clutter's room and shot her. Then he went down to the basement. We had followed him into the bedroom to see him kill Mrs. Clutter but he ran ahead down the stairs. Perry stopped to pick up the shotgun shell casing and we heard the shotgun go off again. When we got down to the basement, we saw the boy dead on the couch.

Mr. Clutter screamed my son my son. He was in the other room and did not see what happened, but he knew.

The kid grinned and reached out with the shotgun to Perry. He said, here, you have to do one. We all have to do at least one. So Perry looked a little dazed at how things were going, but he took the gun as if he wasn't in charge, and he went into the other room. Mr. Clutter was screaming and the shouting kept on, shoot him, shoot him. But it seemed Perry could not shoot with Mr. Clutter screaming. That was when he must have put some duct tape over his mouth, and not before the way we told it, because the screaming lessened to something that happened only in Mr. Clutter's throat. All I could hear over that was do it, do it.

I did not go into the other room just yet because I was putting a pillow under the boy's head. I know this was crazy as he was already dead. I found

247

the shell casing which had rolled partway across the floor. Then I heard Mr. Clutter making a different noise, more gurgling than screaming in his throat. When I went into the other part of the basement I saw his throat had been cut to make him quiet for Perry. Perry was still holding the gun. He yelled to see Mr. Clutter choking his blood away and that is when he finally shot him. Even so it was a few seconds before he was totally still, and all I was aware of was the three of us breathing hard. The boy cursed as if he was sorry it was over, as if he could not get enough killing and was sorry there were no more people to kill. I thought about this later.

There was so much blood in the basement we could not avoid stepping in it. We were afraid of leaving evidence that could come back to convict us, but with the other house nearby, and the chance that people who lived there might hear the gunshots and come to investigate or call the police, we figured we should leave quickly. I said I had two shotgun shell casings, and Perry said he had the one from Nancy's room. He found the other close to his feet, lying in a pool of Mr. Clutter's blood.

When we got in the car the kid put his hand in his pocket and drew out a handful of coins. Here is some change, he said, as he handed it to Perry over the front seat of the car. I found it in a cookie jar in the kitchen when I went to get the knife.

Perry asked him if he still had the knife and he answered yes.

Perry had blood on him from the blow-back of Clutter. The kid was bloody too because of the blow-back of Clutter's son, and because of the blood spurting when he slit Mr. Clutter's throat. I had just a little bit of blood on my clothes from the killing in the basement rather than from Nancy Clutter because I was away from her when I shot her, and the blood went on the wall next to her bed. No one had thought about this in advance and we had to find a creek and wash off.

I watched while they stripped off their clothes and washed them and themselves in the creek. We got back in the car, they were cold and put the heat on. It was November, mind you, and very cold. I was still driving. Perry was a little quiet like me, maybe thinking about what we had done, or the money that was not there, but the boy was talkative. It was as if the whole point of the break-in was the killing, not the money. He seemed very upbeat. No one mentioned how they made fun of me in the Clutter daughter's bedroom. I think they did not want to rile me up again after so much emotion. Either that or it had been forgotten in all the excitement that followed.

We drove back the four hundred miles to Olathe and my parents' farm, and arrived by noon the next day, November 15. I got out of the car myself to ask Mom to let at least Perry stay at our house. At the last second I remembered the splash of blood on the left sleeve of my shirt and covered it with my right hand, reminding myself to hide the shirt in my room. Mom looked at Perry looking out the car window at her and she said no. She probably could not see who sat in the back seat of the car on the driver's side. She did not mention him and neither did I. It went without saying that it was definite that she would not have let the two of them stay at the house.

And that's that part of the story. No matter what you read, the Capote account, or Perry's and my confessions, or even something I wrote at another time, what I have just written is the absolute truth, the whole truth, and nothing but the truth. It makes me feel better than I have felt in a long time. As a matter of fact, I think of a religion study class I took when I was in prison the first time, and a line comes to mind, maybe part of scripture, though I do not know if Jesus said it.

What I have written, I have written.

That was six years ago. How funny that, as I write this, the kid is not a kid any longer. He must be at least twenty, fully grown. It's all I can do to write it here now, I'm so afraid, and I can't even provide the boy's last name because he never told us. His first name was Jerry. That's all I know. Oh, and he said his grandfather's name was Bert, short for Bertrand. But other than that, I do not recall that his grandfather ever came up in conversation after he was left in the field.

What I remember about how Jerry looks is when he came out of the river that night, naked, his wetness reflecting the moonlight a little. He was small, with an out-sized bottom, not like a boy's, but like a little girl too young for breasts. When he got into the car I could see his goosebumps all over. He looked so vulnerable to me, and not like someone I could grow to hate.

Forty-eight

The first thing I thought, of course, was *this could not be*. There had been only two people involved in the Clutter murders. Not three. Not three. This document was just one more made-up version of the many, this one made up by Hickock himself, for what purpose I couldn't tell.

That wishful thinking was followed rapidly by a sudden flash of what definitely was. The only name I had, Jerry, and the odd description of that physical anomaly that a pedophile like Hickock would notice. Not enough on their own, certainly, but added to a long string of suspicious occurrences: Santangelo's convenient death. Finding that Carlo had a sketch of Hickock. The burglary that was similar to others in the neighborhood except that in our house alone the burglar had searched through file cabinets and the library where there would be no valuables. Meadows getting shot just after he spoke with me. The possibilities fell together in what Carlo would call an epiphany, and following that, the shock that I had left Carlo unprotected in Arizona. That he was alone and that his life might depend on Jeremiah Beaufort thinking that what I had could convict him.

Forty-nine

The phone rang again.

Beaufort's mouth went dry, thinking more about what he really wanted from this visit, and he took a sip of his bourbon while the phone rang. Six times. Then silence. He took a deep breath.

Then the message.

"CARLO!" the voice shouted. "PICK UP THE PHONE!"

"Ah, it's Brigid," Carlo said, standing and moving in the direction of the phone. "And she sounds very Brigiddy. You'll have to ex—"

Beaufort stood, too, taking his gun out from where it had been tucked into his jeans, and moved behind Carlo toward the kitchen as the voice continued after a second's pause. "LISTEN!" Brigid shouted. "JERRY IS A KILLER! HE'S AFTER YOU, NOT ME."

Carlo reached out his hand to pick up the receiver, but Beaufort stepped to his side, said, "Let's let that one go, too," and showed Carlo the gun.

She kept on, "DON'T TALK TO HIM, DON'T LET HIM INTO THE HOUSE. CALL MAX AND HAVE HIM WAIT THERE TILL I GET BACK. HE'LL DO IT IF YOU ASK. FLIGHTS ARE DELAYED BUT I'M IN TAMPA AND ON MY WAY."

The two men stared at the phone as if that would do either of them any good. The voice had stopped, and now a blinking light and the number one indicated a second message had been logged. "Sit down, right there." Beaufort indicated a nearby kitchen chair with the muzzle of his weapon.

When Carlo did so, slowly, Beaufort asked, "Who's Max?"

"He's a sheriff's deputy and a friend of mine," Carlo said.

"What does he know?"

"I don't know. I haven't been in touch with him in a while."

Beaufort thought. The woman was in Tampa, so he had Carlo to himself for a good while, at least four hours if she was able to get a flight. She would be nervous about Carlo not answering the phone. Would she call someone herself? This Max person? Would someone come busting in the door any moment? In a pretense of ease, of having time he did not have, Beaufort casually leaned his butt against the kitchen counter and asked Carlo, "Do you ever lie?"

Beaufort reassured himself again about being able to read people, like now. Carlo seemed understandably tense. His eyes were narrow and his body felt rigid even from across the room. Carlo said, "We all lie. Hopefully I lie less than some do."

"Then tell me. What do you fear most?"

"That my wife will kill you." He sounded sad, like it was a certainty, and one he regretted.

Beaufort didn't ask why Carlo would fear this more than anything. Such as his own death, or Brigid's. And why would he, Carlo, care the most about Beaufort, and him dying? He laughed. But the honesty in the man's voice made the laugh feel pretended. What an odd thing to say.

"I want the document that Santangelo gave you."

If Carlo didn't draw a blank on that, he sure gave a convincing performance of it. "I don't know what you're talking about."

"Which part?"

"Well, I knew Father Santangelo, but he never gave me any document. What kind of document?"

Beaufort slapped him, not hard, just enough to show they had reached the real business part of the meeting. "It's what went with the sketch of Hickock. Santangelo told me about you. That's why I'm here. I want to see what else you have. I want to know why Brigid went to Florida."

"But that's—"

"You don't want to spoil your honesty record." He motioned with his gun again, this time for Carlo to get up from the chair. "I want you to show me where you kept the sketch."

Carlo did not rise. He shook his head, and on the second shake Beaufort backhanded him again. "That would hurt a lot more if I used my gun," he said. "Now show me."

Carlo rose now and led the way into the library. He went to the closet there and pulled the left door to the right side. Beaufort silently cursed himself for not continuing to search the closet on the day he'd broken in. But the time was running out then as it was now.

"Whatever you do, do it very slowly," he said, as Carlo reached for the plastic bin on the top shelf.

Carlo pulled it down and set it on the floor.

"Take the top off and dump it," Beaufort said.

Carlo obeyed, standing the plastic top against the wall behind him, and overturning the bin. It was paper. All paper. In a heap so high some of the papers slid off the top like an avalanche. Beaufort stared at it. Carlo looked up, and Beaufort almost thought he could detect a gleam of sympathy in the man's eyes. "I don't think there's anything here," Carlo said. He sorted through the mass of material and said, as if he were an archaeologist at a dig, "This is the level where I pulled out the sketch of Hickock. Remember when I showed it to you, it was taped to a piece of cardboard, and we never even knew there was a letter behind it until I took it to be framed. See, Brigid has always had a fascination for—"

"I know, I know. Shut up and let me think," Beaufort said. Was there enough time to make Carlo go through every single file folder and sheet of yellowing pad before someone came to the house? Could Carlo, with that claim of honesty, be making a fool of him? Trying to stall until his wife got home?

There went that damn phone again. Beaufort made Carlo go ahead of him back into the kitchen and by the time they got there it had already gone to messaging.

Brigid shouted, "IF YOU DON'T PICK UP I SWEAR I'M CALLING NINE-ONE-ONE!"

Beaufort picked up the phone. He might have said something threatening but didn't get the chance.

"CARLO!" Brigid shouted.

"Could you stop shouting like that?" Beaufort said.

There was no response for a while, and then, "It's you," she said, in a voice unnaturally quiet, unnaturally calm.

"That's right. Now as you can tell, I'm at your house. And I heard your last message."

"Where's my husband?" The woman sounded as if she was asking whether it was raining in Tucson.

"What about *please*? Is that a nice way to ask?"

"Where's my husband, you fat-assed little prick?"

"Let me get him for you." Beaufort held up the phone. "Here, Carlo, it's Brigid. Say hi."

"Brigid! Don't come home!" Carlo yelled.

Beaufort put the phone back to his ear. "There, you see? No one is going to get hurt. We've just been talking, trying to get him to give me what I came here for, or tell me where it is. Then I'll be on my way. But two things came up. One is that your husband insists he doesn't lie. The other is"—Beaufort had to figure out how to say this—"how do you know what you know about me?"

"Because, you dipshit, I have Hickock's confession. Carlo doesn't have it. He never did."

Beaufort had tried to sound as cool as she did, but this made him gasp. She must have heard it.

She said, "That's what you want. That's why you've been hanging around. I admit I was mistaken, I thought you were after me and I hoped to find out information about you and maybe even draw you out by going to your old stomping grounds in Florida." She told him how she got the document. "What I have incriminates you. No matter what you do, this will end up with the cops. You're finished, Jeremiah Beaufort. Give it up. Let Carlo call the sheriff to pick you up. Listen to me. Maybe after all this time you won't get the death penalty."

"How do you know my name?"

There might have been a half-second pause before she said, "It's in the confession."

"I never told Hickock or Smith my real name."

"It was a long time ago and you were together for more than two months. At some point you must have. So listen—"

Beaufort felt himself go light-headed as his thoughts skittered around looking for a hold on his control. He knew he was sounding hoarse, but he managed to say, "No. You listen to me. You're at the Tampa airport. By this time you've figured out I have friends in that part of the country."

"So you did have Meadows killed."

"Stop! Shut the hell up!" Beaufort paused to think. "If you just now called Carlo to warn him, that means you hadn't read the document until just now. That means you haven't shared the information with anyone else yet. And I have Carlo." Then he stopped to hear what she had to say.

She spoke calmly, reasonably. "If you don't want to give up, then just go. You've got a head start. I don't care what happens to you and I won't follow. Leave Carlo alone."

"That doesn't seem like the smartest course of action," Beaufort choked.

"Yeah, you're a good judge of smart," her voice whipped over the line.

"Fuck you," Beaufort said, anger taking over.

There was another pause and then her voice continued, calm and cold again. "Do me one favor. Put me on speaker so I can hear his voice again and make sure he's okay. What harm can I do, right?"

Beaufort agreed and pressed the button. Her voice continued. "Hello, Perfesser."

"Hello, O'Hari."

"Has he hurt you?"

"No. I'm okay. You just take care of getting back safely and I'll handle things at this end."

Then it got a little weird, from Beaufort's way of thinking, when she said, "Hey, I'm sorry if I've ever been an idiot."

"You haven't, I have," Carlo said. "An insensitive, unconsciously cruel idiot."

"Okay, you win," she said. "I love you anyway."

There was a pause, and then Brigid went on, speaking to Beaufort while Carlo listened. "All right, then. You and I are going to make a deal. The confession for Carlo, simple exchange. But Jeremiah Beaufort, if anything happens to that man, the law can do their thing, but I'll personally hunt you down no matter where you go. I've done it before and I know how to find you better than you know how to hide." Her voice got as cold and soft as frost on the ground. "And then I won't kill you. I'll keep you alive. Maybe for years. It will be my only remaining pleasure."

Beaufort didn't know how every last thing was going to play out, but he thought he could see the next step now that he knew Quinn had the confession. He had the time to think while the woman made her way to Tucson. There was that. "I won't hurt him," he told her. "Right now I don't have any reason to. We both want the same things. Get here and then we can figure out how to make the exchange." He prided himself on regaining his composure, and already starting to think of a plan. "And you can threaten me all you want, but if I see one funny light out front or hear so much as one chopper blade overhead I'll know I've got nothing to lose. You know what happens when a man has nothing to lose, I bet." There was no response so he finished, "I'm going to hang up now and won't be taking calls on this phone again."

"You have a cell number? Give me that in case I need to reach you."

Beaufort noted the number she was calling from on the phone's display screen. "I'll call you," he said.

He hung up on her. With something close to admiration he turned to Carlo. "Your wife is one crazy bitch."

Carlo moved his jaw where Beaufort had smacked him, and then nodded, clearly troubled more by the past minute than by anything that had gone before. "I'm beginning to get that, yes."

Fifty

I disconnected, shaking with the adrenaline surge from the control I had had to exert over myself during the call. Of course I had lied about the confession incriminating Beaufort, because, after all, Hickock didn't name him. Except for the first name Jerry, a common name, there was no way to undoubtedly connect Beaufort in all the ways I had figured. But Beaufort didn't know that, or was too stupid to remember Hickock couldn't finger him. It was critical that Beaufort stay in the dark about this. If he thought the document was useless as evidence he would have no reason to leave Carlo alive until I got there.

What would he do now? Would he head across the border with Carlo? Would Carlo stay silent as they passed the border guard? I wished I had been able to speak with him more, to give him some warning or advice. If only I had insisted on Gemma-Kate staying with him. At this point I wasn't sure whether I'd ever be able to speak to him again and only hoped he felt some of the courage I was sending him.

What I could be sure of was that Beaufort wouldn't take the chance of remaining in our house. He couldn't know if I would make good on my promise to not call in the cavalry. That's why he said he wouldn't take any more calls on our landline. So where? To Gloria's house?

I thought I knew how Beaufort's mind would be working, but if Gloria was still alive, for me she was the wild card.

On the other hand, as far as Beaufort was concerned, I was the wild card.

"Yes," I said to myself, and looked up, thinking, hardly seeing that I had stepped to the center of the concourse while I'd been talking, instinctively moving away from anyone who might have heard me.

One flight had managed to come from somewhere, and the stream of passengers rolled toward me in a slow wave. Half of them weren't looking where they were going, focused on their iPhones. One of those, a gelled man in a shiny suit with an entitled bag that was bigger than regulation, came straight for me, texting, texting, texting. I didn't want to get knocked over. Neither was I in the mood to give way. I let him collide with me, partly because I was in the mood to hurt someone and partly to test my physical resolve.

It felt good, watching his anger flare before he stepped around me, before the entire wave of people gave me a wide berth. Plus the resistance had focused my mind on the problem. Moving off in the direction of the TSA office, I placed another call, this one to Rising Star, my old acquaintance who was currently in Homeland Security.

When she knew it was actually me, she said, "I believe I can get you to Dallas. I'll call ahead there, but you may have to make other plans. If there's no flight there's no flight."

"Thank you," I said.

"Don't mention it. I'm serious, we didn't have this conversation." And disconnect.

By the time I got to the office I was more in control and knew enough not to burst through the glass door. Bursting is not taken kindly by TSA.

"May I help you?" the woman in uniform at the counter asked, not exactly alarmed at the look on my face, but not completely at ease, either.

"I'm here to see Mr. Holly. He's expecting me." I shook confusion out of my head. "That is, he'll be expecting me in approximately forty-five seconds. Tell him Brigid Quinn is here."

The woman looked at a colleague. I could read her eyes as well as he could, and they said *keep an eye on her*. She disappeared through a door behind the counter, giving me a glimpse of a long hall. She was back in forty-three, forty-four, forty-five . . .

Forty-six. "Mr. Holly will see you," she said, and, shooting a now-puzzled look at her compatriot, showed me down the hall and into an unassuming little office that held a small desk behind which sat an un-assuming man. He was hocking up his postnasal drip with such vigor that when he finally succeeded, I wanted to applaud.

He glanced up at me and then went back to the computer in front of him. "You know so many flights have been canceled." He started clear-ing his throat again, so I interrupted.

"You know this is an emergency," I said.

"So I'm told. Would you care to elaborate on the nature of the emergency?"

"No, thanks."

He frowned at the screen as if blaming it for his being too low on the food chain. "I've got one flight here that leaves in twenty minutes. It doesn't get you all the way, just to Dallas, and it's already overbooked. I can't bump someone without calling attention to the airlines." He rocked his head back and forth a second while I waited without encour-agement.

"There's one seat that would be available to you. It's scheduled for a sky marshal." He examined me over the top of his horn-rimmed glasses and nearly indulged a condescending smile. "How do you do with air-plane rage?"

"I'm good with it," I said, and there was something in my voice that made the smile disappear. "I have to get to Tucson," I said.

"I'll phone ahead. I'm not sure what will happen in Dallas, but some-one will meet you at the gate."

"Give me a badge," I said.

He handed me an official-looking tag which I attached to the collar of my jacket.

"I won't give you a weapon," he said, as if that would be my next demand.

"I don't need a weapon," I said, heading out the door and trotting to the gate while pondering my next move.

Someone once said, when someone tells you who they are, believe them. I took Beaufort at his word and assumed he was desperate enough to kill Carlo. That he might not be thinking clearly. Also, that there was a chance the well-abused Gloria might have become his accomplice. This was an added concern because she was an unknown, possibly dangerous, and doubled the odds of getting either Carlo or me killed.

Even if Beaufort could be proven (and so far this document was all the evidence there was) to have been at the scene of the Clutter family murder, he was twelve years old at the time. And there was no other evidence beyond this that he had actually pulled a trigger.

How bad did it have to be to risk killing Meadows? And what else would he do to prevent being found out? Answer: Meadows was closer than he knew to solving the mystery behind *In Cold Blood*, the solution no one had dreamed of in nearly sixty years. And if Beaufort would take the risk of killing Meadows, he was liable to do anything.

When I arrived at the gate they were boarding and I was in the last group. That gave me time to catch my breath and call Gemma-Kate. She answered with "Sorry, I have to take this." I started to tell her what was going on, but it was a few moments before she responded with "I was in organic chem lab."

"You were right about Hickock and Smith," I said, not troubling to apologize for interrupting.

"About what?"

"Almost everything."

"I missed something?"

"Listen. I never thought I'd be saying this, but I need your help."

She asked help with what, and I think I managed to give her an explanation within three, maybe four seconds. With Gemma-Kate all she needs is a couple of words to get the picture.

"Let me organize things from here," she said.

"No. The guy's worse than crazy, he's stupid crazy. Put the Tucson cops on the scene and you don't know who's going to get hurt. But I have an idea, if you can get something for me."

"Can't you just do your usual, walk in and shoot him in the face or something?"

"He has Carlo. Carlo might get hurt."

"No."

260

"Besides, he knows I'm coming and I'm pretty sure he has a gun."

"Don't you know how to kill someone with a credit card?"

"I'm sure he'll take whatever I have on me. He'll take my wallet."

"Will he be eating anything, do you think?"

"It's not that kind of a situation. Gemma-Kate, just listen. I need a weapon that doesn't look like a weapon."

"That stick of yours with the razor on the bottom?"

"He would see it. That won't get by."

"Okay, what are you thinking? I'll do anything."

"Get me some pepper spray," I told her. "Only it can't be in one of those aerosol canisters marked 'pepper spray.' Understand?"

"That's it, capsicum? That's your plan? And you say this guy is crazy? Do you realize the chance you're taking?"

"Just do it, and I'll take care of the rest."

There was barely a beat of silence before she had thought through several scenarios and I felt her nodding into the phone. "I'll see if I can get the materials and tell you how to handle them without hurting yourself. How much time do I have?"

"I'm in the Tampa airport about to board. I'm seeing a Dallas connection on the departure board, so if I can manage the connection it puts me in Tucson by four fifteen. I'll pick you up. Just call me back to confirm you've got it and tell me what to do."

Gemma-Kate disconnected. I got on the plane to Dallas, found the seat, and buckled myself in, my mind repeating all the connections I'd missed until now. To break the useless flow I went back to reading Hickock's confession because it was all I could do.

Fifty-one

Right from the start Perry and I had agreed that we would split up after the robbery, and then get back together to leave Kansas. If Perry told Capote that we decided to stay together in case we were picked up, that that way we could back up each other's story, that part is true. For now, we were going to leave town together and I wanted to see my parents one last time. They are good people. Were good people. Mom is still alive but Dad is gone.

After I brought the car we had been using back to the garage, I stole a '57 Chevy and changed the plates. When I arrived at the house Dad asked where I got the car and I said it belonged to a friend of mine. He seemed to believe me, but his face drooped a little bit in this sad look he started getting the first time I stole a car (that was what I was in jail for the first time).

Mom did not ask any questions, she just cooked my favorite dinner, fried pork chops, and I must have eaten four big ones. After dinner when the sun was down I hid the shotgun behind a cedar chest. That's where they found the gun later.

On November twenty-first I drove into town to pick up Perry to go to Mexico, planning to kite some checks on the way to fund us. When I pulled up in front of the rooming house I saw the boy standing next to Perry. I suppose I had told myself that the boy would not stick with us. It was a shock seeing him there, I must say.

No, I said. Just no.

Before you go getting upset, wait until you hear him out, Perry said. They both got into the car, Perry in the front passenger seat and the kid making himself comfortable laying across the back seat like he had whenever we drove somewhere.

I still protested, even as I got back into the car. Not Jerry, I said. He made me as nervous as he did before. Worse now, because while we were split up, Jerry had gone to a gun shop and bought a .22 caliber pistol and some shells. He waved it back and forth while we talked. I asked where he got the money for it.

That was when he confessed he had not given Perry all the money he found in the Clutter house. I yelled at him then, thinking he might have found the ten thousand dollars we thought was there, and was holding out on us. But he said he had found a lot, not as much as ten grand, but he would share it with us if we would take him to Mexico with us when we went. He said he would not show me where the money was until we were on the road there, and he wanted Perry to know in advance so I didn't try to kill him.

No one really knows about the money. We celebrated that night, and I felt much better.

Perry talked about his mother who ran out on him when he was a little boy, and about his father who raised him. Perry had helped his father build a tourist cabin up in Alaska but nobody came.

Jerry said he was born in Pascagoula, Mississippi, and had a little brother who he killed with his pop's hunting rifle when he was twelve and his brother was eight. He said it was an accident but he still got sent to a reformatory. When he got out two years later his parents did not want him anymore. That was how he ended up walking across country with his grandfather.

Perry wiped away a tear when he heard this story. I figured some parts of this story might be true, but there was no way of telling which ones. All I could see is that it seemed unfair to kill the one person who stood by you, even if he did so for dirty reasons, but I kept this thought to myself because I could already feel the rift that was forming between Perry and me because of that boy.

They both looked at me so I told about my life, my parents, and my marriages that did not work, and about my four boys who I thought were doing pretty well though I never saw them very much. That's how the kid found out about their names and where they live.

. . .

Jerry now told us where he had buried the money, about a mile outside of Olathe. He said it was more than six thousand dollars and he had found it in Mr. Clutter's office, in one of the file cabinet drawers where we hadn't looked yet because Mr. Clutter interrupted our search. He had found it when we were busy with the Clutters. He repeated that if we took him with us he would share it.

The kid is very generous Perry said. He could have just taken off with the cash instead of funding our getaway.

It would take me nearly two years to earn that much money at the garage. So we headed south through Oklahoma to the Mexico border.

Whoever reads this may already know about our trip around the country, from Kansas to Mexico to California to Florida and back to Nevada where we finally were caught. It was a trip of more than seven thousand miles, and no one ever asked how we were able to make that trip on bad checks. The money the boy had taken from the Clutters, or at least some it, slipped out at my last clemency hearing, but I do not think Perry told it to Capote. What we told about the trip around the country stuck to the facts. The only thing we both left out is that the boy was with us the whole way, right down to him being in the room when I brought in the Mexican whore.

There has been talk that I was trying to prove I was normal or something like that, but the fact was we only had the one room and Perry and the boy refused to leave. So I did it with the two of them watching and I did not care if they looked at each other and grinned as if they knew something between them they would not share with me. But after the woman (and she was a grown woman, not a young girl at all) left, the boy asked if I enjoyed myself. I said yes as a matter of fact I did, and he said good, because I paid for her. I knew what he meant, that we would not have money for anything if it had not been for him finding all that cash at the Clutter ranch, but I kept my cool and left. I passed a few checks one town over and felt better having some of my own money in my pocket.

I talk about this now because it was a continuing sign that Perry and I were not the friends we had been before. Whenever the boy and I had a difference Perry would stick up for him and it was "getting my goat." I remembered thinking of killing him and the boy back at the Clutter ranch, and these days I thought about it more and more.

I was ready to leave Mexico and that was the one time the boy sided with me against Perry. He was as bored as I was.

A good thing about these days is all the interstate highways that have been built. I-10 which runs all the way across the country from Phoenix to Jacksonville, Florida, had been constructed just a couple of years earlier, as if the government was helping us get around the country fast. I passed a few checks along the way and we saved some money by often sleeping in the car. This was especially good because there was less chance of being spotted by someone who might recognize us or the car as we drove through the center of the country.

After a brief time in California we headed east on route I-10 all the way to Tallahassee, Florida, which is where the panhandle meets the main part of the state. When we were getting gassed up at a Standard Oil Perry went into the gas station for some snacks and came back with a map also. We looked at the map and noticed that the only highway in Florida was the Sunshine State Parkway that ran along the east coast. But that was okay. With each day that went by we worried less about being found out, and took our time getting down to Miami.

We stayed there over Christmas, in a nice hotel, reading magazines and swimming in the pool and the ocean. But with Jerry always hanging around I had stopped having any fun. I was feeling pretty much whipped. When Perry said he wanted to head to some place with some action, like Las Vegas, I did not have any will to disagree.

I was afraid to say it is either him or me to Perry. I hated Jerry, but I thought Perry might choose him, and I hated being left by myself even more. People may think that I did not think anything about the Clutters, but I did. I did not want to be left alone with my thoughts. And I did like Perry. I thought he liked me, too, before Jerry came between us.

I sat out by the pool on our last night in Miami and made pretend conversations like, Perry either the kid has to go or I have to go. We cannot keep going on the three of us because that fat assed kid is always riling me. And then Perry said (inside my head) well, you sure make it easy to rile you. And I did not know how to answer that. Even in my head I could not win an argument with Perry. I do not think that imagining conversations makes me crazy.

On the drive north from Miami we stayed in Sarasota for a few days, which is half-way up the coast. Perry was no longer in a hurry to get to Las Vegas, I think he had just been pushing for that to see if I would do what he wanted. Even on the edge of the Gulf of Mexico the motels were very reasonable. Perry bought every newspaper with us in it and read every word aloud. It appeared he was particularly nervous about him being spotted around the scene of the crime, what with being so short and having a limp. I blended in more as my only distinguishing characteristics are some tattoos and one eye that was hurt in a traffic accident when I was younger and never healed properly.

It was very peaceful and I liked it better than Miami or Mexico even without the woman. But after a couple of days Jerry said he was bored, hanging with a couple of old men. Perry and I were maybe ten or even fifteen years older than him. Perry said it was time to head on to Las Vegas.

The day before we left Jerry went out with the car, saying he had some errands to run. Before that we did not know he knew how to drive a car. He was out a long time and Perry put up a fuss about it, whether Jerry had run off. I think he was more upset about Jerry running off than about him stealing our car and even the money. I figured Perry had gotten to think that I could provide anything, pass a check, steal another car, whatever. It made me feel like I was being used.

It was nice to be alone with Perry, however. It occurs to me that was the first time since we had picked up the kid, that it was just Perry and me.

As we were talking we heard the door open and Jerry stood before us. He was all wet, water still dripping off the cuffs of his jeans. Perry asked why and the kid said he had gone for a swim in the Gulf. I said in your clothes but he just shrugged. He did smell of salt water. He went into the bathroom and took a shower with the clothes on, he said to get out the salt water. Then he hung them up to dry because they were the only clothes he had. While he was in the shower we could hear him humming.

I tried once more. That kid is weird I told Perry, we should not keep him with us. Perry said we could not even be sure Jerry still wanted to stick around, he had not committed to the trip to Las Vegas. I said but what about the money, do you have any idea where he stashed the money? Perry just shrugged. Then he went to bed. I looked at the boy's clothes before I turned in. I thought I saw some light pinkish stains on the white T-shirt but I could not be positive of that. At the time I did not think much about it. It could have been wine.

The next morning Jerry got up early, put his clothes back on, they were dry now, and said he was coming with us. He said we should get a move on and he started loading what little stuff we had into the trunk of the car. I said what's the big hurry, but Perry was surprised and definitely pleased.

We left Sarasota and headed north, picking up I-10 in Tallahassee and then west, stopping in Pensacola, Florida, in the evening. Nobody mentioned the stains on Jerry's shirt, which showed up more after the water dried, light pink in the centers spreading to a darker pink around the rim. When we passed a thrift store he asked if Perry would go inside and get him a new shirt. He handed Perry a five dollar bill, and Perry looked at him. But he didn't say anything, he just went into the shop and bought a shirt. Jerry took off the stained one and put on the new one.

Driving at about noon, Perry in the passenger seat and the kid laying in the back like he usually did, with his head on the arm rest attached to the door, it was on the car radio that we first heard about a family by the name of Walker being discovered in their house in a little town near Sarasota. There was a father, mother, son and daughter. It was just like the Clutters, only the children were very young. The report said the mother had been raped, and shot, and the two children shot. The father must have come in the house while the killer was still there, and he was shot, too.

Honey, I said to Perry when I got a breath. That happened while we were in Sarasota.

Just like the Clutters, Perry said, staring out the front window, not looking at me.

If we get tied to the Clutters they'll connect us to this other family, too, I said.

I knew him well enough to know we were both thinking the same thing. The car got really quiet. I felt like my ears got sensitive, like I was hearing the smallest sounds like an animal in the forest. I heard the upholstery in the back seat squeak a little, and in the rearview mirror I saw the kid's face. At first he just looked interested, like he was hearing about this for the first time. It made him smile.

When the news reporter said that the detectives had found a fingerprint and a bloody boot print in the house, his eyes narrowed and he frowned.

Then the reporter said they were looking for a beige '57 Chevy that someone had spotted by the Walker house in the late afternoon of the 19th.

Holy Christ, I shouted.

But the others did not react. The kid kept staring at the radio and Perry kept staring out the front window.

For the first time I began to be scared of the boy, more than before when it was just his grandfather that he killed, or even after I saw what he did at the Clutter place. Here I was, a killer who had done the same thing, but I was afraid of him. I had done it for the money, but this kid did it for the fun. There's a difference.

But after that one shout, I got control of myself, I am very good at keeping control, and I kept my thoughts to myself. I knew enough to keep my mouth shut and we drove on.

Fifty-two

Beaufort knew that Carlo would do as he told him to do. It didn't matter that he held his gun lightly in his left hand while he steered slowly toward Gloria's house, west on Golder Ranch, then down Twin Lakes to Hawser, only a left and two rights to reach the destination.

Carlo sat mournfully in the passenger seat, probably thinking about how he had no way to defend himself. Probably hoping his wife would save him.

Beaufort pulled onto the gravel drive and said, "Aw, fuck."

Gloria's car was there. Beaufort parked behind it and thought. Staring ahead at the house he said, "Okay, I've got it. Here's how it goes. It's a workday so she won't stick around. In the meantime you're going to play nice and not let on that anything is wrong. If you say anything about what's going on, I'll leave you alive and kill her. If I suspect for a second that you're trying to send a message to her about our situation, I'll leave you alive and kill her. Whatever you do, I kill her. Is that simple enough for you?"

Carlo just sat there, folded.

"Tell me you understand what I just said," Beaufort said.

Carlo nodded without turning his head

Beaufort opened his door and got out, instructing Carlo to do the same. He put his gun in the back of his jeans with his T-shirt over it, came around to the passenger side of the car, reached in to open the glove compartment, and took out a roll of duct tape. He said, "Walk ahead of me into the house."

In the meantime Gloria had opened the front door without her usual wide smile that she always gave to Beaufort. She was too old to be on the rag, he thought, but he could deal with her later. Achilles was another matter. Whether he recognized Carlo himself or could smell the pugs on his jeans, the dog went into a frenzy of recognition. Beaufort thought the dog provided a good distraction. He got on his knees and made a show of roughing him up while keeping half an eye on Carlo and Gloria.

Beaufort stood up from petting Achilles and said, "This is Gloria. What are you doing home?"

"I forgot my lunch and there was no appointment scheduled until two." She put her hands up and waggled her fingers in a gesture that described some sort of magic trick. "So voilà, here I am." The words were the old Gloria, but the face . . . had this been going on before now and he was too consumed with his problems to see it? He made a mental note to get more flowers.

"I don't think we've met," Carlo said, treating Gloria the way you do in any normal social situation. "I'm Carlo. Carlo DiForenza."

Good old clueless Gloria. Not seeming to notice the almost palpable current of anxiety coming off of Carlo, she stuck out her hand and gave a tentative "Hi. Can I get you something?"

"I'm fine, thank you," Carlo answered.

Despite the potential harm this meeting could do, Beaufort found himself amused that out in the world such a bizarre circumstance would result in the same boring small talk you got in any social situation. A few minutes of this chitchat and he figured Gloria would be on her way back to work. He sat down in the recliner next to the couch to watch the show. He didn't bother to hide the duct tape, but put it on the coffee table.

"May I sit?" Carlo asked after shaking his head and her hand, his eyes darting between Beaufort and Gloria. When Gloria swung her hand to indicate the couch he took a seat. Achilles jumped up beside him and nosed his hand, which Carlo obligingly applied to scratching behind his ears.

"That's a good idea," Beaufort said. "Let's all sit."

Gloria started to speak.

"Sit," Beaufort said, with an emphasis on the *t* the way you'd command a dog.

She sat, and Beaufort gazed at Achilles. "Did you ever hear the joke about the three-legged pig?" he asked.

The other two shook their heads.

"This guy is visiting a nearby farm and spots a three-legged pig. When he asks the farmer how that happened, the farmer says, 'That pig. That pig is so good he once saved our whole family from a burning house. He squealed and squealed until we were all awake, and even tugged on my son's pajama leg to wake him up to get out.' And the visitor says, 'Wow, that pig is certainly good. Did he lose his leg in the fire?' 'Naw,' said the farmer. 'When you got a pig that good you eat it real slow.'"

The other two stared at him, Carlo with something like horror and Gloria with something like disgust. And something else he hadn't noticed, some angry spark that shows up just before the fire ignites. With an elaborate sigh he said, "What, you don't think that's funny? I don't think I'll ever get used to this world." But he was keeping his eye on Gloria, and decided to test his intuition. "Do me a favor, honey, and put the dog in the bedroom."

"He'll calm down," she said, which, given Gloria, appeared to be full-on rebellion.

"Put the dog in the bedroom," he repeated, and stared at her. "And would you give Carlo and me a minute? We have a little private business to discuss."

She pointed outside. "I was just on my way—"

"One minute," Beaufort said, lifting a finger from the arm of the chair where his hand rested. He gave her a look that did its best to communicate that she was making him look bad, and she gave up and finally did as she was told. When she had wrangled Achilles into the bedroom and shut the door, she didn't give the men a minute, but came out and stood by the couch, her whole body a question.

"I thought you were just leaving," Beaufort said.

"I am," Gloria said, still with the question in her eyes.

"You said we should have friends," Beaufort said to Gloria, answering the question. "Here's one." He couldn't stop himself from chuckling when Gloria looked at him with a slow burn. But not wanting to push her too hard, Beaufort attempted to placate her with "We met at the stables."

Gloria might have tried to stop the words if she'd been given more of a warning, but her anger flared, possibly as much of a surprise to herself as to Beaufort. "You don't work at the stables," she said.

Fifty-three

We landed at the Dallas/Fort Worth airport without incident. I checked in at the Dallas TSA office, showed them my badge, and gave them the name and number that I'd been given. Emergency, I said. So what if it wasn't a national emergency. There was no time for hair-splitting.

Things had been quiet, and it was almost with a sense of relief at some shoe having dropped that the boss jumped into service. This was another man, one without postnasal drip. That's all I can remember about that time. Oh, he looked at me as if with all his soul he wanted to ask who I really was, but at the same time knew that I would not tell him.

I came around his desk and looked at his computer screen.

"The next flight to Tucson leaves in two hours," he said.

"There's this one," I said, pointing to the screen.

"It's a full flight. They're all full flights."

"What about an air marshal? That's whose seat I took from Tampa."

He checked and said, "Sorry, not on this flight. Besides, even if there was a seat open, they're closing the doors. You can't make it."

"You make me make it," I said.

He glanced at my face and picked up the phone. "Hold flight number 6571," he said. "I have someone boarding." He listened. "Yes, I know the flight is full. Can you get the airline to bump someone?" He listened. "What about a steward to deplane without rousing suspicion so our person can take their seat?"

He glanced up at me and shook his head, beginning to feel my frustration.

"You have to get to D concourse," he said. "Skylink—"

"Fuck Skylink. Get me a cart now," I said.

He placed another call, then at my direction typed a few words on a piece of computer printer paper and printed it. Within a few seconds of that, a security cart pulled up outside the office door. I got into the front seat beside the driver, and over her objection pressed the warning button the whole way from the B concourse.

I leaned forward and felt my body trying to increase the forward momentum as we wove through the crowds, the driver saying a loud 'scuse-me when a traveling zombie blocked the way. About halfway there we both spotted ahead of the cart a stooped woman with a walker who tried to wave us to a stop.

"No," I said. "She could have got a wheelchair assist."

The driver looked at me mournfully.

"Oh goddamit, all right, stop." As we pulled up I grabbed the woman's walker and threw it on the cart. I threw the woman after it.

"I'm going to C27," she said.

"Yeah, ultimately," I told her, and to the driver, "No more."

Then we arrived. Without thanks I got off at the gate marked TUCSON. DEPARTED, with my tote slung over my shoulder, nodded to the gate attendant who had been notified of my coming, and entered the jetway. I felt the air sucked out as the door closed behind me. I boarded the craft. The forward steward was on the phone and glanced at me. As I walked down the aisle a few people looked up the way they do when a last person boards a plane alone. I'm sure most of them forgot my face by the time I made it aft, and only figured I was a standby and looked at their watches with the hope I hadn't put the flight off schedule.

By the time I got to the back galley the steward there had hung up the phone. I handed to her the eight-by-ten sign I'd gotten from TSA. Clearly, instructions had already been passed along, and though she looked at me with some concern, not having been told if I was on this particular flight because of some imminent threat, she agreed to do what I said. "Listen, it isn't about this flight," I said softly. "You know if it was, you wouldn't be leaving the gate. You understand."

She took a breath and nodded. I stepped into the port bathroom, locked the door, and sat down. I felt her press the sign against the door and make apologies to the passengers over the intercom, hoping they would just be grateful to be on a flight and please feel free to use the first-class lavatory along with the remaining one aft. It would take two and a half hours to arrive in Tucson. I doubted I would have access to beverage service, but at least I didn't have to worry about having to pee. I made two last calls before the plane taxied to the runway.

"Thank you again," I said when Rising Star picked up.

"You're welcome, Agent Quinn. Good luck and Godspeed."

You might ask why that was all this person would do. If this person could pull strings with the TSA like this, couldn't she send a team of SEALs or something to rescue Carlo from one old codger? Well, it had to do with something about jurisdiction where I was going—and what I might do there—that it was better she didn't know about.

And that's all you need to know about that. My other call was to check in with Gemma-Kate's progress and see if she had any instructions for me. She did.

She told me to have a spray vial of certain dimensions ready.

"Why can't you get that?" I asked.

"I walked over to the campus shop but they didn't have the kind I need."

"But do they have the stuff in the chemistry lab?" I asked.

"I'm sure they do."

"You're sure. Why does this make me nervous?"

"And how do you think I feel leaving the container up to you?"

"I think you don't feel anything at all, but that's beside the point."

"The important thing is that it has to be plastic," she said.

"Why? The canisters I've always had were metal."

"Plastic will be better. Trust me."

With this caution firmly in mind I opened up the envelope and read the rest of what Hickock had to tell.

Fifty-four

All that day I was quiet as the others, wracking my brain to think what to do. Get rid of the car, kill the kid, kept churning over and over in my mind. The murder of the Walker family was as big news as the murder of the Clutters had been, and the newspaper headlines awaited us when we stopped for the night in Louisiana. They had already picked up on the similarities of the two killings, and detectives were asking around the Sarasota area to see if they could find any witnesses. I thought about the times when I might have been seen there. I had a hard time falling asleep that night, wondering what to do.

But it turned out I did not have to make a decision after all. The next morning Jerry was gone! He must have packed up his things and stole out of the room while we were still sleeping. When Perry woke up and saw that Jerry was not in the room, he was not upset at first. But he did go out and look in the back seat of the car to see if he was sleeping there, and found an envelope with one thousand dollars in it. Then he walked down to the water's edge. I followed behind, and I found him crying, not just teary-eyed, but dropping big tears like a child into the surf when it rolled in over his feet.

Maybe he will come back, I said. Maybe he just . . . and then I thought about what had happened to the Walker family the last time Jerry disappeared, and I did not want to say where I thought he might be. I just felt myself shiver in the morning breeze off the gulf and thanked my lucky stars that he was gone.

Perry said he wanted to be left alone and I walked off, unhappy that I got what I wanted but now I was not sure if I would lose Perry, too. We headed on. Perry stayed sad and didn't talk much for a few days. I then thought he had gotten over it, but when I cracked a joke about Jerry's big ass he punched me in the gut so hard I got the wind knocked out of me, so I said no more rather than risk another fight like we had had. Then he got over it, except for picking out the tune of "Humoresque" on his guitar once in a while. Perry said that was the song Jerry was humming all the time. That made me kind of crazy because I did not want him to recall Jerry, but I kept my mouth shut in order to keep the peace and we did not speak of him for a while. Jerry did not come back into the conversation until later. I never realized how close Perry had gotten to him, and how much Jerry stayed in his mind. We ended up in Nevada, but all the fun had gone out of things. That was where Perry got me to swear not to rat on Jerry if we were ever caught.

Anyone reading this will know how we got caught in Las Vegas, and tried, and convicted. We were in all the news, famous even if Capote doesn't publish his book about us. He writes to both Perry and me about once a week and says it is coming along. What he does not say is that he is not going to publish it until after we are dead but I know this is the case.

What people do not know a lot about is that they tried to hang the Walker killings on us because we were in the vicinity at the time. Sarasota, Florida, is close to the town of Osprey where it happened. We were accused of the Walker murders after we had confessed to the Clutter killings and were waiting for trial, only they dropped the investigation after we passed a polygraph test.

Long before the actual trial Perry had changed his confession so that he claimed to have killed the entire Clutter family. He let me off the hook in return for me not betraying Jerry. I thought this would save me, but I got the death penalty just the same. I stewed about this for some time after our conviction. By that time they were not so careful about keeping us apart. We are kept in separate cells on death row, but sometimes take our showers together, or bribe the guards to let us speak.

It was at one of these times that I told Perry we were crazy to not collar Jerry on the Walker killings. We could say we knew the gun used on the

Walkers was .22 caliber and that Jerry bought it. If they would find Jerry, they could match his prints to one found at the scene. It could keep me from being hanged, I said.

Perry begged me not to squeal, he practically got down on his knees and begged me. I asked why he was so stuck on that kid. He said because he had never done anything very noble in his life, and he thought this was a noble thing. I said why do a noble thing for that kid. He said Jerry had his whole life ahead of him, he was just a kid who did not know any better. I said that may be, but the kid had killed six people before the age of sixteen if you counted his own grandfather, two Clutters, and all the Walkers. Maybe it was not such a good idea to leave him loose on the world. Smith said he did not care, he wanted to do this and would I agree. I said I would think about it.

But Jerry must have been in contact with Perry. My father was dead by this time, but my mother came to visit me often. On one visit she told me that a boy had come to the house to say that if I didn't keep to my word she and my whole family could be in danger. He gave her an article about a bunch of dead dogs that was supposed to show he meant what he said. She gave me the article.

That is why I am writing this true and final confession, and true to my word will go to the gallows without turning on Jerry. But I've told Mom that if she or any of my kin is threatened before or after my execution, she should go to Father Santangelo. He has instructions to give this confession to the authorities. I do not imagine Jerry can go long without being picked up on some charge or other, and then his prints can be matched to the Walkers' house.

This finished, I've done everything I can think of to protect my family. Father Santangelo told me that God has forgiven me for the bad things I did in my life, and for the bad things I thought. This is a hard thing for me to believe, but I have to trust him. Now I am prepared to go to the gallows. I even decided what I will say for my last words. I will say, "I just want to say I hold no hard feelings. You people are sending me to a much better place than this has been."

Sincerely,
Richard Eugene Hickock, April 6, 1965

Fifty-five

"Now why would you say that?" Beaufort asked Gloria.

"Because I checked. I called the stables and asked if they had some-one named Jerry Nolan working there. When they said no, I even de-scribed you in case you used a different name. They still said no."

"You went behind my back, asking questions?" It wasn't so much that he didn't understand what she meant by that, as that he couldn't fathom she had that much moxie in her.

But she was in the shit now knee-deep and apparently could not stop. She pointed to Carlo. "I mean, who is this guy really?"

Beaufort snapped the recliner shut and stood up. Gloria remembered who she was and cowered from habit.

"We live," Carlo said, trying to defuse the two of them, responding to Gloria in an amazingly normal way, "we live just about a half mile away. In the Black Horse Ranch subdivision. You might have seen us walking. We have two pugs. You may have met my wife. Brigid."

Well, that set Gloria off again, this time more like a rocket. "*Bri*-gid! So what are you all planning?" Gloria asked. "A threesome, maybe?" Her eyes flickered over the duct tape on the coffee table and she said, maybe without knowing why, "Or bondage? Were you going to invite me?"

Carlo made some vague sound, a combination of protest and groan, while Beaufort advanced on Gloria. When Carlo found his words they were "My dear. Don't."

"That's right, my dear," Beaufort said, and almost sounded sincere. "You have nothing to worry about here."

Maybe because she saw this as a chance to speak in front of a witness, her first without risking Beaufort's private wrath, Gloria seemed to take courage. She lifted her chin to gain an inch on Beaufort and said, "Bullshit. I called that phone number in your wallet. The voice message was her."

"This isn't what you think," Carlo said.

Locked together, Beaufort and Gloria both ignored him.

"You're embarrassing yourself, honey," Beaufort said. "Go back in the bedroom. I'll be there in a minute. We'll . . . talk."

"Why doesn't *he* just leave," Gloria said, pointing at Carlo but with less aggression than she'd displayed only a moment before.

"You could leave," Carlo said. "You can walk out the door right now." He rose from the couch and tried to step between them, but Beaufort gently pushed him aside, the only acknowledgment that Carlo was even in the room.

"Honestly, group sex? Babe, we need to work on getting your confidence back." Beaufort took Gloria by the shoulders and put his face closer to hers. "Where's that old I-can-change spirit? Everything is going to be okay," he said. "You just have to trust me, that whatever I'm doing is for us. You and me. Okay?"

Gloria opened her mouth, part of her still wanting to say yes, but then stopped, searching his face.

Beaufort looked at Carlo to gauge his response to this interaction. He had regretted the way he'd let himself run on over at Carlo's place, and wanted Carlo to understand he was capable of whatever it took to accomplish his purpose. He wanted Carlo to know that women didn't treat him the way Brigid Quinn treated him. Beaufort summoned up all the persuasion he had and said once more, "Now. In the bedroom."

She only had so much fight in her, a muscle weakened from disuse, and it was gone now. As she turned to go Beaufort playfully swatted her rear end, at which she almost smiled. Then he grabbed the duct tape he'd left on the coffee table, and jerked a chair out from the dining room table nearby. "Sit," he said to Carlo.

"You don't have to do this," Carlo said, as he obeyed.

"You don't have to do this," Beaufort repeated Carlo's words, and this time didn't hide the mocking. "Do you know every time that line appears in every movie ever made it never convinces anyone?"

"She doesn't know anything," Carlo whispered.

"Now who's bullshitting?" Beaufort said as he pulled Carlo's hands behind the chair and duct-taped his wrists together. "You think I wanted it to happen this way? I told you to keep your fucking mouth shut but no, you had to talk about Brigid. The pugs." He squatted and taped one of Carlo's ankles to the leg of the chair, stood back up, and said, "There, that should do it for now."

All Carlo could say was "Please. You don't need to. Brigid will be here and give you what you want and you can go away and just leave us all here. Tie us all up so you have time to get across the border. It's only an hour away."

Beaufort shook his head, regretful. He was conscious of feeling full of regret, and he liked it. "She knows too much, and it's all your fault."

Beaufort tore off a small piece of duct tape from the roll and placed it against his shirt, then, thinking about how the duct tape would leave residue around her mouth that could be detected in an autopsy, said "hm," went to the kitchen, and came back with a plastic grocery bag.

"No," Carlo shouted and kicked out ineffectually with the leg that hadn't been taped.

Beaufort opened the bedroom door. Achilles tried to get through, but Beaufort bent down and gently shoved him back, saying, "There you go, boy. That's a good boy."

He shut the door behind him. Gloria still didn't have much of a clue about what was going on, but she did look startled at the shout from Carlo which had come through the closed door. Beaufort figured it was only a matter of time before she started putting things together, especially once the bodies were discovered and things got on the news. At one time he thought he might bring her around to understanding that he was not a bad man, and they could have a life together, but the little scene in the living room told him that was unlikely. He regretted this.

Beaufort was across the room while he thought and regretted, and had Gloria's arms pinned to her sides and her body on the bed before she had time for even one good scream.

It didn't take long to straddle her to where she couldn't fight him off. The plastic bag went over her head easily, and allowed less airflow than the pillow alone would have done. "That's it, go ahead and scream," he said, feeling the vibration through the pillow. When the scream was done he said, "Hush now, babe." He said it more to himself, knowing she couldn't hear much.

He watched the bedside clock as he pressed down. It took a good eight minutes to make sure she was dead, longer than Santangelo but better than leaving marks or blood. Eight minutes is a long time when there's nothing to do but press down. Once she stopped struggling so much Beaufort heard himself humming the old tune, stopping to make that popping sound with his mouth at the end of each musical phrase. What he did when he was enjoying himself.

He was enjoying this. He had been able to assure himself that he hadn't enjoyed killing Santangelo or arranging for the deaths of Meadows and Quinn, but this, this gave him little thrums of pleasure that coursed through his body.

He forced himself to stop humming, hoping that stopping that would stop the feelings, but he could not deny the pleasure. His face grew hot, and a string of *no no no no no* popped like silent firecrackers in his mind.

When Gloria was certainly dead, he got off the bed, reeling a little. He didn't think they'd been noisy, but he could hear Carlo yelling. Had he been yelling the entire eight minutes? Beaufort could also hear Achilles snuffling at the door, like he wanted to get away from what was going on in the bedroom.

Beaufort bent down and petted Achilles. "That's a boy, that's a good boy," he said, and hoped that way to retrieve the feelings of regret. "You stay in here with Mommy now. We'll go for a walk in a bit."

Beaufort came out from the bedroom wiping his right palm on his jeans over and over. He said to Carlo, who watched with horror from his chair, "Too many people dead because of you."

Beaufort thought about taping Carlo's other leg to the chair and then figured it was too much bother. He sagged back down in his recliner to wait for Brigid's arrival, feeling a little old. He was wearied and saddened by what had happened to Gloria. But hopeful, too. The feeling of pleasure had subsided until he could almost think it had never happened. There must be other women like Gloria out there. When that curse that Hickock had laid on him was finally at rest, and he could have peace inside himself, he might be a different man.

Fifty-six

When we landed in Tucson I put the confession back into its envelope and the envelope back into my tote bag. On my phone I found a message from Beaufort, with the caller ID GLORIA BENTHAM. So it was likely he was at her place, using her phone. I called the number back and played dumb.

"Where are you?" I asked Beaufort when I heard his voice. "Are you still at the house?"

"No. Where are you?"

I didn't tell Beaufort I was stuck in the bathroom waiting for everyone else to deplane so I wouldn't be seen. "I'm waiting to deplane. I'm at the back."

"How long does it take you to get home from the airport?"

"About fifty . . . maybe an hour with traffic." I didn't want him to get nervous and do something rash, so I said, "Maybe a little more."

"Then call me again when you get close to your house. I'll tell you what to do when you get there. Do you have the document?"

"I do."

"Good. I'm tired of worrying." I heard his voice catch on this unintended spillage of honesty, and could almost imagine him rubbing his face to get control. Maybe he was losing his grip. That could be good or bad.

Beaufort went on, "So I want you to know, if you made a copy, if you had a notion to leave one in a safe deposit box somewhere—"

"I haven't had the time to do that, you idiot."

"—or you're having my location traced while we talk, I swear I'll stay alive at least long enough to find you, kill Carlo, and make you watch while I do it. Got that?"

"I do. Where's Gloria?"

"She's fine."

"That's not what I asked. I said where, not how."

"In one hour I'll call again and tell you where to go." And he disconnected.

I ran off the airplane and paused for one minute on the concourse, wanting to check one more thing. I accessed the Wi-Fi in the terminal, went to YouTube, and searched *Humoresque*. The even, plodding beat of the melody played on a violin gave me the chills.

Yep, that was what Beaufort was humming at the house when he came for dinner.

I ran down the small concourse, stopping in one of those shops that sell travel-sized everythings along with the supersized packages of Twizzlers and the latest bestsellers. I'd been in enough airports to know where to look and scanned the items hanging against the wall—aspirin . . . tiny nail files—looking for the right container. Dammit, there were no plastic hair spray bottles, just metal ones with the hair spray sealed inside. I chose a vial containing nasal spray. As I paid, I asked the clerk who was charging me somewhere in the neighborhood of five bucks for it, "Does this look like plastic to you?"

She just narrowed her eyes and said, "Do you want to buy that?"

On the way out to pick up my car from the parking garage I tore off the bit of plastic sealing the vial, popped off the lid, and spilled the solution on the ground without breaking my pace. It would work, but whether I would harm myself with it rather than Beaufort remained to be seen. I hoped there were not different kinds of plastic, with some working and some not. Or things that appeared to be plastic but were not? I was focused on putting one foot in front of the other, and put this out of my mind, figuring that with capsicum it wouldn't make a difference, Gemma-Kate was just being overly cautious.

I got my car out of hock and drove the twenty minutes to the college dorm, talking to Gemma-Kate all the while on my phone, getting instructions that she would give me again. And again, just to be on the safe side. When I pulled up, she got in the backseat with her backpack slung over her shoulder.

"Go ahead," she said, "I'm coming with you. I don't trust you with this."

I spent a few precious seconds trying to figure out how to get her out of the car. Her father would kill me if Gemma-Kate got hurt.

She said, "We're losing daylight, Aunt Brigid. And I can work while you're driving." When I recognized the Quinn stubbornness on her face I didn't waste time arguing with her. As I drove, keeping my eyes on the road, skirting ass-draggers when I could, trying to do something more useful than honk, I was aware of her working. She took a black garbage bag out of her backpack, left it folded in half, and spread it over the passenger seat with part of the plastic angled against the back of the seat. That done, she got another, this one a gallon-sized storage bag.

"Where's the manuscript?" she asked.

I reached behind my seat to point out my tote, then put both hands on the wheel again to avoid a crash.

"Jesus, Aunt Brigid, you're going to get us stopped."

"Let them try."

"Oh cool, so you show up with three black-and-whites, lights and sirens, following you. That will send a good message. He's not going to do anything until you get there."

I slowed down some at her logic. She opened my tote and in my rearview mirror I could see her almost fondling the document. Then, by God, she started to read it.

"Gemma-Kate," I yelled.

"We still have a good thirty minutes until we're at the house," she said.

"You can read it later," I said, not commenting that maybe it was time to feel a little something, concern for Carlo, perhaps. A little something.

Gemma-Kate reluctantly folded the document sideways into a tube that would fit inside the zip-lock bag. She handled it like a museum curator. Then she sealed the tab at the top of the bag.

At this point I swung the car on a caution light around the corner of First and Skyline. Not being warned, Gemma-Kate fell against the door of the car.

"You're going to have to stop the car," she said. "I can't do this while you're driving like a madwoman."

"I can't stop," I said.

"I repeat, that guy isn't going to make a move unless you take longer than usual to get from the airport."

"I stopped to pick you up," I said. "I told him I'd be there in about an hour. I'm afraid if it's much more than that he'll get nervous. It will be bad if he's nervous."

"You've more than made up for the time it will take to stop by doing fifty in a thirty-five zone," she said.

"How long will it take?"

"Less than five minutes if nothing goes wrong."

I pulled into the first parking lot I came to, Coco's restaurant at the corner of Oracle and Ina.

"The container thing is in my tote, too," I said.

Gemma-Kate dug around and pulled out the empty nasal spray. She looked somewhat concerned.

"Don't you think it's big enough to do the job?"

"I told you to get a spray bottle."

"They didn't have any. Just use that."

"Aunt Brigid, even an atomizer doesn't have the power of an aerosol canister and it was risky. Now you just want to, what, squirt it at him? I don't think these things squirt all that well. Let's stop at a drugstore."

The thought of what Carlo was going through ate me up inside. "I don't want to waste a minute I don't have to. I'll be careful," I said.

"Suit yourself," Gemma-Kate said. She popped off the lid that I had replaced after emptying the bottle. Then she took two pairs of heavy-duty plastic gloves from her backpack and told me to put on one pair while she slipped on the other.

"You sure are careful with capsicum," I said.

She looked at me. Thought. Spoke. "It's capsicum with a kick," she said. She handed me a small plastic bag "in case I needed it." "Safety first," she added, as she told me what I was to do, with what effect. And smiled.

It had taken us the usual fifty minutes from the airport to the house, plus an extra ten for picking up Gemma-Kate and fixing the vial, which was now in the side pocket of my travel pants. As I headed east on Golder Ranch Road I called the number Beaufort had given me, and told him where I was.

"Great," he said. "Now come to Gloria's house. I understand you know where it is."

As he said that we were passing by Twin Lakes. I pulled off onto the hard-packed stretch on the right-hand side of the road, made a U-turn, and turned right to head to Hawser. "I'll be there in two minutes. If you do anything to Carlo in the next three minutes you're dead."

"Awful lot of talk talk talk about killing," he said. "You don't know killing like I do." He disconnected. I could tell it made him feel in control to have the last word. Let him feel in control.

I dropped Gemma-Kate off under a tree on Hawser and continued on to Gloria's house. We had planned this in advance. Gemma-Kate had her cell phone and I had mine. I told her I would call her when I had Beaufort neutralized. When I said that, I got a *hey, good luck with that* expression. We both knew what neutralized might mean, and how it was by no means a certainty.

Beaufort's car was in the driveway as expected, with the gate un-latched. What I didn't expect was to see Gloria's lime green Beetle there as well. I'd felt certain she would be at work and safely out of the way. It was hard enough to go into a situation like this dealing with Beaufort and Carlo. It was even harder to try to imagine to what extent Beaufort might have Gloria in thrall to him. Was she a victim or an accomplice? A woman like that could go either way.

I picked up the black garbage bag by the top where it fastened, slopping it around in the little clear pool on the plastic covering the seat. Carefully stripping off my plastic gloves, I got out of the car, leaving my phone on the dashboard and my gun in the glove compartment. I had to appear totally helpless in order for this to work.

I slammed the door so he'd know I was coming. Everything on the up-and-up. I was doing as ordered within limits. I had no doubts that before the next thirty minutes were over he expected both Carlo and me to be dead.

He should have no inkling that I could kill him instead. To hide that thought I washed the image of Carlo being hurt out of my mind and off my face. I regretted my threats. It was important that when Beaufort first saw me his impression would be that of a vulnerable, worried, weak, old woman.

Certainly he would have Carlo tied up. Maybe tape over his mouth so he couldn't yell, not that Carlo would. He would do what Beaufort told him to do. I thought I knew Carlo.

Don't think of Carlo. I arranged my face again, pursed my lips and made them tremble.

Beaufort must have been watching through the venetian blinds, because when I reached the door he said, "It's open."

So I went in. I never thought I'd be relieved to see someone standing in front of me with his weapon trained on my face. This was what I expected him to do. So far, so good. Well, not altogether. I didn't see Gloria. But I focused only on what I had to do.

"Close the door," Beaufort said to me, and then, "Hold out your arms."

I did as he directed, and while he ran his hands down my body I saw Carlo tied to a chair as I had expected. I had never seen the look on Carlo's face until that day. His eyes were wide and unblinking, and his bushy brows taut as if they were paralyzed in that spot. His mouth was slightly open with a white circle around his lips. There was no gag. His breath came in fast, tiny sniffs through his nose. It was audible across the room. It wasn't just the inconvenience or even the pain of his restraints. The man was pretending not to be terrified. And he stared at me so intensely it was as if he see anything else. I glanced at a closed door leading off the living room, and then back at him. His eyelids trembled with the strain of not following my glance.

"Carlo."

"Shut up," Beaufort said.

"I want to know if he's been hurt," I said.

"He hasn't hurt me," Carlo said with an effort to smile for my benefit. "My wrists are a little sore."

"Undo his wrists," I said to Beaufort.

He laughed. "You're giving me orders? I'm the one with the gun."

"Are you sure?" I said, and hoped he would see some logic in that preposterous statement. I was at the edge, too, not thinking real clearly, holding the bag farther out from myself and hoping it would neither drip nor dry altogether. I wasn't sure exactly what Gemma-Kate had used.

He might have taken the bag then, but he needed both his hands. Telling me again to hold both arms out, Beaufort held his gun in his right hand as he used his left to frisk me for weapons. He ran over the side pocket of my pants without noticing the empty plastic bag that Gemma-Kate had given me.

A snuffling and scratching sound came from behind that closed door. "How's Achilles?" I asked, hoping to distract him.

Goddammit. Beaufort had reached the buttoned pocket in my travel pants and felt through the cloth. He reached inside and withdrew the vial. I held my breath and prepared to dive away in case he got cute and tried to squirt it on me.

"What's this?" he asked.

"What does it look like? I get congested at high altitudes," I said, praying that he wouldn't tell me to use it. Capsicum up my nose would sting like the devil.

He unscrewed the top and gave it a little sniff, then tossed the container on the rug, and I put all my energy into not crying out, not moving a muscle in my face. I waited for the solution to seep out into the rug.

It didn't. I supposed she hadn't filled it to the brim, and hoped if I could somehow get to it, and use it, I'd be able to apply enough force to get a good stream out of it.

Achilles whined.

"I really like that little guy," Beaufort said, mostly to himself. "I think I'm going to take him with me."

Then he looked at the bag that I held away from my body with my right hand while trying not to look like I was holding it away from my body. "So that's it?" he asked, and ran his thumb over his bottom lip.

I nodded.

"No bogus blank sheets? You wouldn't think I'm stupid enough to fall for that, would you?"

"Not by half," I said. While I wanted to say *go ahead, open it,* I couldn't trust that he was that much of a sucker. Instead, I looked at it sadly as if I hated to lose my last bargaining chip, but what I was thinking was *take the bag, take the bag.*

"I'll make sure you and Carlo can't do anything for a couple of hours, plenty of time to get across the border and get picked up by some friends. Don't worry, I won't hurt you."

The same words that Hickock had used with the Clutters. Maybe the same words that Beaufort had used with the Walkers. I forced my eyes to light up as if I believed him.

"Would you mind if I put it on the table here and untied Carlo?"

As I did so, Beaufort looked at the bag with a mixture of eagerness and fear that I'd never seen before, the door to the basement stairs in a horror movie that he was forced to open. He seemed to have forgotten me for an instant as he focused on it, lying there on the table, and I decided the next safe move was to make sure to get Carlo out of harm's way for what might come next. I stepped slowly to the back of the chair where he sat and tore duct tape from around his wrists. He started to rise, but I put my hands on his shoulders and, without actually moving him, pressed in the direction of the kitchen to his left, hopefully sending a message to go there. He nodded ever so slightly, and I hoped that meant he understood.

First wiping the back of his hand against his mouth as if he was salivating, Beaufort grabbed as I had hoped he would, eagerly, with his whole hand around the bag in which the papers were curled into a tube. Then he seemed to recognize that we were standing off to the side. He trained the gun on me, on us, balanced the bag against the wall, and opened the top with one hand.

It only took a few seconds for things to get interesting as the natural moisture in his palm interacted with the surface of the plastic. While he didn't yet drop the gun, Beaufort reacted with a "shit," and put the palm of his hand instinctively to his mouth, licking it. That was when the shit turned into a shout as the substance hit his tongue and, while he wasn't yet letting go of the gun, the muzzle dropped down and just to the right of Carlo.

It was either save Carlo and get killed or get Beaufort and save Carlo.

I dove to the floor where he had tossed the nasal spray container, grabbed it, and kept rolling away from Carlo, toward Beaufort, to both get closer and draw fire. The one second it would have taken to unscrew the top could have been my last. Beaufort was bent at the waist, close enough. At the last second I wrenched my head away to avoid hurting myself and pressed as hard as I could to spray the mixture at his face.

At the shock of the cold liquid Beaufort spun blindly and got two shots off before the cold turned to little fire bombs that exploded across his face. He dropped the gun and rubbed, no, grabbed handfuls of skin that came away as the fluid ate through his closed eyelids and burned through his corneas. If he had been in less agony, he would have seen that his hands came away bloody after he had clawed at his eyes.

As it was, he dashed without purpose around the room, caroming off furniture, a pinball in a game that couldn't be won.

I swear I could feel the rushing air before hearing the sound of one of the shots Beaufort fired. It passed just over my back, and would have killed me or at least severed my spinal cord and crippled me for life. The other shot went high, hitting a chrome and glass bookcase against the far wall so that the *bang* was followed closely by a shattering sound and then by a slower tinkle as the larger shards drifted to the floor.

Momentarily stunned, I watched Beaufort drop to the floor and writhe while the skin on his face bubbled and dissolved. My own index finger started to burn and I dropped the spray container and the rug under it melted.

292

This wasn't like any pepper spray I'd ever seen. I should have known Gemma-Kate was using acid. I probably did know.

Back to the moment, I had the presence of mind to grab the sandwich bag out of my pocket and use it to pick the gun up off the floor where it had dropped, too late yelling *Run* at Carlo to both get him out of the room and to draw Beaufort's attention toward me. I was glad he had fired the shots and there would be residue on his hand, not mine. We had struggled with the weapon, I thought. I pointed the weapon at his heart, trying to get in a good shot. It was hard to aim because he was twisting about so. On top of that, I couldn't press the trigger with my burning index finger and was attempting to do so with my right-hand ring finger instead.

But I hadn't figured on Carlo. He rushed forward and went to Beaufort. Beaufort grabbed for Carlo's arm with hands reddened and raw from touching the acid in the plastic bag.

"Don't touch him," I yelled over his screaming.

Carlo knelt, keeping his hands raised as if wanting to help Beaufort but not knowing what would help and what would hurt. When he heard me yell, he got off the floor and stood in my way. When I moved a little, so did he.

"Step aside," I said, my vision tunneling through him to the man on the floor.

There was a look on his face that had about a hundred different thoughts in it as his eyes focused on my mouth. Some of the thoughts might have been about what was making me smile. Was it my triumph at having won? Revenge? Divine justice, the pleasure of playing God? Whatever my feelings, my smile seemed to freeze Carlo in place between Beaufort and me.

Then it was Carlo's turn to speak. "No," he said, just loudly enough to be heard over Beaufort's yelling.

My vision cleared and I saw him.

"Don't do it," he said, probably not loudly enough to be heard over the screaming, which is why I said, "What?"

"You may not kill this man," he said, this time with a voice commanding a person he didn't know. Two strangers.

"Why not?" I asked, even in that adrenaline-charged moment

knowing how I was simply stalling. I was going to kill that man, and I wanted Carlo for once to see who, what, I am.

"Because he can't harm us now," Carlo said. "You're not saving me anymore."

Carlo wouldn't know that I hadn't put the acid in the nasal spray, that I thought it was only on the bag that would burn Beaufort's hand. I thought Gemma-Kate was giving me a capsicum solution that would temporarily blind him. This wasn't capsicum, this was the really bad stuff. I was going to shoot him to put him out of his misery. I was also going to do it for the Clutters, the Walkers, Father Santangelo, and Detective Meadows. And Gloria.

"Oh my God, Gloria," I said, and ran through that closed door with my gun raised.

I found her quite still on the bed, a plastic bag over her head and one of the bed pillows at her side. I dropped the gun at the foot of the bed and bent over her, whipping off the bag and placing my fingers at the side of her throat.

Here was the final victim in a long trail of death that stretched from Richard Eugene Hickock and Perry Smith's meeting in that cell in Leavenworth, before they were killers.

I wanted to scream at her. I didn't.

Then, as it always happened at a time like this, thinking of her death made me think of all the other innocents I hadn't saved. And I thought of all the bad guys I hadn't killed, and especially one who didn't suffer enough, who didn't take long enough to die because a shotgun blast to his back ended the pain too soon.

Carlo was right, for reasons he could not imagine. Not shooting Beaufort was much more satisfying.

I picked up the gun, came out of the room, and put the gun on the table, my voice getting a little cold when I said, "She's dead. Again, I advise you not to touch him."

I went into the kitchen area, where I ran cold water over my hand to stop the burning, then turned back to them.

While I was doing that, Carlo had staggered to Beaufort's side, either still in shock or sore from having spent God knows how long tied to the chair. He fell to the floor on his knees, and crawled the rest of the way to Beaufort, who had ceased thrashing about.

Then he looked up at me. "Call an ambulance, for God's sake," he barked.

I pointed out spots on the rug that were burnt as I said, "Be careful. There could be acid anywhere."

If he had questioned whether I knew what was happening to Beaufort, he understood now. I could tell by the way he looked at me, grieving at what he saw. He stayed on his knees but lifted his hands off the carpet. He made a mark with his thumb on Beaufort's forehead, near his hairline where the skin was not burning.

Now. Where are the days when you could find a landline in a house? None there, and neither Gloria's nor Jerry's cell phone was in sight. With another caution to Carlo—Beaufort's screams had subsided and he was only moaning—I ran out of the house and to the car to call Gemma-Kate, where she sat under the shadeless tree with her own cell phone, waiting for the results of her experiment.

"Is Uncle Carlo alive?" she asked first.

"Yes," I said. "I thought you were just putting the hydrochloric acid in the bag. You didn't tell me about putting it in the spray bottle."

"I thought you might object to it," Gemma-Kate said.

"You idiot, you could have killed me."

There was a pause and then she said, "Nobody hurts Uncle Carlo."

I looked at the time on my phone and figured I couldn't wait any longer for Beaufort to die and not look like I was doing it on purpose. I told Gemma-Kate to call nine-one-one with the address and emergency situation. I also instructed her to tell the emergency services to call Deputy Sheriff Max Coyote, and give him my name.

I thought of Gloria. I told Gemma-Kate to say it involved a homicide.

When I got back into the house, Carlo had gotten a pot of water from the kitchen and was pouring it over Beaufort's body. Looked like a baptism. I hoped if there was anything to it, it didn't work this time, that Beaufort would spend eternity burning.

Was that acid on the cuff of Carlo's pants or was it only because they were frayed? When he refused to move away from Beaufort I found a spaghetti pot in one of the cabinets and filled it with water from the tub in the bathroom, then carried it back into the living room to pour it over Carlo's leg without asking permission, without asking whether his leg was burning. Then he looked at me, and something in his dull stranger gaze made me back away with the empty pot.

Did he force himself to look at me? We stared at each other across a room that felt like a chasm. With all the carnage around us, I found my thoughts going back to the time when I was certain he would leave me because he knew in theory what I could do. This was worse. This time he had both seen me in action, and read the satisfaction that I couldn't hide. We knew all of one another's secrets now.

Maybe this time Carlo had been burned after all. Maybe I had burned him beyond repair.

Fifty-seven

Before the cops showed up I opened the door to the bedroom and let Carlo scoop up Achilles so he wouldn't get into the acid. Carlo held him while the cops were there. I was glad that Max Coyote was on duty. He knew enough about all of us that he didn't have to ask so many questions.

"It's your burglar," I said. It was getting on to early evening, and the room had slowly darkened. I turned on a table lamp to help Max see the scene.

"This seems excessive for a burglar," Max said while watching the paramedics load Beaufort onto the gurney after determining that Gloria could wait. He had recommended his screaming. No conning there. I liked the honest sound of it.

"Sorry, I can't hear you over the screaming," I said.

"Excessive force," he yelled.

The morphine they plugged into Beaufort started to take effect rapidly and he quieted. As they wheeled him out I stepped up to the gurney and said, "You were right, Jerry. Hickock never knew your last name. There was nothing in that confession, if it had ever been read, that could have been used to track down Jeremiah Randolph Beaufort. I found out who you were from your booking fingerprints. Now that they have you, they can match your DNA to that from the crime scene. If you had just left things alone, you could have gotten away with killing the Walkers for the rest of your life. You could have just disappeared, you brainless twit."

He moaned, and I took that as an admission of his twittedness. So I turned once more to Max Coyote. "You'll have him on at least five counts of murder going back to 1959. Also murder of a priest in Florida. And a contract hit on a detective in Sarasota County. And the woman in the bedroom." I gave Coyote all the information he needed about Beaufort, including checking his DNA against that found in Christine Walker, via the Sarasota County Sheriff's Office cold case unit. I told Max to use hazmat protocol at the crime scene in Gloria's house. I told him why the bag containing a confession should be handled with plastic gloves. I told him it was the final confession of Richard Hickock. I should have kept it. Max is in his early forties, and from his blank look I could tell he didn't know who I was talking about. He turned to go without asking for an explanation, though I figured once he'd seen to Beaufort and assessed the crime scene, we'd talk at greater length. Just as well; it was time to get out of there, because Carlo was still looking at me in that way you'd look at a spouse who has just, with great zest, nearly killed a guy with acid.

Gemma-Kate accepted a ride back to her dormitory from one of the deputies. Before getting into the car she told me she was royally pissed that I hadn't kept the confession. Seemed I couldn't please anyone that day.

We just had the one car at the crime scene, the Miata I'd driven from the airport. I was a little rattled after something like this, but no more than usual, and trusted myself driving the half mile back to our house with Achilles in the backseat. Carlo was the one I was concerned about. Too obediently, he got into the car and sat hunched over his knees with his hands tucked between them, staring at the glove compartment. He just as obediently got out of the car when I pulled into the garage, walked into the house, and sat in his reading chair hunched over as if he was still staring at the same glove compartment.

I turned on a few lights here, too.

Al and Peg ran up to him and, expecting the usual rubbings, jumped at his knees, then smelled the dampness of them from the water I'd splashed on him. Carlo didn't appear to see or feel them. Achilles sat close to the garage door, waiting to be invited in. When the pugs couldn't get attention from Carlo, they trotted over and sniffed Achilles suspiciously. Then they came over to me by the liquor cabinet in the kitchen and stared with all their WTF bug-eyes. If they were thinking you just can't rely on *Homo sapiens*, I agreed with them.

I opened a bottle of red wine, took a look at Carlo, and, assuming a stronger dose was needed, put the cork back in. We had some Glenlivet. It had been there for years, but liquor doesn't go bad. At least God got that detail right. It's the least he can do. I went into the living room and handed a glass to Carlo, but he didn't take it, didn't look up. I put it on the end table next to his chair.

I knelt in front of him, hoping to catch his gaze and make him see me, I admit, to reassure myself as much as him. "Talk to me," I said. "You can't keep this inside. Sooner or later you have to talk."

I'd been worried about all kinds of things; what Carlo might think of me, for example, watching me in action, seeing what I was capable of. How he might be traumatized by his scrape with death. I ached at what he might have seen Beaufort do to Gloria Bentham, some horror that he couldn't express. So I was surprised when he did speak, at what he talked about.

"When he came over to the house he asked to make his confession. I suspected at first that I was being conned, but there are those times when the job demands . . . well, at first Jerry rattled on. I could tell he thought he was being so clever, and manipulating me. But at some point, he really did start to confess. Not the whole thing. Probably not everything Hickock put in his record. But painful things I'm sure he had never admitted to anyone before. It was the first time I'd listened to a confession in more than thirty years."

Carlo's lips trembled, and then he started to cry. I'd never seen Carlo cry before. Was it the result of the trauma he had been through, or did he want to leave me and go back to the priesthood? I didn't dare to try to stop him so I just hugged him at the knees and let him put his hand on the top of my head, half pulling me to him and half pushing me away. It felt like he was needing to connect with someone, but part of him didn't want it to be me just now. Being the unwanted person hurt.

When he had finished crying, he pulled his hand back from my head and let me look up into his face. "You were going to kill him," he said. "Or at least you were going to let him die."

What I thought I saw there made me understand that you can kill all the people you want, to fix the world, but that doesn't mean you'll ever be able to control the live ones. It again occurred to me I could have blamed it on Gemma-Kate, but what good would that really do when we both already knew what I was capable of? I couldn't win this.

So, tucking up my little protective core in preparation for whatever might come, I said, "I don't understand why that surprises you."

Carlo didn't respond for a long time, and with each second I imagined the chasm between us widening. When he finally spoke, it wasn't with the final judgment I was expecting. Not yet. "I'm different from you," he said. "You see good and evil. All my life I've never seen black on black on black."

"He's evil," I said.

"Is he?" Carlo said. "What about us? Are we good or are we evil?"

Oh for God's sake, did he have to define everything? I said, "Do you remember a while ago when I was in a terrible place? You brought me home covered with someone else's blood, and you put me in the shower and washed me like a child. Then you tucked me into bed. I was afraid that night that you were just responding with your usual kindness. I was afraid that you were getting ready to leave me, because you knew me deep down, what I had felt and thought and done. And that you found me . . . unlovable."

He really saw me now, and was listening. Thank God I was a person, too, not just black on black. It was my last hope. I went on despite my terror of where this was going.

"Do you remember that night?" I asked.

Carlo barely nodded. Oh, the times that he had been so strong and I had been able to lean on him. This wasn't that time.

"Brigid. I'm sorry, but everything is dark right now. I'm having a hard time with clarity." He was speaking in his old Perfesser way, but when he tried to pick up the glass of Scotch his hand was shaking so badly the glass wobbled like a top at the tail end of its spinning.

I took his other hand and put it on the glass so he could hold it without spilling. Then I drew away. Nobody knows dark better than me. I thought about how much he was capable of loving me, and my not knowing whether it was enough. I said, "I understand. I understand."

He shook his head and blinked. "What?"

Hold on to the hardness, I thought. I was going to be needing it while he got out the pictures of his saintly wife. "I understand that I can't become you and you can't become me. It's pretty simple."

He nodded. Oh my God, he nodded. But then he said, "You know, sometimes I wonder if you're as smart as I think you are. You do realize that this whole thing wasn't about you? Without you there still would have been Jerry. I was the one who caused Jeremiah Beaufort to come to Tucson. I was the one he was after, or at least that thing of Hickock's. He would have killed me. You would have been, how would you call it, mere collateral damage. And it's likely that Gloria still would have died, too."

"Well, I guess that's so," I said, sitting back on my heels, though hardly encouraged.

"And then," he said, "then you saved my life. So now I have to live with the fact that he's likely to die and I'm allowed to live. I'll be alive *because* he's dead."

"Perfesser, I wish to God he was dead, but you'll love this part. I checked with the paramedics, who said Beaufort's vital signs were strong. He'll likely be permanently blind and ugly as hell with scarring, but he's going to stand trial for his part in the Clutter family murders, and for the slaughter of the Walker family, too. Not to mention your old friend Father Santangelo. Besides Gloria Bentham."

Carlo didn't full-on sob, but he did choke on my words as if he'd spoken them himself. When I caught his gaze and held it I could see he was embarrassed by his gentleness in the face of however he saw me.

I was still the first one to look away. "But will you be all right?" I asked. Of course I knew even then that I was really asking *will we be all right*.

"Oh, I doubt that there's anything wrong with me that several years of psychiatric counseling and a little Xanax can't ease." He finally picked up the glass of scotch from the table and raised it in my direction. He looked at me, carefully, seeing me for the first time again although through a film of great sadness. His hand was still trembling just a little when he said, "Cheers, honey."

A door that had been momentarily opened between us was closing again. Damned if I'd let that happen. I swatted his knee, which was the closest thing to hand. "Oh, no you don't," I said. "Dammit, Perfesser, I'm the one who does sarcasm. 'Cheers, honey' isn't enough for me." I took a deep breath and released it with the sense that I had removed a glove and was smacking him with it. "You were the one who once told me love isn't so much a feeling as it is a decision." Then I took the glass from him and took a good swig before asking, "So. Are we still on? Are we going to fight for us or just slink off?"

I handed back the glass. Carlo took his time sipping the Scotch. And sipping it again. Good God, he was in thinking mode at a time like this. The thinking seemed to calm him. When he finally put the glass down on the table next to his chair, his hand was steadier as he spoke in thoughts that only after a time blended into full sentences. "This? That inability to reach perfection. Or outright fuckups. Let's call it. Call it sin. Woven into our fabric. Body and spirit. No escape. And then." Carlo's hand started to move in circles, the fingers slightly curved, as if he was pulling the words out of his mind and winding them into a ball only he could hold. "When we look back at the whole thing, the life, the terrible things we've done that often led inexplicably to good, we can see sin as a necessity, even a gift, for making life work in the direction it ought to, to change us as needed. The black hole in the center that keeps a galaxy spinning around it. It's not change per se, but the openness to learning something difficult that's key. Like Wittgenstein says, 'I'm not sure why we're here, but I'm pretty sure it is not to enjoy ourselves.'"

"I have a strong feeling that whatever it is you just said sucks," I said. "Now stop having a roundtable discussion with dead philosophers and look at *me*, dammit."

He stopped, and looked at me as if only now aware that he wasn't alone. That sucked, too. I held my breath waiting for more. When it appeared he was finished, because all the words in the world don't mean anything to me, I said, "I'm sorry. I don't operate on pure logic. I don't even understand half of what you're saying. What does sin have to do with whether we can be together?"

"Now. Well, I guess we say we're sorry to each other not only for what we did or didn't do, but sorry for what we are. Then we go on despite it, because we can change what we say and do, but not what we are at our core. I just remembered something Victor Santangelo told me. 'We fall in love with the person we want ourselves to be, and then they drag us there kicking and screaming.'" Going into abstract thought seemed to calm him again as he wondered, "Where are we dragging each other?"

"Hopefully some place where you stop quoting other people and speak for yourself, because sometimes it gets to be fuckin' annoying," I said without rancor.

We stopped. Then at the same time he started to laugh and I started to cry. The commonality was that both were a little hysterical. Carlo's laughter was the first to fade. He picked up the edge of his T-shirt, held my chin with one hand, and wiped a glop of snot from my wet upper lip with his other. He didn't let go of my chin. It struck me that the last time I had looked into his eyes this way was when we were making love. How strange that a few days ago I wasn't sure I could forgive Carlo, and today I wasn't sure he could forgive me.

What we were dealing with now, what we were, was bigger than my petty jealousy of Jane. That had been before he watched how, without hesitation, I could kill a human being. And worse, with what relish. And I had to face the fact that Carlo loved me, perhaps not as much as he had ever been capable of loving, but enough. Whether it was enough was up to me.

Carlo loved me the way I loved him: maybe not exclusively, but uniquely, and no matter that I wasn't all that good a person. I knew this.

It had to be enough.

Maybe that's the unique difference between romance and marriage; it's not about losing ourselves and changing into the other person, or what we think the other wants. That's for the infatuation stage. No, marriage is about repeatedly forgiving the other person for not being us.

I couldn't remember a romance novel ending that way, but then I haven't read that many. Hm . . . a romance for grown-ups . . . it chafes, but it's where the marital rubber hits the road.

Author's Note

This is a work of fiction. But parts of the story are drawn from fact. Truman Capote made Richard Eugene Hickock and Perry Smith famous in *In Cold Blood*, the "nonfiction novel" about the murder of the Clutter family in Kansas in late 1959. I tried to stay true to Capote's account, and more important, to the facts as I found them in police reports and prison archives. Dozens of links between the story according to Capote and my own fictions are here for the interested reader, making the book different from historical fiction, and more of a puzzle in which fact is not altogether apparent.

For example, meeting the young unnamed boy on the road, and the episode of collecting the bottles, was related by Perry Smith to Truman Capote. That the boy left his grandfather to die, joined up with Smith and Hickock, and was the one who killed the Walkers, is my story.

Capote mentions an article in the Garden City newspaper around the time of the Clutter case which told of the killing of ten local dogs. This is factual, but the perpetrator and the motive are fiction.

The Walker family murder case, which occurred near Sarasota, Florida, in December 1959, roughly two months after the Clutters were killed, is also real. Hickock and Smith have been linked to the crime because of the similarities to the Clutter family murders and because they were in Florida when it happened. It's also true that the men's bodies were exhumed later in order to test their DNA against the semen found in Christine Walker. No match was found, but it's unclear whether the DNA samples were too corrupted to provide conclusive evidence. The Walker family murders are still unsolved.

Some significant discrepancies among police reports, archives, and Capote's book:

In a clemency hearing, Richard Hickock claimed that they took over a thousand dollars from the Clutter house, though official confessions, and Capote's book, put the amount at forty dollars. What would motivate Hickock to change the amount? And how else would he and Smith have been able to afford to travel from one coast to another, staying at hotels along the way?

Capote's version has the killers going to Sarasota first and then Miami, either to make the narrative more interesting, or to help clear them of the Walker murders by placing them elsewhere at the time. My version of Hickock's confession matches the police reports that had them going to Miami before Sarasota.

Smith did change his confession to take responsibility for all the murders at the Clutter home, giving as his motivation that he thought Hickock's mother was "a sweet woman" and he did it to make her feel better. Hickock agreed to the change. Not a single person, including Capote, ever pressed Smith on why he really took the blame for killing all four people.

For further reading, I recommend *Truman Capote and the Legacy of "In Cold Blood,"* by Ralph F. Voss (2011), *In Colder Blood,* by J. T. Hunter (2016), *Mockingbird: A Portrait of Harper Lee: From Scout to Go Set a Watchman,* by Charles J. Shields (2016), and of course the book that started it all, *In Cold Blood: A True Account of a Multiple Murder and Its Aftermath,* by Truman Capote (1965).

The Kansas Historical Society Archives offer well over a thousand documents from, to, and about Hickock and Smith.

The internet also shows an extensive filmography on the topic, with a true crime series aired as late as 2018.

During the writing of this novel a newly discovered manuscript written by Richard Hickock while in prison was discovered, and is expected to be published at some time in the future. Another story surfaces in it, wherein Hickock says that a third person paid Smith and him to kill the Clutters. Why would he say this? Surely if it were true, he would have named the third person and used that information to make a deal for a life sentence. Apparently, in the newly found manuscript, Hickock paints himself as an evil thug, continuing the characterization that Capote created. When Smith shoots Clutter in the head, Hickock says he thought coldly, "he'd like to see the embalmer try to fill that hole." Why would he write such purple prose about himself? To convince us of his guilt? For what purpose?

Sixty years after the Clutter murders were committed, and after the confessed killers were executed, mysteries still abound.

Acknowledgments

As the dedication to this book suggests, *We Were Killers Once* would not have been written without the generous sharing of an idea by my agent, Helen Heller. That day on the phone when she said, "I've always thought, what if there were a third man at the Clutter house that night?" And I stopped pacing and said, "Wow." (I'm more articulate on paper.)

Then came not one but three editors who together provided greater depth for the characters, faster pacing, and more believable plotting: In an effort helmed by Kelley Raglund at St. Martin's Press, with Lara Hinchberger at Penguin/Random House, and Kirsty Dunseath at Orion, all three made this a better book. I'm still humbled and amazed that I didn't see what they saw. Wow.

Also thanks to Helen Smith, the Marsh Agency, and all those who are stepping in now to guide its publication and champion its distribution throughout the world.

India Cooper, best copy editor ever.

Hope Dellon. You worked with me for nearly ten years and, while you may not have edited this book, everything I write is the better for having been influenced by you.

I'm grateful for an all too brief but exciting phone conversation with Michael Nations, the son of journalist Starling Mack Nations, who interviewed Richard Eugene Hickock two years before Truman Capote got involved. That's a whole other story that mine doesn't touch.

Thanks to my brilliant readers, many of whom are authors in their own right: William Bell, Jeannie Johnson, Mickey Getty, Pat McCord, and Rich O'Hanley.

Thank you to Tricia Clapp, a graphologist who helped me to analyze Dick Hickock's handwritten letters from prison and provided suggestions for his character.

Thank you to Fred Segal, who informed me about the history of the Pompano Park racetrack. I know you told me they had flat racing at one time, but I lied. It's what we do.

Finally, thank you, my beloved Fred, for those evenings at The Keg. You might not be magic but you're the closest thing to it.